**James Craig** has worked as a journalist and consultant for more than thirty years. He lives in Central London with his family. His previous Inspector Carlyle novels, *London Calling*; *Never Apologise, Never Explain*; *Buckingham Palace Blues*; *The Circus*; *Then We Die*; *A Man of Sorrows; Shoot to Kill* and *Nobody's Hero* are also available from Constable.

For more information visit www.james-craig.co.uk, or follow him on Twitter: @byjamescraig

Praise for *London Calling*

'A cracking read.'

BBC Radio 4

'Fast paced and very easy to get quickly lost in.'

Lovereading.com

Praise for *Never Apologise, Never Explain*

'Pacy and entertaining.'

*The Times*

'Engaging, fast paced . . . a satisfying modern British crime novel.'

*Shots*

'*Never Apologise, Never Exp* the heartbeat of London. It m reading.'

Also by James Craig

Novels
*London Calling*
*Never Apologise, Never Explain*
*Buckingham Palace Blues*
*The Circus*
*Then We Die*
*A Man of Sorrows*
*Shoot to Kill*
*Sins of the Fathers*
*Nobody's Hero*

Short Stories
*The Enemy Within*
*What Dies Inside*
*The Hand of God*

# Acts of Violence

## James Craig

Constable • London

CONSTABLE

First published in Great Britain in 2016 by Constable

A CIP catalogue record for this book
is available from the British Library.

ISBN: 978-1-47211-512-6 (paperback)

Typeset in Times New Roman by TW Type, Cornwall
Printed and bound in Great Britain by CPI Group (UK) Ltd, Croydon CR0 4YY
Papers used by Constable are from well-managed forests and other responsible
sources

MIX
Paper from
responsible sources
FSC® C104740

Constable
is an imprint of
Little, Brown Book Group
Carmelite House
50 Victoria Embankment
London EC4Y 0DZ

An Hachette UK Company
www.hachette.co.uk

www.littlebrown.co.uk

*For Catherine and Cate*

# ACKNOWLEDGEMENTS

This is the tenth John Carlyle novel. Thanks for dragging it over the line go to: Michael Doggart, Krystyna Green, Clive Hebard and Joan Deitch.

# ONE

Rush hour was over, but the relentless hum of traffic from the King's Road – reassuring and irritating at the same time – never abated. From the direction of Brompton Oratory came the sound of angry horns, followed by the wail of a siren further in the distance – probably an ambulance heading in the direction of the Cromwell Hospital. Gazing up at the darkening sky, Michael Nicholson took a drag on his Rothmans King Size and wondered what exactly he was doing back in London. When he was growing up, the city had seemed impossibly alive and exciting; now, after almost a decade living in Shanghai, it seemed about as dynamic as Derby or Carlisle – and almost as alien.

With a gentle nod of his head, Nicholson expelled the thought along with the smoke; he had never been given to introspection and his forties didn't much seem like the time to start. Focusing his attention on the cigarette, he took a last drag, watching the end flare in the gloom before flicking the stub over the edge of the terrace and into the street below. Throwing back his head, he quaffed the gin and tonic he was holding in one hand, before wiping his mouth with the back of the other. It was his third gin of the night, so far, and he was beginning to feel pleasantly woozy. On average, he would get through six or seven gins, along with a bottle or two of wine over dinner, before falling into bed. It wasn't so much that he was an alcoholic, more that he needed to self-medicate against the boredom.

*How long would he be stuck here?*

It was a question that was impossible to answer. Resisting the temptation to drop the empty glass into the street below, Nicholson watched one of the security team pass in front of the building. 'One of Marvin Taylor's finest,' he hiccuped, as the man disappeared from view round the corner into the alleyway that led to the underground garage and the service entrance. 'Trained killers, all of 'em.' Stifling another hiccup, he tried to remember this particular guy's name but it had gone. As far as he could see, each of the nine guys on Taylor's crew were interchangeable – all in their early twenties, fresh-faced, with crew cuts and the pumped-up torsos of bodybuilders. God, they made him feel old, conscious of a steady decline when he should still be in his prime.

*Bastards.*

At least Marvin Taylor himself was a fair way down the same path towards decrepitude. A small, fifty-something black guy, Marvin liked to complain about his bad back. He looked as if he couldn't fight his way out of a paper bag. His 'boys', however, were something else altogether.

Taylor was an ex-policeman who ran his own security firm, promising '100 per cent professionalism and discretion'. Nicholson was less than impressed at their first meeting, but Taylor had been recommended by a former chum at Eton. Anyway, it wasn't as if Nicholson had much to compare him with. After all, he didn't go round hiring bodyguards every day of the week. And the testimonial from the pal, a rogue called Charlie Simmons, was genuine enough. Simmons was the kind of wheeler-dealer who made Nicholson look almost respectable by comparison. One particularly dodgy scheme left him on the wrong side of a bunch of Nigerian businessmen fearing for his life. In the end, Charlie had survived through a mixture of charm, cash stolen from his parents and Taylor-supplied muscle.

When pitching his services, Taylor was careful to imply that all of his employees were ex-Special Forces, or similar. That was highly questionable. Only some of the men was British; the rest were a random selection of men from around the globe. Perusing their résumés, Nicholson had joked to Wang Lei that they were getting the 'United Colors of Close Protection'. All he got for his trouble was a blank look, quickly followed by a scowl that made Nicholson wince. He had faced up to the woman's lack of a sense of humour a long time ago but it could still grate.

Special Forces or not, the boys that Marvin Taylor had protecting the flat knew how to handle a gun. Each of them carried a Heckler & Koch MP5, the kind of weapon that every other policeman in London seemed to carry these days, as well as a Glock 22 pistol.

Nicholson knew full well that it had to be illegal, armed private contractors wandering round SW7 like it was the Wild West, but Wang Lei was definitely impressed by the show of force. Initially, Nicholson had been determined to raise the issue with Taylor but, in the end, he had avoided the subject. Over the years, he had come to realize that one of his great skills was *not* asking questions.

Turning his glass upside down, he let the ice and lemon follow the cigarette butt towards the street, just as a second guard appeared on the pavement below. As the man looked up, Nicholson hailed him with the empty glass and got the briefest of nods in return. *They must get so bloody bored.* Nicholson knew that there would be a third guy somewhere nearby. Marvin's nine-man team was split into three groups, running eight-hour shifts.

All of this at a cost of £12,000 a day.

*Twelve grand.*

Plus VAT.

And expenses.

Nicholson reflected that Taylor Security Services did not come cheap. *Maybe I went into the wrong business.* The whole set-up seemed to be more than a little over the top for Chelsea, but that wasn't his call; Wang Lei, convinced that a bunch of killer ninjas were about to descend on them at any minute, had insisted that they invest in a full-on close protection service. To be fair, *she* was picking up the tab, although Nicholson could think of a lot of things that Wang would be better off spending her money on: him, for a start.

A familiar sense of frustration washed over him as he fished a cigarette packet from the pocket of his cords. The light was fading now and the last warmth of the day had gone. Shivering in the cool night air, he took the last coffin-nail from the crumpled packet and stuck it between his lips, resisting the urge to head back inside.

'Michael, Mother says "*What are you doing*?"'

Making no effort to keep the annoyance from his face, Nicholson turned to confront the youth. 'I was just having a smoke,' he snapped, wondering where he'd left his lighter. Holding up his hand, he waved Exhibit A for the defence, the crumpled fag packet. 'You know your mother doesn't let me smoke in the house.'

Under an unruly mop of jet-black hair, Ren Jiong grinned malevolently. In the sanctity of his bedroom, the boy could get away with smoking as much weed as he liked. Nicholson himself was kept on a much tighter leash.

'The smoke upsets her.'

Nicholson counted to ten. The idiot was the bane of his life; a spoiled brat with the emotional intelligence and maturity of a ten year old – a ten-year-old monkey, at that. Living in England had totally failed to smooth away the rough edges. Ren's parents must have spent the best part of £600,000 in school fees alone, all of it wasted. The best education that money could buy had done nothing other than refine the youth's taste in expensive booze, fast cars and even faster women. Not yet twenty, he already had the air of a second-rate playboy.

And, Nicholson reflected, I should know all about that.

4

The urge to slap the boy into the middle of next week was tempered by the fact that he was his meal ticket. Ren Junior had been his entrée to the Ren family. The extravagantly rich and powerful father, Ren Qi, and the bored and sexy mother Wang Lei, were like something out of a Chinese remake of a 1980s American soap opera. They were so two-dimensional that only by an immense act of willpower had Nicholson been able to convince himself that they were, indeed, real. Even now, their story was hard to credit. Ren Senior was a long-time political hack, the son of one of the 'Eight Elders' of the Communist Party, a 'princeling' of Chinese politics. His crass populism would have appeared commonplace in the West. In China, however, its novelty helped spur his rise, firstly as a provincial governor, then as a member of the Central Politburo. There was even talk of him getting the top job one day. Nicholson knew the fact that he was being mentioned at all probably meant it would never happen. These things were fairly random, like the election of a new Pope; luck and timing as always would play a decisive part. Even so, Ren Qi was definitely a man worth knowing.

Wang Lei, meanwhile, was the youngest daughter of General Wang Dejiang, a prominent figure in the Red Army when the Party came to power in 1949. General Wang fell out of favour during the Cultural Revolution and his daughter was forced to work in a butcher's shop. However, the family was rehabilitated and Wang studied as a lawyer before meeting her husband at the start of his political career. Ren Junior came along a couple of years later; their only child.

When the time came to further the boy's education, where better to send him than Eton, the home of elites from around the world? And who better to facilitate that than an Old Boy like Nicholson, a smooth fixer who worked in China and could bridge the cultural divide.

Wristwatches had provided Nicholson with his big break into the wider Chinese establishment. He had been selling off a small selection of Breitlings, Rolexes and Omegas for a fellow ex-pat with liquidity problems following a nasty divorce involving a transvestite cabaret singer and a bitter custody battle over the family Shih Tzu. Ren Qi, a connoisseur of such items, had heard of the sale and arranged for a private viewing of the collection at his Beijing home. After inspecting the goods, Ren had handed Nicholson a large tumbler of BenRiach and an envelope filled with cash.

'Will twenty thousand US be enough?' the politician asked.

Nicholson knew better than to check the money. 'I'm sure that is more than sufficient.' Not least as he had told the seller the best he could hope for was $14k. He lifted the glass to his lips and took a mouthful, letting the single malt linger on his tongue as he watched Ren slip a GMT-Master on to his wrist.

'I like a man who delivers,' Ren smiled, still staring at the timepiece.

'That's me,' Nicholson smirked, 'always at your disposal.'

'There is one other thing . . .' Ren reached for his glass.

'Yes?' Trying not to seem too eager, Nicholson slowly drained his glass.

'My wife tells me you went to Eton . . .'

Getting Ren Junior into Eton had been a breeze, on the back of a large donation to the school's social fund. Keeping him there was more of a struggle. Nicholson had to work tirelessly to ensure that the boy avoided expulsion, despite Junior's complete lack of interest in his studies and a steady stream of extra-curricular indiscretions.

This babysitting role meant that Nicholson was spending more time in England than he had done in decades. His profile in China duly suffered; to Nicholson's mind, Ren Senior had not kept his end of the bargain – the anticipated contracts and fees simply never materialized. Increasingly, the family had used him as a glorified servant, little more than an English butler.

Now, under virtual house arrest, Nicholson wondered where it had all gone wrong.

*Probably should have kept my hands off the missus.*

In the first few years, Wang Lei had never looked at him twice. But then she started spending more and more time in the UK, to be close to the boy, and, well, things had just happened. The lady of the house exercised her *droit du seigneur.* The husband, busy climbing the greasy pole in China, may or may not have known what was going on. Either way, he didn't seem to care. Not until the relationship became so open that it was deemed to be a threat to his political career.

Over the last year or so, Nicholson had grown profoundly weary of the whole carry-on. Endless angry phone calls between London and Beijing, Wang refusing to let her son return to China and, now, the paranoid fear that their lives were under threat from some kind of Red Army hit squad. Why didn't they just get a divorce, like normal people did? Nicholson himself had been divorced twice already; it was no big deal.

All he wanted now was to get back to his current wife and family; get back to his rather modest existence in Shanghai in a gated community of cookie cutter houses that were supposed to mimic Prince Charles's idea of a typical English village, complete with cobbled streets, mock Tudor houses and a local pub called the Green Giant which, bizarrely, served only Guinness, Foster's and Coke. The place was deadly dull, home only to a handful of ex-pats who spent most of their time there hiding from the droves of Chinese tourists who came to have their photographs taken in front of the red telephone box (with no phone inside) or the black cab that didn't go anywhere as it didn't have an engine.

Despite its shortcomings, as soon as things settled down, Nicholson was going to head back there like a shot. He would put the whole Ren episode behind him and return to the safer business of selling watches and other luxury items to less well-connected locals.

From somewhere overhead came the whine of a Jumbo's engines as it made its final descent towards Heathrow.

'Michael, come inside.'

It was an order, rather than a request.

Gripping his glass tightly, Nicholson resisted the temptation to smash it down on the kid's head. The need for more nicotine came over him in a rush. Where was his bloody lighter? He must have left it inside. 'I'm just coming.'

'Hurry up.' Ren turned and disappeared through the sliding doors into the living room.

'Fuck off, you little shit,' Nicholson hissed, once he was sure that the boy was safely out of earshot. Tossing the empty cigarette packet over the railings, he watched it float down towards the street. For the briefest moment, he toyed with the idea of throwing himself off the terrace, ending it all here. But the thought quickly passed. There was no way he felt suicidal, he was simply not the type. Anyway, it was time for another G&T; a bloody large one. Yawning, he ran a hand through his greased-back hair and reluctantly wandered inside.

# TWO

Sitting in the cab of his Nissan van, Marvin Taylor watched Michael Nicholson disappear back inside the penthouse apartment four floors above. Finishing off his can of Coke, Taylor stuffed the last mouthful of Coronation Chicken wrap into his mouth. Chewing contentedly, he thought back to a conversation with his daughter in the supermarket earlier in the day.

'Why's it called *Coronation* chicken?' Laurie, nine, had asked in that inquisitive way that all kids had.

For several moments, Marvin stared vacantly at the packet. 'Dunno,' he said finally.

'There must be a reason,' Laurie persisted.

'Dunno,' Marvin repeated. 'It's just chicken.'

'But—'

'Hey, what do you call a crazy chicken?'

Laurie made a face. 'Dad . . .'

'A cuckoo *cluck*,' Taylor chuckled. 'Get it?'

Recalling the conversation made him smile all over again. By now, Laurie would be wrapped up in bed, fast asleep hopefully, while her mum had her feet up watching *Grand Designs*, or something similar, on the telly, a glass of chilled white wine in her hand. He, on the other hand, was sitting here staring at an empty street in one of the richest neighbourhoods in the world. Marvin was cool with working nights but he didn't like Chelsea much. Not because he was a Spurs fan, although that didn't help, more because hanging out with wealthy people always left him feeling uncomfortable and discontented, just like most of his clients seemed to be.

In Marvin's experience, both as a cop and as a private sector businessman, very wealthy people were uniquely unable to distinguish between perception and reality. Invariably, this meant that they made shit clients. Even so, the most important part of his business by a long way involved babysitting the paranoid rich of SW3, SW7, W8 and neighbouring postcodes.

After leaving the Met, Marvin had started Taylor Security Services – TSS – as an all-round security firm: installing alarms, protecting buildings, providing bouncers to nightclubs and so on. However, he quickly realized that the only area where there was any real money to be made was in close protection for SHNWIs. Super High Net Worth Individuals were now something approaching 90 per cent of TSS's business. Over the last few years, he had seen it all: the actor's daughter who wanted protection from her abusive, A-list father; the politician who paid a retainer of two grand a week so that a TSS operative would take his latest mistress shopping at Westfield on demand; the footballer who thought having a bodyguard would help him pull in West End nightclubs.

They were as nothing, however, compared to his latest clients. This trio was easily amongst the weirdest customers he'd ever had. Two foreigners and a Brit under self-imposed house arrest for almost a week now; too scared to come out of their building, only answering their front door for regular takeaways and deliveries from the local off-licence. What precisely they were scared of, he didn't know. The dynamics of their relationship Marvin couldn't quite fathom either. The woman was clearly in charge – she was the one paying the bills – but the English bloke? Was he her boyfriend, or just some lackey? And where did the boy – presumably her son – fit in?

Not that the details really mattered. Marvin had gotten the gig through an old Met contact and he was genuinely grateful for it. Stuffing the food packaging into a small plastic bag, he

10

glanced at his watch. A long, boring night stretched ahead of him. Normally, he would delegate night-shift duties but when there was a no-show, like this evening, he had to fill the gap. All too often, guys just wouldn't turn up for their shift. The people-management side of things routinely drove him mad. The young guys he worked with seemed to have no sense of responsibility. 'Maybe I should have stayed on the Force,' he muttered to himself, as he reached over for a battered copy of *World Football* magazine from the back seat and began flicking through it.

Engrossed in a feature about Liam Brady's time at Juventus in the 1980s, he scowled when the walkie-talkie radio sitting on the dashboard cackled into life.

'All clear.'

Letting the magazine fall into his lap, Marvin picked up the radio and hit the call button. 'Another tough night on the front line, huh?'

'Yeah. Christ, this is *sooo* fucking boring.'

'Think of the money, McGilroy,' Marvin told him.

'Yeah, but still.' James McGilroy was a thickset Irishman who had done two tours in Iraq and one in Afghanistan with the British Army. By comparison, the mean streets of Knightsbridge could be rather tedious. The only civilian he'd seen in the last hour was a woman in a burqa who had politely crossed the street to ignore him as she headed home, a Harrods plastic bag in each hand. 'This is a strange gig, boss.'

Marvin liked it when the boys called him 'boss'; it made him feel that he knew what he was doing, that he was the brains of the operation. 'They're all strange,' he observed. 'At least this one pays well.'

McGilroy grunted.

'Where's Kelvin?' Kelvin Douglas, McGilroy's buddy, was another ex-squaddie.

'Taking a piss.'

11

'OK.' Marvin signed off. 'Keep 'em peeled.' Tossing the radio on to the passenger seat, he returned to his magazine.

'How's Taylor?' Looking vaguely pleased with himself, Kelvin Douglas appeared from round the back of a dumpster, zipping up his flies.

'He's OK,' McGilroy mumbled. 'Not all that happy at having to be out with us tonight, no doubt, but he'll live.'

'Well, Chris said he had a hot date tonight with Annie, what do you expect?'

'I suppose.' Chris Goddard, the third member of their team, had been seeing his nursery teacher girlfriend for almost a year. 'But you would have thought the novelty would have worn off by now.'

'Apparently not.' Reaching into the pocket of his leather jacket, Douglas retrieved an outsized roll-up. 'Fancy a toke?' he asked, gesturing towards the low wall that ran along the back of the flats.

McGilroy frowned. 'Not on duty.'

'Come on,' Douglas grinned, 'it's not like we're in Nahr-e Saraj, is it?'

'No,' McGilroy agreed. 'I suppose not.'

'God. That seems like a lifetime ago, now.'

'I needed a smoke in bloody Helmand,' McGilroy reflected. 'But what I really fancy right now is a nice beer.'

'Good shout.' Douglas gestured towards the end of the alley with his thumb, as if he was trying to hitchhike, searching out an imaginary ride. 'There's an offie just down the road.'

'Regardless of the circumstances, that really would be taking the mickey.' McGilroy ran his hand over the grip of his Glock. The MP5s were safely locked up in TSS's offices, but even the handgun made him nervous. He understood that they were only to reassure the clients – Marvin liked to call it his USP for the high-end market – and the woman in the flat above them was clearly paying through the nose for *armed* protection. But it still felt wrong. Their handguns were unloaded but it was still totally illegal to be carrying a concealed weapon on a London street; possession of a firearm and ammunition was in clear breach of the standing orders familiar to every British soldier and fundamentally was contrary to the law of the land.

In his head, McGilroy ran through the list of crimes he could be charged with: possession of a firearm with intent to endanger life; possession of ammunition with intent to endanger life; possession of a prohibited firearm; possession of ammunition for a Section 1 Firearm without a certificate. If they got caught, jail was inevitable. He remembered the case of a guy in Cardiff – a regular family guy – who had brought back a pistol from his tour in Afghanistan and kept it in his sock drawer as a souvenir. A judge had given him two years in jail. McGilroy seemed to remember that the sentence had been overturned on appeal, but only after a right palaver. If it came to it, he and Kelvin wouldn't be so lucky.

Marvin Taylor liked to imply that he had it all covered; if necessary, he could call in a few favours from old colleagues to make any charges go away. But that was highly doubtful. McGilroy liked Marvin, but he knew a bullshit story when he heard it. 'Ah, well,' he mumbled to himself, 'you've made your bed. You signed up for this gig. No point in blaming the boss if it goes tits up.' He watched Douglas amble over to the wall, sit down and light up his spliff. Inhaling deeply, he began coughing.

'Good stuff?' McGilroy asked.

'Not bad.' Kelvin extended his arm, offering up the spliff.

McGilroy hesitated.

'Don't worry,' Kelvin continued, taking another quick puff, 'it's going to be another quiet night. You know it and I know it. The clients are safe and sound upstairs. Marv is probably having a kip in the van. Anyway, we're entitled to a five-minute break, aren't we?'

\* \* \*

The dope – a none too shabby Moroccan black – was pleasant enough but had little effect when it came to making McGilroy feel relaxed. Sitting on the wall felt like slacking off, and slacking off had always made him nervous, even when he was a young kid. On the other hand, the thought of walking aimlessly round the block for the next six-and-a-half hours did not appeal much either. The night before, McGilroy calculated that he had made 279 circuits of the building, moving at the slowest walking pace he could manage. It felt like being a rat in a lab experiment.

In the alley, shielded from prying eyes on the street, the two men finished the joint and fell into a rambling conversation that exhausted the usual topics – girls, guns and booze – before getting on to the subject of darts. Kelvin was opining on the relative merits of Phil Taylor and someone called Barney, when McGilroy sensed a movement off to his left. Slowly turning his head, he felt something cold brush against his cheek. At the edge of his vision, he could just make out the silhouette of a silencer. Oh, shit, he thought, stifling a nervous giggle, Marv is not going to be pleased.

'Jesus.' Jumping up from the wall, Kelvin Douglas reflexively reached for his empty weapon. There was a gentle pop and he went sprawling face down into the gutter.

*Marv's not going to be pleased at all.* Staring into the middle distance, McGilroy let his eyes lose their focus. Keeping his breathing under control, he concentrated on turning his body to stone.

'Boss? Boss, are you there?' The words finally began to penetrate Marvin Taylor's brain and he jolted himself awake, sending the half-read magazine sliding out of his lap and under the van's steering column. *Hell.* How long had he been dozing? What would happen if the bloody clients had seen? Fumbling with the radio, he hit the Call button.

'Yes?' he said tersely, trying to hide the grogginess in his voice. 'What is it?'

14

James McGilroy's response was equally terse. 'We've got company.'

'What?'

'Contact.'

*What?* The fog from Marvin's brain refused to clear. It was dark now. The street in front of him was deserted. 'Repeat,' he demanded. But McGilroy did not respond. Instead there was a burst of static from the radio, followed by the soft click of the van's passenger door opening. Someone slipped into the seat beside him and Marvin felt something going round his neck. Dropping his head to his chest, he gulped as a thin strand of wire tightened against his skin. His brain was screaming at him to fight but his arms would not move. Marvin's eyes teared up as the wire gently cut into his flesh. How far would they go? Would his head come right off? Gritting his teeth, he willed his last thoughts to be of his daughter, asleep in her bed.

*What do you call a crazy chicken?*

Closing his eyes, he brought up an image of her earlier in the day, in the supermarket, laughing at his crap joke. Was this dying happy? he wondered. It was as close as he was going to get.

# THREE

'For God's sake, will you stop coughing? Are you not taking something for that?'

Scratching at his stubble, Alexander Carlyle looked at his son apologetically before launching into another machine-gun bark. It was a relentless, rasping cough that sounded like he was going to deliver his lungs up onto the table at any second. The couple at the next table looked at the old man nervously before turning away.

Lifting his shot glass, Inspector John Carlyle sincerely wished he was still at work. Criminals could be a pain in the arse, but at least he could park them in cells and go home. And they were nowhere near as emotionally draining as his father.

After his mother had died, Carlyle had hoped he would have a more 'normal', less stressful relationship with his old man. Instead, he felt more and more like Harry H. Corbett in *Steptoe and Son*, the frustrated offspring of a hopeless parent. Finishing his whiskey, he gestured towards the half-full pint of Guinness in his father's hand. 'Get the rest of that down you,' he ordered, 'and I'll get another round in.'

Alexander placed his free hand over the top of his glass. 'I'm fine,' he croaked, before embarking on another extended bout of coughing.

Carlyle scowled as he got to his feet, convinced that at least half of the drinkers in the Princess Louise were now staring at them. 'Are you sure?' he enquired, once his father finally got his latest round of barking under control. 'I'm having one.' *Or maybe two.*

'To be honest, son, I've kind of lost the taste for it.'

'Suit yourself.' Fumbling in his pocket for some change, Carlyle limped towards the bar. Two days earlier, during one of his increasingly rare visits to the gym, he had sprained his ankle, leaving him hardly able to walk. The sudden, embarrassing incapacity had done nothing to improve his mood.

'You should get that seen to,' his father called after him, drawing on all the wisdom of his many years on the planet, 'before you do yourself some permanent damage.'

*You don't say.* Gritting his teeth against the pain, Carlyle hobbled faster. While waiting to catch the barmaid's eye, he watched the TV at the end of the bar. On the small screen, he could make out the rolling news ticker. A young reporter – they all looked young these days – was broadcasting live from outside a block of flats less than a mile away. Down an alley, behind the oh-so-familiar police tape, there had been some kind of fatal altercation. Details about what had happened were still sketchy, but it seemed to revolve around a dispute between local residents who, as the TV man put it, *'were not thought to be UK nationals'*.

'Bloody foreigners,' Carlyle muttered, only half-joking, 'forcing up property prices and bringing mayhem to the streets.'

Returning to the table with a double Jameson's – and a half of the black stuff for the old man, just in case – he was dismayed to see his father still struggling to control his cough. 'What's the matter?' he asked, belatedly trying to show a bit of compassion. 'Is it the flu?'

'Don't know, son,' Alexander replied, taking a quick sip from his previous pint during a brief lull in the coughing. 'Had it a while. Been feeling a bit under the weather since the turn of the year.'

'But that's been months.'

'Aye.'

Carlyle looked his father up and down. He was getting on, no question about it, but his health had always been good. And, after Carlyle's mother had divorced him, he had taken to the single life with a surprising gusto. Still, it was clear that he was now nearing his sell-by date.

*Looks like he's lost a bit of weight; maybe a bit pale. Definitely tired.*

How big was their age difference? Carlyle did the calculation. Twenty-three, twenty-four years? Something like that. It wasn't such a lot when you thought about it. Carlyle realized that he was looking at a picture of himself in the not too distant future and the thought weighed down on him like a concrete slab sitting on his chest.

'Been to see the GP?'

'Nah. I'll be fine.'

'Dad.'

'You know what it's like,' his father protested. 'They'll give you a few tests and tell you to stop smoking.'

Carlyle frowned. 'But you don't smoke.'

'Exactly. The doctor's a nice lad – quite a bit younger than you – but I don't like going to the surgery. It's depressing.'

*I know what you mean.* 'You should go, just to be on the safe side.'

Alexander gestured under the table with his glass. 'Anyway, have *you* been to see the GP?'

'Me?'

'About your foot?'

'No, but—'

'Exactly.'

The argument was ended by another bout of coughing. Sitting in sullen silence, Carlyle retreated into his drink. His father could be a stubborn sod – in a passive-aggressive kind of way – and he had never bought into the idea that he could take advice from his son.

Letting a mouthful of Jameson's linger on his tongue, Carlyle decided that he would need to consult Helen on this one. His wife had always had Alexander's measure, striking the right balance of daughter-in-law deference and no-nonsense female authority. Finishing his whiskey, he contemplated ordering another. Across the table, his father nibbled ineffectively at the remains of his pint, the fresh half still sitting untouched on the table. It was time to change the subject. 'I was wondering if you might fancy coming to the Cottage next weekend?' Father and son had been going to see Fulham together since Carlyle was six. They had given up their season tickets a few years ago but still went to see three or four games a season.

Alexander didn't look up from his pint. 'Who's playing?'

'Villa.'

'Ach. They're rubbish.'

'That's why they've still got seats on sale. I can get a couple of tickets in the Home end.' *At fifty-five quid each. Plus a booking fee.*

Alexander finally looked up, distinctly unimpressed. 'I don't know.'

*Come on, show a bit of enthusiasm.* 'OK, let me know.' Getting to his feet, Carlyle stretched. 'I need to get going. I'll see you soon.'


Standing by the window, Sergeant Alison Roche wearily shifted her weight on to her left foot, in order to prevent her SIG Pro pistol from digging into her side. Roche's shift was coming to an end and she felt knackered. Standing around doing nothing was one of the most exhausting parts of the job, always had been. And she was no spring chicken these days either. Looking down the road, she wondered just how much life this particular crime scene had left in it. They had been here for hours now, and all of the standard protocols had been executed. Just beyond the police tape, she could see the bright lights of the last remaining TV crew broadcasting from the middle of the road. The journalists' barely concealed delight at being able to report

19

on the mayhem and misfortune suffered by others annoyed the hell out of her. She thought of them as vampires. Surely they had bled this story dry by now? Even the BBC had packed up and taken their toys off to Buckingham Palace, in toadying anticipation of the next royal sprog popping out.

'Roche.'

The sergeant instantly recognized the reedy voice of her boss. 'Sir.' She turned and watched the Chief Inspector slouch down the corridor. He looked crumpled and not a little careworn. Your uniform could do with a press, she thought, looking him up and down like a mother inspecting the return of her offspring from a particularly hectic day at junior school.

As far as Roche was concerned, the problem with Chief Inspector Will Dick – or rather, *one* of the many problems with him – was that she just couldn't take him seriously. The more the man tried to affect gravitas and establish his credentials as the Commanding Officer of SO15, the more the sergeant had him pegged as a complete bluffer. In fairness, he wasn't the only one; the lack of proper leadership in the unit had been a major concern for Roche almost since her first day in the job. Staff rotated in and out with alarming regularity. After a while, she came to accept it as just one of those things. Thank God the place more or less ran itself.

All thinning hair and beseeching eyes, Dick was the unit's third CO in as many years. He had arrived in London after a spell running a training college in some provincial police force. His appointment would have been genuinely baffling were it not for the fact that baffling appointments appeared to be the norm in the higher echelons of the Metropolitan Police Force. On a day-to-day basis, Roche worked hard at being phlegmatic. As long as she managed to keep her distance from the hapless Chief Inspector, why should she worry too much about his ineffectiveness? After all, his replacement would doubtless be along soon enough.

All of which made his current unexpected presence at the

actual crime scene rather disconcerting. As he came closer, Roche patiently waited for the Chief Inspector to articulate what he wanted from her. When no explanation was forthcoming, she gave him a gentle prompt. 'What can I do for you, boss?'

A pained expression crossed Dick's face, as if he was suffering from the after-effects of a dodgy lunchtime curry. 'Slacking off, Sergeant?'

*What?* Roche felt herself stiffen. *Hardly.* 'No, sir,' she said evenly. 'Inspector Craven told me to keep this floor clear.'

'Good.' Inspector John Craven was the unit's second-in-command and just about the only person in the unit prepared to kowtow to Dick. Both divorcés, the two men shared a rather sad enthusiasm for real ales and middle-class sports. To the general amusement of the rank and file, the pair played golf together out at Epping and were rumoured to be planning a hiking holiday in the Alps. All in all, their relationship looked like a fine bromance.

Roche gestured at the ceiling. 'I think he's upstairs.'

Dick looked puzzled. 'Who?'

The man had the attention span of a goldfish. 'Craven.' *In case you want to get on with your holiday planning,* she thought sarkily.

'Ah yes.' Dick was a good two inches shorter than his sergeant. Unwilling to acknowledge this by looking her in the eye, he stared at his shoes. With his head bowed, Roche was gratified to see that the bald patch on the crown of his head was becoming more obvious.

'Can I help you with something?' she repeated.

'No,' Dick said stiffly, 'not really. I'm just checking up on how things are progressing here. Need to be able to justify the use of the manpower – overtime and all that.'

'And?' Roche knew she should keep her mouth shut, but she couldn't resist putting the little sod on the spot.

'And what, Sergeant?'

21

'How *are* things progressing, sir?' she asked sweetly, as if genuinely interested in his answer.

For a couple of moments, the Chief Inspector seemed totally stumped by the question. 'Satisfactorily,' he said finally, lifting his gaze towards her ankles.

Roche waited patiently for him to look vaguely in the direction of her face. 'It's just that I was wondering,' she continued, her voice containing just the right tone of innocent curiosity, 'why exactly are we here?' She was rewarded with another blank look. 'I mean, why are we guarding an empty flat?'

'Counter Terrorism Command has a broad remit,' Dick replied, adopting the kind of tone you would use when doing community outreach at a sixth-form college or WI group, 'and don't forget, three people have died, one of whom was a former colleague.' For a moment, it looked as though Dick was going to cross himself, but the Chief Inspector thought better of it at the last minute. News of Marvin Taylor's decapitation had spread like wildfire; the poor man's identity had been kept from the press so that the family could be informed, but his face would be on every website and TV news show in the next couple of hours. 'He had a wife and child, so I hear.' Dick shook his head mournfully. 'It's such a sad state of affairs.'

At least I've got no one to get too upset, Roche thought, if something like that were to happen to me. Feeling a twinge of discomfort in her lower back, the sergeant grimaced. It was the kind of niggling pain that she experienced more and more often these days. She regularly vowed to go and see someone about it but never managed to get round to it. 'Yes, but—'

A mobile started ringing in Dick's pocket. Roche recognized the theme from *Mission: Impossible*.

*Original.*

Holding up a hand, the Chief Inspector answered his phone. 'Yes?' Then, turning away from the sergeant, he marched back down the corridor without another word.

*Rude.* 'I didn't sign up for SO15 to act as a bloody security guard,' Roche muttered after him. The truth was, after almost three years in CTC, she struggled to remember why she had wanted to join it in the first place. One thing was for sure, the supposed glamour of working for one of the Metropolitan Police's elite units had failed to materialize. In a city like London, there just wasn't enough drama to go round. There were at least half-a-dozen different units chasing after the sexy jobs, which was why you ended up standing in an empty corridor for an entire shift. Days like today left her thinking that it had been more fun being an ordinary plod.

The sergeant was wondering just how much longer she would be left here, guarding precisely fuck-all, when SO15's newest recruit, a fresh-faced young officer called Oliver Steed, appeared from the nearby stairwell.

'Ali . . .' The boy, barely twenty-five, almost blushed as he approached her. It hadn't escaped Roche's attention – nor that of the rest of the unit – that Steed fancied her something rotten. Given that her would-be suitor was more than a decade her junior, most people assumed that the sergeant would be flattered by the attention. The reality, however, was that she found his interest embarrassing and annoying in equal measure. Roche had an iron rule: no boyfriends who were on The Job. It was a rule born out of bitter experience: she had learned all about the pitfalls of dating colleagues long before this particular one had finished school.

Roche folded her arms and kept her expression blank. She didn't want anything in her body language that might give the kid any kind of encouragement. 'What's up?'

'We've been told to stand down,' Steed explained, almost apologetically. 'Apparently Forensics have finally finished their work inside the building. They're just about to let the neighbours back into their flats.'

'Better get out of the way then,' Roche quipped, 'before there's a stampede.' The building, as far as she could tell, was largely empty. The cheapest apartment went for somewhere north of £2.5 million, and the only people who could afford to buy them could equally afford not to live in them. They no doubt had multiple properties scattered around the globe and used their London bolt holes rarely, if at all.

'A few of us,' Steed continued, blushing properly now, 'are gonna head down the pub after the shift for a few drinks and I was wondering—'

'Thanks for the offer,' Roche said curtly, pre-empting his question, 'but all this standing about doing nothing has done me in. I need a hot bath and a good kip.'

'Hm.' Contemplating the prospect of Alison Roche soaking in the bath, Steed blushed a little more.

'Anyway,' the sergeant concluded, moving swiftly on, 'if we're done, I'm outta here. Thanks for letting me know.' Slipping past the kid, she headed for the stairs. 'See you later.'

# FOUR

*I need a coffee.* Still feeling rather thick-headed from the night before, the inspector limped into the lobby of the Charing Cross police station with his sergeant, Umar Sligo, in tow. Carlyle reflected unhappily that he should have gone easier on the whiskey. That was the problem about having a drink with his father; you kept going back to the bar in order to break up the uncomfortable silences. The reality was that Alexander Carlyle wasn't the only one getting on a bit. These days, the effects of even a modest amount of drinking would stay with the inspector well into the following day.

'Home sweet home,' Umar murmured. Another sleep-deprived night had taken the edge off his pretty-boy good looks, but to the inspector's jaundiced eye, he still looked more like a male model than a policeman.

Shifting his weight from his sore foot, Carlyle grunted something suitably dismissive as he surveyed his domain. Given the early hour, the place was rather busier than he would have expected. At the front desk, a middle-aged man in a suit was arguing with the duty sergeant while a random selection of other customers waited their turn on the benches provided. Conducting a quick head-count, the inspector came up with a total of twenty-three people. As you would expect in this part of London, they were of all ages, shapes, sizes and ethnic origin. For a moment, he wondered what had brought them to his door, before shaking his head sadly. Twenty-three people, each with their own tale of woe, represented rather too much humanity for one policeman to contemplate before breakfast. 'It's like the number 15 bus,' he said aloud.

Turning to face the inspector, Umar offered up one of his trademark blank looks. 'Huh?'

Carlyle gestured towards the front desk, where the sergeant, an amiable North Londoner called Frank Stapleton, was trying to placate the increasingly upset businessman in front of him.

'We're the only station in London that still has an old-style front desk, with a sergeant who will interact – like a normal human being – with whoever drops in off the street. Everywhere else, it's like walking into a call centre: *Take a ticket and a customer-service operative will be with you shortly.* After two hours, some intern working for a support-services company – nothing to do with the police at all – gets you to fill out a form and gives you a Crimestoppers number, so you can claim on your insurance.' As he spoke, Carlyle could feel himself getting worked up by it all, but he wasn't quite sure why. This had been the norm in police stations across the capital for years now – and it wasn't like it was his problem. 'You might as well be dealing with a computer. In some stations, you probably are already.'

'Yeah.' Umar nodded, not sure where this particular rant was going. He had been working with the inspector long enough to realize that his random moaning was not to be taken too seriously. Whatever had rattled his cage would normally be forgotten once he'd had his morning fix of both caffeine and sugar. 'Want me to go to Carluccio's?' he asked, gesturing towards the door. There was a branch of the upmarket café just up the road and he knew it was close to the inspector's heart.

Carlyle gave the proposal careful thought before deciding, 'Nah. Here's fine.' Carluccio's had far better coffee than the basement canteen in the station, and the cakes were to die for, but if he didn't start rationing his visits, the place would bankrupt him.

'Suit yourself.' Glancing up at the clock behind the desk, Umar wished he was back in bed. He had always hated the early starts; now that his daughter Ella had arrived, they had become even harder to endure. Yawning, he thought about how his recent plan to quit the Met – and bin his alarm clock – had been stymied. Christina, Umar's wife, had wanted to go back to work. For his part, Umar had been more than ready to embrace the role of house-husband. But the job market was tough and Christina had found nothing that could come close to matching his sergeant's salary. So the status quo was maintained – *hurrah for traditional family values* – and here he was, stuck with the ever-complaining inspector at bastard o'clock.

Umar liked to think that Carlyle was pleased that he had stayed on. He knew that the reality was that the old sod simply took whatever happened in his stride. If he left, another sergeant would take his place. That was the thing about Inspector John Carlyle, he always moved on with a minimum of fuss.

'It's like the old Routemaster buses on the 15 through the centre of Town,' Carlyle continued, oblivious to Umar's lack of interest. 'A bit of heritage for the benefit of the tourists. The only buses you can still jump on and off between stops, with a conductor. Far more fun than those crappy modern driver-operated ones.'

Umar gestured towards the desk sergeant, who was growing visibly exasperated with the unhappy suit. 'I'm not sure I would call Stapleton a tourist attraction,' he grinned.

'No,' Carlyle conceded, 'but you know what I mean.'

*Not really, old man.* 'Yeah, yeah.'

'He exists to create the impression that we give a fuck about people and customer service, rather than just hiding behind our desks. We want the public to think that there are still some traditional standards left here and there.'

What the hell are you on about? Umar wondered.

'Gentlemen.' Seeing the two officers loitering by the door, Frank Stapleton beckoned them over to the desk.

Carlyle approached warily. 'How's it going, Frank?' he asked, ignoring the customer.

'This, er, gentleman,' Stapleton said carefully, pointing at the suit with the chewed end of a blue biro, 'could do with some assistance.'

'Uh-huh.' Carlyle took a quick step backwards so that Umar was to the fore.

The suit turned and looked at the sergeant expectantly.

'Um, yes,' Umar said reluctantly, 'what is the problem?'

The man offered a hand. 'Brian Yates.' He was of medium height, maybe five foot eight, with thinning grey hair and a day's worth of stubble on his chin. The wrinkles around his pale brown eyes were pronounced and he had the haunted look of a man who hadn't slept much the night before. His creased suit and the absence of a tie added to the overall effect.

You look even worse than I feel, Carlyle thought. He imagined Yates to be an insurance salesman from Birmingham, or maybe something in IT from Manchester. The inspector's metropolitan snobbery kicked in and he felt a pang of sympathy for the bloke. *More to be pitied than scorned, no doubt.*

Umar looked at Yates's outstretched hand but made no attempt to shake it.

'Mr Yates feels that he has been a victim of fraud,' Stapleton smirked, his exasperation evaporating as he effortlessly passed the buck to his colleagues. 'But I am sure that you officers will be able to help him.'

Umar glanced at Carlyle, but the inspector simply took another step backwards to underline his disinclination to get involved.

'Like I said to the sergeant,' Yates said brightly, happy now that his complaint was finally being acknowledged and that he was moving up the food chain, 'I tried calling 999, but couldn't get any joy. No one would take me seriously.'

'So he came to the station,' Stapleton explained with the tone of a man building up his joke in anticipation of the punchline.

'So what was the fraud?' Umar asked.

'Contravention of the Sale of Goods Act 1979,' said Yates, with all the authority of a man with Google on his side. 'I checked it on the internet.'

Letting his smirk mutate into a full-blown grin, Stapleton looked at Carlyle. 'He wasn't happy with Sonia.'

'Sonia?' the inspector asked, allowing himself to be drawn into the conversation despite his better judgement.

'Sonia Coverdale,' Stapleton explained.

Carlyle recognized the name but said nothing.

'Who's Sonia Coverdale?' Umar asked.

'Sexy Sonia,' Yates jumped in, 'a Platinum girl from Royal Escorts. Except that she wasn't.'

'Eh?' said Carlyle and Umar in unison.

'I paid three hundred quid for a quote-unquote "stunning beauty" – one of their top girls – and that's not what I got. The law says goods must be of satisfactory quality, be fit for purpose and match the seller's description.'

Carlyle took a moment to retrieve a mental image of the hooker. He probably hadn't seen her in the last year or so, but, as far as he could recall, Sonia was a perfectly good-looking girl.

'I mean she was all right, but nothing special. It was a clear case of mis-selling if ever there was one. But when I asked for my money back, she told me to get stuffed and stormed out of the hotel.'

'You paid in advance?' Umar asked.

'Yes,' Yates blinked. 'I said – three hundred quid. Why?'

Careful not to make eye contact with the chortling Stapleton, Carlyle gestured towards the stairs. 'I think you'd better come with us, sir.'

More blinking. 'Aren't you going to make a report?' Yates asked, his tone more pleading than demanding.

'First things first,' said Carlyle, leading the way. 'Let's go and get a coffee.'

* * *

29

Sitting in the canteen, Carlyle rested his injured foot on a free chair. Should he put some ice on it? Deciding that it would make too much mess, he distracted himself by watching one of the dinner ladies chalk up a list of the day's lunch specials on a blackboard on the wall next to the serving area. Seeing nothing that took his fancy, he then considered where else he might take his lunchtime custom. Unable to reach a decision, he turned his attention back to Brian Yates, who was morosely toying with a packet of sweetener.

'So let me get this straight.' Yates tossed the sachet on to the table and leaned back in his chair. 'I'm three hundred quid down, the woman nicked my cash, and *I'm* the one who broke the law?'

'Soliciting is a crime,' Umar pointed out, 'under the Street Offences Act 1959.'

'But I didn't solicit,' Yates protested. 'I only looked at Sonia's picture on the internet; her very *flattering* picture. I'm not even sure it was her. It was airbrushed to hell, at the very least. Or Photoshopped, whatever they do to pictures these days. And they say that the camera never lies.'

Let's not go there again, Carlyle thought. 'You contacted her. You met. You handed over the cash. It's an open and shut case.'

Yates shifted uneasily in his seat. 'But the bloody internet didn't even exist in 1959,' he wailed.

'Even if we didn't go for soliciting,' Umar said cheerily, 'there's the Criminal Law Act of 1967.'

Carlyle looked at his sergeant in disbelief. When did you swallow a copy of Black's *Law Dictionary*? he wondered.

'Oh?' Yates looked as if he might have a stroke at any moment.

'Yes,' said Umar, dropping a piece of chocolate chip muffin into his mouth. 'If you'd taken a look at it, you'd have found out that wasting police time is a serious offence, one which carries a maximum sentence of six months' imprisonment.'

Yates's face crumpled and he looked like he was going to start crying. 'But . . .'

Tiring of the conversation, the inspector held up a hand. 'Don't worry, Mr Yates,' he said gently. 'We are not going to take this any further.'

Hope battled with despair on Yates's face. 'No?'

'No. But you need to put this down to experience.'

'What would your wife think?' Umar added.

'Haven't got one,' Yates muttered. 'We got divorced four years ago.'

*Why am I not surprised?* 'Even so,' Carlyle advised, 'I think you should maybe give the escort agencies a rest for a while.'

Yates looked at each of the officers in turn. 'So I'm not being prosecuted but I'm not getting my money back either?'

'Get a few blank taxi receipts,' Umar ventured, 'claw it back on expenses.'

Yates thought that one through for a few moments, saying nothing. Then, glancing at his watch, he jumped to his feet. 'Goodness, I'm going to be late for my next appointment.'

'What is it you do?' Carlyle asked.

A renewed look of concern passed across the man's face. 'Why do you ask?'

'No reason,' the inspector shrugged. 'Just curious.'

'I sell satellite capacity to telcos and ISPs.' Pulling a business card from the pocket of his jacket, he handed it to the inspector.

'I see,' Carlyle nodded, none the wiser. 'Anyway, good luck. And I don't want to see you back here.'

'Yes, well, quite.' Skipping towards the door, Yates didn't look back.

Umar watched him disappear before turning to the inspector. 'Why did you let him go?'

'Good old-fashioned customer service,' Carlyle grinned.

'Like the 15 bus.'

'Something like that,' Carlyle replied, surprised that Umar had been paying attention to their earlier conversation. *We should be grateful to Mr Yates; he gave us a rare opportunity to use our common sense. Arresting him for time-wasting would* simply have wasted more time. And it wasn't like we were going to go after Sonia, was it?'

'I wonder if she's as bad as he made out?' Umar asked, stuffing the last piece of the muffin into his mouth.

'Not as far as I recall.'

'You know her?'

'I've met her a few times,' Carlyle admitted.

'And she's a looker?'

'She's a pretty girl.' Noting the wheels turning in his sergeant's brain, the inspector quickly added: 'Not that it should be of much concern to you.' Now that Umar was married, with a kid, the inspector felt some kind of vague responsibility for trying to keep him on the straight and narrow when it came to the ladies. Never a player himself, the setting of the younger man's moral compass made Carlyle distinctly uncomfortable. Still, he had been quite happy when the boy's hopes of leaving the police were dashed; Umar was his third sergeant in quick succession and a bit of continuity was most welcome.

Umar wiped the corners of his mouth with a paper napkin, sending crumbs cascading on to his Kasabian T-shirt. 'Just making conversation,' he mumbled.

'Better get on.' Not wishing to discuss the matter any further, Carlyle got up and headed for the lifts.

# FIVE

Reaching the third floor, Carlyle passed a red collection bucket that had been chained to an empty desk. A notice next to it read: *Collection for family of Marvin Taylor (Charing Cross 2008– 2010) who died last week. Please give generously.* Sighing, he took out his wallet and removed a twenty-pound note. Folding it up, he pushed it through the slot, while eyeing the anti-tamper seal on the lid suspiciously. I hope that holds up, he thought. I wouldn't trust the buggers round here for a minute.

Umar appeared at his shoulder and scanned the notice. 'Who's Marvin Taylor?'

'He was a sergeant here,' Carlyle explained. 'Nice guy. Took redundancy in one of the rounds of cost-cutting we had and went off to set up his own security business.'

'OK. So what happened to him?'

'Someone sawed his head off in Chelsea the other night.'

'Ah,' Umar replied, 'so he was one of the guys in the massacre?'

'The what?'

'That's what they're calling it on TV – the Chelsea Massacre.'

'Wankers,' Carlyle hissed. 'I bet they pissed themselves with excitement when they found out what had happened.'

'That's the media for you,' said Umar philosophically.

'Yes, it is,' Carlyle agreed, heading for his desk. 'But Marvin was a good guy, a family man, so put some money in the collection.'

'Eh?' A look of consternation crossed Umar's face. 'But I never knew the bloke; he was before my time. And, besides, I'm skint.'

'Twenty quid minimum,' the inspector added, dismissing his protests with a wave of the hand. 'You never know, we might be doing it for you one day.' Stumbling into his chair, he reached across the desk to switch on his PC, grabbing a Post-it note that had been stuck to the screen before slumping back into his seat. If anything, the pain in his sprained ankle was getting worse. He lifted his foot on to the table and tentatively wiggled his toes in the hope that it would somehow ease his discomfort.

'You should get that seen to, you know.' Standing at the next desk, Umar began sifting through a pile of mail that had been left in his in-tray.

'Thank you, Dr Findlay.'

'Who?'

'Never mind.' Eschewing his glasses, Carlyle squinted at the square of yellow paper in his hand. *Naomi 0203 405 5958.*

*Naomi?* His foot throbbed angrily as he tried to put a face to the name.

*Naomi? Who the fuck was Naomi?*

Giving up, he turned back to his sergeant. 'Do we know a Naomi?'

Umar thought about it for a moment and chuckled. 'I don't know about you, but I know a couple.'

Exasperated, the inspector waved the Post-it note at his minion. 'I mean, professionally speaking. Some woman called Naomi wants me to give her a call.'

'Give her a call then,' Umar shrugged, going back to his mail.

'I'll give her a call then,' Carlyle parroted. With his computer still struggling to come to life, he reached across the desk and picked up the receiver on his landline and punched in the woman's number. The call was answered on the second ring.

'Naomi?' Carlyle demanded, settling back into his seat.

'Yes.' The voice sounded small and distant.

'This is Inspector John Carlyle at Charing Cross police station. I got a message to give you a call.'

'Yes.'

*And?* His hackles rising, Carlyle said nothing.

'You don't remember me, do you?'

'Should I?' Carlyle asked, his voice rather more brusque than he intended.

'I am . . . was Naomi Sage. I'm a friend of Susan Phillips.'

'Ah, yes,' Carlyle nodded, none the wiser. Susan Phillips, a police pathologist working out of the Holborn station, was an old friend. He couldn't place the other woman, however.

'Susan suggested that I give you a call.'

'OK,' said Carlyle warily, wondering what he was going to be lumbered with now. His computer finally made it through its start-up routine and a prompt appeared on the screen demanding his username and password. His mind ran through the overdue reports that needed to be written and the other crap that he should be dealing with.

'My married name is Taylor,' her voice wavered.

*Taylor.* The inspector glanced across the room in time to see one of the uniforms drop a handful of coins into the collection bucket.

'You worked with Marvin, didn't you?'

'Er, yes,' Carlyle coughed, 'yes, I did.'

'I'm his wife.'

Putting down the phone, the inspector scratched his head. Feeling listless and unable to focus on matters of a professional nature, he pondered a quick return to the café for another snack but ruled it out on the grounds that he wasn't hungry in the slightest. Looking across the room, he was dismayed to see his sergeant hard at work on his Facebook page.

*Crime-fighting really can be a bitch.* He was just about to chide Umar when he was distracted by a whiff of expensive perfume. Sniffing the air like some small animal in the desert, he watched Amelia Elmhirst float by.

Carlyle cleared his throat. 'Morning.'

'Good morning, Inspector.' She eyed him with the wry

amusement of someone who knew that *she* would be the boss around here soon enough, before taking up a perch on the corner of Umar's desk. Sergeant Amelia Elmhirst was the talk of the Charing Cross station. Six foot one, blonde, with deep blue eyes, the sergeant had the kind of über-healthy, Leni Riefenstahl-approved look that belonged on a catwalk, rather than walking the beat on the grimy streets of WC2. A graduate of King's College, with a first in Psychology and an MA in Social Anthropology, Elmhirst was being fast-tracked through a graduate trainee programme that would see her make inspector well before her thirtieth birthday. The fact that she lived with her long-term boyfriend – a social media entrepreneur called Simon – in a loft in Shoreditch did nothing to stop her from being an object of desire for every man in the station.

'Hi, Amelia,' Umar grinned, quickly abandoning Facebook in order to give the new arrival his full attention.

Careful, Carlyle thought, you don't want your tongue dragging on the floor.

Never slow when it came to the opposite sex, Umar was a man on a mission. At a conservative estimate, the inspector calculated that around a quarter of his sergeant's working day was currently devoted to flirting with his colleague or devising strategies to try and get into her knickers. 'How's it going?'

'Fine. Nothing particularly exciting.' Pushing a strand of hair behind her ear, Elmhirst glanced at Carlyle, who was settling in to shamelessly eavesdrop on their conversation. Keen to assess the state of Umar's quest, the inspector smiled sweetly, making no effort to pretend to be working. 'Had to deal with a landlord yesterday, who tried to evict his tenant by shooting him.'

'It's a way of speeding things up, I suppose,' Carlyle quipped.

Umar shot him a look that said *Get lost*.

'Anyway, he missed. Or things could have been much worse.' Elmhirst turned away from Carlyle to give Umar her full attention. 'About that photo . . .'

'Did you like it?' Umar grinned.

36

Leaning forward, Elmhirst lowered her voice. 'Don't do it again. If Si saw it, he would have a fit.'

'I thought he was in San Francisco,' Umar protested.

'Yeah, but if he came back and picked up my iPhone . . .' Elmhirst got to her feet. 'I've deleted it, but just don't do it again. It's not very funny. And,' she giggled, 'I was really quite surprised. It's not very big, is it?'

Umar sat up in his chair. 'It was just the angle,' he said stiffly.

'Whatever.' She began walking away but stopped after a couple of paces and turned back to face him. 'Look, Umar, I know it's just supposed to be a joke. But some people might not be so . . . broad-minded as me.'

'Mm.' Umar squirmed in his seat as he contemplated Elmhirst being broad-minded.

'Just be careful.'

'What do you mean?'

Elmhirst smiled. 'I know you've sent pics to some of the other girls. If someone were to make a complaint, you could be in big trouble.'

'Fancy a drink tonight?' he called after her as she finally walked away.

'Sorry. I'm going to meet Si at Heathrow. Next time.'

'Lucky bugger,' Umar muttered under his breath. 'And he's such a total waste of space. Completely useless. I don't know what she sees in him at all.'

*Not your problem, is it?* Carlyle took one last breath of Elmhirst's scent as she disappeared. 'What was all that about?' he asked.

'Nothing,' said Umar glumly, before returning his attention to the computer screen. 'Nothing at all.'

The inspector couldn't resist twisting the knife just a little. 'She's not responding to your charms, then, eh?'

'Sod off,' was all he got by way of reply.

# SIX

Sitting in a Lebanese café on the Edgware Road, an occasional haunt over the years, Carlyle reluctantly put on his glasses, the better to inspect himself in the mirror that covered the entire wall opposite. Groaning inwardly, he noted every line on his sagging face and every additional grey hair on his head. It seemed that just as he had reconciled himself to uncomfortable middle age, he was exiting that stage of his life at some speed. At what time would he formally become old? Not for the first time, thoughts of retirement flitted through his head. The idea seemed as ridiculous as ever.

The grumpy old sod staring back at him seemed equally unimpressed with what he saw. The inspector had to resist the considerable temptation to flick him a few angry V-signs. At least he didn't seem to be going bald. If nothing else, the Carlyle family genes should ensure he kept a full head of hair well into his advancing years. His father was testament to that. It wasn't much of an inheritance but he supposed that it was better than nothing.

'Inspector?'

Reluctantly, he returned his attention to the woman in front of him. Naomi Taylor was a small, fragile-looking woman, with short auburn hair and black rings under her eyes, which stood testimony to the stress she had been under, the last few days. If he had ever met her before now, Carlyle couldn't recall it; she wasn't the type of person you were likely to remember unless you had a particular reason to do so.

'Susan said you might be able to help me.'

'Yes.' *Bloody Phillips.* From a radio behind the counter came the sounds of Daft Punk's 'Get Lucky'. The song was a current favourite of Alice's and he liked to listen to her mooching around the flat singing the chorus to herself. It was well past time for his daughter to start developing her own tastes in music – she could only limit her interests to The Clash, The Jam and the rest of his old CD collection for so long. A question popped into his head. 'Did you . . . I mean, do you have kids?'

Naomi nodded and her eyes filled with tears.

*You moron. Surely you should be better at this by now.* Grabbing a napkin from the table, he handed it over.

'Thanks,' she mumbled, before blowing her nose with surprising force. 'A girl. She's with my mother.'

'Yes.'

She waited patiently until it became obvious that he wasn't going to say anything else. 'Did you work with him?' she asked finally.

'Marvin? Er, yes, a few times.' It was a complete lie. During Taylor's time at Charing Cross, the two of them had barely spoken to each other. It was a period when Carlyle seemed to be landed with endless night shifts, and his interaction with the majority of his colleagues had been severely curtailed. Convinced that night shifts were very bad for your physical and mental health, the inspector had nothing but unhappy memories of that time. He had known the sergeant by sight but they were barely on nodding terms when they passed in the corridor or on Agar Street. 'We covered a few cases together when Marvin was at my station. He was a good man, a valuable colleague . . . very dependable.'

Her eyes filled again and a large tear rolled down each cheek. Stifling a sob, she rocked forward until her face was barely two inches from the top of the table. Carlyle reached for another napkin. On the radio, 'Get Lucky' had been superseded by another cheery tune. This one he didn't recognize. Time seemed to slow down and he was conscious that the other customers were looking at them, their own conversations put on hold while they tuned in to the human drama nearby. Clearly, a café had been the wrong choice of venue for this meeting. He offered her the napkin but she waved it away, wiping her nose on the sleeve of her jacket. Fair enough, Carlyle thought. This is not the time to be standing on ceremony.

'They say . . .' her voice quavered and she fought for a breath. Carlyle glared at a couple on the next table who were shamelessly eavesdropping until they reluctantly went back to their own conversation. Naomi Taylor placed her elbows on the table and leaned forward. 'They say,' she whispered, 'that his head . . . was almost sliced off.'

Squeamish at the best of times, Carlyle grimaced. 'Who told you this?'

She shuddered, as if someone had just stuck a blade through her ribs. 'I overheard someone joking about it.'

The inspector shook his head in dismay 'Have you not seen the body yet?'

If anything, the woman's face became even more anguished. 'No, they won't let me see it.'

Carlyle thought back to this morning's papers. The grisly details had been there for all to read. 'But they told the press?' *Very strange. Someone must have sold the information.* So much for the new Commissioner's promise to clean up the Met; the organization still had more than its share of officers who were as bent as a nine-bob note, willing to sell juicy details of a crime to journalists for some beer money.

His unhappy musings were interrupted by the phone vibrating next to his left breast. 'Sorry, I need to take this,' he told her as he pulled it from his pocket.

'Carlyle.'

'Where are you?'

Taken aback by the brusqueness of his boss's opening gambit, the inspector took a moment to get his bearings. 'Er . . .'

'I spoke to Charing Cross and they just said you'd gone out.' Commander Carole Simpson sounded like a pissed-off headmistress. Come to think of it, that was increasingly her default tone when speaking with her erratic underling. Maybe it was simply a reflection of her advancing years. Remembering that, however old she was, the Commander was still younger than him, Carlyle dropped that line of thinking immediately.

'I'm in a meeting. Not far from you, as it happens.' Simpson was stationed at Paddington Green, barely five minutes' walk from where he was sitting.

'How convenient,' Simpson drawled sarcastically. 'So I take it that you could manage to put in an appearance with us, then?'

*Bollocks.* Whatever Simpson wanted, it would inevitably involve more work. As he got older himself, the inspector was less inclined to take on the cases he was given and more determined to pick and choose the ones he wanted. As far as he could see, it was one of the few perks of longevity in the organization. Normally, the commander was happy enough to keep him on a long leash. There were times, however, when she enjoyed bringing him to heel.

'Of course, boss,' he replied, throwing an ounce of fake cheer into his voice, 'I'd love to.'

'Good,' said Simpson, her good humour equally false. 'I look forward to seeing you in what – the next ten minutes or so?'

Carlyle looked at Taylor, patiently waiting for him to finish the call. The disappointed look on her face made it clear that he should have left the phone unanswered. He felt like a heel. 'Make it twenty.' Ending the call, he dropped the phone back into his pocket. 'Sorry,' he repeated. 'That was my boss.'

Taylor nodded. 'You must be very busy.'

*Not really.* The inspector thought about the random odds and sods currently on his desk; nothing to get the adrenaline pumping. 'Yes.'

'I'm sorry to have taken up so much of your time this morning.' She began fumbling in her bag for her purse. Carlyle leaned across the table and put a hand on her arm.

'Don't worry. I'll get this. Tell me what I can do to help.'

She looked at him doubtfully.

Taking his hand from her arm, he said, 'Marvin was a good bloke and a good colleague. If there is anything I can do to help you and your . . .' Did they have a boy or a girl?

'Daughter.' It wasn't so much a word as a cry.

'Yes.' The couple on the next table had tuned back into Carlyle's conversation. He tried to ignore them.

'Laurie.'

'If there is anything I can do to help you and, er, Laurie, I am at your disposal.'

'Well, if you could see what you could find out.'

He looked at the hope mingling with despair on her face and tried to smile. 'About . . .'

'About anything,' she sniffed. 'What happened, why someone did this to him, when we can have him back. Anything.' From the pocket of her jacket she pulled a business card and handed it to him. 'This is the person I've been dealing with so far. He's been very nice but hasn't been able to tell me much. That's why I spoke to Susan and she suggested I get in touch with you.'

'Yes.' Putting his glasses on the top of his head, Carlyle scanned the card. *Oliver Steed, Liaison Officer, SO15.* Below the name and title, there was a landline number but no mobile, suggesting that Mr Steed didn't really want to be contacted at all.

*SO15? What did this have to do with Counter Terrorism? What had Marvin bloody Taylor gotten himself into?*

Taylor caught him frowning. 'Do you know him?'

'No.' Carlyle carefully entered Steed's details into his phone,

42

handed back the card, and then took Taylor's own numbers. 'I do know some people in SO15 though,' he added, still peering at the mobile's screen. 'So maybe I *can* find out something.'

For once, Simpson didn't keep him waiting. Arriving at Paddington Green, he was ushered directly into the Commander's office by her latest PA – a greasy-looking boy with too much fake tan – and offered a coffee, which he declined. After his meeting with Naomi Taylor, he had more than enough caffeine in his system already.

'But we have some really nice Jamaican Blue Mountain roasted beans,' the boy protested, fiddling with the collar of his fuchsia-coloured polo shirt. 'I got it from Waitrose this morning.'

*Waitrose? Jesus.* Even Helen complained about the posh supermarket's prices, and his wife rarely noticed such things. There were times when he wondered if the gentrification of his city had not gone too far. Carlyle shook his head. 'I'm fine, thanks.'

Simpson appeared from behind her assistant and grinned. 'Not like you to say no to a coffee, John.'

Not like you to offer me one, the inspector thought grumpily. 'Helen's been trying to get me to cut down for a while now. And, anyway, I just had one.'

'Ah, yes.' Simpson's grin grew wider. 'Your meeting.' She looked up. 'I'll have half a cup, please, Jason. Black.' The boy nodded and hurried out of the room.

'New?' Carlyle asked, happy to prolong the small talk for as long as possible.

'I've had him about a month.'

'Any good?'

'We'll see.' Jason reappeared almost instantly, placing a faded *London 2012* mug on the Commander's desk, and retreated out of the door doing something that looked to Carlyle suspiciously like a moonwalk. If Simpson noticed, she didn't let on. Taking a sip of her coffee, she gave a small nod of approval. 'At least he can make a decent cup of coffee – and in double-quick time too. Not that it matters much, none of them last very long. I worked out recently that the average life expectancy of one of my PAs is about four months. I try not to get too attached to any of them.'

'Very wise.'

'So . . .' Simpson smiled over the top of her mug in a way that was, frankly, unsettling. Trying to look at her without maintaining eye contact, the inspector noted that she looked tanned and relaxed; just back from holiday, perhaps, or a long weekend in the country. 'Thank you for coming.'

'My pleasure, boss.' Carlyle braced himself, wondering what he was about to be carpeted for. He ran through his recent indiscretions. Nothing major sprang to mind, but he knew from painful experience that it was always the things you didn't think of that caught you out.

Sensing his discomfort, the Commander said, 'Don't worry, John, you're not here for a bollocking.'

'No?' he enquired, failing to keep the surprise from his voice.

'No,' Simpson replied firmly. 'You're here because of a woman called Barbara Hutton . . .'

'OK.' Sitting up straight, he placed his hands in his lap and adopted a formal *paying attention* pose.

'. . . aka Sylvia Tosches. Maybe.'

'Maybe?'

'Hutton, maiden name Grozer – according to her papers at least. Born in Germany, a UK citizen living in a Georgian pile in Bloomsbury. Her husband is a lawyer.'

'So far, so boring.'

'Tosches, on the other hand, is a German national. Born in Frankfurt in 1949, she was a lesser light of the Baader-Meinhof gang, a terrorist group in the seventies.'

Carlyle held up a hand. 'I know who they are. Helen took me on a date to see *The Baader Meinhof Complex* once.'

Simpson looked at him blankly.

'It's a movie.'

'Ah, yes.'

'Not exactly what you would call a date movie. It was her idea of a joke, I think.'

'I see.' Not unduly interested in the dynamics of the inspector's marriage, Simpson moved swiftly on. 'Tosches was believed to be involved in a bank robbery in Kassel and also in the kidnapping and murder of a businessman by the name of Uli Eichinger. She was arrested by the police but got away.'

'And now she's turned up in London forty-odd years later?'

'Our colleagues in Berlin had a tip-off that Hutton is, in fact, Tosches. They have asked us to investigate.'

'Now?' Carlyle pursed his lips. Of all the weird stuff he'd had to deal with over the years, this was right up there with the strangest. 'Almost half a century on?'

'Eichinger's body was found in a wood,' Simpson said matter-of-factly. 'His hands were bound and he had been shot in the back of the head. A bank teller was also killed in the robbery. Two murders. There's no time limit on these crimes.' She paused, reached for her mug and then thought better of it. 'And apparently, Eichinger's family have considerable political influence. Even after all this time, they continue to lobby hard for the cases not to be forgotten.'

Stands to reason, Carlyle thought. If it was just the bank teller we were talking about, no one would be interested.

'They want justice,' Simpson continued primly. 'Which is understandable.'

Folding his arms, the inspector stared in the general direction of the window. 'So what do you want me to do?' he asked eventually. 'Go and beat the truth out of some granny who may or may not have been there at the time?'

'She's not a grandmother,' Simpson observed, 'as far as we know.'

'And what proof do we have that she is, in fact . . .'

'Tosches. Sylvia Tosches. They don't have any proof – but they can get some. Sylvia has a sister, a retired librarian living in Gelsenkirchen. They want to do a DNA test.'

'Doesn't sound legal to me,' Carlyle grumped. 'Not without a warrant.'

'All you have to do, John,' said Simpson patiently, 'is to accompany the German police officer who will present himself at Charing Cross tomorrow, on a visit to Mrs Hutton's home.' She mentioned the address and he committed it to memory. 'It will be a preliminary meeting before, inevitably, lawyers get involved.'

A wave of annoyance swept over Carlyle at the thought of being used as a babysitter but he let it pass. 'Fine.'

Simpson raised an eyebrow.

'No problem.'

The Commander smiled. 'But?'

'But I was wondering if there was something *you* could do for *me*.'

The smile evaporated. 'Why is it,' the Commander wondered, 'that everything with you has to be a matter of negotiation?'

'I'm not haggling,' Carlyle said evenly, 'it's just that I wondered if you could help with something.' He quickly ran through his conversation with Naomi Taylor and the secrecy surrounding her husband's death. 'Maybe you could see why the Counter Terrorism guys are all over this?'

Simpson shook her head. 'If SO15 are involved, I suggest that you leave it alone. Apart from anything else, the last time you got mixed up with those guys, you almost got yourself killed.'

And almost got kicked off The Job, Carlyle reflected ruefully. 'That was a long time ago.'

'Not that long ago,' she countered. 'So keep your distance.'

'But—'

'Do as I say.' Simpson eyed him sternly, then let her visage soften. 'I haven't heard something. If I come across anything relevant, I'll pass it on.'

'Thank you.'

'But only if you keep out of it. For once, see if you can surprise me by *not* causing any trouble.'

# SEVEN

Carlyle was dozing in front of the television when he felt a hand on his shoulder.

'Sleeping?'

'Not any more,' he grumped, shuffling along the sofa in order to let his wife sit down beside him.

Helen glanced at the half-empty bottle of Jameson's sitting on the coffee table, and the empty shot glass next to it, but said nothing.

'What time is it?' Carlyle asked groggily.

'Just after ten.'

'You've had a long day.'

'Yeah.' Helen took a sip of peppermint tea from the chipped mug she was holding. 'There was a Board meeting tonight.'

'Ah.' Helen worked for a charity called Avalon. It was the kind of place where everyone had to express an opinion on everything, at considerable length. 'I suppose you should be grateful that you made it home before midnight.'

'The whole thing basically degenerated into an argument about whether or not we should take money from Chase Race.'

'Who he?'

Helen grabbed a cushion, tossed it on the floor and sat down. 'He's a rapper who's got convictions for drug use and also for beating up his girlfriend.'

'Lovely.' Carlyle was in no doubt as to which of those offences was the more serious in his wife's book.

'On the other hand, he has offered us fifty grand for a project in Liberia which no one else will support. It really needs the cash.'

'Why?'

She looked at him. 'Why what?'

'Why did he offer you the cash?'

'I dunno. PR, I suppose. Apparently his management is worried that if he doesn't get his act together his career is toast.'

'Not exactly a business geared to longevity though, is it?'

'No,' Helen agreed, 'but that's hardly my problem. Trying to get the Board to agree, *that* was my problem. Fifty grand . . .' She heaved a sigh. 'They're worried about the risk to our reputation.'

'Understandable.'

'As well as the impact on staff morale.'

'Staff morale?' Carlyle never paid too much attention to the touchy-feely stuff.

'People work for us out of principle,' Helen explained. 'If they think we're willing to grab money from anyone, some of them would just up and leave.'

*What you mean is that they're a bunch of highly strung primadonnas.* Knowing better than to pass judgement on Helen's co-workers, Carlyle restricted himself to some sympathetic tutting. 'Decisions, decisions.' Helen's job often made the humble policeman's lot seem very straightforward.

'What would you do?'

'Me?' Carlyle thought about it for a second. 'I'd take the money. If you can put it to good use, who cares where it came from? Money is just money.'

'After four hours, going back and forth, we decided to turn it down.'

'It must be hell having principles.'

'I know. It's not as if we don't need the money. And *I'm* the one who has to make sure that everyone gets paid at the end of the month.' The bitterness in Helen's voice was obvious.

Carlyle wondered if she could do with a change of job. So many years in such a physically and emotionally challenging position was bound to take its toll. He gave her a consoling peck on the cheek.

'All you can do is do your best.' *Jeez. That was something his father used to say.* Inwardly, he groaned.

'Yeah, right. How was your day?'

'Pff.' Carlyle took a moment to recall what had happened and select a suitable highlight. 'I went to see Carole Simpson. Have you ever heard of a woman called . . .' he thought he was going to forget the name, but it tripped off his tongue after the briefest of delays, '. . . Sylvia Tosches?'

'I don't think so. Why?'

'Apparently, she was a member of Baader Meinhof and the Red Army Faction. I don't remember her in that movie, do you?'

Helen shook her head. 'It was a movie though, hardly a document of historical record.'

'I suppose not.' He repeated what the Commander had told him about the woman. 'And I looked her up on Wikipedia this afternoon.'

'So,' Helen chuckled, 'you think Jimmy Wales is a more reliable source of information than your boss, do you, Inspector?'

'Being someone who has to collect and evaluate information for a living,' Carlyle said airily, 'I think that multiple sources are a good thing. Especially when they tell me the same story.'

Pulling her legs up under her bum to get comfortable, Helen smiled. 'Which, in this case, is what?'

'That it was all a very long time ago.'

'So why is this woman of interest to the Met?'

'The German police think she might have turned up in London. Well, not really turned up, more been living here for decades under an alias.'

'And they want her back?'

'Of course, assuming it is her.'

'What if she's paid her debt to society already?'

'How?'

'I dunno. Maybe she's spent the last forty years working with disabled homeless kids or something.'

'Maybe,' Carlyle said doubtfully, recalling the Bloomsbury mansion and the lawyer husband.

'Hopefully it's just a case of mistaken identity,' was Helen's final observation on the subject. 'That would save everybody a lot of hassle – especially you.'

'Quite.'

She gestured at the TV. 'What are you watching?'

'No idea.' Carlyle rubbed his eyes. He felt exhausted. It had been a long day, doing essentially nothing. Grabbing the remote, he clicked on to one of the rolling news channels. For a few moments he stared blankly at the ticker scrolling along the bottom of the screen; it was the usual mix of the irrelevant, the banal and the inevitable. 'Maybe it's time for bed. I've got an early start in the morning.'

'I spoke to your dad this afternoon.'

'Oh yes?' Suddenly on alert, he pushed himself up into a sitting position.

'He gave me a call at the office. He's obviously worried about that cough of his.' Helen gave Carlyle an admonishing look. Her own father had died years ago and she was close to Alexander, closer than Carlyle himself was, anyway.

'He should go and see a bloody doctor, then.'

'He's got an appointment for the day after tomorrow.' She took another sip of her tea. 'I think you should go with him.'

'I'll see.' The last thing Carlyle wanted to do was sit about in a doctor's surgery for hours on end. If he wasn't unwell when he went in, he would be when he came out. 'Things are quite busy at the moment.' A story about a footballer who had killed two guys in a car crash came on and, trying to let the conversation wither, he waved at the screen, saying, 'Can you believe it? The bloody Prison Service released him by mistake. No wonder the families of the blokes who were killed are pissed off.'

'John,' she said, not interested in his diversionary tactics, 'this is important. Your dad's getting on. He needs our support.'

'I'll see,' he repeated.

'OK.' Helen was clearly not happy with his response. 'But you should do it.'

'Yeah, yeah.' Irritated, Carlyle tried to change the subject. 'Does Alice still want to go on the school trip?' Along with his father's health, their daughter's class study tour to the USA was another current bone of contention. Two weeks in America was all well and good, but how were they going to pay for it? It was hard enough coming up with the fees each term; the 'extras' were killing them. He had always felt somewhat ambivalent about sending his only child to a private school – Helen had insisted – but he realized that he mustn't burden Alice with any of his concerns.

'I think so. She understands that it's expensive though.'

Lifting the remote, he switched the TV off again. 'God, in my day we were lucky to get a trip to Margate. Now the kids are off to New York and Washington DC.' Carlyle, who'd never been to America in his life, suddenly felt a pang of self-pity.

'It'll be good for her. All her friends are going.'

'I know, I know.' Placing the remote back on the coffee table, Carlyle forced himself to his feet and shuffled towards the door. 'Don't worry. We'll sort it out. It's just a question of money.'


Was he awake? Slowly coming to, he rolled on to his back and focused on getting his breathing right – deep and regular breaths – before reluctantly opening his eyes. Blinking, he gazed at the ceiling. It looked diseased. Dirty white emulsion was flaking off in various places and a thick crack ran from one corner towards the centre. Out of the crack a spider appeared, scuttling along its length before disappearing again.

'Urgh.'

Lifting his head off the pillow, Michael Nicholson threw back the tatty duvet, slowly swung his legs over the side of the bed.

For several moments, he dangled his bare feet over the lino-leum floor, scratching his head while he checked that he still had the usual number of toes. Happy to confirm that was the case, he then inspected each hand in turn. A pedicure wouldn't go amiss, but there were no digits missing. Finally, crucially, he stuck his hands down his trousers and gave his balls a vigorous scratch.

'All present and correct,' he mumbled. Yawning, he looked around. Directly in front of him was a small window, with bars on the outside. Through it, he could see that the sky was grey and the light was fading. Overhead was a light fitting but there was no bulb.

In the distance was the hum of traffic. Nicholson assumed that he was still in London but that was by no means certain. God knows how long he had been out for. They could have bun-dled him into a crate and taken him anywhere in the world. For all he knew, he could be back in China right now.

At least they hadn't killed him.

Yet.

Running his tongue across his teeth, he realized that he had a low-level headache, caused by dehydration, and his mouth felt like it was full of cat litter. He tried in vain to raise some spit before noticing that a two-litre bottle of Evian had been placed in the far corner of the room, next to a large red plastic bowl and a roll of pale green toilet paper. Nicholson tutted unhappily. He had a thing about coloured toilet paper; if it wasn't white, he couldn't go. It was an immutable law that he'd learned to live with over the years. He looked at the bowl. 'No matter,' he said to himself, 'I wouldn't be able to crap in *that*, anyway.'

Getting to his feet, Nicholson felt dizzy, but the feel-ing quickly passed. It took him two steps to cross the room. Picking up the bottle, he checked the seal then unscrewed the top. Lifting the water to his mouth, he gargled, spitting it out into the bowl before taking a second mouthful and swallowing. Replacing the cap, he put the bottle back on the floor and took a cautious stretch. Pushing back his shoulders, he rotated his head and tried to massage his neck with the thumb and forefinger of his right hand as he recalled what had happened at the flat in Chelsea.

What was the last thing he could remember? Stepping through the sliding doors, in search of the gin, to be confronted by two large figures in black, like something out of a James Bond movie. He froze. Ren Jiong and Wang Lei were nowhere to be seen. Without Ren's rap music blasting from the bedroom, the place seemed eerily quiet. On the muted TV, two middle-aged women were comparing carriage clocks on the *Antiques Roadshow*, one of Wang's favourite programmes.

One of the intruders approached Nicholson, a syringe in his hand. The businessman opened his mouth in protest, but no sound came out. He watched as the needle was thrust into his arm and the plunger pressed down. For a moment . . . nothing; and then everything went black.

And now he was here.

As the crappy B-movie in his head came to an end, Nicholson chuckled grimly. Wang Lei might have been paranoid, but she had been right. They had come for them and they had taken them. When things got tricky, the expensive security she had hired hadn't been worth shit. *Twelve bloody grand a day.* The thought of all the money that could have been going into his pocket made him want to cry.

Putting his own frustrations to one side, Nicholson fleetingly wondered what his captors had done with Wang, and with the boy. Quickly, however, he returned to his main interest: himself. If he made it out of here, wherever 'here' was, he renewed his vow that he would head back to Shanghai for good and opt for the quiet life.

Having sorted out the rest of his life, Nicholson looked slowly round the room. Apart from the bed, there was no furniture. Decoration was limited to a faded poster of the Victoria Falls advertising the Zimbabwe Tourism Authority. To his right was a door; he knew it would be locked but he stepped over and tried the handle anyway. When it didn't open he gave it a couple of desultory slaps and listened for any activity on the other side. There was none. Nicholson hit the door again, harder this time.

'Hello? Hello . . . HELLO!'

Mumbling to himself, he counted to a hundred.

Five hundred.

A thousand.

No one came. Sitting back down on the bed, Nicholson realized that he was quite relieved about that. No doubt, someone would check on him soon enough. In the meantime, he was in no particular hurry to find out what they would do to him next.

# EIGHT

A mixture of amusement and dismay washed over Alison Roche's face as she watched the familiar figure approach from behind a police car that had been lazily parked at a thirty-degree angle to the kerb.

'Inspector.'

'Long time no see,' Carlyle said.

'Yeah.' The sergeant eased her forefinger off the trigger of the MP5 slung over her shoulder and gazed down the Horseferry Road. 'And I suppose you were just passing?'

Carlyle stared at the tarmac. His stomach rumbled; leaving home in a rush, he hadn't had any breakfast and was feeling more than a little hungry. What he really needed was a good greasy spoon but the places he'd passed on his way over from St James's Park were not yet open. 'This is my patch,' he observed, 'kind of.'

'How are things at Charing Cross?'

'You know – same old, same old.' Looking up, Carlyle gestured at the roadblock that was stopping cars in both directions. 'What's all this about?'

'Just a routine exercise,' the sergeant explained. 'A bit of PR to show the public we're earning our corn.'

'Yes.'

'Anyway,' said Roche, 'what do you want?' There was no malice in her voice, just a recognition that her ex-boss wouldn't drop in on her without a reason. The concept of a social call was alien to Carlyle. And anyway, it wasn't yet a quarter to seven in the morning.

Out of habit, Carlyle looked around, checking that no one was paying any attention to their conversation. 'Marvin Taylor,' he said quietly.

'The guy who got his head chopped off?'

Carlyle nodded. 'I used to work with him.'

Fifteen yards down the road, a taxi driver started arguing with one of the two officers who were checking his car. The second officer stepped over to support his colleague but the driver was a big guy who would be more than capable of giving the pair of them a run for their money. Roche's expression suggested she would like nothing better than to put a couple of 9mm rounds through the cabbie's windscreen.

'His wife came to see me,' Carlyle went on. 'She isn't being kept in the loop.'

'And what makes you think I can help?' Roche asked, keeping her eyes on the argument.

'You were at the scene,' Carlyle said evenly.

Roche shrugged.

'And your boyfriend is the family's liaison.'

Her face darkened. 'My *boyfriend*?'

'Oliver Steed,' Carlyle replied cautiously, suddenly not so sure about the quality of the intel he'd gleaned from the station grapevine.

'He's not my boyfriend,' she snapped. 'He's just a kid who fancies me.' Her face set into the hard mask that he remembered from their time working together in Charing Cross. It was the kind of expression so many women in the Force adopted when they had to be more macho than the men they worked with. 'He's clueless. Probably still a bloody virgin.'

'There's nothing wrong with that. You could be a . . . whatsitsname,' an image of a well-preserved American actress with over-inflated boobs popped into the inspector's head, 'a cougar.'

'Ha.' Roche snorted. 'What would that make *you*, Grandad?'

'An old git,' Carlyle smiled, happy that he could still get on the right side of her.

'No change there then.' Down the road, the taxi driver had been coaxed back into his cab and sent on his way. One of the officers at the roadblock checked his watch and waved Roche over. 'I'm up,' she said. 'Gotta go.'

'Taylor,' Carlyle reminded her.

'I'm off at one. You can buy me lunch.' They agreed a venue and she walked quickly off.

'Try not to shoot anyone,' Carlyle shouted after her.

'I'll do my best,' she replied over her shoulder.


Fortified by a cooked breakfast at the Pitstop, a former public convenience that had been converted into a café, Carlyle sauntered through St James's Park, wondering how best to utilize his morning. Reluctant to put in an appearance at the police station, he ran through the 'to do' list in his head. The number of overdue reports with his name next to them was getting longer by the day, but they could wait. The thought of giving himself over to paperwork for a few hours was so unpleasant that he had to stop at the next park bench. Sitting down beside a well-groomed woman reading a copy of the *Financial Times*, the inspector pulled out his BlackBerry and began scrolling through his email contacts. Finding the name he was looking for, he composed a short message and fired it off into the ether. To his surprise and delight he got a reply almost instantly. Stifling a burp, he ignored the irritated look of the businesswoman and got to his feet, heading past the Canadian War Memorial, in the direction of Lower Regent Street.


'You were quick.' Looking over the top of her iPad, Susan Phillips gave him a warm smile. She was standing in the middle of the lobby of a bank on Regent Street. The place had been cleared and they were alone, apart from the body wedged between two ATM machines.

'I was in the neighbourhood,' Carlyle explained, watching bemused as the pathologist began waving the tablet in front of her face. 'What are you doing?'

'I'm trying to connect to the Cloud,' she explained.

Carlyle looked up at the ceiling. 'What cloud?'

'*The* Cloud, with a capital "C".' Phillips lifted the device higher. 'It's where we store our crime-scene data these days – some of it, at least. I can't seem to get a bloody connection.'

Not having a clue what she was talking about, Carlyle watched as a couple of paramedics appeared from outside and set up a portable trolley. On Phillips's nod, they lifted the corpse on to the trolley and wheeled it out to a waiting ambulance.

Giving up on the Cloud, Phillips let the tablet fall to her side. 'I've been here since four this morning,' she yawned.

'Bummer. What happened?'

'Guy comes in to get some money. Doesn't realize that a dosser is sleeping in the lobby. Dosser wakes up. Whacks man over the head for his cash. Hits him a bit too hard. Man smacks head against side of cash machine as he goes down. Smashes his skull *and* has a heart attack. Dosser goes back to sleep until police turn up some time later.'

'Sounds like my kind of case, nice and simple.'

'When they found him, he had the bloke's money and his ATM card in his pocket.'

'Even better.'

'Still the same amount of paperwork though.' Phillips gestured towards the congealed blood that had pooled on the floor. 'Poor bloke was from Belgium.'

'The tramp? Or the tourist?'

'The tourist. The tramp is from Osterley, apparently.'

'A well-known den of thieves,' Carlyle observed. 'Then again, you shouldn't really be wandering around here in the middle of the night.' He recalled the tagline for a recent movie: *same streets, different city*.

'No, I suppose not.' Phillips dropped the iPad into a holdall near her feet. 'Have you had breakfast?'

Still feeling rather over-full, Carlyle patted his belly. 'Yep, afraid so.'

'Well, I'm starving.' Picking up the bag, Phillips marched towards the door. 'Come on. You can watch me eat.'

Resisting the temptation to scoff a second breakfast, Carlyle daintily sipped on a peppermint tea as he watched Phillips polish off some mango slices from a small plastic pot. They were sitting in an insanely busy branch of an ubiquitous café chain, just off Piccadilly. Behind the tills, a group of eight staff expertly relieved customers of their money, while a couple of baristas behind them frantically worked massive coffee machines to deliver the orders of an ever-lengthening line of jumpy, caffeine-deprived customers. Carlyle grinned at the sight of one man, a youngish guy in a grey pinstripe suit, hopping from foot to foot as he waited impatiently for his beverage, desperate to be on his way. Surely, he thought, this place should have more people making coffee and fewer people taking money.

If only.

Phillips popped the last piece of fruit into her mouth and washed it down with a mouthful of her Americano. 'So,' she said brightly, dabbing the corners of her mouth with a paper napkin, 'what can I do for you?'

Carlyle shot her a look of mock hurt. 'Why does everyone think I only make an appearance when I want something?'

'Because,' she grinned, 'you only make an appearance when you want something.'

'Fair enough.' They had known each other long enough; he didn't feel that he had to mess about. 'Tell me about Naomi Taylor.'

Phillips's face fell. 'She gave you a call, did she?'

'Yeah.' Carlyle's foot was still playing up; he gingerly lifted it on to an empty chair next to him. 'I met with her yesterday.'

'Sorry if I dropped you in it.'

'No, no,' the inspector replied quickly. 'I vaguely remember her old man, but I never really worked with him.'

'I knew Marvin from when he was at Holborn,' Phillips explained. 'I was going out with a lawyer at the time – the four of us went out together a few times.'

Carlyle had long since given up trying to keep abreast of Phillips's private life. Glamorous and single, she always seemed to be either just going into a relationship or coming out of one. As a bloke who hadn't had to worry about the dating game for more than thirty years, he found it stressful even thinking about such things.

'You know what it's like,' Phillips continued. 'You socialize quite a lot over a relatively short period and then something happens and you don't see them for a while. Of course, when Marvin left to set up his own business, I don't think that he and Naomi had the time or the money to go out very much.'

'No.'

'And then their daughter was born. I don't think I'd seen them for two or three years before Naomi called.' She shook her head. 'I'd been away with Danny in Istanbul for a few days.'

*Danny?*

'And I hadn't even realized that it was Marvin who . . . well, you know.'

'Yes,' said Carlyle, surprised. It was the first time he'd ever seen Phillips show any squeamishness around death.

Phillips cradled her coffee cup in both hands. 'They say he was a terrible mess. Why would anyone do that to him?'

'I don't know,' Carlyle admitted. A sour-looking woman with a pretzel in one hand and a coffee in the other appeared in front of him and gestured at the spare seat. Reluctantly, the inspector removed his sore foot. With a disgusted huff, the woman sat down. Edging away from her, the inspector turned back to Phillips.

'Naomi is lovely,' Phillips said. 'She needs some help.'

Carlyle nodded. 'I'm gonna see what I can do.' *Which is probably nothing.*

'Thanks.'

'I just wanted to ask—'

A phone started ringing and the pathologist reached into her pocket. 'One second.' She answered, 'Phillips. Yes?'

Tuning out of the conversation, Carlyle watched the woman next to him stick the last of the pretzel into her mouth before letting his gaze slide across the room. It was well past the rush hour, but people were still flooding through the door faster than the staff could serve them. How many of these places were there in London? he wondered. Fifty? A hundred? Whoever set this place up was obviously a genius. There was more money in coffee than there was in crack. Thinking of drugs, his mind turned to his old ally, Dominic Silver. A retired drug dealer, Dom was in the process of reinventing himself as an art dealer. Gazing out of the window, Carlyle attempted to get his bearings. Dom's gallery wasn't much more than a couple of minutes' walk away. Maybe he should pop in and say 'hello'. They were overdue a catch-up; like Phillips and Naomi Taylor, he and Dom had rather lost contact recently. With Dom's career change, their professional interests no longer intersected in the same way and it was more of an effort to hook up. Did he feel sorry about that? Carlyle wasn't sure.

'Sorry, I've got to run,' Phillips sighed. 'One of those mornings.'

'Yeah.'

'What did you want to ask me about?'

It took Carlyle a second to get his brain back on the right page. 'Oh, yes. Marvin Taylor.'

'Yes?'

Carlyle looked around. Pretzel Woman was lingering over her coffee. Staring vacantly into space, she showed no interest in their conversation. He lowered his voice anyway. 'Everyone agrees Marvin was a nice bloke. But was he bent?'

# NINE

Resplendent in a pair of baggy shorts and a truly hideous pink and yellow Hawaiian shirt, Umar Sligo was standing on the bottom step of the entrance to the police station, smoking a cigarette as he chatted to a youngish bloke in a Nirvana T-shirt and scruffy jeans. Carlyle vaguely recognized the guy, an undercover officer working out of the Waterloo station who had spent the last three years spying on a bunch of hippies who were opposing the building of a new power station somewhere near the Kent coast. The rumour was that the guy had gone so deep undercover that he'd had kids by two different women in the group. There had to be some sort of law against it. No doubt the tree huggers would sue the arse off the Met in due course.

Seeing the inspector approach, Umar said something to the scruffy Lothario, who nodded before scuttling off in the direction of the Strand. Taking one last drag on his smoke, the sergeant let the stub fall onto the pavement, grinding it into the concrete under the toe of his Puma trainers.

'Boss . . .'

'I didn't know you smoked,' said Carlyle by way of a greeting.

'Pressures of married life.'

'Dirty habit.'

'Aren't they all? It helps me deal with the stress.'

Stress, what fucking stress? Carlyle thought irritably. Maybe if you stopped chasing every piece of skirt that crosses your path, life would be a little less fraught. He was finding Umar's juvenile behaviour increasingly annoying. The guy was in his thirties now, he had a wife and a kid; surely it was time that he grew up a bit. Instead, he just drifted along, all ambition seemingly gone. The idea of becoming a house-husband had apparently turned his head. *He probably fancies a few years hitting on the mums at the school gates.* An image of Umar hosting a coffee morning for a bunch of yummy mummies appeared in his head and Carlyle let out a small yelp of amusement.

Umar shot him the *pissed-off teenager* look that he had been perfecting over the last few months. 'What's so funny?'

'Nothing, nothing.' Carlyle let the smile fall from his face. After a couple of years establishing a decent enough working relationship with his colleague, the inspector felt like things had gone into reverse. He was losing the boy. Worse, he didn't know if he had the will or the ability to retrieve the situation. He contemplated his sergeant in all his finery. Today, Umar looked more like an extra from *Miami Vice* than one of the Met's finest. The silly bugger had never been undercover in his life. If Simpson caught sight of him like that she'd have a total fit. At times like this, the inspector just wanted to give the berk a good slap. But he knew that would only get him the sack. So Carlyle kept his mouth firmly shut, telling himself that it really wasn't his problem.

Feeling thoroughly fed up with the situation, he nodded at a couple of uniforms heading down the steps and out on patrol duty before turning his attention back to Umar. 'Busy?'

'Not really. I had to go and see Mrs Miller about her bomb this morning, but that's about it.'

'Oh yes?' Agnes Miller had lived in the neighbourhood since just after World War II. Her fiancé, a young police constable from Islington called Eric Davis, had fought and died for the International Brigades in the Spanish Civil War. His body had never been found. Agnes had swallowed her grief and got on with her life as best she could. Now well into her nineties, and never married, she refused to be moved from her flat on the tenth floor of a block just off Kingsway on the grounds that *'this is my home and I'm going to die here'*.

Carlyle had discovered all of this one night, a week or so earlier, sitting in Agnes's tiny living room, nodding politely as the old woman gave him a potted history of Covent Garden over the last sixty years. He had been responding to her 999 call, regarding the explosion that had blown up her kitchen just before 1 a.m.

'It's the bloody council,' Agnes had hissed, as they watched a procession of firemen stomp up and down the hall. 'They want me out.'

Carlyle clucked sympathetically.

'They say I've got too many bedrooms. The damn cheek. I've been here since this place was built in the sixties.' Rocking gently in her chair, she pulled a shabby blue housecoat tightly around her shoulders. 'Why decide now that I shouldn't have a second bedroom?'

'I think it's something to do with the government,' Carlyle mumbled. He vaguely recalled reading something about attempts to get tenants to give up properties that were deemed too big for them – the latest stab at crass social engineering by the over-privileged idiots who tried to run the country as if it were an edition of *The Sims*. 'I don't think they'd blow up your kitchen though.'

'Why not?' Agnes shot back. 'Those buggers have got no shame. They want to put me in a home in Theydon Bois.'

*Theydon Bois. A fate worse than death.*

'They say they'll give me a thousand pounds to go and not come back. But this is my home.'

'Yes.' Carlyle stifled a yawn. Unable to think of anything else to say, he was rescued by the Fire Brigade Commander sticking his head round the door to give them the all clear. Promising to check in on the old woman in a few days, he had made his excuses and left.

A VW hatchback rolled past, windows down, rap music

blaring from its speakers. The inspector felt a sudden urge to arrest the driver on the spot. As the car lurched round the corner, taking its aural pollution with it, he reluctantly let the idea slide.

'She says that you promised to pop in and see her,' Umar reminded him.

'Yes, yes.' Carlyle wondered if he could get Helen to do it, or maybe Alice.

'Turns out that the "bomb",' the sergeant chuckled, 'was a large jar of home-made rhubarb chutney that she'd been keeping in the fridge. Apparently there was a build-up of fermented gases – and *boom*.'

'Ah well,' Carlyle reflected solemnly, 'just shows, you can never be too careful when it comes to fermented gases.'

'It took the Fire Brigade a few days to work out what had happened.'

'I'll bet. On the bright side though, think of it as another case successfully closed. I just hope Agnes isn't going to get any more of the stuff.'

'It comes from her cousin in Kent.'

She never mentioned a cousin, Carlyle thought. Not that it mattered.

'I told Agnes to have a word with her to be careful.'

'Better send an alert to the Kent Constabulary,' Carlyle quipped. 'The stuff should carry a health warning.'

'Yeah.' Pulling a packet of Benson & Hedges from the back pocket of his shorts, Umar contemplated another cigarette.

The inspector glanced at his watch. 'Look, if you're not busy, you might want to join me for lunch.'

'Oh?' Umar's eyes narrowed. It wasn't like the inspector to make that kind of an offer without a reason. 'What's the catch?'

'No catch,' Carlyle said. 'You can meet your predecessor.'

'OK, sure.' Umar still wasn't convinced.

'A woman called Alison Roche,' Carlyle told him. 'Good cop. She works for SO15 now.'

'A Counter-Terrorism babe,' Umar grinned. 'Sounds good.'

Carlyle grimaced. 'Just don't call her a "babe". Roche doesn't stand for that kind of thing.'

The sergeant's grin grew wider. 'A *feisty* Counter-Terrorism babe.'

'Fuck's sake, Umar.' This was turning into a bad idea.

'OK, OK.' Umar juggled his cigarette packet. 'I'll be on my best behaviour.'

'You'd better be. We'll just go round the corner. In about an hour.' Heading up the steps, he wondered if Roche might have any advice on how he could get Umar back on the straight and narrow.

'Oh,' Umar shouted after him, 'by the way. There's a couple of guys inside waiting to see you. They're in Interview Room Six.'

The inspector eventually found the men in Interview Room Four. Walking through the door, he was dismayed to discover two suits sitting behind the room's only table, heads bowed, each tapping frantically on the screen of an iPhone as if their lives depended on it.

*Communing with the great God, Apple.*

Carlyle took an instant, irreversible dislike to both of them.

After a couple of seconds, each one looked up in turn. The inspector found himself confronted by two very unhappy faces. Clearly, these were men not used to being kept waiting. 'Gentlemen.'

The younger man placed his iPhone on the table. 'Inspector . . . Car . . .'

'Carlyle. Pronounced like the town . . . well, technically, it's a city, but spelled differently.'

All he got for his trouble was two uncomprehending looks.

'We were told that you were expecting us,' the older man said gruffly. His English was precise, with no trace of an accent. A deep tan offset the silver in his hair and he had the

67

well-groomed look of a banker or some other form of highly paid low-life.

The George Clooney Eurotrash look, Carlyle mused. Pulling out a chair, he sat down at the nearside of the table. Out of habit, he glanced up at the CCTV camera hanging from the ceiling, in the far corner of the room.

The older man followed his gaze. 'You're not recording us, are you, Inspector?'

'No, no,' he said quickly. 'Not at all.'

'Good. Maybe we can begin, then. You have kept us waiting more than long enough this morning.'

'Yes.' The younger man had a pair of business cards lined up next to his phone. He slid them across the table towards Carlyle. 'This one is me,' he said, tapping the card to Carlyle's right. 'Sebastian Gregori.' Again, his English was flawless, although his accent was evident.

Carlyle carefully studied each card in turn. After several moments, he looked up. 'What is Max Drescher Associates?'

'It is my company,' Gregori said smugly.

'What kind of company?' Carlyle asked a little too sharply. These men were annoying him intensely; and it was almost time for lunch.

'We are private security consultants,' Gregori explained, 'providing a wide range of range of services for—'

Carlyle cut him off. 'You're a private detective?' In his experience these were creatures only suited to the pages of cheap thrillers.

'We provide a range of services,' Gregori repeated. He gestured towards the man sitting next to him. 'We are representing Herr Kortmann and the family trust in this matter.'

Playing dumb, Carlyle looked at each man in turn. 'And which matter is that?'

'The murder of my uncle,' Werner Kortmann said tersely. 'Uli Eichinger.'

*Eichinger.* The inspector nodded as he recalled his

conversation with Commander Simpson about the slain businessman.

'And the long-overdue arrest of the murderer Sylvia Tosches.' Kortmann gave his retainer a less than playful smack on the arm. Puffed up with anger, the older man looked to have aged a further ten years in the two minutes or so since Carlyle had walked through the door. 'I thought that this . . . detective had been fully briefed on the matter and had been deployed as our local liaison.'

'My Commanding Officer spoke to me about it yesterday,' Carlyle stated, not wishing the tone of the conversation to degenerate further on the grounds that it could only delay his exit from the room. 'However, I was under the impression that this was an official police matter.'

The atmosphere had become uncomfortably warm. Kortmann's face was getting redder. Carlyle wondered if the man might be on the brink of a heart attack. In a fatuous show of goodwill, he got up and began fiddling with the air-conditioning control panel on the wall.

'The police in Berlin have other priorities,' Gregori explained. 'They will not move on this until there is clear proof that this lady, Barbara Hutton, is who we think she is.'

'We *have* proof!' Kortmann slammed his palm down on to the top of the table. 'We have had the damn proof for years now. More than enough to put this . . . this she-devil away for ever.'

Carlyle wasted a few more seconds pushing random buttons on the AC. He heard the faint sound of something wheezing into life, but it died almost immediately. Giving up, he sat back down and asked, 'Can I see the evidence that you have?'

Gregori lifted an outsized black leather briefcase from the floor and hauled it on to the table. Opening the top of the bag, he pulled out a small bottle of Evian and handed it to his flagging client. Unscrewing the cap, Kortmann drank deeply while Gregori went on to produce a folder several inches thick, held together by a couple of thick rubber bands. 'This is all the paperwork that we have brought with us.'

'I see.' Carlyle's heart sank. *Bloody Simpson*. He would be speaking to her the moment he got out of this room.

Werner Kortmann finished his water, replaced the cap, and set the empty bottle on the table. 'We were told,' he said firmly, 'that you would take us to see the Tosches woman tomorrow.'

'I see.'

Gregori resumed rooting around in his case. 'This,' he said, pulling out an A4-sized photograph and offering it to Carlyle, 'is Sylvia Tosches.'

Reluctantly, the inspector took the photo. The black and white image showed a painfully thin young woman, lounging against a wall. Dressed in jeans and a white T-shirt, she had cropped black hair and an intense but rather distant stare. It reminded Carlyle of Robert Mapplethorpe's portraits of Patti Smith. *Just Kids* indeed. He handed the photograph back to Gregori. 'A long time ago.'

'That doesn't matter,' Kortmann snorted. 'She's still a killer.'

# TEN

The inspector finally got rid of the Germans by promising to meet them at their hotel at 9 a.m. sharp the next morning, fudging the issue of a trip to see Hutton on the grounds that he didn't have the remotest clue on what authority he was supposed to be acting. Retreating up to the third floor of the station, he passed Umar playing on his computer.

The sergeant looked up expectantly. 'Time to go?'

'In a minute. I just need to make a quick call.'

'Check this out.' Gesturing towards the screen, Umar offered Carlyle a set of headphones.

'What is it?' Carlyle squinted at the YouTube video. It looked like Lego.

'It's an animation of Eddie Izzard's *Death Star Canteen* skit.'

'Huh?'

'Darth Vader is trying to get his lunch in the canteen of the *Death Star*.' Pointing on the screen, Umar adopted the tone of an adult explaining something important to his dull five-year-old nephew. 'But no one knows who he is. It's brilliant.'

'You've really got way too much time on your hands at the moment,' his boss observed, 'haven't you? Maybe we should find you some traffic duty or something.'

'Sod off,' was Umar's heartfelt response.

Taking the Sylvia Tosches file from under his arm, the inspector contemplated smacking his sergeant firmly across the back of his head with it. Once again, he reluctantly decided against resorting to physical violence on HR-related grounds. Instead, he dropped the papers on to his own desk, where they landed with a dismaying thud. 'Five minutes.'

'OK.' Putting the headphones back on, Umar returned to his screen.

Grabbing the phone on his desk, Carlyle dialled Simpson's mobile number. She picked up on the fourth ring. *Big mistake.* 'Explain to me what the hell we are doing getting involved in this German thing?' he demanded.

After years of dealing with his moods, the Commander took her underling's brusqueness in her stride. 'So I take it that you've met with Mr Kortmann?' The noise in the background suggested that she had already made it to lunch.

'Yeah. What an arrogant git.'

Over the clatter of the restaurant, he thought he heard her groan. 'Hold on, let me step outside.'

'This,' Umar giggled, staring at his computer screen, 'is not a game of *do you know who the fuck I am?*'

'Shut up,' Carlyle hissed, 'I'm on the bloody phone.'

'What?' asked the Commander.

'Nothing, nothing.' Carlyle quickly ran through his meeting with the two Germans. 'If their own police have got better things to do, why are we getting involved?'

'There's still an arrest warrant out for Tosches,' Simpson informed him, 'one of the oldest Interpol Red Notices still outstanding in Europe.'

'Yeah,' Carlyle replied sarkily, 'and remind me, how much did we have to pay out to Hamzeh Kamalvand?'

Simpson bridled at mention of the recently revealed Interpol debacle. A young asylum seeker had been wrongly accused of premeditated murder, destruction of property, and possession of firearms, ammunition and explosives without a permit. After three years in detention, threatened with deportation, a judge had thrown the whole thing out. The Met had been left with a compensation bill of over £2 million.

'Red Notices can't be taken at face value,' Carlyle persisted. 'Countries send them out all the time these days, trying to track down people they don't like for one reason or another.' He knew a little bit about this from his wife; Helen's charity had launched a campaign to support one of their doctors who had recently turned up on one of Interpol's 'wanted' posters. According to Helen, the guy's only crime was to have criticized his home government. The number of Red Notices being issued had almost doubled, to reach 30,000 in the previous year. Increasingly, the system was being abused by dictatorships wanting to hunt down opponents in exile.

'Yes, but this is Germany we're talking about,' Simpson countered. 'The Germans don't do these things on a whim. And this one has been out for a long time. The issue is whether this woman is really Tosches, not whether Tosches should be sent home to face justice.'

'She could be dead,' Carlyle suggested.

'Let's find out, shall we?'

Reluctant to admit defeat, Carlyle stared at the ceiling. 'Bit of a wild-goose chase, if you ask me.'

'I didn't ask you.'

'Should this really be a priority? I still don't understand why these guys appear at the station and I have to jump to attention.'

'John . . .' Simpson kicked out at an empty cigarette packet which had been discarded on the pavement, sending it flying into the gutter. Despite her lengthy experience of dealing with the inspector, he could still try her patience, quibbling over every request and instruction. As the saying went, he was the kind of man who could start an argument in an empty room. Every time she thought he might be mellowing a little with age, something would set him off again and he would be right back in her face. The Commander thought back to all the times she had pulled his balls out of the fire. Was it really worth it? Carlyle was a good cop, but maybe that was no longer enough. One day, he would stray too far over the line.

'Kortmann,' she said finally, 'has clout.'

'Not with me, he hasn't.'

'Maybe not,' said Simpson curtly, 'but with the Commissioner he does. His family firm donated more than a million pounds to various Met-related good causes last year. Apparently, they are also being lined up to be a major sponsor of the new police sports facilities in Ealing.'

'And you get what you pay for.' Like all frontline officers, Carlyle was aware of their increasing reliance on the financial support of private companies. The Force took support in the form of everything from concert tickets and football shirts, to high-end SUVs for use by Special Branch and Royal Protection Officers. Cash donations were funnelled into specialist investigation units. It was the kind of creeping privatization that had been eating away at all manner of public services for years and it created a *rent-a-cop* image that was, at best, unhelpful.

'Yes, you do,' Simpson agreed. 'I don't like it any more than you do, but that doesn't do anything to change the facts of the situation.'

'Which are—'

'Which are,' she said shrilly, 'that we have been instructed to investigate the Hutton matter properly.'

What's all this 'we' business all of a sudden, Carlyle wondered grumpily. I'm the one left holding the baby.

'Do you understand? I don't want to find another memo about you on my desk in the next few days,' she paused, as if to catch her breath, 'or ever for that matter.'

'Fat chance of that,' Carlyle said ruefully. They both knew that he could rarely manage more than six months between complaints.

'Well, quite. Let's aim for a realistic target then, shall we? Just mind your Ps and Qs for the next day or so, while you help facilitate Mr Kortmann's query.'

'During which time I will, of course, be paying due care and attention to the rights of Mrs Hutton.'

'Yes, yes. Of course.' Simpson was interrupted by the sounds of an argument erupting in the street.

'Sounds like you might have to make an arrest, boss,' Carlyle quipped.

'Don't think I wouldn't,' Simpson shot back, 'if the situation demanded it.'

Happily for the Commander, however, the dispute died as quickly as it had begun, both parties heading on their way. She returned her attention to the vexatious inspector. 'How good is the evidence against Hutton, by the way?'

Carlyle stared morosely at the file on his desk. 'I dunno. Haven't had a chance to look at it yet.'

'Very well, but keep me posted.'

'Will do.'

'Good. Thank you.'

*Maybe I'll get Umar to take a look at it.* Glancing across the room, Carlyle watched his sergeant still surfing YouTube and wondered if he might not just dump the whole case on to the lazy bugger's lap. At the very least, he could get Umar to do a quick Google search, check if Baader Meinhof had its own online TV channel or whatever.

'Look, John,' mistaking his silence for acquiescence, Simpson adopted a more conciliatory tone, 'I know this is a bit of a hospital pass but we've just got to get on with it.'

There was that '*we*' again, getting on his nerves.

'I don't like it any more than you do,' Simpson repeated.

'No.' Normally, Carlyle would give his boss the benefit of the doubt, but today he wasn't in the mood.

'But just remember, if this woman does turn out to be Tosches, she's wanted for some very serious crimes.'

There was more shouting in the street. From his end, it was impossible for Carlyle to make out if it was the same dispute being revisited.

'Christ,' Simpson groaned, 'I'm never going to get any bloody lunch at this rate. Look, one final thing – I managed to dig out some information that you can share with Naomi Taylor.'

'Great,' said Carlyle, cheered that Simpson had at least managed to make good on that particular promise.

'The body should be released to the family tomorrow.'

There was a pause while Carlyle waited for her to continue. The commotion in the background had dissipated again, to be replaced by the generic hum that rose from a thousand city streets.

'It's not a hundred per cent,' Simpson added, 'but that is the hope . . . at this stage.'

'Is that it?' Carlyle tried to sound disappointed and incredulous at the same time. 'I think Mrs Taylor was looking for a bit more info, like who killed her husband? And is his head still in any way attached to his body?'

'It will be a closed casket,' Simpson responded, 'under the strict instructions of the undertaker. It is a matter for his discretion.'

'Jeez. He must be a right old mess then.'

'Apparently so. But that is not something you want to have to get into with the widow.'

'No.'

'Leave it to the liaison officer.'

'Sure. So who killed him then?'

There was a long pause, filled by the sound of traffic.

'Commander?'

'All I can say is that it appears to be really quite complicated.'

*It's always complicated*, Carlyle observed, *when you don't want to explain it.* 'So what am I supposed to tell Naomi Taylor?'

'Just tell her that we're doing all we can,' Simpson said irritably. 'Didn't you go on the Emotional Outreach Training Module that was run last year?'

'No,' Carlyle scoffed. 'Of course not.'

'Then you'll have to damn well work it out for yourself, won't you.' Simpson ended the call and stalked off in search of her lunch.

76

Placing the receiver on the cradle, Carlyle got to his feet. Sensing movement, Umar looked round hopefully. 'Time for lunch?'

Carlyle smiled. 'Slight change of plan.' He gestured towards the file on his desk. 'Take a look at that lot and see what you think. It's about a woman called Sylvia Tosches. See what you can find out about her online as well.' Umar started to protest, but Carlyle kept going. 'And see if you can dig up anything on a woman called Barbara Hutton. Her address is in the file. I'll be back in an hour or so.'

'But I'm starving,' Umar spluttered.

'I'll bring you a sandwich,' Carlyle promised. 'I won't be long. It'll do you good to have some work to do for a change.'

# ELEVEN

Sipping from a glass of Evian, Wang Lei paced around the room in ever-decreasing circles until she felt dizzy. She had spent the last hour trying to clear her head and decide how best to handle the situation. To her immense frustration, however, no plan presented itself. As a lawyer, improvisation was not one of her strong points. Coming to a halt in the middle of the floor, she let her head flop to one side in a half-hearted attempt to clear the pressure that was steadily building at the top of her spine. As it became clear that wasn't going to work, she spun around, projecting her ill temper onto her host.

'What is the interest of the MSS in all of this?' she demanded, in a staccato Cantonese that threatened to blow the top off her skull. 'What are *you* doing here?'

Standing by the window, Xue Xi looked on impassively. Years of training had taught her not to respond to this kind of desperate aggression.

'You are from the Ministry, aren't you?' Sitting in an over-stuffed armchair in the corner, Ren Jiong didn't look up from his Wii console. The boy had been playing a soccer game for almost four hours straight; it was an excellent way of keeping him quiet.

*The opium of the masses.*

Xue smiled to herself, which only served to enrage Wang further.

'What is so funny?' she thundered. 'You have no right to keep us here. Your actions are completely illegal.'

*Illegal? The mission of the Ministry of State Security, of which I am an important member, is to control the people, in order to maintain the rule of the Party. Legality doesn't come into it.*

'I know the Deputy Under-Secretary responsible for the MSS,' Wang continued. 'He is a close personal friend.'

*I very much doubt that, not now. After your little foreign adventure, I'd be surprised if you have any friends at all back in Beijing.*

'Think about that. Your boss's boss's boss.'

'Times ten,' Ren chipped in.

'When they get to hear about this,' his mother added, 'they will crush you like a bug.'

*And who do you think ordered this mission?* Xue said nothing.

'Like a bug!' Wang squawked, pushing an unruly strand of hair from her tired and puffy face. Dressed in baggy grey sweat-pants, trainers and a ratty red cardigan over a grimy T-shirt, she looked far removed from the creature who had, until recently, been described as one of the most powerful women in the People's Republic.

*What did Ren Qi ever see in you,* Xue wondered. *And how does he feel now, after so much of his power and influence has been squandered in chasing his unfaithful wife around the world, only to drag her home in shame?*

Wang's eyes bored into her, as if she was reading the young security agent's thoughts. 'Where is my husband? Is he here?'

Tired of the woman's ranting, Xue finally broke her silence. 'We must wait.'

Draping a leg over the arm of his chair, Ren looked up from his game and shot Xue a lascivious look, his tongue hanging out of the corner of his mouth like a parched dog. When Xue stiffened, the boy made a show of checking out her backside. 'You are quite sexy,' he said insolently, speaking English in a mid-Atlantic accent that spoke of too many wasted hours spent watching American police shows on TV. 'You know, for a spy.'

Xue allowed herself the smallest of smiles. The boy was appalling, but all the same, he was easier to deal with than the grotesque mother.

'Ren.' Wang glared at her son. 'Now is not the time.'

'It's always the time, Mama,' the boy smirked as he returned his attention to *FIFA 22*.

For a moment, Wang looked as if she was on the point of an aneurysm. Lifting the glass to her mouth, she gulped down the last of her water, before returning her gimlet eye to Xue. 'And where is my adviser, Michael Nicholson? What have you done with him?'

A snort of derision came from the corner. 'Who cares about your *adviser*?' Ren gestured towards Xue with his controller. 'I hope she's killed the bastard. I never understood why you were fucking him in the first place.'

'Enough.' In one fluid movement, Wang arched her back, raised her right arm and hurled the glass at her son's head.

Her aim was high and wide. Ren did not even flinch as the glass smashed on the wall behind him.

*What a family.* Xue Xi watched the glass fragments bounce across the oak floor and come to rest near her feet. *If it were down to me I would have shot the lot of you.* The MSS agent was not yet out of her twenties, but she liked to think of herself as a traditionalist when it came to matters of personal deportment and discipline. Her father, a Commissar in the People's Armed Police, had always taught her that there could only be one fate for people who betray the faith and the Party: a single bullet to the back of the head with the cost of that bullet invoiced to the surviving family members. All of this skulking around in the shadows, trying to gather up the Politburo's dirty laundry, was both demeaning and an abuse of privilege. She had no doubt what her father, dead almost a decade now, would have made of it all.

Wang stepped forward until her forehead was almost under Xue's chin. 'Well? Where is he?'

'You'd better tell her what she wants to know,' Ren Junior warned Xue. 'She can be terrible when she's angry.'

*Maybe you would be worth two bullets.* 'He is in a secure location,' was all Xue offered by way of reply, her English clean and classical by comparison to the boy's drawl.

'More important than the fate of that English fool, what about my mother and I?' Ren asked. Getting to his feet, he dropped the controller onto the chair and took up a position at his mother's side. 'What are you planning to do with us?'

Steely Dan's 'Dirty Work' was playing in his head as Carlyle finally walked into the Box Café on Henrietta Street.

'Hey.' Alison Roche looked concerned as he hobbled towards her table. 'What happened to your foot?'

'Nothing, nothing.'

Folding her copy of that morning's *Metro*, she dropped it on the chair next to her and watched him sit down opposite.

'Sorry I'm late.'

'No worries.' After a year or so working with the inspector during a stint at Charing Cross, Roche took his shortcomings in her stride.

Carlyle tried to catch the eye of the owner, Myron, so that he could place his order. Ignoring his loyal customer, Myron allowed himself to be distracted by a pretty blonde who proceeded to order a complicated smoothie. Carlyle's stomach rumbled with dismay and he stared forlornly at Roche's empty plate. 'What did you have?'

'Just a salad. Look, I don't want to be rude, but I've got a few things I need to do this afternoon and—'

'Sure, sure.' Carlyle sat back in his chair and looked her up and down. Catching him staring, Roche grinned from behind her cup of builder's tea.

'Are you checking me out, Inspector?'

'No, no.' Blushing slightly, he quickly turned his attention to the street outside. Across the road, on the south-west corner of the Piazza, they were turning an office building into a selection of eye-wateringly expensive flats. Carlyle calculated that the cheapest studio cost more than he had earned in the last twenty-five years. The thought made him more than a little depressed.

'So . . . Chelsea.'

'Yes. Marvin Taylor.'

Roche placed her tea cup on her saucer. 'It's all a bit of a mess.'

'So I've heard.' Carlyle was distracted by the sight of the blonde girl leaving the café with her drink. This time he waved at the owner for some service but Myron had already ducked into the kitchen. Turning back to the smirking Roche, he tried to look philosophical. 'But all Naomi really needs is a few kind words and the return of the body. That shouldn't be so difficult, even for you geniuses at SO15.'

'Ha,' said Roche mirthlessly, 'you'd be surprised.'

Carlyle raised an eyebrow. 'Getting a bit bored with the big guns and the fast cars?'

'Mm. Maybe a little. Sometimes.' Roche gestured at Myron, who had reappeared behind the counter. Waiting patiently for him to lumber over, she let the inspector order some food before continuing. 'Marvin,' she said *sotto voce*, 'as you know, had his head sliced off. Two of his staff were shot in the head; both of them were serving soldiers who were supposed to be on leave.'

'Yeah,' Carlyle said, 'a massacre.'

'The official line is that it was some kind of organized crime dispute,' Roche continued, 'and people have bought that, so far.'

Carlyle folded his arms. 'But that wouldn't explain why you are involved.'

'No. SO15 took control of the scene less than two hours after the initial 999 call. A man reported six quote-unquote "ninjas" entering the building Taylor's men were guarding around the time of the murders.'

'Have you spoken to him?'

Roche shook her head. 'He didn't leave any details. We haven't found him.'

Showing some belated urgency, Myron arrived with a cheese and tomato sandwich and a Diet Coke. Carlyle nodded his thanks, opened the can and took a swig. 'Neither have the media though, which is a big plus.'

'Whoever he was, the guy sounded a bit drunk on the tape but he definitely described them as "ninjas".'

'So what were Marvin and co. doing there?' Carlyle took a bite of his sandwich, chewing rapidly.

'They were looking after some clients in one of the penthouse flats. The assumption is that the ninjas got rid of the bodyguards, grabbed the clients and took off. We've got a bit of CCTV coverage showing a van going into the basement garage and then leaving twenty minutes later. That's about it.' Roche fished a tenner out of her pocket.

'Don't worry about it. Lunch is on me.'

'OK, thanks.'

'Who were the people in the flat?'

'We don't know.' Picking up her newspaper, Roche got to her feet. 'But we think that they might have been Asian.'

'Indian?'

'No.' Roche edged round the table, towards the door. 'Chinese. Japanese. Something like that. Thanks for lunch. I'll give you a shout if I hear anything else.'

'Thanks.' Carlyle wiped the corner of his mouth with a napkin. 'But what'll I tell Naomi Taylor in the meantime?'

Roche reached for the door. 'I'm sure you'll think of something,' she grinned. 'After all, if I remember rightly, you're good with grieving widows.'

Umar eyed Carlyle expectantly as he approached the sergeant's desk. 'Where's my sandwich?'

*Shit.* The inspector stopped in his tracks. 'Sorry, I forgot.'

'But—'

Carlyle dismissed the protests with a wave of his hand. 'What have you found out about our terrorist?'

'Terrorist *suspect*,' Umar said grumpily.

'Yeah, yeah. Thank you for that vital clarification, Clive Stafford Smith.' Carlyle picked a sheaf of papers from Umar's desk, a selection of pages gleaned from various websites, and began leafing through them. 'So what have we got?'

Pushing his chair backwards, Umar lifted his trainers on to the desk. 'Sylvia Tosches looks like she was a fairly minor figure in Baader Meinhof, aka the Red Army Faction, or RAF. Also known as Hitler's Children or the 68ers, after the social protests of 1968.' He looked at his boss and grinned. 'Were you part of all that?'

'I'm not that old,' Carlyle said gruffly.

'Anyway, Tosches. Not as well known as Andreas Baader and Ulrike Meinhof or, indeed, people like Gudrun Ensslin or Jan-Carle Raspe – all of whom are dead, by the way – but sufficiently well known to have her face on *Wanted* posters in police stations all over Europe in the seventies.'

Carlyle rattled the papers in the air. 'I can read all this stuff for myself. Anything to suggest that she might be in London?'

Umar shook his head. 'She's not on our system. I haven't even found anything written about her in the last ten years.'

'And Barbara Hutton?'

'Nothing, so far.'

'OK, why don't you go and get something to eat? I'll take a look at what you've printed off.'

'Fair enough.' Grabbing his coat, Umar scuttled towards the exit.

Flopping into his chair, Carlyle settled in for some quiet reading.

# TWELVE

*Not bad. Not bad at all.* Pushing back his shoulders, Ren Qi flicked an imaginary piece of dust from the shoulder of his Hermès suit and contemplated himself in the floor-to-ceiling mirror. The man staring back at him – tall, elegant, relaxed – was clearly a member of the international elite; someone who belonged in the pages of *GQ* or *Esquire*, whose natural habitat was the streets of Manhattan, or Barcelona . . . or Knightsbridge.

Ren glanced at his Parsifal Gold Chronograph. He was due in Savile Row in under an hour for a fitting with his tailor, followed by a drink at the Atlantic Bar and dinner with a couple of close business partners at the Delauney. After that, it would be time for some fun.

A polite cough woke him from his reverie. Turning away from the mirror, Ren blinked at Guo Miao.

'What do you want to do?' the MSS man asked, pointing at the TV in front of them. On the screen, Wang Lei continued to shuffle in and out of shot, while Ren Jiong played with his computer game.

*Does the boy ever do anything else?* his father wondered. *All that money spent on his education and all he can do is fornicate, drink and play games.* He let out a brittle laugh. *Maybe we have turned him into an English 'gentleman', after all.*

'Sir?'

Ren Qi looked at Guo carefully. The Major was one of his most trusted retainers in the Ministry but Ren knew that his loyalty was being stretched to the limit. Overseas adventures like this took a lot of explaining away back in Beijing. 'The flight is ready?'

'Yes. We can leave when you wish.'

Ren nodded. 'Good.' He turned to go.

'But—'

'Yes?' Ren paused.

'What about the Englishman? Wouldn't it be better to leave him here?'

'Definitely not,' Ren snapped. 'He comes too.' Clearly not happy, the Major nevertheless declined to argue the point any further. 'Think of it as a special delivery.' Ren let his frown melt away. He placed a hand on Guo's shoulder and gave it a firm squeeze. 'I am very grateful for all of your assistance in this matter.'

'Yes, sir.'

'Good.' This time he did head for the door. 'Now, I need to see a man about a suit . . . or two.'

Two doors down from the Charles Dickens Museum, number 46 Doughty Street looked like it had been spruced up recently. The front door of the four-storey Georgian terraced house had been given a coat or two of bright red paint and the wooden-framed windows had been newly installed. Compared to the crumbling pile next door, the place looked very sprightly indeed.

Pressing the doorbell, Carlyle gazed down the street, counting three houses with scaffolding outside. Clearly, the tree-lined street was going through one of its periodic bouts of gentrification.

Having reflected on the state of the local property market, he was just about to reattach his finger to the bell when the door opened and a head appeared. 'Yes?'

Ignoring the cross tone in the woman's voice, Carlyle said politely, 'Mrs Hutton?'

'I'm her daughter.' Suspicion personified, the woman kept the door between them. 'Who are you?'

'I was wondering if I could have a word with your mother.'

'About what?' The woman's eyes narrowed; she rocked backwards as if getting ready to slam the door in his face.

'It's all right, Caroline.' The door opened wider and an older woman appeared. Somewhere in her sixties, she had a neat bob of grey hair and a friendly face. Tall and slim, with high cheekbones and warm eyes, she must have been quite a looker thirty years ago. Hell, she was quite a looker now, Carlyle thought. Whether or not she was the woman in the picture that Gregori, the German private eye, had shown him, however, was another matter entirely. It was impossible to tell. 'I can handle this.'

Caroline gave an irritated sigh before disappearing back inside.

The woman gave Carlyle an apologetic smile. 'I am Barbara Hutton. Can I help you?'

The inspector couldn't help but notice that her accent was pure Home Counties. Flashing his warrant card, he invited himself inside.

Hutton led him to a large reception room on the ground floor at the back of the house. She gestured for him to take a seat on a sofa that had been covered with a pale yellow throw.

'I hope I'm not in any kind of trouble,' she said lightly, remaining on her feet, even when he sat down.

*So do I.* Having decided to pre-empt Sebastian Gregori and Werner Kortmann by coming to see Barbara Hutton for himself, the inspector had given careful consideration as to how he would explain his presence on her doorstep. At the time it had seemed plausible; now, as the woman folded her arms and fixed him with an amused stare, it seemed woefully inadequate. Playing for time, he made a show of glancing around the room: *the policeman analysing his surroundings.*

The room was dominated by a large black and white image,

which hung on the wall to his right. At first glance it looked as if it was a photograph, but on closer inspection he decided it was a painting. It showed the profile of a woman lying on her back, eyes closed, her dark hair merging with the black background. Mesmerized, Carlyle fumbled for his glasses. Slipping them on, he pointed at the picture. 'There's a line around her neck.'

Hutton turned to study the painting. 'That is the German . . . terrorist, Ulrike Meinhof. She hanged herself on the bars of her cell.' She saw the look of surprise on Carlyle's face and added: 'It's a very arresting image but rather intense, in my view. My husband bought it but I insisted that he put it in here. I don't think I could bear to look at it every day.'

'Is it valuable?' was all he could think of to ask.

'No, not that one. It's just a print. The original is in the Museum of Modern Art in New York.'

'Aha. A particular interest of your husband's, is it?'

She shot him a curious look. 'Art?'

'Terrorism.'

'Not particularly, I don't think. He was simply taken by the image.'

'When did she die?'

'Pff.' Hutton looked back at the picture. 'A very long time ago.' Did a tiny smile cross her lips – or did he imagine it? 'Anyway, Inspector, what is it that I can do for you?'

'Well . . .' Bracing himself, he launched into a fictitious tale about a serial burglar who was thought to be targeting the street. 'He has been known to go for works of art,' he concluded lamely, nodding in the direction of Ulrike Meinhof.

'I should be so lucky,' Hutton muttered.

'So we are just going round talking to local households about their security arrangements.'

'I see.'

The conversation was interrupted by the sound of the front door slamming and footsteps in the hallway. Carlyle got to his feet in time to see a short, rotund man walk into the room, loosening his tie as he did so. Clocking Carlyle, the man stopped in his tracks.

'Derek,' Barbara Hutton explained, 'this is Inspector Carlyle, from the police. He's come to warn us about a cat burglar in the neighbourhood.'

Derek Hutton grunted something that sounded very much like '*bollocks*' to Carlyle. Pulling the tie from his neck, he tossed it onto the sofa, close to where the inspector had been sitting. His wife rolled her eyes.

'Inspector, my husband.'

'Since when do the police send an inspector round to talk about a *potential* burglary?' Derek Hutton huffed, removing his jacket and throwing it on top of his tie.

Carlyle remembered that the bloke was a lawyer and began edging towards the door.

'He also likes your print.' Barbara Hutton offered a wry smile in the direction of Ulrike Meinhof.

'What?' Flicking a bead of sweat from his brow, the lawyer glared at his unwelcome visitor.

Ignoring the husband, Carlyle gave Mrs Hutton a big smile as he slipped into the hall. 'Well, nice to meet you. Remember, if you see anything suspicious, please let us know immediately.' Not waiting for a reply, he made a break for the door.


'What the hell is this?' Carlyle waved the letter in the direction of the kitchen doorway.

'What?' asked Helen, over the sound of the kettle coming to the boil.

'This letter.' He was momentarily distracted by the opening bars of Blondie's 'Atomic' coming from Alice's bedroom. Further proof that his daughter lived in something of a musical time warp; then again, a good song was a good song, however old it was.

Helen appeared from the kitchen, a mug in each hand. One

bore a picture of Captain Haddock, the other the legend: *Keep Calm and Drink Tea*. 'I haven't read it.' She handed the Captain Haddock mug to her husband. 'What does it say?'

Carlyle peered into his mug.

'It's green tea.'

Carlyle would rather have had a whiskey, but he kept his mouth shut.

'What does it say?' Helen repeated, leading him into the living room.

'It's from a TV production company called Laxative Productions,' he said, following after her.

'Charming!' Helen picked up a copy of that afternoon's *Standard* from the floor and eased herself into the armchair by the TV.

'Listen to this.' Carlyle placed his tea on the coffee table and dropped on to the sofa. '*Does your child take drugs? Are drugs destroying your family? We are an award-winning independent production company, responsible for hit shows such as* Britain's Biggest Chavs, Travellers from Hell *and* Born in Prison.' He looked at his wife. '*Born in Prison*?'

'Never heard of it,' Helen said innocently. Before he could interrogate the truthfulness of that statement, she opened up the newspaper and started scanning the pages.

'*We are currently researching a show called* My Teenage Drug Hell *and are looking to talk to potential interviewees aged ten and above.*' A thought crossed his mind and he let out a low chuckle. 'Maybe Alice could do it.'

Not wishing to be reminded of their daughter's problems with drugs at school, Helen glared at him over the paper.

'I was only joking.'

'That's not funny.' Helen went back to her reading. 'We've put all that firmly behind us.'

'Let's hope so.'

'Make sure he doesn't see it,' Helen commanded. 'Tear it up and put it in the recycling bag.'

After doing as he was told, Carlyle recovered his tea and took a sip.

'How was work?' Helen asked.

'Fine.' Not sure which recent lowlight to recount for his wife's amusement, he finally plumped for the conversation between Umar and the statuesque Amelia Elmhirst about the former's mysterious photograph.

Looking up from the newspaper, Helen eyed him suspiciously. 'Is she good-looking, this girl?'

Trying to affect the air of the mythical male creature who never considered such things, he took a moment to pretend to give the matter some thought. 'Yes,' he said finally, trying to make the whole thing sound as abstract as possible, 'I suppose you would say that she is.'

'Then he'll be sexting her, or sending her photos of his willy or something,' Helen said.

'Eh?'

She looked at him as if he was particularly dense. 'That's what boys do these days, if they fancy a girl. Apparently, sending someone a photo of your privates is considered a part of normal social discourse among the younger generation.'

'But he's not a boy,' Carlyle protested.

Arching her eyebrows, Helen shot him a look that said *All men are boys, present company included.*

'He's married.'

'And Christina will no doubt have a total fit when she finds out.'

'Not to mention Simpson.'

'Yes,' Helen agreed. 'If someone complains at work, I expect he'll be out the door in almost less time than it takes to email your todger round the world. We had to sack a guy for something similar last year. When it comes to the Met, he's bound to be breaking dozens of employment rules. I doubt if even the Police Federation would be able to save him.'

Carlyle lifted his feet on to the coffee table. 'I'm beginning to think he has a bit of a death wish about The Job. It's almost like he *wants* to get the sack.'

'Maybe. It happens. But the sexting thing is more about him coming on to women, rather than a cry for help about his job. Probably, in his mind, it's just an extension of flirting.'

There was a lull in the conversation. Helen returned to her paper. Carlyle tuned back in to the sounds of Blondie coming from the back of the flat. 'Do you think we need to speak to Alice about this kind of thing?' he asked. 'You know, in terms of the boys at school?'

'Only if you want *her* to explain it more to *you*,' Helen said drily. 'Alice has had to be alert for this kind of nonsense ever since she got her first smartphone.'

Carlyle grimaced at the thought of some degenerate little scrote sending . . . *aaargh*. He didn't want to imagine it. 'And?'

'And what?'

'Has she ever received—'

'No, thank God.' Helen, not wishing to dwell on it either, cut him off. 'At least, not as far as I know.' She gestured at the letter on the table. 'It's like the drugs issue, just another thing we have to try and keep an eye on.'

'I suppose,' said Carlyle glumly, wondering if he would ever get to the point where he could feel like he had this parenting thing even remotely under control.

# THIRTEEN

This time of the morning was far too early for the beautiful people who haunted the Garden Hotel to make an appearance. For a few moments, it seemed as if he was the only person in the entire building.

Tapping the toe of his shoe on the limestone floor, Carlyle contemplated the empty lobby. They'd changed the artwork again, he noted, inspecting the massive canvas that ran almost the whole length of one wall. Paint of all colours had been smeared on with gusto and, to his mind at least, it looked like nothing so much as the contents of an ill child's nappy. *Even Derek Hutton's picture looks better than that*, muttered Carlyle's inner peasant.

'Striking, isn't it?'

Carlyle turned to find a pretty, twenty-something girl at his shoulder. She wore the grey Mao tunic that denoted a member of staff, and her flat shoes meant that he could just about avoid having to look up to her. Her blonde hair was pulled back into a ponytail and she had the fresh-faced look of someone who had just started her shift. Above her left breast was a small badge that said: *Deborah Burke, Chief Concierge*.

'What happened to Alex?' Carlyle was well acquainted with Alexander Miles, who had been Chief Concierge at the hotel for many years. During that time, Alex had benefited on several occasions from the inspector's ability to overlook a range of indiscretions on the part of both staff and guests. As a result, he still owed Carlyle more than a few favours.

'He left a couple of months ago,' the new Chief Concierge smiled. 'He was headhunted to go and work in a new destination hotel in Battersea.'

What's a 'destination hotel'? Carlyle wondered. No matter, if the silly sod had gone south of the river he was unlikely to be of much use to anyone working out of Charing Cross. For Carlyle, the ultimate metropolitan snob, London stopped being London by the time you got to Fulham Broadway. As for Battersea, it might as well be Bournemouth.

'Did you know Alex?'

The all too appropriate use of the past tense made Carlyle smile. He whipped out his warrant card and held it up for the late Mr Miles's replacement to see.

The woman did a double take, glancing over her shoulder to check that no one was listening in on their conversation. 'A policeman?'

'That's right, Debbie.' Carlyle stuffed the ID back into the inside breast pocket of his jacket. 'I work just round the corner at the Charing Cross station.'

'It's Deborah,' she said stiffly.

'OK, Deborah. Anyway, don't worry, I'm just here to meet a couple of guys who happen to be staying in this place. Nothing to do with the hotel.'

'Good, good.' She edged further away.

'But Alex and I had a good working relationship. We should have a chat about that when I've got a bit more time.'

The young woman smiled nervously, once again looking over her shoulder, this time for someone to come to her aid. 'That would be great, thanks.'

'Fine, I'll see you later then.' Not wishing to cause *Deborah* any more discomfort, he strode off in the direction of the reception desk to try and track down his two Germans.

\* \* \*

94

Five minutes and four attempted phone calls later, he was none the wiser as to the whereabouts of Sebastian Gregori and Werner Kortmann. Neither man was answering the phone in his room. Their mobiles were going to voicemail. Gregori had not responded to the email Carlyle had sent earlier. The inspector looked at his watch. He had been late arriving and it was now more than forty-five minutes past the time they had agreed to meet. 'If they've gone to see Barbara Hutton without me,' Carlyle mumbled under his breath, 'I'll . . .'

*You'll what?* said a voice inside his head. *Why do you care what that pair get up to? This is not your problem. Leave it alone.*

'Good advice,' Carlyle agreed, staring at the ground as if he was conversing with his shoes. 'But what should I do now?' Looking up, he caught sight of Deborah Burke watching him from behind her desk in the corner of the lobby. Not wishing to waste all of his morning talking to himself, he gave her a brisk wave and headed towards the exit.

'Hey, Inspector!'

Carlyle turned and smiled. 'Hey. How are you?'

Sonia Coverdale danced across the limestone floor of the hotel, wearing a flowery dress.

'I hear I owe you an apology.'

'Me?' Carlyle frowned.

'Yeah. I heard you had to deal with the guy who was demanding his money back.'

'Ah, yes. The unhappy Mr Brian Yates.'

'I never knew his name,' she shrugged. 'But what a nerve.'

'It was a strange one,' Carlyle agreed. Standing in front of him, the girl looked tanned and healthy. To his eyes at least, she was very attractive too.

She gave him a cheeky grin. 'Did you nick him?'

'Nah. I just sent him on his way with a flea in his ear.'

'Shame.'

'I don't think he'll do it again.'

'That's not much good to me,' Sonia said, her face turning serious. 'Word gets around.'

Carlyle gestured in the direction of the rooms upstairs. 'It's not like business has dried up completely.'

'No,' she conceded, 'but I've got my reputation to consider.'

'Well, it was the best I could do, under the circumstances.'

'I know, and I'm very grateful.' The smile returned and she slipped her arm through his and led him towards the door. 'And, to show my appreciation, I've got something for you in return.'

Carlyle felt himself stiffen. He glanced nervously towards the concierge's desk but Deborah Burke had disappeared.

'Don't worry,' Sonia chuckled, pulling him closer, 'it's not that.'

'What is it, then?' Carlyle asked, relieved and disappointed at the same time.

'In a minute.' Reaching the revolving door, she gently pushed him in front. 'First, I need some breakfast. It was a long night.'

He watched the last piece of toast disappear into Sonia's mouth and wondered if he could have managed something more than a cup of tea. They were sitting in a café near Seven Dials. It was the kind of place whose name you could never remember, even when you were in it; not really a tourist trap, but not a hangout for the locals either.

'Long night?'

'Yeah,' the girl grinned. 'The pair of them kept me at it till almost five o'clock.' She took a slurp of her tea. 'That's the problem with all this Viagra and stuff; people want to feel they're getting their money's worth.'

Carlyle's eyes narrowed. 'Two guys? They weren't German, were they?'

'Nope. Americans. Why do you ask?'

'Doesn't matter.'

'Rich college kids.' She made a face. 'I much prefer older guys, like you.'

'Thanks a lot.'

'Apart from that wanker who made the complaint, obviously.'

'Yates,' Carlyle reminded her.

'Whatever. The older blokes usually just hand me the cash there and then. Ten minutes of slobbering and it's over and done with.' She appraised the inspector coolly. 'I reckon six or seven for you. Eight max.'

'Good to know,' said Carlyle, less than pleased with her assessment, even though he knew it was somewhat on the generous side.

'The younger guys though, they're popping the blue pills and trying to go all night. It's an abuse of the fair usage policy.'

'The what?'

'Fair usage. Like with your internet company. You use too much and they cut you off. Happens to Darren all the time. Mind you, the silly sod spends all day downloading all the illegal crap he can lay his hands on.'

Carlyle wondered who Darren was, but wasn't curious enough to ask.

'Anyway, I've complained to the agency about it, but they don't want to know.'

'I suppose not.'

'At the very least, we should be thinking about changing our pricing structure, to take account of that kind of thing.'

*Christ, when did you do an MBA?* 'I don't suppose Royal Escorts has given much thought to changing its business model,' Carlyle observed drily, 'given that they're operating in the oldest profession of them all.'

'No,' Sonia nodded, 'but you would have thought Harry would have been prepared to at least think about it. After all, it's all about him making more money.'

Carlyle raised his eyes to the heavens. Harry Cummins, the cheery public schoolboy owner of Royal Escorts, had more than enough money already. For Harry, being a pimp was more about a lifestyle choice than putting bread on the table. 'How long has he been out of jail now?'

'I dunno,' Sonia shrugged, 'A couple of years, maybe?'

Carlyle tutted. 'I don't know how he gets away with it.' Even when sending him down, the judge had commented favourably on Harry's 'remarkable' and 'enlightened' business, which paid Corporation Tax, National Insurance, VAT and council tax, as well as refusing to have anything to do with trafficked women. 'The whole operation had been kept as legitimate as a criminal enterprise could have been,' the beak had concluded, before passing a ridiculously lenient sentence. So far, it had been Harry's only spell inside.

'He's OK, really,' Sonia claimed.

'If you say so.' The inspector took a sip of his tea and signalled to the waitress behind the counter for the bill. 'Breakfast is on me.'

'Thanks.'

'So,' he continued, finally getting down to business, 'you said you had something for me?'

'Yes.' Finishing her tea, Sonia placed the cup back on the saucer. 'I hear you were asking about Marvin Taylor?'

Jeez, Carlyle thought, how is it that everyone always knows my business? 'How did you hear that?'

'I have my sources,' she said cheekily, 'just like you.'

Another thought popped into his head. Instead of batting it away, he asked: 'Did you know him?'

'In passing. I'd seen him around a few times.'

*Thank God for that.* The last thing he needed were skeletons to start falling out of cupboards.

Recognizing the look of relief on his face, Sonia waved an index finger at him. 'No, no, you dirty-minded sod, he wasn't a punter. Although, if you want, I could give you a list of cops round here who are. It'd be quite a long list too.'

'No, thanks.' He thought of the havoc that such information

98

could wreak and shuddered. 'Let's just get back to Marvin, shall we?'

'It wasn't so much about Marvin as that place in Chelsea he was guarding.'

'What about it?'

'I've been there a lot. One of my best clients lives there, on the top floor.'

Carlyle's eyes narrowed. 'Has anyone spoken to you about this?'

'No, why would they? I've haven't been there for over a month. The place is always deserted anyway; you never see another soul there.'

'What about Harry?'

'What about him?'

'Presumably he would know that you went there.'

'Yeah, but he hasn't mentioned it. Probably hasn't made the connection. Harry isn't the kind of guy who spends a lot of time following the news.'

'Smart bloke. So, who is the client?'

'He was a businessman. About fifty, I'd say.' Sonia let out a chuckle. 'He was a seven-minute man . . . like you.' Reaching into her bag, she rummaged around for a few moments, finally pulling out a business card and placing it on the table in front of Carlyle. '*Voilà*.'

Picking up the card, Carlyle squinted at the script.

'You need glasses,' Sonia observed.

'I've got glasses,' Carlyle told her 'but I don't really need them for reading. I tried varifocals, but they didn't work for me.' He squinted harder. *Tallow Business Services, Michael Nicholson Managing Director.* There was a mobile number and an email address. He looked at Sonia. 'Tallow?'

'It's a kind of Chinese tree,' she explained. 'The guy did a lot of business in China, apparently.'

*China.* He thought back to his conversation with Roche and the mysterious call about the 'ninjas'. It vaguely felt like he could be on to something, even though he didn't really want to be. Holding up the card, he waved it at Sonia. 'Can I keep this?'

'Sure.'

'And if Nicholson gives you a call, can you let me know?'

'Yeah, but I wouldn't hold your breath. He goes off on his business trips and I might not see him for months.'

The waitress appeared with the bill and Carlyle dropped a tenner and some change on the table. 'I've got to get going.'

'OK,' Sonia smiled. 'I'm in no rush.'

'Thanks for the info.' He got to his feet. 'And I hope you don't have too many hassles with the punters.'

The smile vanished. 'You know what it's like, Inspector. You never know what you're gonna get when you walk through that door.'

# FOURTEEN

The first thing Carlyle noticed when he walked into the room was the urn, a small metallic pot squatting on the mantelpiece. At first glance, he imagined that it was glowing slightly, as if it was radioactive. Distracted by its malevolent presence, it took the inspector a couple of moments to acknowledge the woman's presence. Perched on the sofa, Naomi Taylor seemed to have shrunk since their last meeting.

Rocking backwards and forwards, she blew her nose into a handkerchief as he sat down in an armchair by the fireplace. 'I'm sorry,' she whispered.

'Don't worry.' Embarrassed, Carlyle pointed towards the pot. 'What happened?'

Taylor's face crumpled. 'They cremated him,' she sobbed.

'Yes.'

'We went to collect the body and they gave me . . . *that*.'

Carlyle took a deep breath. 'Did you give your consent for the cremation to take place?'

'No. I wasn't even there when they did it.' She looked up. 'I was just given the ashes. I don't even know that it's him.'

'I'm sure that—'

'Why would they cremate him,' she wailed, 'without my permission? Why would they do that?'

Because they're berks, Carlyle thought wearily. 'What did they say?'

She mumbled something that sounded like 'bureaucratic error'.

Carlyle scratched the back of his head. There was nothing useful he could tell the poor woman. 'You could sue,' he said finally.

'No.' Trying to compose herself, she sat back on the sofa and wiped her eyes. In a pair of jeans and a *Breaking Bad* 'I am the one who knocks' T-shirt, she looked about sixteen, even though he knew that she must be pushing forty-five. 'They made me sign something before I could take the ashes away. My lawyer says it was a declaration that I am happy with what was done, even though I'm not, obviously.'

It looked like she was going to start sobbing again, but she blinked back the tears and pulled her knees up under her chin. Her feet were bare and the inspector noticed that her toenails were painted different colours. He looked away, focusing his attention on the far wall, which was dominated by a large photographic print of the New York City skyline at night. After some ill-tempered debate inside his head, the inspector decided that it was not hanging straight.

'Anyway,' Taylor continued, 'I don't want money.'

'No.'

'I want to know who killed Marvin. And why.'

Money would be easier, Carlyle thought glumly. He reluctantly met her expectant gaze. 'Well, I have spoken to some people who are working on the investigation and there does not seem to be a lot for them to go on at the moment.'

She waited patiently for him to say more.

The inspector rubbed a hand over his face. Now was the time for him to get up, make his apologies and scarper. Only he couldn't. On the one hand, the decapitation of Marvin Taylor was nothing to do with him. Indeed, the irony was that it probably wasn't much to do with Marvin himself either. On the other hand, the inspector felt unable to just ignore it and walk away. Sometimes cases chose you, rather than the other way round.

'I was, er, wondering what you might be able to tell me about Marvin's business. In particular, whether you knew anything about the people he was working for on the night that he was killed.'

'The other people asked me about that.'

*The other people. SO15.* 'Yes.'

'But I couldn't tell them anything much. Marvin and I never really talked about his work.'

'No.'

'He was big on client confidentiality.'

'Of course.'

She pointed towards the ceiling. 'We use the spare bedroom as an office.'

'Jolly good.' Carlyle got to his feet.

'The anti-terrorism people came and searched it the other day.'

'Ah.' He sat back down again.

'They took the computer, a couple of laptops and our back-up hard drives. I asked the bloke how long till we got them back but he just said, "how long is a piece of string?".'

'Helpful.'

'Marvin's mum had to go down to PC World and get another one, so Laurie could do her homework.'

'Yes.' The inspector stole another glance at the urn. *Marvin, you silly sod, if only you knew the trouble you've caused.* He looked back at the wife. 'What did the SO15 boys say that they were looking for?'

'Dunno,' she sniffed. 'The same as you, I suppose.'

'OK.' Carlyle wondered what to do next. Maybe he should go back to Roche; see if he could do a trade with the information that Sonia Coverdale had given him. Maybe SO15 already knew about Michael Nicholson and Tallow Business Services, but maybe they didn't.

'They didn't take the paper records though.'

'Sorry?'

'We keep paper copies of all Marvin's files. I mean, you

103

never know with all that electronic information, it could all just disappear in a puff of smoke one day and then where would you be? Marvin was always paranoid about losing all the data, so we had a back-up to the back-up.'

*Good old Marvin.* 'Only the paranoid survive, as they say.'

Naomi Taylor blinked away a tear.

*Carlyle, you idiot.* 'Sorry.'

She struggled to her feet. 'Would you like to see them? They're in the kitchen.'

After an hour of sifting through a pile of papers six inches thick, Carlyle was none the wiser as to the job Marvin Taylor had been doing on the night of his death. Marvin and Naomi might have been keen on keeping duplicate records, but they hadn't been too interested in filing them in any discernible order. Moreover, it was clear that Marvin's clients were not the kind of people who liked to provide too much information for the purposes of an invoice. Pushing his chair back from the kitchen table, he closed his eyes and yawned.

'Who are you?'

Opening his eyes, Carlyle saw a young girl standing in the doorway. He smiled. 'I'm John. Who are you?'

She didn't answer his question, but went on: 'Why are you here?'

'I'm a policeman.' Taking his warrant card from his pocket, he held it out for her to inspect. 'I'm looking at some information for your mother.'

The girl thought about it for a moment, then stepped into the kitchen and took the ID from his hand. Studying it carefully, she read aloud: 'Inspector John Carlyle, Metropolitan Police.'

'That's me.'

She looked at him doubtfully. 'You don't look like your picture.'

'That was taken a while ago now,' Carlyle said, 'when I wasn't as old as I am now.'

The girl took one last look at the photo and handed the card back to him. 'Not so much grey hair. And no glasses.'

'I'm getting old,' Carlyle shrugged, dropping the card back into his pocket. 'It happens.'

'Are you older than my dad?'

Carlyle felt a sick feeling in his stomach. 'Yes, a few years older.'

'My dad's dead,' the girl said matter-of-factly. 'His ashes are in the living room.' She stared at him defiantly, as if challenging him to deny it.

Trying to hide his embarrassment, Carlyle began trying to tidy the papers on the desk. 'What's your name?'

'I'm Laurie.'

'Nice to meet you, Laurie.'

'Did you know my dad?'

'Yes, I did. We worked together when he was in the police. I liked him a lot. He was very good at his job.'

Laurie nodded. 'Are you going to be here long?'

'Not very long.'

'Do you want to hear a joke?'

'Sure, why not?'

'OK, and maybe you want this for your pile.' From behind her back she produced a sheet of A4 paper that was covered in crayon of different colours and placed it carefully on the table.

'Thank you.'

'You're welcome.' She looked at him earnestly. 'So, what do you call a crazy chicken?'

'A crazy chicken . . .' Carlyle rubbed his chin thoughtfully. 'I don't know.'

'A cuckoo *cluck*, ha. Geddit?'

'That's a good one,' Carlyle chuckled.

The girl folded her arms. 'Your turn.'

'OK.' Carlyle thought about it for a moment. He only ever had the one joke but it was a good one. 'What do you call an exploding monkey?'

'A what?' The girl frowned.

'An exploding monkey.'

'No idea.'

'A ba-*boom*.'

He watched her face fall.

'That's terrible.' Pushing herself away from the table, Laurie skipped out of the room and disappeared down the hallway.

'I quite like it,' Carlyle mumbled to himself. Returning to the mess on the desk, he picked up the sheet of paper the child had left behind. It was immediately clear that Laurie had spent quite a bit of time colouring in one of her dad's invoices. The mess reminded him of the art on the wall of the Garden Hotel. He should show it to Deborah Burke; maybe she could hang it in the lobby. Underneath a smear of orange crayon he noticed the date; the invoice had been raised barely a week ago.

Then he saw the name. *Tallow Business Services.*

'Bingo.'

Folding the sheet of paper into quarters, he stuffed it into his pocket. Getting to his feet, he headed quickly for the door, leaving the mess of papers for someone else to deal with.


Fifty yards down the road, the phone started vibrating in his pocket.

'Carlyle.'

'Boss, where are you?'

'Tsk.' The inspector was in no mood to be quizzed by his sergeant.

'I think you'd better get back here sharpish,' Umar continued. 'Simpson's on the warpath.'

'What's the problem this time?' Carlyle asked, adopting the blasé tone of a man long past caring.

'It's your Germans.'

*My Germans? When did they become* my *bloody Germans?*
'What about them?' he snapped. 'We had a meeting scheduled for this morning. They didn't turn up.'

'That might be because they were beaten to a pulp in Soho last night.'

'Fuck,' Carlyle sighed, lengthening his stride. 'OK, I'm on my way.'

# FIFTEEN

Standing on the top floor of one of London's most expensive private hospitals, Carlyle looked over the nearby rooftops. It had turned into the kind of typically grey London morning that suited the inspector's sombre mood perfectly. Having spent the morning running around like a blue-arsed fly, he wanted nothing so much as a sandwich and a decent coffee. More than that, however, he just wanted to be left alone. There was nothing that irked him more than feeling the Commander's controlling hand on his shoulder. Carlyle simply did not respond well to being *managed*.

Following the call from his sergeant, he had rushed over to A&E at St Thomas's, only to be cheerily informed by a senior staff nurse that his quarry had flashed his Platinum health insurance card on arrival and had been promptly transferred to the Len Cohen Medical Centre. There was nothing your average NHS operative liked better than being able to pass a patient off to the private sector with a minimum of fuss.

'He wasn't even British,' the woman observed, shaking her head at the temerity of these bloody foreigners, coming over here and getting sick just so they could take advantage of our wonderful health service.

With a growl of frustration, the inspector had turned around and retraced his steps as far as Portland Street, in the heart of Fitzrovia. Twenty-five minutes later, he was standing in the hotel-style reception of the LCMC, being told that Mr Gregori was undergoing 'tests' and could not be seen for another half an hour at least.

'Fuck's sake.'

The nurse, who looked barely half his age, shot Carlyle a disapproving look.

'Sorry,' he stammered. 'What about the other one?'

'The other one?' the girl asked. He noticed the name on her badge: *Siddle*.

'Yes.' Carlyle tried to recall the name of the second German, but his mind was resolutely blank. 'There was another one.'

'I don't know about that,' Nurse Siddle said, 'but let me see what I can find out for you.' And she scurried off before he could ask any more questions.

Nurse Siddle did not reappear. However, after nipping out to a nearby sandwich shop to rebalance his blood-sugar levels, Carlyle felt somewhat calmer. Eventually, after flicking through various back issues of *Motorboat Monthly*, he was collected by another nurse who escorted him up to the HS Thompson Suites on the eighth floor. As they exited the elevator, turning right, Carlyle immediately knew the room he wanted; it was the one with the guard outside.

'Thanks,' he said to the nurse. 'I know where I'm going.'

'Very well.' Turning on her heel, she headed off down the corridor in pursuit of her next chore. From somewhere nearby came the sound of a daytime TV programme. There was a smell that he couldn't quite place; it made his stomach feel a bit queasy after its recent lunch. Nodding at the constable sitting by the door, he flashed his ID and stepped inside.

Sitting up in bed, a brief look of panic spread across Sebastian Gregori's face until he belatedly recognized his new visitor. Ignoring the two chairs, Carlyle took up a position at the end of the bed. 'How are you feeling?'

Gregori smiled weakly. The private investigator looked like he'd taken a bit of a beating, but he was hardly on life support. He had the beginnings of a shiner around his left eye, beneath which there was a plaster on his cheekbone. Otherwise, apart from a gash on his chin, he looked in reasonable condition.

Hardly enough cause for me to rush halfway across London and then back again, Carlyle thought sourly. 'What happened?'

'We were heading back to our hotel from dinner at the Countdown Club just after midnight,' Gregori explained. 'We were walking down a kind of alleyway and some guys jumped us from behind.' He looked aggrieved. 'I thought London was supposed to be a safe city?'

*It is.* 'You can be in the wrong place at the wrong time, anywhere,' the inspector mused.

'I suppose so.' Gregori sounded less than convinced. 'Anyway, I was punched in the face and went down. They were kicking me on the ground and then it all went black. The next thing I knew, I was waking up in the ambulance.'

'And what about Mr Kortmann?' Carlyle felt pleased with himself for finally remembering the name.

Without any warning, Carole Simpson appeared at his shoulder, making him jump. 'Werner Kortmann,' she said grimly, 'appears to have been kidnapped.'

'Kidnapped?'

Taking a sheaf of papers from her briefcase, Simpson thrust a single sheet into his hand. 'This is a copy of a picture that was sent to the hotel earlier this morning.'

Scowling, Carlyle scanned the image: Kortmann sitting cross-legged on the ground in front of a brick wall. It looked like he was inside a garage. His clothes were dishevelled, but he appeared to have taken less of a beating than Gregori. In his hands, he held a copy of *The Times*. The date wasn't discernible, but Carlyle assumed it was today's edition. There was a picture of a member of the Royal Family on the front page; then again, there was a picture of some royal or another on the front page most days.

'History is repeating itself,' Gregori groaned. 'It's the same as Uli Eichinger.'

The poor sods in these types of pictures all looked the same to Carlyle. 'That was a very long time ago,' he pointed out.

'We have to assume there's a connection of some sort,' Simpson put in, 'for the moment at least.'

'It was certainly not a random mugging.' Carlyle handed the picture back to Simpson. 'What are they asking for?'

'So far,' she said, 'they haven't made any demands.'

*Was that a good thing?* Carlyle tried to retrieve what little he knew about kidnappings from the recesses of his brain. There was, however, next to nothing to recover. Other than a young boy who had been snatched by his father – a nasty domestic from years earlier – he had no real experience of dealing with this kind of thing. 'Who've you got on the case?'

Simpson looked at him as if he was an idiot.

'Hold on a sec.' Stepping away from the bed, Carlyle lowered his voice to the point where it would be impossible for Gregori to hear.

'Your mess,' Simpson hissed. 'You have to clean it up.'

'My mess?' Carlyle stifled a wail. 'But this has nothing to do with me.' He gestured half-heartedly towards the bed. 'It's hardly my fault what happened.'

'The kidnappers think differently,' the Commander said tartly, stuffing the picture back into her case.

Carlyle frowned. 'What makes you say that?'

'The picture. They sent it to you.'

Back on the front step of 46 Doughty Street, Carlyle peered through the ground-floor window, searching in vain for any signs of life. He counted to ten as he gave another blast on the front-door bell, waiting patiently as it reverberated through the old Georgian house. Still nothing; no one was coming out to play. Looking over the wrought-iron railings, he stared into the well that ran along the front of the house, a six-foot wide, ten-foot deep trough that separated the building from the pavement. A small set of iron stairs led down from street level to a basement door. At the top of the stairs was a gate set into the railings.

The gate was open.

Carlyle looked up and down the tree-lined street. Giving the doorbell one last try, he waited a few more seconds then nipped down the stairs.

Like the house proper, the basement appeared to have been spruced up recently. Turned into a granny flat perhaps, or rented out to give the Huttons a little extra income. Either way, a quick squint through the window suggested that the place was also empty. Carlyle rapped on the window with his knuckles.

'Hello? Anyone home? Police.'

Not getting any response, he turned his attention to the door. The top half consisted of six small panes of glass; wood on the bottom. It looked flimsy. The inspector considered giving it a good kick, then thought better of it. It wouldn't look too clever if he left an identifiable footprint. Instead, he pulled out a pair of latex gloves from his jacket pocket and slipped them on. On the pavement, above his head, a young woman walked past, squealing on her mobile phone.

*'Whatever. That little cow's gonna get a good slap when I see her, skanky bitch.'*

*Ah, the solidarity of the Sisterhood.* Listening to the young woman disappearing down the street, Carlyle smacked the pane nearest the handle with his elbow.

'Fuck. That hurt.'

It took three more determined blows before the glass gave way. Pulling out the largest pieces of glass, he made a hole large enough to get his hand inside and unlock the door. Careful not to stand on the broken glass, he then slipped inside.

The flat had a heavy, musty smell. Carlyle quickly checked out the three rooms – a bedroom, kitchen/living room and a tiny bathroom with the smallest shower he had ever seen.

Everywhere was clean and tidy, but there was no evidence that anyone was currently residing there. On a counter in the kitchen was a set of tourist leaflets and a ring binder on which someone had written USEFUL INFORMATION + THINGS TO DO IN LONDON in black marker pen.

*Holiday let*, the ace investigator concluded. In the distance, he heard a siren and froze, letting out a deep breath as he realized it was moving away from him.

'Let's get on with it, shall we?' At the back of the flat were stairs leading to the house. At the top was a door. He tried the handle.

Locked.

'Shit.' Carlyle stared at the door for several moments, on the off-chance that it might open of its own accord. When it didn't, he scratched his head.

'OK, genius, what are you going to do now?'

'Well, stop talking to myself, for a start.' Returning to the kitchen, he rummaged around the drawers until he found a substantial-looking knife. Having already faked a break-in (or rather, *committed* a break-in) now was no time for subtlety. Knife in hand, he climbed the stairs and set about jimmying the lock.

Two minutes later, he was standing in the room where he had previously spun the line to Barbara Hutton about a burglar being on the prowl. He glanced up at the painting on the wall and gave Ulrike Meinhof a quick nod of recognition. She didn't respond.

Belatedly, an alarm went off somewhere in the house. Carlyle glanced at his watch. A couple of minutes and then he was out of here. Even *his* recklessness had limits.

Clearly he didn't have time to search the whole house, so where should he start? He contemplated the idea of grabbing a DNA sample – from a hairbrush perhaps – that could be compared with the sister. But how could he explain acquiring it? Moving into the hallway, he began climbing the stairs.

Reaching the second floor, he found a small study, situated at the back of the house, with a window overlooking a walled garden. Almost half of the floorspace was taken up by a large oak desk on which sat an Apple Mac, largely hidden behind piles of papers. On the wall to his left was a large framed movie poster, showing a couple embracing under the legend *Angst essen Seele auf.* Below the poster was a small bookcase on which sat a framed black and white photograph. In the picture, a man and a woman seemed to be aping the pose of the couple in the poster. Carlyle lifted the picture in front of his face. The pair were standing outside in the sunshine. From the selection of people and banners in the background, it looked like they were taking part in a demonstration of some sort. Carlyle guessed it had probably taken place some time in the 1970s, or maybe the eighties. The man was a youthful Derek Hutton, hidden behind a thick, bushy beard. The woman he didn't recognize; it clearly wasn't Barbara Hutton, however. *An old girlfriend? Wouldn't that be a strange thing to keep on display in the family home?*

He was still staring at the picture when the doorbell rang.

*Stay calm.*

Putting the photograph back in its place, Carlyle slowly counted to ten. Nothing. Relaxing, he went back to his task. The bookcase was filled with legal texts. On the bottom shelf was a battered red box-file. Opening it, Carlyle stared at a jumble of yellowing newspaper cuttings, some in English, some in German. At first glance, they all seemed concerned with Baader Meinhof and various terrorist attacks in Germany in the seventies. He glanced at his watch. His time was up. But what had he learned from his little criminal adventure?

Then he saw it.

It was an undated clipping from a German newspaper. Only four paragraphs and the headline had been cut off. Beside the text was a grainy photograph of a pretty girl and, beneath, the name: Sylvia Tosches. Interesting. It wasn't exactly proof of anything, but it was *something*. He squinted at the image. It could have been Barbara Hutton. It could have been a million other women.

From outside came another blast on the doorbell.

*Time to go.*

Placing the clipping back in its place, he returned the file to the shelf and headed for the stairs. As he descended, a third blast led him to conclude that there was no merit in trying to exit through the basement. Instead, reaching the ground floor, he pulled open the front door to find a young PC standing on the doorstep. At the kerb, his partner sat in their police vehicle, watching developments with interest.

'Excuse me, sir. Is this your house? Your alarm's been going off.'

Carlyle turned to look at the blue light flashing insistently from the box above the front door before reaching for his warrant card.

The constable looked at it suspiciously and glanced at his partner.

'I was just passing and saw there had been a break-in.' Putting his ID back into his pocket, Carlyle pointed to the mess in the basement. 'So I went to have a look.' He knew it sounded lame, but as long as he stood his ground he would be able to get away with it.

'Without calling it in?'

'No, sorry. It was kind of an impulse thing.'

'Didn't you hear the bell when I rang it the first time?'

'No.'

The PC clocked the latex gloves Carlyle was still wearing. It was clear that he was becoming more suspicious by the minute.

It was time to go on the offensive. 'What is your name, *Constable*?'

'Wilson,' the uniform said stiffly.

Carlyle eyeballed the officer in the car, who was now busy talking on his radio. 'And your partner?'

'Garner.'

'From the Holborn station?'

A nod.

'OK,' Carlyle sighed. 'There is a bit of damage downstairs but nothing serious. Difficult to say what, if anything, was taken. The owners are out, obviously. You probably just need to leave them a crime number and we can be on our way.'

'What about Forensics?'

Carlyle shot the youngster a look of disbelief. 'Are you kidding? Have you guys got nothing better to do?'

'Standard procedure.'

'Not if you're broke, it's not. And the Met is most definitely broke.'

'But—'

His irritation rising, Carlyle pushed open the door and invited Constable Wilson inside. 'Want to take a look around?'

Sitting on the stairs, Carlyle checked the messages on his BlackBerry while Wilson poked about upstairs. After five minutes or so, the constable reappeared on the first-floor landing, filling out a pre-printed *sorry you've been robbed* form.

Is there any organization in the world that is as addicted to forms as the Met? Carlyle wondered. Getting to his feet, he yawned. 'All done?'

'I'll just leave this for the owners,' Wilson replied, coming down the stairs. 'They can give me a call if they see anything on the CCTV.'

'Huh?'

With his biro, Wilson pointed towards a small wall-light in the hallway. 'They've got cameras all the way up to the top. Set them up to look like lights. Not bad.'

Carlyle stared at the camera. It looked like a normal light to him.

'If you look inside, you'll see that the "bulb" is a camera.' Carefully placing the form on the bottom step of the stairs,

Wilson went and stood directly underneath the fitting. 'You can just see the little red light to indicate it's on.' He gestured for Carlyle to come and take a look.

'It's OK,' the inspector said grumpily. 'I need to get going.' *Who the fuck has CCTV inside their house?* He cursed Derek Hutton under his breath.

'I'll let you know if they find anything.'

'Thanks.' Bolting from the house, he gave Constable Garner the briefest of nods before heading down Doughty Street and turning on to Gray's Inn Road. Seeking out the sanctuary of Andrews Café, he ordered All Day Breakfast Number 3 and dialled Umar's number.

'I need you to get up here,' he commanded when the sergeant finally answered.

'Why?' Umar whined.

'I'll explain when you get here.' Carlyle gave him the Huttons' address. 'Meet me there in half an hour . . . no, make it twenty minutes.' The service in Andrews was always quick; he would have enough time to finish his food before trying to clean up this latest self-inflicted mess.

# SIXTEEN

'Ren Qi is not going to be happy.' Guo Miao looked down at the body of Michael Nicholson lying peacefully on the bed. 'What happened?'

'They gave him a sedative,' Xue Xi explained, 'in preparation for the journey. Maybe they gave him too much. Or maybe his heart just gave out. He might have had a pre-existing medical condition. We have no way of knowing.'

The State Security man shook his head. 'The boss does not deal in "maybes". He will want to know.'

'That is a matter for the doctor,' Xue replied, her tone a shade more dismissive than she had intended.

'We're hardly going to do an autopsy,' Guo snapped back.

'No. Of course not.' For a moment, the pair of them stared at the corpse in silence. The man didn't look any more appealing dead than he did alive. An image of Nicholson on top of the tiny Wang Lei flashed through Xue's mind and she shuddered. 'What are we going to do with the body?' she asked finally.

'That remains to be seen.' The major eyed his underling carefully. Xue Xi was turning into something of a disappointment and it pained him more than he would have imagined. She had been his star student but her efficiency was beginning to be undermined by a lack of discipline. First she almost takes the security guard's head clean off, and then this. Perhaps the deaths were indeed due to circumstances beyond their control.

But wasn't it the job of Ministry personnel to control all circumstances at all times?

Sensing her boss's displeasure, Xue stared at her boots. A gift from her father when she had joined the MSS, she knew that they would last her whole career. As always, they were polished to an impressive shine. Flexing her toes, she felt the leather creak.

'Did you hit him?' Guo asked.

'What?'

'Did you hit him?'

Xue paused. She should deny it but she could not lie completely. 'I used appropriate force,' she said quietly, 'when it came to restraining the prisoner. He struggled when the doctor came to give him the injection. It was hard to find a vein.'

'Is that right?' Guo was old enough to remember the Cultural Revolution. 'Appropriate force' meant anything up to and including throwing people out of tenth-floor windows.

'Yes, sir.'

Guo looked around the room. I should have installed a surveillance camera, he thought, up there in the corner. In the event, there simply hadn't been time. It was just one more way in which this wasn't a secure location. That's what happened when you went off on these private adventures; everything got compromised. He had always considered his loyalty to Ren Qi as unwavering but now he could see that it had its limits. His patron was becoming increasingly erratic in his decision-making. Driven by hubris and lust, it seemed that the man's fall from grace was written in the stars. It was a story as old as the hills. The final chapter was only a matter of time and there could only be one ending.

The chatter in Beijing was getting louder. Guo had already been approached on two separate occasions, with offers to dish the dirt on his boss. So far, he had refused. Next time, however, his answer might very well be different. His gaze once again fell on the dead Englishman. 'Leave him for now,' he commanded. 'He's not going anywhere.'

* * *

Looking exceedingly pleased with himself, Umar sucked down another mouthful of Coke. 'It was really straightforward. Once we found their box of tricks under the stairs, all I had to do was erase the hard drive.'

Carlyle grunted. His All Day Breakfast had settled in his stomach and he was feeling less than chipper. What he really needed was a lie-down in a dark room with a damp towel over his head.

'Basically, everything gets stored for a month.' The sergeant paused, taking another mouthful of his drink. 'I've cleared it all and set it to start up again in a couple of hours.'

'And there's no back-up?'

'Let's hope not,' Umar played with his can, 'for your sake.' Acknowledging the look of vague distress on his boss's face, he quickly added: 'I couldn't see any evidence of anything else. It'll be fine.'

'Thank you,' Carlyle said grudgingly. 'Seems like a lot of kit to have in your house.'

'Not really,' Umar countered. 'It's quite common these days. Apart from deterring burglars,' he shot Carlyle a look, '*attentive* burglars, that is, people use it for spying on the nanny, things like that.'

Umar finished his drink. 'Bit risky, wasn't it?'

No more risky than sending everyone in the station pictures of your willy, Carlyle thought sarkily. 'I just wanted to take a look.'

'What were you doing in there anyway?'

With what he liked to think was commendable brevity, Carlyle brought his sergeant up to speed on the situation with Gregori and Kortmann and his earlier visit to see Barbara Hutton.

'So you think she is this other woman?' Umar asked. 'The German terrorist?'

'That,' Carlyle replied rather wearily, 'is what we're gonna have to find out.'

The receptionist at Horse, Kellaway & George was not in the mood to take any nonsense from the man who had just dropped in on the off-chance of a word with one of her senior partners. A sturdy fifty-something, the woman had clearly spent decades perfecting various looks of displeasure as she contemplated the broad array of miscreants that arrived at her desk. Smiling lamely, Carlyle imagined that she couldn't have looked more put out if she realized that he had recently broken in to her boss's home.

'I do not have an appointment,' he said patiently, 'but I think that Mr Hutton will want to see me.'

'What is it concerning?' the woman asked brusquely, making it clear that she doubted that very much.

Resisting the temptation to start flashing his warrant card, the inspector went for the enigmatic approach. 'It's a private matter.'

Without another word, the woman shot out of her seat, buzzed herself through the door to the left of her desk and disappeared, leaving Carlyle to peruse the mug shots of grinning lawyers that lined the wall behind the desk. He found the chubby, cheery face of Derek Hutton on the top row, directly underneath HK&G's mission statement. With nothing better to do, Carlyle read it carefully: *Our human rights experts provide access to justice for our clients, despite the notoriously expensive and complex UK legal system. Combining civil liberties, discrimination and social care expertise, we act for individuals, groups and organizations who find themselves challenging the lawfulness of decisions, acts, omissions and policies of public bodies and authorities.*

'*Guardian*-reading, sandal-wearing, lentil-sucking lefties,' Carlyle scoffed.

'Sorry?' The receptionist pushed her way back through the doors looking even more irritated than she had when she'd left her station.

'Nothing,' Carlyle mumbled, blushing slightly as he moved away from the desk.

'Mr Hutton is not here,' she said firmly. Sliding back into her seat, she began tapping at the keyboard of her computer, in order to underscore the inspector's dismissal.

'Not here?' Carlyle acted bemused. Rudeness rarely bothered him and he had made a conscious decision that he wasn't going to let this woman wind him up.

'He's not in today,' the woman said huffily, keeping her eyes on her computer screen.

'On holiday?' Carlyle persisted. 'Off sick? With a client?'

'Out.' Was all he got by way of reply.

Deciding not to push the matter any further, Carlyle admitted defeat. 'OK. Thank you for all your help.' Ignoring her petulant toss of the head, he headed for the exit.

Walking down the street, he checked his phone and was dismayed to find he had four missed calls and a text from Helen that simply said: *where are you?* 'I'm at work,' Carlyle muttered crossly, almost dropping the phone as he walked into a young woman pushing a pram. 'Where do you expect me to be?' Glaring at the woman, he jumped into the gutter and continued on his way.

'Here. You can hold the baby while I make some coffee.' Before he could protest, Caroline Hutton placed the sleeping infant on Umar's lap and headed for the kitchen. Shifting uncomfortably on the sofa, the sergeant grimaced.

'What's his name?' he called after her.

'Sssh,' she admonished him, before adding in a theatrical whisper: '*Her* name is Mary.'

'Ah.'

'She was named after my grandmother, on my father's side.'

'I see.' Although he was now a father himself, Umar felt anxious about the responsibility of holding someone else's child. Mary, on the other hand, seemed perfectly content. Wrapped in a blanket, in a red babygro, she snored peacefully as he took stock of his surroundings.

Tracking them down hadn't been difficult; a quick check of the Electoral Register had brought him to a crumbling block of flats off Gower Street, south of Euston Road. The one-bedroom flat was a third-floor walk-up, clean but in need of a lick of paint. Some random pieces of cheap furniture were clustered around a small TV. The usual baby paraphernalia was scattered everywhere. The decoration consisted of a few family photographs taped to the far wall next to a framed poster for a movie called *The Marriage of Maria Braun*. The image – a woman in a black basque doing up her stockings – seemed completely out of place in this room. Umar had never heard of the film, but the image certainly commanded his attention; maybe he would check it out.

The politest word you could use to describe the place was *modest*. Compared to her parents' digs, less than a mile away, this looked rather like genteel poverty. Most importantly, however, as far as Umar was concerned, there was no evidence of a bloke in residence.

Mary sighed and wriggled in his lap. He scanned the room again to reaffirm his assessment. No discarded trainers, no men's mags, no football DVDs under the telly. All the evidence pointed to Caroline Hutton being a single mum.

His observations were interrupted by a familiar noise from inside the romper suit.

'Urgh.' Getting to his feet, he took three careful steps towards the door. 'I think she's just—'

'The Pampers are on the sideboard,' Caroline shouted back, 'behind you.'

He was just tying up the nappy sack when Caroline walked in with two steaming mugs of black coffee. Lying on the changing mat, Mary was still happily asleep. Swapping one of the mugs for the sack, her mum inspected his work. 'Good job,' she grinned. 'Far better than her father ever managed, anyway.'

Umar took a sip of his coffee. 'Her dad isn't around then?' Trying to sound casual about it.

Handing him the second mug, she gently lifted Mary from the mat and placed her in a cot in the corner of the room. 'He was released back into the wild before Mary was born.'

'Bummer.'

'These things happen.' Caroline picked up her coffee and took a seat on the ratty green sofa. 'It's not the end of the world.'

'No, but still . . .' Plonking himself down on the room's only other seat, an uncomfortable black swivel chair, Umar checked out the curve of her breasts under her crumpled white blouse before lifting his gaze to give her some empathetic eye contact.

Glancing at the wedding band on his right hand, she said, 'So, how can I help you, Sergeant? Do you work with that creep I met in Doughty Street yesterday?'

'Yes,' Umar laughed, not bothering to correct her impression of the inspector, 'that's right.'

'And it seems like the demon burglar has struck.'

'There was a break-in, yes.' He took another mouthful of coffee and placed his mug on the carpet. 'It doesn't look as if anything was taken, and the mess is fairly minimal, but we've been trying to contact your parents to inform them.' He pulled a small business card from his pocket with the details of a lock-smith on Gray's Inn Road. 'Give these guys a call, they can make it secure.'

'Such service,' she said archly. 'I'm sure that they will be very grateful.'

Umar gave a small bow. 'In the Metropolitan Police we are always working hard to enhance our customer-service culture.'

'That's good to know.'

'Next time though, I would get your parents to keep their gate locked,' he added, gilding the lily somewhat. 'Someone walks down the road, sees easy access to the basement . . .' With a shrug, he let the story play out in her head.

'Yes, of course.' Pulling her legs up underneath her, she sat back, waiting patiently for him to get to the point.

'So – we've been trying to get hold of your parents,' he repeated, 'and we wondered if you might know where they are at the moment?'

'No idea, sorry.' She gestured airily in the direction of the window. 'My folks like to take off every now and again. Lets them imagine that they're still free spirits.'

'Free spirits?'

'My dad always wished he'd been ten years older. He was a bit of a radical when he was younger, in the 1970s and early '80s. But he would really have liked to be around in the 1960s.'

'An old hippie.'

'No, no.' She shot him a disapproving look. 'Absolutely not. He would have loved to be a student back then. Paris 1968, Grosvenor Square – that kind of thing. Before the forces of the state got their act together properly, as he likes to put it. Now, with the legal practice and the big house in Bloomsbury, he frets endlessly about selling out.'

'And your mum?'

'Technically, Barbara's not my mum,' she corrected him. 'She's my step-mum. She and my dad hooked up when I was little. She was a client of his, a bit older than Dad. She really was around in the sixties. And quite the firebrand, by all accounts.'

'Oh?'

Sensing his interest, she backtracked. 'They're just a pair of old lefties really. They like to run off now and again, get pissed, shag like superannuated rabbits and pretend they're both twenty-one again.'

'Yes.' Dazzled by her smile and talk of youthful couplings, Umar momentarily quite forgot why he was sitting there. He was only brought back to reality by the baby starting to cry in the corner.

Jumping to her feet, Caroline Hutton began unbuttoning her blouse. 'Time for a feed.'

Unable to control himself, Umar licked his lips.

She shot him an amused look. 'Apologies for kicking you out.'

'Er, yes.' Slowly, he stood up.

'Thanks for the visit.' Reaching into the cot, she recovered the child and began manoeuvring her into position. 'I'll call the locksmith and get my parents to give you a call when they resurface.'

'That would be great,' he replied, reluctantly heading for the door.

# SEVENTEEN

On closer inspection, the mess on the pavement was a dead mouse. It had been squashed across the concrete, like a cartoon character or a mini art installation. How did that happen? Carlyle wondered. What has flattened a poor mouse in the middle of a London street? It was a mystery.

People were walking past it, backing up and queuing to get round it. He watched a procession of people going past but none stepped on the expired rodent. That was the city; you quickly learned to watch where you put your feet.

'Boss?' Miffed by his boss's apparent disinterest in what he had been saying, Umar did a little dance on the pavement as a couple of tourists appeared and started photographing the mouse on their smartphones.

'Huh?' Reluctantly the inspector focused on his Sancho Panza.

'Derek Hutton.'

Carlyle recalled his meeting with the sweaty lawyer. 'He didn't seem like much of a revolutionary to me,' he said.

'He's gotten old, that's all,' Umar chortled, 'just like you.'

'Ha.' Looking at his younger colleague, an unhappy thought entered the inspector's head. 'You didn't hit on her, did you?'

'What, the daughter?' Umar tried to look offended. 'Of course not. She's got a tiny kid, for God's sake.'

*Liar.*

For a moment, they contemplated each other in sullen silence.

'What do you want to do now?' Umar asked finally.

Carlyle scratched his head. 'I want to go home.'

'Sounds like a plan. I'm fairly knackered myself.'

'You, on the other hand, can do a bit more digging.'

Umar's face fell. 'Into what, exactly?'

'Into the Huttons. Try and get a line on where they might be . . . check their credit cards, track their mobiles. Whatever works.'

'Ooh,' Umar sucked in some air. 'Dodgy.'

'I know, I know. But Simpson will back us up. She needs to find this Kortmann guy more than we do.'

'And you think these two old lefties have got him?'

'What other leads do we have?'

'Fair point.'

'So let's find the old buggers then.'

'OK, your call.' Umar began ambling off in the direction of the station.

Yes, Carlyle thought as he watched him go. My call.

With a spring in his step, Carlyle bounced along the pavement mumbling the words to The Clash's 'London Calling' as he danced between the oncoming pedestrians. The German case, as he had come to think of it, was in his bloodstream now and he felt energized. Whatever he had told his sergeant, he had no intention of heading home, not yet at least. Instead, he was off to do what he did best, tease out bits of information from unwilling sources that would allow him to inch closer to a resolution of the matter.

Walking into the lobby of the Garden Hotel, he checked his phone. There was another irritated message from Helen, but even that could not dent his mood. Deleting it with a flourish, he felt the handset vibrate in his hand. Casting caution to the wind, he answered without first checking the screen.

'Carlyle.'

'Inspector, you're sounding very chipper.'

*Shit.* Carlyle cursed silently. *Bernard Gilmore Esquire. The*

*Fourth Estate's finest. And a royal pain in the arse.* 'What can I do for you, Bernie?'

'Just checking in,' Bernie said lamely. 'Keeping in touch with my contacts while I've got time on my hands. All this royal baby crap is making it impossible to get into the bloody paper at the moment.'

'Uh-huh.' The inspector couldn't give a toss.

'The bloody woman goes into labour and it's the first sixteen pages of the first edition, for fuck's sake. Imagine what it'll be like when the damn thing pops out. At this rate there won't even be any bloody sport.'

Carlyle yawned. 'Didn't have you pegged as a republican.'

'I'm not, particularly. Then again, I'm not a seventeenth-century peasant either. All the fawning and grovelling does your head in.'

'Helen says the same thing.' On autopilot, Carlyle headed towards the lifts. Veering left, he came to the threshold of the Light Bar and peered into the gloom. 'Look, I'm just about to go into a meeting . . .'

'Yeah, right, so I was wondering what you could tell me about the Oakwood case.'

'The Oakwood case?' The name didn't ring any bells.

'Yeah,' Bernie replied, his voice gaining strength as he got to the reason for his call. 'I hear that arrests are imminent.'

'Could be.' Carlyle imagined that he could hear Bernie licking his lips.

'And that there are some big names involved.' He mentioned a couple of celebrities.

'I wouldn't know about that.' He paused. If Bernie wanted a quote, he would have to beg.

'Can you give me something?'

'On background? No fingerprints?'

'Of course.'

'And you owe me?'

'I'll add it to your balance in my famous book.'

'Fair enough.' Carlyle took a deep breath. 'So, how about something like this: An unnamed police source said: *"We are very pleased with the way in which things are progressing and hope to be able to update the public on developments soon. Rest assured that no one will be given a free pass. Everyone will be required to account for their actions".*' Rather pleased with himself, he waited for Bernie to scribble it down.

'Great.'

'Maybe make it: *"Everyone will be required to fully account for their actions".*'

'You're a natural.'

'Whatever,' Carlyle said modestly. 'Hope that helps you knock the sprog off the front page.'

'Hardly. It might make page twenty-two, if I'm lucky.'

'A good day to bury bad news,' the inspector murmured. *Who had said that?* He couldn't remember. It didn't matter. Taking a second look around the bar, he finally located his target in a booth at the back just as another thought popped into his head. *Might Werner Kortmann be on Bernie's radar?* Better not to ask. 'Got to go. Keep me posted on . . .'

'Oakwood.'

'Yeah, right.' Carlyle suddenly realized he was in the mood for a ridiculously expensive beer. Dropping the phone into his pocket, he strode manfully towards the bar.

For a man who had seen his client kidnapped and also just been released from hospital, Sebastian Gregori looked to be in pretty good shape. Without waiting to be asked, the inspector took a seat and placed his bottle of Kirin on the table, along with the glass that he wasn't going to use. Looking up from his newspaper, Gregori smiled thinly.

'I see that everyone is very excited about this royal baby.'

Carlyle made a face.

Closing the paper, Gregori tossed it on the seat next to him. 'We don't have this kind of thing in Germany.'

'That's why you are Europe's leading nation,' the inspector observed drily, 'loved and respected around the world.'

'That is good to know.'

'How are you feeling?'

'I am getting better, thank you.' Gregori lifted his glass from the table and took a cautious sip of his carbonated mineral water. 'The doctor said I should have no lasting effects from my unfortunate experience.'

'That's good.' Carlyle reached for his bottle. The private eye watched him closely as he took a swig of beer. 'I was wondering if you could remember anything else about what happened. About the men who attacked you, for example.'

All he got in response was a blank look and a shrug. 'No. I am sorry, I do not.'

'OK.' Carlyle chugged down the rest of his drink; ten quid well spent. 'So what will you do now?'

Sitting back on the banquette, Gregori folded his arms. 'I will wait.'

'For what?'

'For you to find Herr Kortmann.'

Carlyle suddenly tuned into the music playing quietly from a speaker above his head. The song, a track from South Korea of all places, was so ubiquitous that even he recognized it. It was also profoundly annoying. 'That may take some time.'

Gregori raised an eyebrow. 'So I am beginning to understand.'

'Which is why,' Carlyle continued, 'I would be extremely grateful for anything else that you might have that might help us in our investigations.'

'Such as?'

*No idea.* 'Anything.'

'I'm sorry, Inspector, but I have told you all I know.' Catching the eye of a passing waitress, Gregori signalled for the bill before finishing his drink. When the woman appeared with the tab he signed it with a flourish, adding his room number in a large child-like script at the bottom. Even with his dodgy

131

eyesight, Carlyle could make it out: 226. Getting to his feet, Gregori toyed with the top button of his jacket. 'You will let me know of any progress that you make?'

Carlyle nodded. 'Of course.' Playing with his empty bottle, he watched the German cross the lobby and head out on to the street. When the waitress appeared to claim the bill he ordered another Kirin with a whiskey chaser. They didn't have Jameson's, so he settled for Bushmills. As she cleared the table, he thought he caught a glimpse of Sonia Coverdale at the bar with another girl, but when she turned so he could see her face he realized it was someone else. The waitress reappeared with his drinks, slipping the tab on the table. Taking a mouthful of the whiskey, he let it linger on the back of his throat while he fumbled in the inside pocket of his jacket. Pulling out a biro, he squinted at the bill, wincing at the price.

'Ah well, never mind. It's only money.'

With a flourish, he scribbled a rough approximation of Gregori's signature and added the room number. It's the least you can do, he thought, for dropping me in this shit. Reaching across the table, he retrieved the newspaper and began flicking through its pages. He was almost at the middle before he found anything that wasn't in some way related to the royal baby. Bernie Gilmore was right, he thought, it's all a load of crap. Given all the domestic excitement, 'World News' had been relegated to half a page, next to the horoscopes. His eye caught a small story across three columns, under the headline REN QI FACES FIGHT TO SAVE HIS CAREER: *High-flying Chinese politician Ren Qi is at the centre of China's most serious political in-fighting for decades as Communist Party leaders try to clamp down on corruption and abuse of office.*

Carlyle shook his head. *Politicians; it doesn't matter where you go, they are all the same. A right shower.* For a moment, his thoughts veered off in the direction of Marvin Taylor and Roche's ninjas, but that would have to wait. Dropping the newspaper on to the table, he pulled out his mobile and brought up

132

a number he hadn't used in a while. Happily, the number was still working. Even more happily, the call was answered on the third ring.

'Alex Miles.'

'Mr Miles, John Carlyle.' He paused, the better to enjoy the low groan from the other end. 'How's the new job going?'

'It's good, thank you,' Miles said stiffly.

'I'm at your old place at the moment,' Carlyle explained. 'I met your successor. She seems very nice.'

'Debbie will do well.'

'She prefers Deborah, apparently.'

'Yes. Very proper,' Alex chuckled. 'You might not find her as easy to do business with as me.'

'That's exactly why I'm ringing, Alex.'

Another groan. 'I'm at work at the moment. Up against it a bit.'

'This won't take long.'

'Very well.' Miles lowered his voice. 'So what is it that I can do for you, Inspector?'

# EIGHTEEN

Making sure that the policeman hadn't followed him out of the hotel, Sebastian Gregori headed down St Martin's Lane, slipping round the corner and onto the Strand. After ducking into a mobile phone store, he bought a £20 pay-as-you-go sim card with cash. Exiting the shop, he crossed the road and hurried down Villiers Street, which ran down the side of Charing Cross station, towards the river. He had discovered Victoria Embankment Gardens while wandering round the area the day before. Now the scruffy park was empty apart from a few dossers. Taking a seat away from the entrance, he put the new sim into the cheap handset he'd bought from a different vendor earlier in the day. There was one number in the memory. He hit Call and waited for it to ring three times, as usual.

'I'm listening.'

'Everything is proceeding as planned.' Gregori spoke clearly and slowly. 'It should not be long now.'

'Good.' There was a pause. 'We await your confirmation.'

The line went dead.

Gregori removed the sim from the handset and walked out of the park. Two minutes later he was standing on Hungerford footbridge, looking down into the Thames. A nearby beggar sitting on the pathway invited him to give alms. Gregori ignored him. Such a dirty river, he thought. Letting the sim fall from his hand, he watched it flutter downwards and disappear into the murky water.

*Such a dirty city.*

*   *   *

Carlyle followed the woman along the corridor and waited patiently while she opened the door to Room 226 with her key card. Pushing the door open, she invited him to step inside.

'Thanks.'

'No problem.' Rosalind McDonald, the Garden's Head of Security, gave him a big smile. 'Don't be too long.'

Carlyle took a pair of latex gloves from the pocket of his jacket and pulled them on. 'Five minutes, max.'

'OK. I'll wait here. The desk will call me if Gregori reappears, in which case we'll have to leg it.'

'Sure.' Stepping inside, Carlyle let the door close behind him and went straight to the closet. Finding the safe, he punched in the management override code that McDonald had supplied and let the door click open. Inside, Gregori had stashed his passport, an iPad and a sheaf of papers. Removing the lot, Carlyle sat down on the bed to see what he could find. On first glance, the papers were simply a copy of the Tosches file, which he'd already been given during their meeting at the station. Dropping them by his side, he powered up the iPad.

'Shit.'

It was locked. Looking at the screen, he scratched his head. Then he called Umar. Listening to the phone ring, he drummed his fingers on the screen. 'C'mon, c'mon.'

*'You have reached—'*

'Bollocks.' So much for Phone a fucking Friend; who else might know how to open the bastard machine? He pulled up another number and hit Call.

'Hiya, Dad.' Alice's cheery voice made him smile.

'Hiya, sweetheart, how's it going?'

'It's going,' Alice replied, her voice expressing a level of weariness that only a teenager could reach. 'Mum's pissed off though.'

*Why?* He glanced at his watch; he had used up his five minutes already. 'You can tell me later. Right now I just wondered if you could help me with something.' He explained his problem.

Alice thought about it for a moment. 'You'd have to restore it to its original factory settings.'

'Great. How do I do that?'

'Are you sure you want to? You'll delete everything that's on it at the moment.'

*Damn.* 'Are you sure?'

''fraid so. One of the girls at school lost all her stuff last week.'
*Bollocks.*

'By the way, Mum says you're a useless git.'

'What?' Half-crazed with frustration, he struggled to deal with the switch in the conversation.

'You missed Grandpa's doctor's appointment.'

'Bloody hell,' he hissed. 'Now's really not the time.'

'Just sayin',' she replied, offended.

'OK, OK. Tell your mother I'm sorry but it's been a bit of a tough day.'

'She said you'd make some kind of lame excuse,' Alice responded with gleeful malice.

*Good for her.*

'Just like you usually do.'

'Tell her I'll be home soon.'

'OK. I'll make sure I'm hiding in my bedroom when that happens.'


Deborah Burke stifled a gasp as she saw Mr 226 himself slip through the revolving door and head across the lobby. *Going back to the bar?* From behind her desk, she watched as Sebastian Gregori veered to the left and came to a stop in front of the lifts.

*Apparently not.*

Folding his arms, Gregori waited patiently behind a Chinese couple who had just checked in with more than enough luggage for a two-month stay. They were VIPs of some sort or another – Burke had seen a memo about it – but they didn't seem to have any entourage. Gregori smiled at the woman but she ignored him. Casually picking up the mobile on her desk, Burke hit the text message she had pre-prepared – *he's back* – and hit the Send button. She then checked the lifts. One was on the top floor, the other making its way steadily upwards. That should give Carlyle more than enough time to get out of there. The Chief Concierge was very unhappy about being dragged into the policeman's little scheme which was doubtless illegal and would certainly result in the sack should it come to light. But Rosalind had insisted. Deborah heaved a sigh; the girl could be so cavalier at times. She watched as one of the lifts finally made it back to the ground floor, disgorging its collection of guests heading out to sample London's nightlife. The Chinese couple struggled in with their luggage – *where was the bellboy?* – and she could see Gregori hesitate. Should he squeeze in beside them or wait for the next one? Eventually, just as the doors were beginning to close, he jumped inside. The doors shuddered then finally came together. Deborah watched as the lift stopped at the first floor then continued on to the second.

*Plenty of time.*


Scrolling through her emails, Rosalind McDonald heard the lift open and someone get out. Conscious of a figure coming towards her, she looked up.

*Bloody hell.*

Sebastian Gregori shot her a quizzical look as he headed towards the door of his room.

'Excuse me, sir.' Stepping in front of him, she dropped the phone into her pocket and pulled out her ID. 'Hotel Security. I'm afraid you'll have to go back downstairs.'

'But I want to go to my room.' Gregori made a half-hearted attempt to brush past her, but McDonald stood her ground. Waving his key card in front of her face, he said, 'This is ridiculous.'

'I'm very sorry, sir,' she smiled, 'but we've been informed of a health and safety problem on this floor.'

137

Gregori let his arm fall to his side. 'What problem?'

'We have had a report,' she said, not missing a beat, 'of multiple carbon-monoxide monitors going off. We've had to evacuate the entire floor.' McDonald allowed herself a quick peek up and down the corridor. *Please God, let no one come out of their rooms right now.*

From inside the room came a distinct whirring noise. Gregori stared at the door and then at McDonald. For a moment it looked as if he was about to force his way past but she pushed back her shoulders, making best use of her height advantage, in order to appear as intimidating as possible.

'There's someone in there.' It was part-observation, part-cry.

'One of our operatives, sir. Checking for fumes.' She cast a grateful glance towards the door behind which her selfless colleague was risking life and limb before adding: 'He's got his own oxygen supply, obviously.'

'They said nothing about all of this downstairs,' Gregori grumbled.

'It's probably just a false alarm,' she said soothingly. 'We had one last week.'

'You should get it properly fixed,' he tutted.

'We're trying, sir. Hopefully it will only take a few minutes.' She gestured in the direction he had come. 'In the meantime, we have to follow the correct protocol. I'm afraid I need to ask you to return to the lobby.'

Gregori glanced back at the lifts. 'Should I take the stairs?'

'Yes, please.' She felt her pulse slacken slightly as it became apparent he would buy it. 'If you want to go back down to the bar, all drinks for second-floor customers are complimentary at the moment. Just mention my name and give the waitress the code word, which is . . .' for a moment her mind went blank, 'er, starfish.'

'Starfish.'

'That's right.'

'And it won't be long?' Gregori looked wistfully at the door to his own room. 'I wanted to have a shower.'

'Just a few minutes. As soon as we have the all clear, I will come straight down and let you know.' Reluctantly, he turned and headed back down the corridor. Only when he had disappeared into the stairwell did McDonald allow herself a deep breath.

Hearing voices outside the door, Carlyle froze for a moment. Then, reminding himself to breathe, he gathered up all of the material on the bed, shoved it back into the safe and gently closed it, grimacing as the lock whirred shut. Stepping up to the door, he could clearly hear Rosalind McDonald trying to talk her way out of a tricky situation. Looking round, he considered his options, quickly coming to the conclusion that he didn't have any.

'. . . *we have to follow protocol.*' The inspector smiled. Good for McDonald; the security chief was giving it her best shot, thinking on her feet. He concentrated on keeping his breathing under control. He felt a tightening of his chest and wondered if he might be having a heart attack. That would be great timing – typical. But the feeling quickly passed and instead a sense of calm enveloped him. He would just have to wait and see what happened.

To his left was the bathroom. The door was open and he tiptoed inside, carefully closing the toilet lid and taking a seat, while his fate was decided.

'. . . *starfish.*'

*Starfish.* Carlyle stifled a giggle as he scanned the range of products lined up by the sink. Gregori certainly had a lot of toiletries for a gumshoe. Folding his arms, he counted a dozen small vials of different shapes and colours, all neatly lined up in front of the mirror. At the end of the row was a squat grey bottle of prescription tablets. Getting to his feet, Carlyle stepped over to the sink, picked it up and studied the label. 'Well, well, well.'

As he dropped the bottle in his pocket, there was a click as the door to the room opened. He turned to find McDonald in the doorway, giving him a funny look.

'What are you doing in the loo?'

The search of Kortmann's room on the fifth floor was far more straightforward but yielded nothing of interest. The man's clothes were all neatly put away and his shoes lined up next to the desk.

The inspector checked the safe: empty.

In the wardrobe, he found a bag from the Calvin Klein store on Long Acre, containing three unopened packs of boxer shorts, along with a receipt, showing that they had been purchased just after Kortmann's visit to the police station. Carlyle was hit by a sudden feeling of listlessness as he looked around the spacious room; the bed had been made and the bathroom cleaned. Aside from a toothbrush and some toothpaste, there were no other toiletries and no bottles of prescription pills.

When they returned downstairs, there was no sign of Gregori in the bar. Taking a seat in the VIP area, McDonald ordered a mineral water, while Carlyle opted for a whiskey.

As the waitress hurried away, McDonald gave him a crooked smile. 'I thought you weren't supposed to drink on duty?'

Now it was the inspector's turn to smile, a tad sheepishly. 'And I would have thought you would have realized by now that there're quite a few things I do that are not strictly by the book.'

'Alex did mention that you could be a bit unorthodox.'

'Ha. That was uncharacteristically understated of him.'

'He likes you.'

'I don't know about that.'

'He said that you were very fair.'

The waitress reappeared, placing their drinks on the table, along with a small bowl of olives. Looking at the olives, both of them decided to pass. Carlyle took a sip of his Jameson's. 'I try to be *realistic* about things.'

'I suppose you have to be.'

'Yes. Over the years, I've learned the hard way that you

should pick your battles carefully.' He watched her take a drink and for a few moments they sat in silence. Finally, he asked: 'What should I call you, by the way?'

McDonald made a face. 'I prefer Rosalind, but everyone calls me Ros.'

'I shall call you Rosalind then.' The inspector raised his glass in salute. 'Or Ms McDonald, if you want to keep it formal.'

The Head of Security laughed ruefully. 'I think it's a bit late for that, don't you?'

'Yes,' the inspector agreed. 'Thank you for bailing me out back there. That could have been tricky.'

'Find anything useful?'

'Maybe.'

Lifting the glass, he let the remains of his drink moisten his lips. 'I like the "starfish" thing. Very good.'

McDonald nodded.

'Quick thinking.'

'No, no. It's for real. We have a code that changes every month or so. At the moment it really is "starfish", although I nearly forgot. My mind went blank for a second and I couldn't remember the bloody word. Before that, it was "donkey". It's very handy if you've got a guest who's pissed off about something or other. Nine times out of ten a free drink is enough to placate them. It was something I introduced when I arrived here.'

Carlyle took a more substantial mouthful of whiskey. 'How long have you been here?'

'I got the Head of Security job about four months ago. Before that, I was at the Imperial in Sloane Square.'

Carlyle shook his head. 'Don't know it.'

'It was fine. A bit boring. Not as interesting as this place.'

'In my experience,' Carlyle grinned, 'boring is good.'

'Yeah,' McDonald played with her glass, 'but you know what I mean.'

'Sure.'

'Before the Imperial, I was in the Army. An electronic warfare specialist in the Royal Signals.'

'I see.' He gave her the once-over: quite tall, maybe five eight but stocky with it, not yet thirty, open, guileless face under a black fringe.

'Bomb disposal. One of the team would go in to cut the wires and my job was to block any signals that could set it off.'

'Sounds like a barrel of laughs. How long did you do that for?'

'I was in the Army for almost five years – did two tours in Afghanistan.'

Here we go, Carlyle thought, bracing himself for a tale of shell-shock and body parts. 'So why did you pack it in?'

'Well,' she grinned, 'in the end, it wasn't really compatible with being a single mum.'

'Ah.' *Quite the surprise package, aren't you?* The inspector was beginning to take a shine to Ms McDonald. 'And this job is?'

'Well, I was hoping to get into the police, but what with the cuts and everything, that was a complete non-starter.'

'Tell me about it.'

'So I got the gig at the Imperial through a mate and then ended up here. My mum helps out a lot, so it's manageable. You've got to juggle a bit, but then so does everyone, don't they?'

'Yes.' Finishing his whiskey, he placed the glass on the table.

'Fancy another?' she asked.

'No, no. I've got to get going. Thanks again.'

'No problem. Alex says you owe him though.'

'In his dreams.' A most unsavoury thought popped into Carlyle's head. 'Did he get you this job?'

'No. He might have had a say, but it was Debbie who got me in the door.'

'Deborah,' Carlyle corrected her.

'I call her Debbie.'

'You didn't tell her what we were up to, did you?'

'Yes – I had to. It was only prudent.'

142

Carlyle grimaced. 'Prudent?'

'Yes.' McDonald lifted her gaze past his shoulder. 'Speak of the devil.'

'Here you are.' Pulling up a chair, Deborah Burke sat down without even acknowledging the inspector's presence. 'I thought you might have been nobbled.'

'It would have helped if you'd given me a heads-up,' McDonald shot back.

Uh, oh, Carlyle thought, ready to make a speedy getaway. The last thing he wanted was to get stuck in the middle of a row. He had his own domestic waiting for him when he got home.

'I sent the bloody text as soon as the bloke appeared,' the concierge protested.

'Oh yeah?' McDonald pulled out her mobile and waved it above the table. 'Where is it then?'

'Ladies, ladies . . .' Getting to his feet, Carlyle tried to inject some calm into the conversation. 'All's well that ends well and all that.' Looking up, they grunted at him in stereo. It was, the inspector imagined, like dealing with a pair of truculent sixth-formers. 'I am very grateful to *both* of you for your help,' he continued, 'and look forward to repaying the favour in due course. If I can ever be of assistance, you know I'm only round the corner. For the moment, however, let's just keep this under our hats, shall we?'

There was a pause, followed by some gentle, synchronized nodding. 'Good.' He began shuffling backwards, trying to get out of earshot before the bickering resumed. 'I'll see you both later.'

# NINETEEN

Waiting for a muffin to toast, Carlyle looked at the picture of the fluffy caramel tabby cat. *'Lovely Wilf the cat has gone missing from Flat Nine,'* he mumbled to himself. *'He is not used to being on the street, so we think he may be in hiding somewhere.'* The toaster clicked off and the muffin popped up. Crumpling the flyer in his hand, he tossed it in the direction of the sink. 'Poor bugger is probably in a kebab by now.'

'What are you chuntering on about?'

Reaching for the butter, he turned to find Helen in the doorway. She was wearing a pair of shorts and one of his old Fred Perry polo-shirts. The towel wrapped round her head finished off the ensemble nicely.

'Enjoy your bath?' he asked innocently, adding before she could reply, 'Cup of tea?'

Leaning against the frame of the door, Helen folded her arms. 'Yes please. Peppermint.'

'Jolly good.' Maybe the lovely long soak had mellowed her mood, but he couldn't be sure. Grabbing the kettle, he filled it at the sink. 'Look,' he said, his back still turned, 'I'm really sorry about missing Dad's GP appointment. It just turned into a hell of a day.'

Appearing by his side, she slipped an arm round his waist. 'It's OK.'

'Oh?' he asked, relieved that he wasn't going to get royally bollocked. Flipping down the lid, he plugged in the kettle and switched it on.

'I went.' Helen turned off the tap for him. 'We had to wait almost an hour.'

'Sorry, I know you're busy too.'

'It was fine. I didn't want him to have to do it on his own.'

'No.' Carlyle opened a cupboard above his head and reached for some cups. 'So, what's the verdict?'

'They're sending him for a scan.' She gave him a stern look. 'You really must be there for that one.'

'Of course,' he said stiffly.

'And you should give him a call.'

'Yes.'

'Go and do it now.' She shooed him away, in the direction of the hall. 'I'll sort the tea. What do you want on your muffin?'

Conscious of someone hovering in front of her desk, Deborah Burke looked up and stifled a small gasp. 'Can I help you, sir?' she asked.

'Someone has been in the safe in my room,' Sebastian Gregori said flatly.

The concierge frowned. 'Has something been stolen?'

'Nothing was taken. However, someone has been snooping around. I want to see the audit trail of the safe.'

Placing her hands on the top of the desk, Burke pushed herself to her feet. 'Let me go and find the Head of Security for you.'

A pained expression settled on Gregori's face. 'I'm not interested in the Head of Security. Get me the manager. Right now.'

After a fairly pointless couple of minutes on the phone with his father, Carlyle tucked into his muffin with relish. Wiping a blob of butter from his chin, he sat back on the sofa and contemplated a second.

'Want another?' Helen smiled.

'Thinking about it.' Taking a mouthful of his tea, he caught an unmistakable whiff of body odour. 'I need a shower.'

Helen murmured her agreement.

'Presumably,' Carlyle reflected, returning to the matter in hand, 'it must be quite serious if they're sending him for a scan.'

'He *is* getting on. But at the moment, they're just trying to find out what's going on. You know what it's like with doctors; they're never going to commit to any definitive diagnosis if they can help it.'

Carlyle nodded at his wife's wise words.

'I should know,' Helen continued, 'I've worked with enough of them over the last twenty years.'

Make that thirty, Carlyle thought, but he let it slide.

'Anyway, it's best to know for sure,' she said.

'Depends what it is. If it's cancer, I think he'd rather not know.' For a few moments, the pair of them sat in silence, thinking about the mortality of their parents. Helen's father had died years ago; Carlyle's mother more recently. It was a grim business. Grim but inevitable.

'How's the rapper thing coming along?' he asked finally, trying to lighten the mood.

'Chase Race,' Helen sighed, 'is not a man who is used to being told *no*. We turned down his fifty grand, so he came back and offered us a hundred.'

'Bugger. So what are you going to do?'

'There's another meeting to discuss it next week. On the plus side, he's back with his girlfriend. On the minus, he was in the papers again yesterday, pictured snorting cocaine out of the bellybutton of a stripper.'

'Sounds like Umar,' Carlyle commented. 'Those two would get on like a house on fire.'

'What would you do?'

'Same as you, sweetheart.' Struggling to his feet, Carlyle planted a smacker on her forehead. 'Take the money and run.'

'My hero,' Helen swooned. 'Ever the pragmatist.'

Carlyle tentatively sniffed the air. 'A smelly pragmatist. I'm going for that shower.'

* * *

He was just drying himself off when Helen handed him his mobile. 'It's your favourite sergeant.' Smirking at his nakedness, she retreated towards the living room.

'Great,' Carlyle groaned. Jamming the handset under his chin, he wrapped a towel around his rather too thick waist. 'What is it?'

'I'm at the Garden Hotel,' Umar explained, keeping his voice low. 'There's a bit of a palaver.'

*A bit of a palaver?* When did the bloody boy start mimicking his speech?

'I've just spoken to a woman called Ros McDonald,' Umar went on, barely whispering now, 'and I think you'd better get down here asap.'

Fifteen minutes later, Carlyle burst through the Garden's revolving doors and strode purposefully towards the concierge's desk. The look on Sebastian Gregori's face hardened as he watched him approach.

'Why are *you* here?' he ground out.

'Because,' the inspector said as cheerily as he could manage, 'it looks like I'm turning into your own private policeman.' He gave a brisk nod to Burke and McDonald in turn, before glaring at Umar. Until he learned how much the sergeant knew, Carlyle was determined to play things straight. 'What seems to be the problem?' All four voices started at once, forcing Carlyle to hold up both hands. Noticing that they were beginning to attract a crowd, he took the opportunity to get rid of Umar by sending him off to disperse the gawkers.

Turning to Gregori, he smiled unctuously. 'Sir, why don't *you* tell me what happened?' Nodding at every opportunity, the inspector focused his attention exclusively on the private eye while he listened to his suspicions about the safe.

Reaching his conclusion, Gregori pointed at McDonald. 'And *she* was in on it.' Saying nothing, the Head of Security kept her gaze fixed on an indistinct point in the middle distance. 'When I demanded to see the manager, they refused, so I called the police.' He jerked a thumb over his shoulder. 'They sent your boy.'

Suppressing a grin, Carlyle looked across the lobby to see the sergeant deep in conversation with a very attractive middle-aged woman. For once, he was happy to let Umar get on with his flirting. Knitting his brows together, he turned back to the two women. 'This is a very serious matter. Where is Nicky?' Nicholas Lezard had been the manager of the Garden for almost fifteen years. The inspector knew him well enough to have a contact number programmed into his phone.

Burke coughed. 'I haven't been able to get hold of him, Inspector.'

'Is that the manager?' Gregori demanded. 'She didn't even try.'

Once again, Carlyle held up a hand for silence. Taking out his mobile, he pulled up Lezard's number and hit Call. Almost immediately, it went to voicemail. With a sigh, he turned to Gregori. 'Just give me a moment,' he requested, heading for the reception desk. 'I will sort this out for you.'

'Thank you,' Gregori mumbled, unconvinced.

He found Nicky Lezard in a serviced apartment on the top floor of the Garden, eating popcorn and watching a DVD. 'Don't you remember tonight is movie night?' was all the hotel manager could bring himself to say when he finally responded to the persistent rapping of the inspector's knuckles on the door. 'We've got the latest Jennifer Aniston movie,' he added, flouncing back into the living room. 'At least, I think it's the latest. The girl certainly knows how to churn them out.'

Carlyle mumbled something suitably banal and followed him inside. Nicky flopped back onto the sofa and took the remote from his viewing companion – a young-looking guy with a crew cut and a Madonna T-shirt which harked back to the singer's

*Like a Virgin* period. His host reluctantly gestured towards a nearby armchair. 'Take a seat.'

'It's OK.' Carlyle positioned himself in front of the TV and shoved his hands in his pockets. 'This will only take a minute, then you can get back to your film.'

Letting the remote drop from his fingers, Nicky let out an unhappy cluck. His companion considered Carlyle for a moment then slithered off the sofa and swanned out of the room.

'Ma-artin,' Nicky shouted after him, 'get me a Coke, will you? Sugar-free.' When he got no response, he turned his attention back to the policeman standing on his carpet. 'You really have ruined the mood, you know.'

'Sorry,' Carlyle fibbed. 'We just need to sort something out.'

Nicky arched an eyebrow. 'We?'

Carlyle nodded.

'What's all this "we" business? Just because you had Alex Miles doing your bidding for you, it doesn't mean you can come running upstairs now that he's gone. From what I hear, you always were too demanding, Inspector.'

'I am the hotel's best friend,' Carlyle countered, 'and you know it. All the crap I spare you and your guests on a regular basis—'

'All right, all right.' Recovering the remote, Nicky looked at it longingly – keen, no doubt, to get back to the lovely Jennifer Aniston. 'What is it this time?'

Carlyle kept his explanation short and to the point, omitting any mention of his own wrongdoing.

Trying to work up a sense of outrage, Nicky shook his head. 'So you went rummaging about in one of our guests' rooms, eh?'

'The man is mistaken,' Carlyle replied blithely. 'No one went into his room.'

Shifting in his seat, Nicky released a large fart to let the inspector know what he thought of the story he was fabricating, an amused grin dancing across his lips as he watched Carlyle move away in a futile attempt to escape the smell. 'But?'

'But this gentleman is involved in something else I am dealing with at the moment, so I need to make this little problem go away.'

Grunting, Nicky tried to repeat his gas trick, failing miserably. 'What's this guy called again?'

'Gregori.'

'Gregory?' His gaze drifted off into the middle distance. 'I knew a boy called Greg once.'

'Gregori's the surname. With an *i* on the end.'

Martin reappeared, minus the drink and Nicky shooed him away again, saying, 'All I wanted was a bloody Coke.'

'Houseboys,' Carlyle opined, 'they just don't make 'em like they used to.'

Nicky turned his nose up at the plod's feeble attempt at humour. 'This Gregori with an *i*. Why's he so important that you had to go snooping around his room?'

'That doesn't matter.'

'Well, maybe you could at least share some details regarding your proposed plan of action?'

Nicky insisted on watching his Jennifer Aniston laughathon through to the bitter end before doing the inspector's bidding. With twenty minutes to kill, Carlyle went in search of Rosalind McDonald. He was still looking for her when his mobile started vibrating in his pocket. Assuming it was Helen, he hit Receive and held it to his ear.

'Hi, sweetheart.'

'Inspector? It's Naomi Taylor.'

'Ah, yes, sorry. I thought you were someone else.'

'Is this a bad time?' Her voice sounded even more fragile than he remembered.

Gritting his teeth, Carlyle glanced at his watch. *Of course it's a bad time.* 'No, no, not at all. What can I do for you?'

'I just wondered how things were going?'

'Ah.'

'My lawyer wants me to sue the Police Service for what they did to Marvin but I wanted to see what you were able to find out first.'

Carlyle thrust his free hand into the pocket of his jacket. The crayon-covered invoice that Laurie had handed him was still there. Since leaving the Taylor household, he had done precisely nothing. 'I'm still following up a couple of things.' It was a lame response, but she was too polite to call him on it.

'So I should tell the lawyer to hold off?'

'Tell them to give us another couple of days.' *Us.* A nice touch. Pleased with his own verbal dexterity, he smiled. 'We should know where we stand by then.' *Neck-deep in a sea of shit, most likely.*

'All right. Thank you, Inspector.' Her pathetic gratitude in the face of his sloth made him cringe.

'How's Laurie doing?' he asked feebly.

'We're doing OK.' She struggled to fight back a sob. 'One day at a time and all that.'

'Yes.' Embarrassed, he shifted his weight from foot to foot as he stared at the carpet. 'Look, I've got to go.'

'Of course.'

'I'll be in touch.'

'Thank you.'

'No problem.' Ending the call, he immediately pulled up another number.

'Are you stalking me, Inspector?' Alison Roche sounded groggy.

'Sorry, were you asleep?'

'Like you care,' she grumbled. 'What time is it?'

'Not that late.'

'All things are relative. What do you want?'

'The Chelsea massacre. Did you come across a company called Tallow Business Services?'

For a moment, he listened to silence on the line.

'Alison?'

'How do you know about that?' she asked, all sleepiness disappearing from her voice in an instant.

Once the final credits of the movie had rolled, Nicky Lezard followed the inspector down to the lobby to placate the irate Sebastian Gregori. They found him in the bar, sitting behind the rope in the otherwise empty VIP area, nursing a large glass of white wine. Carlyle noted the half-empty bottle of Chablis in a bucket by the side of the table and smiled.

*Starfish.*

The free booze seemed to have somewhat taken the edge off the German's irritation. He shook the manager's hand and politely listened as he parroted McDonald's explanation of a carbon-monoxide scare on the second floor.

'This would never happen in Germany,' was his only observation when the tale was concluded.

'No.' Lezard glanced at the inspector, who remained inscrutable. 'Well, I can only apologize. We will, of course, waive your bill for the duration of your stay.'

Gregori gave a satisfied nod. 'What about the audit?'

'What?' Nicky asked, flustered.

'The audit trail for the safe.' Gregori looked at the inspector. 'Was it opened while I was out of the room?'

'Er . . .'

The inspector placed a calming hand on Nicky's shoulder as he returned Gregori's stare with interest. 'I'm afraid that the particular model of safe that the hotel uses does not have this facility.' It was a lie, but he had taken the precaution of getting McDonald to wipe all the incriminating data while waiting for Lezard's movie to finish.

Gregori started to say something but thought better of it. A waitress appeared with a bowl of roasted macadamia nuts. Placing them on the table, she smiled at Carlyle. 'Would you like a drink, sir?'

'No. I've got to get going. Thanks for your help, Mr Lezard.'

'My pleasure,' said Nicky archly.

The inspector watched Gregori as he took a handful of nuts. 'I will keep you posted on the other matter.' No longer interested in their conversation, the German simply nodded and looked away.

# TWENTY

Sammy Baldwin-Lee, founder and part-owner of the Racetrack, the West End's premier entertainment complex, clasped his mojito to his breast and looked out over the balcony, surveying his domain. The dance floor wasn't as full as he would like, but then again, tonight's main attraction, DJ Oscar 451, wasn't due to take the stage for another couple of hours at least. Initially, Sammy had baulked at the cost of bringing Oscar over from Ibiza to play three mid-week sets in London. That was until his Marketing Manager, a rather louche woman called Wendy, had produced a set of spreadsheets showing that punters paid a minimum of £80 to get into one of Oscar's gigs and the average spend at the bar was almost £125 a head.

'You'll be able to clear six figures, easy,' Wendy had told him at their weekly finance meeting, 'maybe seven. He's the new David Guetta.'

Sammy didn't have the first clue who the *old* David Guetta was, but he kept his mouth shut. He was a major nightclub-owner, after all, and he should know such things. He watched Wendy scratching at the sleeves of her cardigan. Maybe she's on heroin, he thought. You never see her arms.

'It's a no-brainer, Sammy.'

'When someone tells me something's a no-brainer,' he grumbled, 'I usually run a mile in the opposite direction.' She started to protest. 'But in this case, let's do it.'

'Yay.' Wendy made a feeble attempt at punching the air.

'Just make sure there are punitive penalties in the contract if he doesn't turn up.'

'Don't worry,' Wendy chuckled, 'I've already spoken to his manager. And Oscar's a consummate professional; one of the hardest working men in showbiz, according to *Heat* magazine.'

'Good for him.' Sammy raised his eyes to the heavens. Instead of a nightclub, he should have opened an old folks' care home, just as his mother had advised him. It would have been a lot less hassle and much better cash flow. 'Make sure we have the penalty clauses in the contract anyway.'

That had been three months ago. Now, on the second night of Oscar's mini-residency, Sammy had to admit that it was a case of *so far, so good*. The tickets had been sold, at £87.50 (plus a £6.50 'industry standard' booking fee) and the first night's bar takings had been even better than Wendy had forecast. By all accounts, Mr 451 had put in a storming performance, not that Sammy had been around to see it. He would never admit it, but the music gave him a terrible headache. He could stand it for a maximum of an hour a night, tops, and even then, only when the volume was kept to a reasonable level. Once the party really got started, he took himself off to another part of the complex or just headed back to his Shaftesbury Avenue crash pad. A creature of routine, he liked to be in bed with a cup of organic tea and a nice juicy crime novel on his Kindle well before midnight.

If all three nights went well, the Racetrack might almost break even for the week. It would be the first time since the refurb that this had happened – a milestone worthy of celebration, had it not arrived six months later than forecast. That, and the fact that there would be no Oscar 451 next week. On the back of last night's efforts, Sammy had already enquired about the DJ's availability, only to be offered some dates more than a year away. Despairing, he had sent Wendy off to try and rustle up some alternative names.

'There must be more than one guy who is the next . . .'

'David Guetta,' she reminded him.

A lightbulb went off over Sammy's head and he waved his arms around excitedly. 'Couldn't we get the real David . . . thingy?'

Wendy shook her head. 'Never in a million years. Even if you could get a slot in his diary, which you couldn't, we could never afford him.'

'But he's just a DJ,' said Sammy, miffed.

'Sammy, DJs are the new rock stars. It's not like your day. Look how much we're paying Oscar.'

'We could charge more.'

'We're hitting the ceiling on ticket prices already.'

'Not just tickets, I'm talking about booze. Once they're inside, these kids will pay anything.'

'We're already asking almost a tenner for a bottle of lager. This is the most expansive venue in Town.'

'OK, OK.' Dismayed at being lectured on the financial facts of life by a marketing girl, he sought to bring the conversation to a swift end. 'Just see who you can get.'


Taking a sip of his mojito, Sammy settled back into his seat as the numbers kept whirring through his head. However many times he did the calculation, he always came back to the same conclusion: *you're sinking.*

From the outset, the Racetrack had always been marketed as a long-term investment. At least that was what Sammy had told his backers. The problem was, the investors' idea of 'long-term' was eighteen months, two years max. On current projections, they were on course to get their money back in about two *decades*, if you factored in a significant, steady improvement in trading from this point. Not that clubs lasted that long – certainly not Sammy's clubs. Waving at the hovering waitress for another drink, he turned to his guest. 'You know, I've invested almost fifty million pounds restoring this place to its former glory.'

'And how much of that came from your own pocket?' Gunning his Grey Goose vodka, Ren Qi cradled the empty glass in his hands. With his London trip taking a turn for the worse, the last thing the Politburo chief needed was the hard sell from some nightclub-owner desperate to snare new investors willing to throw money into the financial black hole that he'd created. The whole point of investing in London was to protect the politician's net worth, not see it evaporate into thin air.

Ignoring the question, Sammy slipped into his established spiel: 'We're open twenty-four hours a day, offering a casino, two restaurants and four bars, as well as a disco and a bowling alley. You can even get a massage on the top floor.'

Ren raised an eyebrow.

'All totally kosher,' Sammy chuckled. 'Swedish, deep tissue – you name it.'

Ren nodded. Rolling his head, he could feel the tension in his shoulders; he could certainly do with a massage. Maybe he should check it out.

'Last quarter, we pulled in almost 35,000 people a week, well ahead of our original forecasts. Highest ticket price in town. Highest in-venue spend.' He gestured towards the dance floor. 'And with gigs like these, those numbers are going to increase substantially.'

'Impressive,' Ren lied. He stared at the ice in the bottom of his glass. He currently had far more pressing matters to attend to than the London entertainment market. His energy levels had been depleted to the point where he knew that he had to step back for a short while, or risk making further mistakes. Things were bad enough already. Wang Lei was on the warpath and even Ren Jiong couldn't be kept quiet with an endless diet of computer games for ever. Both of them would need to be dealt with, one way or another.

Ren Qi couldn't risk further details of their London activities getting back to Beijing. There were plenty of people who would feast on the news of his family's final, incontrovertible implosion. His career – thirty-five years of unstinting hard work – would be over in an instant as he was transformed into a poster boy for the latest clampdown on graft and corruption.

His trial, a carefully scripted affair in some hitherto unheard-of provincial Intermediate People's Court, would be a classic Tiger-thrashing – the elite throwing one of its own to the mob in an attempt to show the masses that no one was above the law. Of course, everyone would see through the sham but it was a tried and tested technique that the Politburo would cling to for as long as they could. Ren himself had never had any problem with it, so long as he was not the one on trial. Now that he was facing the dock himself, the best-case scenario would be twenty years in jail, the rest of his life, more or less; the worst, a firing squad. Ren could sense them closing in. He was deeply uncomfortable about having to rely so completely on Guo Miao after the State Security man had messed up so badly with the death of Michael Nicholson. On the other hand, this was the first time in the many years they had worked together that the major's competence had ever been an issue. Just as important, Guo's dedication to Ren was not in any doubt. Nor was his willingness to undertake the dirtiest of dirty work without complaint.

After being told of Nicholson's demise, Ren had ordered that the body be disposed of. He was confident that Guo would not fail again. No traces of his wife's lover would ever be found.

Now, sitting with the nightclub-owner, the thought made him chuckle. He had hoped that Nicholson would be shipped back to China where he would be assured of a slow, painful death. In the event, however, this was retribution enough.

Seeing his guest muster a smile, Sammy ploughed on. 'We are forecasting a profit within the next couple of years. Around half of our visitors are Asian, many from London and the South East, but we get many Chinese tour groups too. They do a circuit of Bicester Village, Bond Street, Buckingham Palace and the Racetrack.'

The waitress reappeared with another mojito and a large vodka. Although he hadn't asked for the fresh drink, Ren began mechanically drinking the vodka. Never much of a drinker, he was already feeling slightly woozy. It was hot and he fumbled with the top button of his shirt before loosening his tie. The music, some unidentifiable mush, was beginning to give him a migrane.

'Send all the information to my financial advisers in Mayfair,' he said. 'I will see what they have to say.'

'Good, good.' Sammy poked at the ice in his drink with a green straw. 'I will make sure they have it tomorrow.'

'Fine.' Ren took another mouthful of Grey Goose and felt his eyelids slowly begin to droop. 'But now is not the time for business,' he muttered.

'No, no.' Jumping to his feet, Sammy raised a hand, clicking his fingers.

Three tables away, Sonia Coverdale nudged her co-worker for the evening, a redhead from Scotland called Morag, who already looked like she'd had one glass too many. 'C'mon.'

'About time,' Morag slurred, struggling to her feet.

Sonia tenderly pushed a strand of hair from her companion's face. 'Get a grip, girl – Harry won't be happy.' Harry Cummins expected his girls to live up to certain standards when they were working. In particular, the boss did not tolerate drunkenness, which he considered 'prole-like behaviour'. If he found out about Morag, she would be out on her ear faster than you could say '*sorry sir, but I'm afraid that you do have to wear a condom*'.

'Harry's a wanker,' Morag grumbled.

'Fair comment, but keep it to yourself, eh?' Sonia nodded at Sammy as she helped Morag stop swaying as discreetly as possible. 'We're on. Just try not to puke in the guy's lap.'

With Sammy leading the way, Ren headed up the stairs, a girl on each arm. It was a struggle to hold the redhead up straight, but Ren took each step with the same grim determination with which he had risen up through the Party hierarchy. At least his reward tonight would be a lot quicker in coming. Reaching the top-floor landing, Sammy turned left and ambled down a long, dimly lit corridor. As his eyes adjusted to the gloom, Ren saw there was a set of double doors at the end, guarded by the largest bouncer he'd ever seen.

'That's Kendrick,' Sammy shouted over his shoulder, as if reading his guest's mind. 'He's from American Samoa.' On mention of his name, the bodyguard reached down and opened the door. With the air of a reigning monarch, Sammy disappeared inside. The redhead stumbled and Ren had to strain to stop her from falling. The other girl gave him an apologetic smile.

'Morag'll be OK,' she whispered. 'I think she might have just had a dodgy prawn or something.'

Or something, Ren thought. With a sense of weary shame, he realized that this was the type of place better suited to his wastrel son. Pushing that thought as far away as possible, he kept moving forward. 'Let's just get her inside.'

'Welcome to the *ultra*-VIP suite!' Sammy shouted over the relentless drive of generic rap lyrics blaring out of speakers built into the ceiling. Extending an arm, he bade them contemplate what looked like the scene from a particularly debauched music video. In front of a buffet table groaning with food of all descriptions, a dozen or so women lay around the floor in various states of undress. As far as Ren could make out, there were only two other male guests. One, sprawled on a white leather sofa pushed up against the far wall, underneath a large poster advertising the residency of Oscar 451 downstairs, had his trousers around his ankles and an almost empty bottle of Jim Beam in his hand. Despite appearing to be asleep, he was being fellated by a white girl while her black colleague filmed the action on a smartphone and offered up the occasional shout of encouragement.

'You should be able to watch that on the internet in about five minutes,' Sammy grinned. 'Hey,' he called to the girl with the phone, 'make sure you get the branding in the background.'

The second man was sitting in the middle of the room on what could only be described as a throne. A flunky stood beside him with a flute of champagne while the man tapped repeatedly on the screen of his phone. Ren felt Morag wobble again and reflexively tightened his grip on her arm. However, she wriggled out of his grasp and staggered towards the King.

'Oh my God. You're . . .' Unable to finish her sentence, the hapless girl sent a stream of projectile vomit straight into the man's lap.

'What the fuck?' Before anyone had the chance to react, the man jumped up. Tossing his sick-covered phone to the flunky, he began frantically wiping at his clothes. 'You stupid fucking bitch. What have you done?' He raised his fist but Morag was so far gone that she was halfway to the floor before the punch was unleashed.

The sour smell rising from the throne sent people scurrying for the door.

'Towels,' Sammy squealed. 'Someone get some towels and some hot water.'

'Fuck that,' the King screamed, 'I need a whole new outfit – and a shower.' Eyeing Ren for the first time, he bared his fangs. 'What you doin', man,' he poked at the comatose Morag with the toe of his defiled Nikes, 'bringin' *that* in 'ere?'

Edging backwards, Ren looked for Sammy. But his host had now fled, along with most of his guests.

'Well?' The King grabbed the lapels of Ren's jacket.

Not able to think of any kind of reply, Ren tried to pull himself away, stumbling on the slick floor as the man released his grip. Righting himself, he tried to make for the door, only to find his escape blocked off by the flunky. There was a groan as Morag disgorged the further contents of her stomach at their feet. Ren felt bemused. *How could such a small creature have so much inside her?* He felt a hand on his shoulder, spinning him round, followed by a succession of blows, which smashed the cartilage in his nose. As he went down for a second time, he tried to angle his fall away from the pool of vomit soaking into the carpet.

# TWENTY-ONE

Playing with his BlackBerry, Carlyle stood patiently in line, waiting to be seen. He knew it was his turn when the old codger who was standing behind him gave him a quick poke in the ribs.

'Hurry up, son,' the man muttered. 'Some of us haven't got all day.'

Ignoring the old git, Carlyle nodded at the woman behind the counter.

Vicky Collingridge, manager of the Drury Lane pharmacy, gave him a cheery smile. 'Good morning, Inspector. How's the foot?'

Carlyle winced. 'So-so.' The truth was it had been less painful of late but he knew that the respite would only be temporary.

'Are you wearing the support?'

'Well, sometimes.' In reality he found it too much of a hassle; he couldn't get his shoe on with an athletic support under his sock.

'You've got to stick with it.'

'I'll try.'

'Anyway, what can I do for you this morning?'

'I wondered if I could ask you about something.' Conscious of the pensioner shuffling behind him, Carlyle moved further along the counter and lowered his voice. 'In my professional capacity.'

'Oh, I see.' Vicky gestured towards the small storeroom at

the back of the shop that doubled as her office. 'Why don't we go in there?'

'I need my bloody prescription,' the man huffed.

'Don't worry, Mr Halliwell, I'll get Hayley to come over and sort it out for you.'

With Hayley despatched to deal with the grumpy Halliwell, Carlyle stood next to a pile of cardboard boxes, while Vicky perched on the edge of a tiny desk that looked as if it had been nicked from the infant school round the corner.

'He's a cheery old sod, isn't he?' Carlyle said about the pensioner.

'Mr H? He's OK, just a bit lonely. He lives on Stukeley Street, just above the tattoo parlour. He's been in the neighbourhood for almost sixty years. His wife died a few years ago and he doesn't get out that much these days.'

That could be me, soon enough, Carlyle thought morosely. He tried to push the idea from his mind. 'Do you know the names of all your customers?'

'Just a few of the regulars. How's the family?'

'All good, thanks.' Reaching into his pocket, he produced the bottle of pills swiped from Sebastian Gregori's hotel room. 'I was wondering if you could tell me what these are.'

Vicky took the bottle and inspected the label. 'Triazolam is a sleeping pill. Probably not the most common type that we would see prescribed these days, but fairly common.'

'Could you abuse them?' He realized it was a stupid question before it had even left his mouth.

'Trust me,' Vicky grinned, 'you can abuse anything. With prescription drugs, you have to follow the instructions to the letter.'

'Of course,' Carlyle nodded.

'Why do you ask?' She took another look at the label. 'Has Mr . . . Kortmann come a cropper?'

'Come a cropper?' Carlyle laughed.

'You know what I mean.' She handed him back the bottle. 'Did you find the victim face down in his own . . .?'

'That's CSI Miami, not boring old Covent Garden.' Carlyle put the bottle back into his pocket.

'Come on, Inspector, it's not that boring.'

'No, I suppose not. But there is no victim.' *Not yet, anyway.* 'And all this is strictly between us.'

Vicky knitted her eyebrows. 'Yes, of course.'

'Just a few preliminary enquiries.'

'So I won't be reading about it in the papers then?'

Carlyle stood up straight. 'I most certainly hope not.'

'Is that it?'

'That's it. Very helpful.'

'Glad to be of assistance.' Vicky slipped off the desk and led him out of the room. 'Give Helen and Alice my best.'

'Will do.'

Heading back through the shop, Carlyle saw Mr Halliwell chatting away happily to Hayley, wilfully oblivious of the queue of people that was building up behind him. Heading behind the counter, Vicky opened up a second till and got back to work.

Approaching the police station, Carlyle was still pondering the significance – if any – of finding Kortmann's sleeping pills in Sebastian Gregori's hotel room. Waiting to cross the road, he saw a council worker steam-cleaning the pavement at the spot where the flattened rodent had previously come to rest. RIP, Mousey, Carlyle thought, your fifteen minutes of fame are over. From the other side of the street came the sound of a dozen cameras whirring into action. Looking up, he saw a well-built black guy hurrying down the front steps of the station, trying to ignore the snappers as he pushed his way into the back of a black Lexus which slowly pulled away from the kerb. A couple of the photographers made a half-hearted attempt to follow it down the road but most reckoned that they'd already got their shot. By the time the car had disappeared round the corner, the majority were sitting on the pavement, laptops out, emailing the best shots to their picture desks.

'Whoever that guy is,' Carlyle mumbled to himself, 'he'll be all over the internet before I manage to get my computer switched on.'

On his way to the third floor, he bumped into Sergeant Elmhirst on the stairs. 'Who was that who just left?' he asked, manoeuvring himself up a couple of steps so that she was not towering over him.

'Dunno. It's been a total circus downstairs this morning and I've been keeping well out of it.' Wearing no make-up, with her hair pulled back into a ponytail, Amelia Elmhirst looked ridiculously pretty and it was a struggle not to gawp.

'Smart.' He edged up another step. 'And how's Umar getting on?'

She frowned. 'Sorry?'

'No more photographs, I hope.'

'I wouldn't know about that either,' she replied frostily.

'But—'

'You'd really need to ask *him*.' Taking hold of the handrail, Elmhirst continued on her way before he could quiz her any further.

'What are *you* doing here?' Sitting at Carlyle's desk, Sonia Coverdale looked up from the game she was playing on his PC. There were dark bags under her eyes and she looked like she hadn't slept. 'And how did you get on to my computer?'

'Your sergeant got me started,' she explained, adding: 'He's quite cute, isn't he?'

'He's married with a kid,' Carlyle grumped.

'Lots of men are . . . you, for example.' She returned her attention to the screen.

'What are you doing here?' he repeated.

'There was no room downstairs, so they brought me up here.' She giggled. 'It's like me getting an upgrade on my points, I suppose.'

'Eh?'

'I must have a lot of points on my police loyalty card by now. I'm one of your best customers, surely.'

'That's one way of looking at it.' Resting on the edge of a nearby desk, Carlyle folded his arms. 'Sonia,' he said wearily, 'why were you arrested?'

'There was a bit of a fight at the Racetrack last night. Someone called the police.'

'And your involvement was?'

'Innocent bystander,' she said, carefully tapping on his keyboard.

'You are turning into a right shit magnet, aren't you?'

She giggled again. 'More like a puke magnet.' Pushing the chair back from the desk, she gave him a blow-by-blow account of the night's events. 'Poor old Morag was sent to A&E at UCH. The rest of them are downstairs.'

'I suppose I'd better go and take a look, then.' Heading for the stairs, he shouted over his shoulder, 'Can I get you a coffee, or anything?'

'I'm fine, thanks,' she said cheerily. 'Umar's gone to get me something from the canteen.'

'Good for him,' Carlyle muttered, 'the smarmy sod.'

A look of profound disappointment swept across the face of Constable Mike Proctor as the inspector appeared in front of him. 'I was hoping you were Vaughan,' he said dolefully.

Having no idea who Vaughan was, Carlyle simply nodded.

'He should have relieved me by now,' Proctor yawned. 'I've been here all night.'

'Think of the overtime,' was the only consolation that the inspector could offer.

Proctor patted his already ample stomach. 'I'm thinking of a bacon sandwich.'

'I can imagine.' Carlyle gestured over his shoulder towards the cells. 'I hear that you had a busy night last night.'

Proctor raised his eyes to the heavens. 'It was like Piccadilly Circus in here. Most of them have gone now though. Sammy Baldwin-Lee was screaming and moaning till his lawyer got him out.' He looked up at the inspector. 'You know who he is, don't ya?'

'Oh yes,' Carlyle said, making a mental note to go and visit Sammy in his lair before too long – encouraged by a vague sense that he might be able to dig up something to his advantage. 'Everyone knows Sammy.'

'Great club, the Racetrack. Great grub too.'

Carlyle shot the portly constable a sharp look.

'So I've heard,' Proctor added swiftly.

'So who's left?'

'Just the one bloke. Sonia's punter.'

Stands to reason, Carlyle thought tiredly. 'Why hasn't he been sprung yet?'

'Refuses to give his name. Not sure he speaks English. He's a Chinese bloke, I think.'

Wrinkling his nose at the smell, Carlyle stopped Proctor from closing the door behind him. Happy enough to oblige, the constable lumbered off back down the corridor to dream of bacon and await his tardy replacement.

Not venturing any further into the cell than was absolutely necessary, the inspector surveyed the figure lying on the bench in front of him. Even in his dishevelled and malodorous state, the man had a patrician air. Long-limbed and lean, he had a shock of expertly dyed black hair, and his firm jawline was encased in salt and pepper stubble. His dark suit, albeit crumpled and stained, was clearly of excellent quality, and his brogues, which had been placed neatly by the door, bore the logo of an ultra-expensive English brand.

From down the corridor came the sound of voices; it looked like Vaughan had finally turned up. Slowly, the mystery man swung his feet off the bench and slid into a sitting position.

With his hands by his sides, he looked at Carlyle through expressionless eyes.

'OK.' Placing his hands in his pockets, the inspector remained in the centre of the doorway. 'I assume you speak English, otherwise you wouldn't have been in Sammy's VIP room last night. My name is Carlyle, I am an inspector at this police station. From what I understand, you were the victim of an assault. You could have been out of here hours ago, if you had simply explained who you were and given a statement. I assume you're keeping schtum because you're embarrassed about the hookers.' The man kept his expression blank, but Carlyle could see that he understood. 'Well, I don't care about that.' He looked down the hallway. 'Let's get out of here. You can get cleaned up, make a phone call if you need to. We'll grab some breakfast and I'll help you get this sorted out.'

Sitting stock still, Ren Qi looked at the inspector suspiciously. Finally he spoke: 'What does *schtum* mean?'

# TWENTY-TWO

Edna Holmes, the head dinner lady at Charing Cross, was chalking up the Specials for the day on the blackboard when Carlyle walked into the empty canteen, a rather sheepish Ren Qi in tow. 'We're closed,' she told them.

Turning on the Celtic charm, Carlyle put a friendly hand on her shoulder. 'Not for me, surely.'

She shrugged off his hand. 'Don't try to schmooze me, Inspector Carlyle. And as for your friend there,' she waved a piece of chalk in the direction of Ren, like a referee administering a red card, 'tough night, was it? He looks like he was dragged through a hedge backwards.' Sniffing the air, she added, 'Amongst other things.'

'I know, I know,' Carlyle sighed, 'he doesn't quite meet the dress code, but we are in dire need of sustenance. And anyway, I thought this fine establishment was supposed to be a twenty-four-hour operation.'

'Maybe in the minds of folk who don't have to actually run a kitchen,' Edna grumbled, her accent as pronounced as it had been on the day that the young Miss Edna Hardy had left Kilkenny, almost thirty-five years earlier. She tapped on the board with her chalk.

He scanned the menu. 'It can't be goulash again, surely?'

Edna, whose culinary heritage was strictly 1970s fare, had long since dispensed with any pretence of interest in customer feedback. 'Whaddya mean? It's good for you. It's just stew. I gave it to my own kids all the time.'

'How are the family?' Carlyle asked. He knew that the longer he kept the conversation going, the more likely Edna was to relent and let them have something to eat.

Crossing herself, the dinner lady raised her eyes to the heavens and muttered a reference to the power of sin. Taking that as his cue, the inspector ordered a couple of coffees and directed Ren to go and sit at a table in the corner.

'And Father Zukowski?' he asked, keen to keep Edna talking as she moved automatically to the ancient coffee machine behind the counter. Aside from family, religion was the one totally reliable area of small talk he could fall back on. The woman would visit nearby Corpus Christi after work almost every day.

'He's struggling, Inspector, to be honest.' She placed two mugs of black coffee on a tray, spilling both of them in the process.

'Oh? How so?' Peering over the counter, he tried to locate any filled rolls that had been hidden away back in the kitchen.

'The congregation, Inspector, it's all Filipinos these days. The Father and I, we're the only white people left. It's hard for the poor man. How can he relate to his flock?'

'That's the thing about our great city,' Carlyle said cheerily, not wanting to get drawn into a discussion about the changing composition of the faithful, 'there's a home here for everyone.'

Edna mumbled something that suggested she had a slightly different take on multi-culturalism. Choosing to ignore it, he rooted around in the pocket of his jeans for some change. 'You wouldn't have any bacon rolls left, would you?'

'You're out of luck,' she replied, with just the merest hint of malice. 'Young Proctor took the last three.'

*Three? The fat bastard.* Reluctantly settling for a couple of apples, he paid for breakfast and headed over to the waiting Ren. His guest looked nonplussed at the fare on offer.

'Sorry, I'm afraid that's all I could get.' Carlyle cast an accusing glance at Edna, but she had disappeared into the kitchen to start on the goulash.

Ren picked up an apple, looked at it and then decided to give it a polish with one of the paper napkins Edna had tossed onto the tray. When he was satisfied with his efforts, he took a large bite. Once the first apple had gone, he repeated the process with the second.

Help yourself, Carlyle thought sourly. Sipping his coffee, he scrutinized the man on the other side of the table. He had spent a good twenty minutes trying to clean himself up, but still looked a terrible mess. The smell wasn't getting any better either. Finishing his apple, the man took a sip of his coffee and winced.

'I know,' Carlyle said, 'the coffee here is terrible. Do you want any milk? Or sugar?'

'No.' Ren shook his head as he placed the mug back on the table. 'Black is fine.' As Carlyle had suspected, there was nothing wrong with his grasp of the language. The accent, the inspector guessed, was somewhere between Seattle and Shanghai.

Ren belatedly pressed his face into a smile. 'Thank you. I must apologize for last night.'

'I don't think there's anything to apologize for, sir.' For a reason he didn't quite understand, Carlyle had slipped into full-on deferential mode. He recalled a phrase his late mother liked to use: '*you get more with honey than vinegar*'. The irony was that his mum, God rest her soul, liked to sprinkle the vinegar at every opportunity. This morning, however, something deep in his consciousness told him that a bit of sweetness would yield some as yet unspecified reward. 'It is a most unfortunate situation.'

Murmuring his assent, Ren returned to his coffee.

'And we will need to do a little bit of paperwork before you leave.'

'My people will sort that out.'

*My people*. The first thing Ren had done on leaving the cells was to reclaim his mobile phone. Carlyle had stood by his side as he barked orders in Mandarin (or maybe it was Cantonese) to some minion before stalking off to the cloakroom. The inspector glanced at the clock on the wall, above the door. Presumably the minion would be here imminently.

'How do you know Sonia?'

Ren shifted in his seat restlessly. 'I know the agency. There has never been any problem of this sort before.'

'I'm sure that Harry will be mortified.'

Ren said nothing. If he knew Harry Cummins, he wasn't letting on.

Time to change tack. 'Why are you in London?'

'I'm a businessman,' Ren replied casually, 'I travel a lot.'

'And do you like it? The travel? It must be very tiring.'

Ren gave a dismissive shrug. 'It is necessary.' In the doorway, Umar appeared, gesturing that Ren's entourage had arrived upstairs. Carlyle nodded and got to his feet. Following suit, Ren turned and marched to the door. As he did so, an idea occurred to the inspector.

'I was just wondering . . .'

Without showing the slightest interest, Ren kept walking. Heading out of the canteen, he took the stairs two at a time, rather than wait for the lift.

'Doesn't he like your hospitality?' Umar quipped.

'Ungrateful sod,' Carlyle groused.

In reception, a very expensive-looking lawyer was berating the desk sergeant about the most horrendous infringement of his client's human rights. Ignoring the brief, Carlyle's eyes were drawn to the impressive Amazon standing next to him, deep in conversation with the unfortunate 'businessman'. Tall, for a Chinese, she had the lean, hard look of an athlete. The most striking thing about her, however, were the dark, dead eyes staring out from under a fringe of black hair.

Carlyle elbowed Umar in the ribs. 'Put your tongue back in,' he whispered. 'Who is she?'

'No idea. His daughter? Some kind of PA, perhaps?'

'PA my arse,' Carlyle murmured. The word that came to mind was *ninja*.

Once the necessary paperwork was signed and the lawyer felt he had spouted enough dire threats to impress his client, the woman said something to Ren and they started towards the door.

Skipping in front of them, Carlyle made a performance of opening the door. 'I was just wondering,' he repeated, ignoring the woman's glare. 'A friend of mine does a lot of business in China. He's got a company called Tallow Business Services. I wondered if you might have come across it at all?'

Ren shot an irritated glance at Xue Xi before giving the inspector a gentle shake of the head. 'I'm sorry,' he replied, his English slowing to almost glacial speed. 'I don't think so. China, as you are aware, is a massive country. You can't know everyone.'

'Yes, of course.' Stepping aside, Carlyle let them pass. 'I just thought I'd ask – on the off-chance.'

When he made it back to his desk, Sonia was gone, although she had left him a message – *see you later xx* – in pink lipstick on the screen of his PC monitor. The passing Sergeant Elmhirst clocked the childish scrawl and gave him a big grin. 'Got an admirer then, boss?'

'How am I supposed to get that off?' Carlyle said crossly.

Sitting at the inspector's desk, the youthful figure of Harry Cummins looked up from his copy of *The Economist*. 'A little bit of washing-up liquid should do the trick,' he suggested.

'Get out of my fucking chair,' Carlyle growled.

'Nice to see you, too,' the posh pimp replied as he moved to a seat nearby.

Pulling open the top drawer, Carlyle half-heartedly looked for some paper napkins. 'What do you want, anyway?'

Temporarily distracted by the sight of Elmhirst sashaying across the floor, Cummins said nothing.

'Well?' Carlyle demanded.

'Blimey,' Cummins blurted out, still staring at Elmhirst's bottom, 'where did you find her? She belongs on a catwalk.'

'She was on a catwalk, I think, but decided to come here instead.'

Leaning back, Harry let out a laugh that sounded a bit like a hyena confronting a baby antelope. 'Not right in the head, is that it?'

'Not at all. Sharp as a tack.'

Harry scratched at the logo of his pink Lacoste polo shirt. 'She could make a fortune working for me. An absolute bloody fortune.'

'Harry, leave it out.' Giving up on the napkins, Carlyle decided just to leave the lipstick where it was. Maybe the cleaners would sort it out.

'I'm just saying.'

'If you "just say" anything more,' Carlyle retorted, 'I've got a nice empty cell downstairs that has just been vacated by one of your clients. Smells a bit, mind.'

'That's what I'm here about.'

'What?'

'The guy who was downstairs.'

Carlyle fell back into his chair, almost parking his arse on the carpet in the process. 'Mr Li Hang,' he yawned. 'Great name.'

'That's just the point,' Harry said, tossing *The Economist* into the cardboard box that served as a bin. 'It's not his *real* name.'

*Oh, really?* Carlyle began to sit up and then resumed his slouch. There was no point in appearing too keen. He forced another yawn. 'Why would he lie on his release form? He was the victim of an assault.'

Harry leaned forward. 'How much do you know about Chinese politics?'

'About as much as you know about morals,' was Carlyle's instant response.

'That's hardly fair,' Harry protested.

'OK, I apologize. Give me the short version. And keep it simple.'

'Well, to start with, Mr Li Hang's real name is Ren Qi.'

'Hold on . . .' Carlyle grabbed a Post-it note and a black biro that had been leaking out on his desk. 'Spell it.'

Harry obliged, going on to give the inspector the helicopter view of Ren's role at the centre of the current spate of Politburo infighting.

Carlyle gestured at the magazine peeking out of the top of the box. 'All very interesting, *Mr Economist*, but what does any of this have to do with the price of beans?'

'Because,' Harry said excitedly, 'the word is that Ren is building himself a little business empire over here. He wants to make London one of his primary bolt holes.'

None the wiser, Carlyle stuck out his lower lip and nodded.

'A bit like a Chinese Abramovich,' Harry explained, offering up the Russian tycoon as a point of reference.

'What?' Carlyle frowned. 'He's gonna buy Chelsea?'

'You know what I mean, you berk. He needs an escape route. That's what London is these days, or hadn't you noticed? This place isn't really for the likes of you and me, it's just a refuge for the rich. Ren certainly has the cash to play in this market. He might be more of a politician than a businessman but in places like China the line is very blurred indeed.'

'I suppose.'

'They say all political careers end in failure,' Harry continued, 'but whereas over here that might mean retiring to the country with wife number three and a collection of directorships, there it can mean a bullet in the back of the head. Ren is just being prudent.'

'He wasn't prudent enough to avoid getting caught up in a nightclub brawl with a hooker on each arm,' Carlyle observed.

'He was just a bit unlucky, according to Sammy.'

'So you know Sammy then?' Carlyle was hardly surprised.

'Yeah, 'course I do. He's tried to get me to invest in the Racetrack a couple of times.'

Carlyle raised an eyebrow. 'Business is that good?'

'Sure. Pretty girls never go out of fashion.'

The inspector glanced at the lipstick on the computer screen. 'Even poor old Sonia.'

'She does fine. That guy who complained, Yates, he was just a total dick. Thanks for sorting that out, by the way.'

'It was nothing.' Carlyle shrugged it off.

'No, seriously. Consider the heads-up on Ren a bit of quid pro quo.'

*A bit of quid pro quo?* Those educated pimps; you had to laugh.

'He has a son over here – got him into Eton, God knows how. Must have pulled a lot of strings. The kid's turned into a bit of a rascal by all accounts. The wife spends a lot of time in London too. There are rumours she's playing away with a Brit.'

'Doubt that bothers him too much,' Carlyle interjected, 'given his preference for your girls.'

'You know what such men are like, Inspector.'

*Not really.*

'They want to have their cake and eat it.'

'I'm sure. By the way, the other girl, the one who isn't Sonia. What happened to her?'

'Morag? The silly cow's gone home.'

'To Scotland?'

'No, no.' Harry shook his head. 'Studio flat in Putney.' She claims it was a stomach bug, but that half bottle of vodka she downed before arriving at the Racetrack was doubtless a factor. I think a return to the land of the midges beckons for that young lady. She's just not cut out for this.'

'Make sure she's looked after properly,' Carlyle said, but it was less a command, more of a plea.

Harry made a face. 'I'll do what I can, but I'm not social services.'

'Fair enough.' Carlyle scratched behind his ear. 'By the way, who was the Chinese woman – the one who came to pick Ren up this morning? She seemed quite something.'

'No idea,' Harry said. 'Whenever I've met Ren, he's always been on his own.' Just then, Umar appeared with a coffee in each hand. Placing one on his own desk, he handed the other to Harry.

'Thanks, pal.'

A look of dismay fell across the inspector's face. 'Where's mine?'

'Didn't know you wanted one,' Umar grinned as he sat down.

Not wishing to intrude on a domestic dispute, Harry got to his feet. 'I'd better be going.' He offered his free hand and the inspector gave it a firm shake.

'Thanks for coming in,' Carlyle said mechanically. 'Let me know if you come across this guy . . .' he glanced down at the Post-it '. . . Ren, again.'

'Will do.'

Umar gave Harry a wave as he headed for the stairs. 'Nice bloke.'

'For a pimp,' Carlyle grumped, still put out that he hadn't been offered a coffee.

'By the way,' Umar said airily, 'Commander Simpson wants to see you.'

'Great,' the inspector complained. 'It's not like I haven't got enough to do without schlepping over to her office.'

'She's not at Paddington Green,' Umar corrected him. 'She's got a fitting.'

'A fitting?'

'That's what she said.' The sergeant mentioned an address just off Regent Street. 'Wants to see you there. Said she'd be there for the next hour or so. You'd better get your skates on.'

# TWENTY-THREE

Stepping off the street and into Nixon de Brunner's Bespoke Headwear Emporium was like stepping back in time. Assistants dressed like Edwardian servants scuttled about under dim lighting, fetching boxes from wall-to-ceiling shelves at the behest of invisible customers. Catching the attention of one of them, a flustered-looking woman with a red face, Carlyle asked for the Commander and was directed to the fitting rooms on the second floor.

Climbing the stairs, he found Carole Simpson in a tiny room at the end of a long, dusty corridor. Standing in front of a full-length mirror, she was adjusting her headpiece, a black number that looked a bit like a bowler hat that had been squashed into an oblong, with a white flower sticking out of the top. To Carlyle's untrained eye, it looked like something left over from the French Revolution.

'What the hell's that? It looks like—'

'It's a Napoleon-style bicorn hat with a black and white feathered plume.' The flustered assistant appeared at his shoulder. 'We've been making them using the same craft skills for more than two hundred years.' She turned her attention to his boss. 'How does it look, Commander?'

'I think we're there,' Simpson smiled. 'It feels fine.'

'Not too tight?' the woman enquired anxiously.

'No, just right.' Removing the hat, Simpson handed it to the assistant. 'If you could put it in a box for me, I'll be down in a minute.'

'Of course.' The woman took the hat and hurried away.

'Thank you.' Listening to her stomp down the stairs, the Commander turned to her charge. 'Why do you have to be so snide about everything?'

'Me?' Carlyle lifted a hand to his breast, signalling the wound he had suffered. 'What did I do? I didn't say anything.'

'It's just a bloody hat,' Simpson snapped back. 'Couldn't you say something nice for once? Or, better still, just keep your mouth shut?'

'What's it for?'

'Ceremonial.'

'Aha.' None the wiser, Carlyle waited for her to explain.

'The Met needs a relatively senior officer to take part in Trooping the Colour, in order to help secure the event. One of the Assistant Deputy Commissioners was going to do it but she fell off her horse a couple of weeks ago at a point-to-point meeting and broke her back. So it looks like I've got the nod.'

'I didn't know you rode,' Carlyle replied.

Simpson gave him a cold stare. 'There's a lot you don't know.'

'How very true. For example, I didn't know that we had to provide someone to dress up in a funny hat and ponce around on a horse behind Her Maj.'

'See what I mean?' Simpson shook her head. 'Snide.'

'It's a nice hat,' Carlyle grinned. 'Kind of.'

'When it comes to ceremonial riding hats,' Simpson continued, 'you've got to have a fitting. It has to be fitted because there's no chin strap.'

Carlyle barely stifled a yawn. 'Sorry, I should have realized. Ceremonial duties are not something I've ever been called on to do.'

'I wonder why?'

'How much does it cost, by the way?'

'The hat's not cheap. About £800, plus VAT.'

*£800. That might be a story worth punting to Bernie Gilmore.* Filing the globule of information away for a later date, Carlyle

couldn't resist a little dig. 'Good to know the police force can still afford such essentials while frontline services are getting the chop right, left and centre.'

'John.'

*Time to move the conversation on.* 'At least you're back in favour with the powers that be.' Simpson's career had been in the toilet for several years, but she had stuck at it and was gradually rehabilitating herself. 'Don't fall off Dobbin and maybe you'll get a promotion yet.'

'I wouldn't bet on it,' Simpson said grimly.

Leaning against the frame of the door, he folded his arms. 'So, what did you want to talk about? Other than the hat, of course.'

'Ah, yes.' On the floor, by the mirror, was a large red shoulder bag. Bending forward, Simpson unzipped it and began rummaging around inside. After a few moments, she pulled out a folded sheet of paper and handed it to Carlyle. 'Here.'

Opening up the paper, Carlyle squinted at the image. 'Which way up is this supposed to go?'

'Whichever way you like,' Simpson said tartly.

Carlyle flipped the sheet of A4 round. 'I see what you mean.' The man in the picture, naked from the waist down, was in a state of some excitement. His face wasn't visible but Carlyle knew well enough who it was. Refolding the picture, he handed it back to the Commander.

'You can keep it.'

'No thanks. Bloody Umar.'

Reluctantly, Simpson took the picture and shoved it back into her bag. 'Sergeant Sligo is in quite a bit of trouble.'

Carlyle nodded. 'Who complained? Elmhirst?'

'There have been two complaints from colleagues who both received a copy of that picture but I don't believe that Sergeant Elmhirst was one of them.' Simpson removed her purse from the bag. 'That is one of the problems the Federation is going to have; once disciplinary proceedings begin, more complaints

181

may well emerge. It's going to be hard enough for Umar to survive this as it is, but if there are four or five, well . . .'

'Quite.' The Police Federation might be one of the most successful trade unions ever, but even it would have trouble saving a member who liked to flash his member so indiscriminately. 'What the hell did he think he was doing?'

'People do strange things,' was all Simpson could offer in response.

'I suppose. Anyway, thanks for the heads-up. What happens next?'

'I need to conduct a preliminary inquiry,' Simpson said briskly, her inner line manager kicking in, 'and then, if there is deemed a case to answer – which seems a formality in this situation – we will have a meeting with Sergeant Sligo and ask him to explain his side of the story. Then, barring some miraculous explanation, he will be suspended pending a formal hearing.'

'OK.' Carlyle thought about that for a moment. 'The thing is, I could do with him right now, what with this German business.' *And the 'ninjas'.*

'I can't sit on it for too long but one of the girls who made a complaint is on holiday this week and next, so you've got a bit of time. Of course, you have to keep this under your hat,' Simpson chuckled to herself, 'no pun intended.'

'I understand.'

'Umar will have plenty of time to prepare his response but you mustn't warn him in advance. We can't have him running around trying to nobble the witnesses.'

'I don't think he'd try to do that.' Carlyle felt a sudden urge to protect his wayward colleague. 'He might be a bit immature but he's not threatening.'

'That's not really for you or me to decide, is it?'

'Perhaps not. But you know what I mean.'

'Whatever we think privately,' Simpson stated, 'we have to be above reproach in the way that we are seen to handle these matters. Apart from anything else, this kind of thing is manna from heaven for the papers.' Picking up her bag, she hoisted it onto her shoulder. 'Which reminds me, I see that your journalist chum Bernie Gilmore has been writing about Operation Oakwood.'

'He's hardly my chum,' said Carlyle rather defensively.

Simpson waved away his protests. 'There is considerable unhappiness upstairs about leaks on this one.'

'Nothing to do with me, this Operation . . .'

'Oakwood.'

'Don't know anything about it.'

'Is that right?' Simpson looked disbelieving.

'Speaking of leaks,' Carlyle said brightly, 'do you think we should let the press know about the Kortmann kidnapping?'

'Ah, yes, exactly. That was the other thing I wanted to discuss. Where are we on that?'

Carlyle explained about the sleeping pills he had discovered at the Garden Hotel, glossing over how exactly they had come into his possession.

'And that's your only line of enquiry?' she scoffed. 'Kortmann's private eye? What about Sylvia Tosches?'

'If you mean Barbara Hutton and her husband,' Carlyle replied, 'we're still looking for them. But there's something about this guy Sebastian Gregori . . . I think he's trying to run some scam.'

'Well, get some proof, dammit. Used to be you'd never act on a hunch; now it's all you seem to do.'

'Hardly.'

Simpson jabbed an angry finger in Carlyle's direction. 'Getting old and lazy, that's what it is.'

'Thanks for the vote of confidence, boss.'

'Prove me wrong.' She gestured for him to get out of the doorway. 'Have you informed Kortmann's family yet?'

'No. I was waiting to see if Gregori did that.'

'And?'

'He's not made any contact, as far as I know.'

'Hmm. Maybe he *is* bent. Keep digging. But don't be too long about it. At the very least, we will have to speak to the German Embassy before your mate Bernie gets the scoop.'

'He's not—' Carlyle began, but Simpson darted out into the hallway. He chased after her. 'One final thing.'

Pausing at the top of the stairs, Simpson checked her watch. 'Make it quick, Inspector, I'm due to see Maverick in less than an hour.'

'Maverick?'

'My mount for the Trooping the Colour. He's quite a specimen.'

'Good for him.'

'After that, I've got to go and talk to an MP who claims he's been the victim of a bullying campaign on Twitter.'

Carlyle gave a sympathetic tut. 'Busy day.'

'People are so bloody thin-skinned these days.' Simpson heaved a sigh. 'Tea and sympathy, that's just about all I do.'

'And riding the horse.' Ignoring her glare, the inspector quickly ran through what he had come across in relation to Marvin Taylor's death, Tallow Business Services and the mysterious Li Hang, aka Ren Qi.

'Give it to SO15.' Digging out a credit card from her purse, the Commander began down the stairs. 'No doubt Alison Roche will make sure it gets properly looked at. After all, she learned at the feet of the master – John Carlyle himself.' Laughing at her own joke, she disappeared to collect her fancy titfer.

On the way back to Charing Cross, he put a call in to Roche. The phone rang for what seemed like an eternity before the sergeant picked up.

'Inspector. What can I do you for?'

Carlyle was conscious of a strange humming noise in the background. 'This isn't a bad time, is it?'

'I'm not on duty,' Roche pointed out, 'but it's OK. I can talk.'

The noise was getting louder. 'Where are you?' Carlyle asked.

There was a pause before Roche said: 'I'm at the Beekeeping Club.'

'The what?'

'The Beekeeping Club,' she repeated. 'SO15 set it up a couple of months ago to help firearms officers de-stress.'

'And is it working?' Carlyle asked, intrigued.

'This is only my second visit, but I'll keep you posted.'

'Just make sure you don't get caught in any sting operations,' the inspector giggled.

'Yes, yes,' Roche said flatly. 'Very good. Never heard that one before. Not in the last ten seconds anyway.'

'Sorry.' The inspector bit his upper lip.

'Was there something I could help you with?'

Was there? Distracted by the bees, it took Carlyle a moment to remember the purpose of his call. 'I was just wondering,' he said finally, 'did you ever find out any more about those "ninjas"?'

'Nah. They eventually tracked down the bloke who made the call but he turned out to be a complete alkie. I spoke to him myself, or at least I tried. It was barely eleven in the morning and the guy was already sozzled.'

'A quality wino then?'

'Oh, a perfectly nice bloke. Lives in a flat that's probably worth a couple of million, if not more.'

Carlyle let out a low whistle.

'Easily. Gerald Howard's certainly no dosser. More of your nice middle-class dipso. A functioning alcoholic, at least up until lunchtime. The problem is, he was probably on bottle number four or five by the time it all happened. By that stage he could barely remember his own name. Hardly what you could call a reliable witness.'

Carlyle recalled the statuesque associate of Ren Qi who had turned up at the police station. 'I was wondering if one of the ninjas could have been a woman.'

'Boss,' Roche responded, exasperated, 'they could have been

little green men for all we know. There's nothing to show that they existed at all.'

'Someone sliced Marvin's head off,' he reminded her. 'That was hardly a figment of Mr Howard's imagination.'

'No.'

'Could a woman have done it?'

'Yes, in theory. You'd need a strong stomach, as well as strong arms though.'

Stepping off the pavement, he was almost knocked down by a Lycra-clad cyclist racing round the corner. 'Watch where you're fucking going,' the rider snarled. Carlyle flipped him the finger but the guy was already fifty yards down the road, shooting through the next red light.

'I hope you get taken out by a bus, you git,' the inspector shouted after him, to the amusement of his fellow pedestrians nearby.

'What?' Roche demanded on the other end of the phone.

'Nothing,' he replied, stepping back onto the pavement.

'So, have you got anything? How's the widow bearing up?'

'Nothing worth reporting – not so far, at least. Naomi's doing OK, I suppose, under the circumstances. Your boyfriend hasn't been to see her again, has he?'

'Oliver Steed is *not* my boyfriend,' Roche responded curtly, 'and no, he hasn't been to see Mrs Taylor again.'

'Just as well,' Carlyle chuckled.

Ending the call, Carlyle approached the next crossing with care, looking round for any more rogue cyclists before stepping tentatively off the kerb.

# TWENTY-FOUR

Lying on the bed in Room 226, staring at the ceiling, he finally realized what was bothering him. Swinging his feet on to the floor, Sebastian Gregori padded into the bathroom and stood in front of the sink. All of his pots and bottles were lined up in front of the mirror, in the usual fashion. Missing, however, were the sleeping pills: Werner Kortmann's prescription.

'Hell.'

The only possible explanation was that the cop had taken the tablets.

His plan was beginning to unravel. Gregori had assumed that the Huttons would have been arrested by now, paving the way for Kortmann's brutalized body to be found in a remote ditch, a final victim of a long-forgotten class war. The Huttons, however, were refusing to play their part in the drama that he had so carefully constructed. With their unexpected disappearing act, his whole timetable had been thrown out of kilter. Worse still, that arsehole cop was making no effort to track them down. Instead, he seemed more interested in Sebastian himself.

For several moments, Gregori stared blankly at the mirror. Then he grabbed his wash bag and began packing.

Carlyle was walking along Orange Street when his phone started vibrating.

'He's leaving.'

'What?'

'He's leaving,' Rosalind McDonald repeated. 'Sebastian Gregori just came downstairs and said he was checking out. I thought that you'd want to know right away.'

'Yes, thanks.' Calculating that he was only a couple of minutes from the hotel, Carlyle upped his pace as he passed the back of the National Gallery. 'How much luggage has he got?'

'Just a weekend bag, I think,' McDonald replied, understanding immediately what the inspector was getting at. 'He hasn't asked for a cab. Then again, there's roadworks outside at the moment, so he'll have to walk a bit to find one.'

'OK. I'm not far away. Get the desk to delay him for a couple of minutes if you can. I'll see if I can pick him up when he comes out.' Breaking into a brisk jog, he ended the call and immediately pulled up another number.

Umar picked up on the third ring. 'Are you all right?' he asked. 'You sound like you're out of breath.'

Ignoring his sergeant's amused tone, Carlyle explained what he needed.

'I'll see what I can do.'

'No rush,' said Carlyle sarcastically, ending the call. This time he didn't worry about the traffic, challenging drivers and cyclists alike as he strode across Charing Cross Road and nipped down the pedestrianized Cecil Court.

In the event, he had a good two minutes to spare. Using the cover provided by a utility company van, one of several that had been parked on that stretch of St Martin's Lane, Carlyle watched the entrance to the hotel.

He was just starting to fear that he had missed his man when Gregori appeared. Hesitating on the pavement, he began moving in the direction of Trafalgar Square before turning 180 degrees and heading north. The inspector let the man get twenty yards ahead; as he started following, Umar fell in step next to him.

'Did you see our man?' Carlyle asked.

'Yeah,' Umar nodded. 'Gapper's trying to make his way up

Charing Cross Road, if we need him.' Joel Gapper was one of the drivers at Charing Cross. 'He's in a green Astra.'

'Nice,' Carlyle scoffed, keeping an eye on Gregori on the far side of the road. 'Not going to be much use in this traffic, is he?'

'If it's gridlocked for us,' Umar said chirpily, 'it's the same for the bad guys.'

'Yeah,' Carlyle mused. 'Maybe he's not going very far.'

'Or maybe he'll take the tube.'

Irritatingly, the sergeant's prediction was almost instantly proved to be correct. Reaching Long Acre, Gregori hustled across the road, heading west.

'Looks like he *is* going underground,' Carlyle groaned, ignoring Umar's smirk as he upped the pace. 'Bugger.'

Following his quarry into Leicester Square station, the inspector assumed that Gregori must be heading for the Piccadilly Line and the airport. Instead, however, the private eye took the escalators for the Northern Line, ducking into a passage for the northbound platform when he reached the bottom.

'What do we do?' Umar asked.

'Keep following,' said the inspector, elbowing a tourist out of the way as he clattered down the left-hand side of the escalator, his sergeant following reluctantly behind.

'What are we looking for?'

'How the hell should I know?' the inspector muttered under his breath. 'We'll know it when we see it.'

'What do we do if he recognizes us?'

'Let's just see what happens, shall we?' Carlyle said impatiently.

'You're the boss,' Umar responded sullenly.

'God give me strength.' Jumping off the escalator, Carlyle headed after his man.

With the Northern Line enduring one of its all too frequent service glitches, the platform was almost completely full. After some searching, Carlyle caught a glimpse of Gregori under the indicator board, staring at an advert for Greek holidays. In the event, he let two Edgware Road trains go through the station without getting on either. According to the board, the next train, due in three minutes, was for the High Barnet branch. Carlyle consulted the map on the wall on the far side of the tracks. 'If he's going on the High Barnet line, that means he's not gonna get off before Kentish Town at the earliest.'

'There's another nine or ten stations after that,' Umar fretted.

'I know, but we'll have to busk it.' Carlyle gestured back towards the escalators. 'Get Gapper and head towards Kentish Town. I'll give you a bell once I know what's going on.'

'Not much of a plan,' Umar grumbled.

'Thank you for your support,' Carlyle replied politely. 'Now bugger off and find the driver.'

By the time the tube train rumbled into Finchley Central, the passengers had thinned out to the point where, apart from a pensioner and a couple of schoolboys playing hookey, Carlyle had an entire carriage to himself. Gregori was in the next carriage along, towards the far end; far enough away to be unconscious of the inspector's presence but close enough to make it hard for Carlyle to disembark unnoticed. They were back above ground now; once the mobile operator had finally condescended to provide him with a signal, he sent Umar a text: *go to the end of the line.*

Someone had discarded a copy of the *Telegraph* on the seat next to him. Picking it up, Carlyle was disappointed to find the Sport section missing. Ignoring all the political nonsense, he went to the Obituaries section, alighting on the story of a Spitfire pilot from Tunbridge Wells who had been shot down over Sicily during World War II. After escaping from a German firing squad and trekking over the Alps to Switzerland, the guy had survived to the ripe old age of ninety-one.

'Not a bad innings,' the inspector mumbled to himself. 'Not bad at all. If you offered me that, I'd bite your hand off.'

As the train pulled into Woodside Park, two stops from the end of the line, Carlyle returned the paper to where he had found it. Looking up, he saw Sebastian Gregori get up out of his seat and move towards the doors. *'Shit.'* Quickly he rang Umar's number. The sergeant answered on the first ring.

'Where are you?' the inspector demanded.

'About ten minutes or so away.'

'Change of plan – he's getting off at Woodside Park.' He paused while Umar held a quick conflab with Gapper.

'We'll meet you there.'

'OK, hurry up.' Keeping the line open, Carlyle glumly surveyed the empty platform. With no one else around, it would be impossible for him to follow Gregori undetected. As the tube came to a halt, he watched the doors open and gave a quick glance to his right to confirm that the German had indeed got off. Fortunately, he was walking away from the inspector. Jumping to his feet, Carlyle hovered at the doors for as long as possible. As they began to close, he slipped on to the platform, head bowed.

To leave the station by the main exit, you had to take a bridge over the tracks. Jogging up the steps, Carlyle kept himself out of Gregori's line of vision, staying well behind the German until he had disappeared into the station building. Counting to ten, the inspector followed cautiously. As he stepped through the ticket barriers, he heard the sound of a car engine revving up, and saw Gregori driving out of the car park behind the wheel of a black BMW.

'Brilliant,' he hissed. 'What are you going to do now, genius?'

It was almost fifteen minutes later when Gapper screeched up to the kerb in the green Astra. The passenger window buzzed down and Umar looked at his boss expectantly.

'What time do you call this?' Carlyle complained.

'Sorry, boss, the traffic was a nightmare,' the sergeant explained. He looked around. 'Where's your guy?'

'He legged it in a black Beemer.'

There was a pause while all three men contemplated the myriad frustrations of police work.

'So what do we do now?' Umar asked finally.

'Fuck,' Carlyle said emptily. 'I dunno. Let's go and get a coffee.'

Leaving the car in a side street off the High Road, they picked a café at random, Carlyle ordered a smoothie and began checking the emails on his BlackBerry while Umar and Gapper played a game of table football in the back. The smoothie, when it came, was rather sharp. Sucking on his straw, Carlyle winced, his mood not helped by a message from Alice's school about a proposed hike in fees for the next school year. He was forwarding the email to Helen when there was a whoop of delight from behind him. Moments later, Umar pulled up a chair and sat down. 'Eight-three,' he announced. 'A massacre.'

'Glad to know our little day trip hasn't been a complete waste of time,' Carlyle said coolly.

'It was your idea,' Umar reminded him, opening a bottle of Coke.

'That makes me feel a lot better.' Looking out of the window, he scanned the ugly main road. For many years, Finchley had been Maggie Thatcher's constituency. A Conservative stronghold. That figured. To Carlyle this part of the city – N12 – had absolutely nothing in common with 'his' London. And then, from the corner of his eye, he caught a flash of movement. An expensive-looking car was pulling out of the road opposite.

A black car.

A black BMW.

'It's him!' Carlyle jumped to his feet, spilling the remains of his smoothie over Umar.

'Hey!'

Ignoring his sergeant's protests, Carlyle gestured at Gapper. 'Get the car, quick.' Sitting at the junction, Gregori patiently waited for a break in the traffic, before turning right and heading north towards High Barnet. Fumbling for some cash to pay the bill, Carlyle pushed his driver out of the door. 'Quick,' he repeated. 'Let's not lose him again.'

'Urgh. This stuff is all sticky.'

Carlyle looked in the rear-view mirror. 'Stop whining,' he chuckled, his good mood restored as much by his sergeant's misfortune as the renewal of contact with Sebastian Gregori.

'But it's all over my jeans,' Umar wailed. 'It looks like I've pissed myself.'

'Don't worry, your secret's safe with us.'

Gapper and Carlyle exchanged grins. Putting his foot down on the accelerator, the driver eased them past a lumbering bus and through Whetstone. The traffic had finally begun to thin out slightly and they were soon making steady progress along the A1000. Gregori's black BMW could be glimpsed half a dozen or so cars ahead of them.

'So where do you think he's going?' Umar asked as they eventually passed Barnet Playing Fields.

'Dunno,' Carlyle yawned. 'Maybe he's heading for the M25.'

In the event, Gregori ignored the orbital motorway, instead taking the A1, in the direction of Stevenage. The inspector glanced nervously at the dashboard. 'How much petrol have we got?'

'Enough,' was Gapper's only response.

The BMW was still safely in sight, moving at a steady speed, when Umar piped up from the back seat. 'I need a piss now, for real . . . all that Coke.'

'For God's sake.' Carlyle shook his head.

'If you mess the seats,' Gapper said grimly, 'I'll kill you.'

Almost an hour later, the BMW turned off the motorway at a place called Biggleswade. Careful not to get too close, Gapper followed suit. For several minutes they headed down a narrow two-lane road without seeing another vehicle. On both sides of the road were fields, surrounded by low hedges. Apart from the occasional group of sheep, the fields were empty. It reminded Carlyle of the landscapes of Skåne where a fictional Swedish detective ran around dealing with a non-stop crimewave that was far worse than anything a real-life London copper ever had to deal with.

'Where the hell are we?' he asked, as they passed a sign for the John O'Gaunt Golf Club.

'Bedfordshire,' the driver explained.

'There's nothing here,' the inspector observed dolefully.

'My grandparents used to live round here.' Gapper glanced at the speedometer, careful not to go above 40 mph. 'It was very handy for London.'

'I suppose it would be.' Failing to feign any interest in Gapper's family tree, the inspector gestured at the road ahead. 'How are we going to do this?'

'We just have to keep far enough back that he doesn't see us, and hope that we don't lose him.'

'Not very inspired,' Carlyle sighed.

'Always happy to hear a better idea.' Straying into the middle of the road, Gapper eased the Astra round a bend and almost straight into the back of the Beemer, which had been parked on the side of the road.

'Shit.' Carlyle ducked down under the dashboard as Gapper took evasive action.

'What do you want me to do, boss?'

'Keep going!' Carlyle shouted. 'Find a place further along where we can stop.' Cautiously checking in the rear-view mirror, he looked for signs of Gregori. 'Where is he?'

'Maybe he's taking a leak,' Umar said pointedly.

'All right, all right. Hold on.'

A hundred yards further on, the road curved left and fell away into a hollow containing a few diseased-looking trees. 'This'll do.'

Gapper edged the car off the road as far as he could and they got out. Showing a hitherto concealed turn of speed, Umar sprinted up to the nearest tree and relieved himself.

'Aaahhh.'

'Happy now?' Already marching back up the road, Carlyle checked his phone to see if he had a signal. Two bars. Ah well, he supposed he should be grateful for that. He waved the phone at Gapper. 'What's your mobile number?' Gapper had to recite it three times before Carlyle managed to correctly store it on his phone. 'OK, good,' he said finally. 'You stay with the car. I'll give you a call when we need you to come and pick us up.'

'Sure,' Gapper said, reaching for a packet of Benson & Hedges in his jacket pocket. 'Suits me.'

Umar reappeared, zipping himself up while still trying to scrape the worst of Carlyle's smoothie from his crotch.

'You look a right mess,' Carlyle sniggered.

'And whose bloody fault is that?'

'Yeah, yeah.' The inspector gestured for Umar to follow him. 'C'mon, let's go and see what this bent bugger is up to.'

# TWENTY-FIVE

'Where's the Beemer?' Standing where the car had been, Carlyle scanned the horizon like a lost sailor searching for land. Hands on hips, he turned through 360 degrees in the vain hope of catching a glimpse of black metallic paint. All he saw was grass; lots of grass. Suddenly he felt hungry. Wishing he'd had something to eat in the café in North Finchley, he wondered how far away they were from food of any description. Miles, probably.

Ten yards along the road was a gap in the hedge, with a low, wide metal gate. Umar climbed up on the bottom rung and peered over. 'Looks like he went in here.'

Carlyle sauntered over to take a look. 'It's an empty field.'

Umar pointed to a set of muddy tracks leading from the gate to nowhere in particular. 'That's the car.'

'Maybe.'

'Let's go and take a look.' Without waiting for his boss, Umar vaulted the gate and began jogging across the field.

Wearily, Carlyle hauled himself over the gate and followed at a more sedate pace. 'Let's just hope,' he said to himself, 'we don't come across some farmer with a loaded shotgun.'

It took the best part of twenty minutes for the inspector to cross the first field, by which time Umar was through another gate and halfway across a second field, heading towards a wood. Quite the little Boy Scout, Carlyle thought, panting. Tired and hungry, he pulled out his phone to call Gapper to come and pick them up. The screen, however, showed no signal.

'Great.' Shoving the phone back in his pocket, the inspector soldiered on.

He caught up with Umar at the edge of the woods where the sergeant was having another piss.

'Weak bladder?' Carlyle enquired. 'Maybe you should get your prostate checked.'

'Maybe you should get *yours* checked, *old man*.' Umar gestured towards where the vehicle tracks came into the wood. 'There's a gravel road down there. It'll be to provide access for farm vehicles; more than big enough to get the Beemer down.'

But the inspector was in no mood for further adventures. 'It could go on for miles,' he demurred, taking a seat on a conveniently located tree stump.

'There's only one way to find out.'

'Have you got a signal on your phone?'

Umar checked his handset. 'Nah.'

Remembering that this whole palaver had been his idea in the first place, Carlyle reluctantly pushed himself to his feet. 'OK then,' he sighed, 'having come this far, I suppose we might as well go and take a look.'

They walked in silence for nearly half an hour, each man keeping his thoughts to himself. The inspector was fantasizing about a Flat White from the Monmouth coffee shop when Umar put a hand on his arm.

'Did you hear that?' he whispered.

For several moments, Carlyle did an impersonation of a man straining to distinguish the different sounds around him. Holding his breath, he focused all his attention on trying to pick apart the soundwaves bouncing off his eardrums.

After a while, he exhaled, shaking his head. 'Nothing, just the wind in the trees.'

'Listen!' Umar hissed.

The inspector tried again. Still he could make out nothing of note. No point in telling Umar that, he thought. After all, it was nice to have the boy enthused about a task for a change. 'Yes,' he nodded. 'You're right.'

'See?' Umar grinned. 'I told you.'

Carlyle looked at his sergeant expectantly. 'What is it?'

Umar, however, was distracted by something over his shoulder.

'Step backwards,' a voice barked.

Lifting his hands in surrender, the sergeant did as instructed.

'Fuck's sake,' Carlyle tutted. 'I knew we shouldn't have gone wandering about in the countryside.'

'No,' Sebastian Gregori concurred, 'you should have stayed in your own little world and done your own little job. That shouldn't have been too difficult, should it?' Bouncing on the balls of his feet, he clubbed the inspector across the back of the skull with his pistol. Falling to his knees, Carlyle flinched as a shot rang out above his head.

As the ringing in his ears subsided, the inspector slowly opened his eyes. In front of him, Umar was rolling on the ground, holding his left thigh.

'Shiiiit . . .' the sergeant screamed. 'I've been shot. The fucking bastard shot me.'

'It's only a flesh wound,' Gregori said contemptuously. 'Show some balls. You could be dead by now. As it is, worst-case scenario, you'll have a slight limp for a while.'

Or you could have no balls at all, Carlyle thought, as he watched the smoothie stain on Umar's crotch disappear under a slowly spreading bloodstain. Staying down, the inspector watched the German circle round in front of him, keeping the prostrate sergeant between them.

'That was just to let you know that I am serious.'

'I never doubted it.' Carlyle kept his eyes on the gun.

'Not that I want you dead, you understand. I just have to even the numbers up a bit, seeing as there's two of you and only one of me.'

*Good to know.* Carlyle glanced at Umar, who was muttering to himself through gritted teeth as he tried to staunch the flow of blood.

'Help him up,' Gregori commanded.

Slowly, Carlyle got to his feet and stumbled over to Umar. Squeamish at the best of times, the sight of blood made his stomach do a somersault. What should he do? A tourniquet perhaps? For the first time in his career, he wished he'd taken one of the First Aid courses regularly on offer at Charing Cross. He offered a hand to his stricken colleague. 'Can you get up?'

Still holding his leg, Umar showed no inclination to move. 'I've been fucking shot, you dick.'

Looking around helplessly, Carlyle's gaze alighted on Gregori's tie. The German might be psycho, but at least he was a well-dressed pyscho, with a white shirt and a very nice red and green number around his neck. The inspector held out a hand. 'Gimme your tie.'

'Huh?' The German wiggled the gun irritatedly at his captives. 'Get on with it.'

'Give me the tie,' Carlyle repeated, 'and I'll try to get him up.'

'But it's Hugo Boss,' Gregori objected.

'Just give me the sodding tie.' Reluctantly, the German complied, clawing at the knot with his free hand, while keeping the gun trained on Carlyle.

'Here.' Pulling the tie from around his neck, Gregori threw it towards them.

'Thank you.' Ignoring Umar's protests, Carlyle set about tying it around the top of the sergeant's thigh before carefully helping him to his feet.

'That way.' Gregori gestured down the path. 'Keep going. It's not very far.'

Entering a small paddock, in front of a group of three low buildings, Carlyle helped Umar sit down on a large stone. Off to the left, their BMW was parked next to an ancient Land Rover. Behind the vehicles, a single-lane tarmacked road led away from the buildings. Presumably this was where Kortmann had been brought. Maybe the businessman was still here. The motive for his 'kidnapping' was still a mystery, but the inspector had seen enough in his time to know that there was no reason to assume that things had to make any sense at all. His gaze alighted on a small patch of ground next to a fallen tree that looked as if it had been recently dug up. Maybe Kortmann's in there, he thought grimly.

Keeping his distance, Gregori circled the two policemen. There was a vaguely satisfied look on the German's face. For the first time, the inspector wondered if he might really be bonkers.

With his free hand, Gregori pointed towards the building, furthest from the vehicles. 'You are going in there, gentlemen, so if you please . . .'

The building looked like a barn, with a large wooden door at one end and no windows, at least on the side that Carlyle could see. Even from this distance, it was clear that the door was badly warped and rotting at the bottom. Its green paint had flaked off in large patches and there was no sign of a lock. Not much of a prison.

'*Please*,' Gregori repeated.

With a troubled sigh, Carlyle leaned over and helped Umar back onto his feet. The sergeant's skin was cold and clammy and his eyes were glazed. He's gone into shock, Carlyle thought. Flesh wound or not, the boy needs some medical attention. Slowly, he led him over the rough ground towards the building. Walking ahead of them, Gregori pulled open the door and gestured for them to enter.

Inside, the barn was cool and dark. The smell of damp and decay filled his nostrils as Carlyle let his eyes adjust to the gloom.

'In there.'

*Oh shit.* Feeling his knees buckle, Carlyle had to quickly

adjust his stance to prevent himself and the sergeant from both falling over. Bolted on to the back wall of the barn was a cage, a lattice of narrow metal bars roughly twelve feet wide and twelve feet high. The floor of the cage was covered with dirty-looking straw and, next to the door were lined up a dozen two-litre bottles of water, a couple of toilet rolls and a metal bucket. The whole scene was like something out of a torture porn movie.

'In you go.'

Reluctantly, the inspector led Umar inside, laying him carefully on the straw as Gregori padlocked the door behind them. 'Make yourselves comfortable,' the man advised them. 'You may be here for a little while.'

'My colleague needs a doctor,' Carlyle replied, trying to keep his voice from cracking. On cue, Umar let out an anguished groan.

Gregori dropped the key into his pocket, saying tersely, 'He'll live.'

'He's lost a lot of blood,' Carlyle persisted.

'He'll still live,' Gregori said. 'The human body is a wonderful thing.'

Reaching for one of the bottles, the inspector knelt down by his colleague. Unscrewing the cap, he lifted the bottle to Umar's lips and forced him to drink a little water. 'Slowly, slowly,' Carlyle said, 'there's no rush.'

Smiling weakly, Umar signalled that he'd had enough.

Over his shoulder, the inspector shouted: 'What about food?'

'Later.'

'You know they'll be looking for us.'

'Looking is one thing,' Gregori replied. 'Finding is another.'

*Don't I know it.* Just then, the inspector caught sight of something lying in the corner of the cage; it was a newspaper. Was it the one Kortmann had been holding in his photograph? Maybe. Getting back to his feet, he turned to face Gregori. 'You brought Werner Kortmann here?'

Smirking, Gregori said nothing.

Taking a gulp of water, Carlyle rinsed his mouth before spitting it onto the ground. 'What I don't understand is why you would kidnap your own client?' Replacing the cap on the bottle, he placed it back with the others. 'Perhaps you could explain it to me?'

The German's smirk grew wider. 'Do you really want to know?'

'Of course.'

Contemplating his answer, Gregori scratched his temple with the muzzle of his gun. 'In that case,' he said finally, 'you'll have to see if you can work it out for yourself. However, with your track record I doubt very much that you will be able to manage it.' Argument won, their captor turned and headed towards the light.

'Wanker.' Lowering himself to the floor, Carlyle leaned back against the side of the cage and yawned. For a while, he sat staring into space, thinking about nothing in particular, his Zen-like calm only interrupted by the sound of a car starting up and driving away.

'There goes the Beemer.' Carlyle looked over at his sergeant who was staring into space. 'What do you suggest we do now, then?'

Umar's only response was to turn on his side and throw up.

After dozing for a while, Carlyle woke with a start. It was properly dark now, after 10 p.m. according to his still signal-less BlackBerry. Helen will be pissed off, he thought dolefully.

In the middle of the cage, Umar muttered something in his sleep. His breathing was heavy but he seemed comfortable enough. *Christina won't be too happy, either.*

Enough light from the paddock trickled under the doorway for the inspector to glimpse something rustling in the hay near Umar's head. Hoping it was just his imagination, he struggled to his feet, his stiff joints protesting all the way up. Conscious of his aching bladder, he stepped up to the bars and unzipped his trousers.

In mid-flow, he was interrupted by a noise outside. There was the sound of multiple vehicles, followed by footsteps and hushed voices. He just had time to finish up before the main door creaked open and a light was switched on. He had to shield his eyes against the sudden glare.

'So there you are.' Carole Simpson strode up to the cage and placed her hands on her hips. An amused grin played at her lips as she took in the scene. 'Inspector John Carlyle behind bars. I have to say I rather like it.'

'This is no time for jokes.' Carlyle gestured towards Umar, who was still flat out on his back, seemingly unmoved by the new arrivals. 'Get us out of here.'

From behind Simpson, Gapper appeared and stared at the padlock. 'Get an axe, or a set of bolt cutters, or something,' Carlyle hissed. With a nod, Gapper turned and headed off to see what he could find.

'You should be a bit more gracious, John,' Simpson admonished him, once the driver had disappeared. 'If it wasn't for young Gapper, you would have been in a world of trouble.'

'And here's me thinking we were in Butlins,' Carlyle said sarcastically.

'When you went AWOL, at least Gapper had the sense to call the station. Who would you rather have, turning up to rescue you? Us, or the local plod?'

Not wishing to concede the point, Carlyle simply glared at her.

'Or we could have decided it could wait and then taken a leisurely stroll up here sometime tomorrow.'

Carlyle was momentarily distracted by further rustling in the straw. 'All right, all right. You've made your point. Just get us out of here.'

# TWENTY-SIX

In the event, it took Gapper the best part of twenty minutes to find an axe and smash the lock. Once the cage had been opened, the driver used the First Aid kit from the boot of the Astra and carefully cleaned up Umar's wound.

'Do you know what you're doing?' Carlyle asked.

'I did the First Aid course last month,' Gapper explained evenly, not looking up as he wrapped a gauze bandage around the sergeant's thigh. 'I know enough to patch him up until we get to hospital.'

'It's just a flesh wound,' Umar said, decidedly more chipper now that they had been rescued. 'Let's get back to London. You can drop me at UCH.' University College Hospital, at the top of Tottenham Court Road, was barely fifteen minutes from Charing Cross police station.

Simpson looked on doubtfully.

Taping up the bandage, Gapper handed Umar half a dozen ibuprofen in a foil wrapper. 'At this time of night we can be there in an hour or so,' he pointed out. 'At least we know where it is. It could take us almost as long to find a local hospital.'

'And you don't want to leave him out in the sticks,' Carlyle chimed in. 'We'd have a lot of explaining to do.'

'We'll have a lot of explaining to do at UCH,' Simpson said moodily.

'Nothing we can't talk our way out of,' Carlyle countered. 'And at least we'll be on home turf.'

A gust of wind swept through the barn, causing Simpson to shiver. 'You don't really operate very well outside of Zone 1 of the tube map, do you, John?'

'The fresh air doesn't agree with me,' Carlyle grinned. 'Not enough lead in it.'

'You should have protected your colleague.'

Carlyle gave Simpson a disbelieving look. *The colleague you are going to hang out to dry in the next few weeks?* 'Look,' he started, 'if you want to play the blame game, who got us into the mess in the first place? You were the one who told me we had to help Gregori and Kortmann.'

Ignoring him, Simpson stalked out into the paddock. Following her outside, Carlyle gestured towards the other buildings. 'Anything of interest in there?'

Relieved that the inspector was not looking to continue the argument, she shook her head. 'Not really. We can check who owns the property in the morning.'

'No sign of Kortmann, I suppose.'

'Nothing. Only the newspaper in your cell to suggest he's been here.'

'There was some freshly dug ground.' Carlyle gestured towards the fallen tree. 'Over there. Maybe—'

Simpson shook her head. 'It's someone's vegetable garden. There's no body.'

The inspector looked almost dismayed. 'So we're pretty much back at square one.'

'Hardly,' Simpson corrected him. 'We now know that Gregori is our man. I'll call in Forensics, see what else they can discover.'

Carlyle bridled at the suggestion. 'Maybe that is not such a good idea. Not right now, at least.' The lights were on in one of the buildings. Through a ground-floor window, he could see a fridge. Further along was an open door. Carlyle began walking towards it. 'We don't have the remotest clue about what's going on here. Who the hell *is* this guy Gregori? What's he

205

playing at? And how was he able to dupe his client? That's what we need to find out. Not to mention, what the hell is he going to do next?' Not waiting for a reply, he went in search of the kitchen, hoping that the crazy kidnapper had at least left some decent food behind.

Pulling open the fridge door, Carlyle gave silent thanks to Gregori for at least being organized enough to buy some groceries. Helping himself to a Jamaican beer, some Dutch cheese and the remains of a baguette, he began filling his stomach.

Stepping into the kitchen, Simpson watched impassively as her underling stuffed his face. 'I hope you've left something for Umar,' she said.

Chugging down the beer, Carlyle stifled a burp. 'Don't worry, there's plenty.' He gestured towards the fridge with his can. 'Want a beer?'

The Commander thought about it for a moment. 'Why not? It's been a long day.' Stepping over to the fridge, she pulled out a can of Red Stripe, cracked it open and took a long drink. 'Aaah.' Wiping her mouth with the back of her hand, she rested her behind on the edge of a workbench. 'You know,' she said, staring at her can, 'even by your standards, today has been quite a cock-up.'

'I know,' Carlyle replied unapologetically, shoving another chunk of cheese into his mouth and washing it down with the last of his beer. Crushing the can, he dropped it onto the table. In the corner was a pile of neatly folded plastic bags; grabbing one, he opened it up and placed the can inside. 'We don't want to leave any rubbish with our fingerprints on it, do we?' Placing the bag on the table, he returned to the fridge. 'Just in case Forensics do happen to turn up, one day.'

'You're going to wipe that down, as well?'

'Of course,' Carlyle said airily. 'There's no harm in being paranoid.' Grabbing the last can of lager, he closed the door and wiped down the handle with a grubby tea towel. Opening the can, he took a swig as Simpson gave him a look. 'Well,' he shrugged, 'it's not like Umar can drink it. And Gapper's driving.' With Simpson making no further objections, they drank in silence for several moments. 'By the way,' Carlyle said finally, 'how did you find us?'

'Gapper played a blinder,' Simpson told him. 'By the time I made it up here, he had followed your trail and found the road that comes in from the other side. He assumed that you were in here as there's nowhere else for miles.'

'Good for him,' Carlyle said, finishing off the last of the cheese and speaking with his mouth full. 'If he thought we were here though, why didn't he come in and get us out? Gregori legged it hours ago.'

'He had no way of knowing that. For all he knew, he could have stumbled right into a nutter with a gun.' Lifting the can to her lips, she smiled. 'Just like you did.'

'Thanks for reminding me,' Carlyle grumbled.

'Like I said,' Simpson teased, 'you just can't function outside of Zone One.' Taking a final mouthful of beer, she poured what remained into the sink and dropped the can into the plastic bag. 'So, what do you want to do now?'

'We'd better put the word out about Gregori,' Carlyle said. 'We can't have him scampering around the Home Counties, armed and dangerous.'

'Leave that to me,' Simpson replied. 'I'll make sure that it's done in a way that doesn't scare the horses.'

'OK. Then let's get back to London. See what else we can find out about him. Think how we can manage the mess when the news gets out that we helped a nutter to kidnap some German industrialist.' Sweeping up the bag of rubbish, he looked at Simpson. 'Who put the two of them on to you in the first place?'

'Someone in the Commissioner's office.' The Commander exhaled. 'There was nothing particularly surprising about that. Like I said before, it was the kind of referral that you get on a fairly regular basis. "Just make sure that so and so feels that they are being properly looked after." You know what it's like; plenty of VIPs turn up expecting us to do their bidding.'

'Tell me about it,' Carlyle agreed.

'I just passed them on to you.'

'Maybe you need to have a word with the Commissioner.'

'Ha.' She waved the idea away with a dismissive flick of her hand. 'What exactly would I say? Anyway, I'm sure he knows nothing about it; it was just a name on a piece of paper that came across his desk that he delegated.'

And we don't want to lose the Trooping the Colour gig, do we? Carlyle thought. But it was a cheap shot and he knew it. 'In that case, maybe we need to speak to some people in Germany.'

She looked at him doubtfully.

'Don't worry,' he told her. 'I think I know where to start.'

With Umar bundled into the back of the Astra, Carlyle took up Simpson's offer of a ride in her Range Rover. Setting off in convoy, they headed back towards London. Once his network coverage was restored, Carlyle called home. Helen sounded like she'd been asleep. Skipping any mention of his rustic adventure, he told her he should be home in a couple of hours and let her get back to bed. That done, he made a second call. The phone rang for several moments before someone finally picked up.

'Hello?'

'Ben? Look, sorry for ringing you so late. It's John Carlyle, from Macklin Street.' Ben and Elizabeth Crane lived in a townhouse just off Seven Dials and played a leading role in the Covent Garden Residents Association, which was active in trying to keep the local nightlife to manageable levels. Carlyle had first come across the couple a few years earlier when the Association had helped get a kebab shop closed on Macklin Street. Since then, he and Helen had been out with the Cranes a couple of times socially. The inspector had never been entirely clear what Ben did for a living. Elizabeth, on the other hand, was a Registrar at University College Hospital and therefore a good contact to have at times like this.

'Ye-es?' The man sounded more than a little drunk.

'I was wondering if I could have a quick word with Elizabeth. Bit of a work-related emergency.'

'She's not here,' he mumbled. 'She's on shift.'

*Perfect.* That was a better result than he could have hoped for. 'OK, I'll call her at work. Sorry again to have phoned you so late.'

'OK. No problem.'

Ending the call, Carlyle found a number for UCH on his BlackBerry and phoned the hospital. After what seemed like an eternity, he was finally put through to Dr Elizabeth Crane. She listened patiently while Carlyle explained the nature of Umar's injury, without going into any of the details regarding how it happened.

'I'm not on A&E,' she responded, taking the matter in her stride, 'but I'll see what I can do. All the usual paperwork will have to be done, of course, and the police have to be informed immediately. But then again, you are the police, so we'll take that as read.'

'Thanks. I appreciate it.'

'I suppose Helen knows what you're up to?' Elizabeth Crane asked finally. 'Out all night playing cops and robbers. I don't know how she puts up with it.'

'It's a living,' Carlyle laughed. 'She would get pissed off if I was under her feet the whole time.'

'Ben's the same,' she confided. 'He likes his space.'

And his booze, Carlyle mused. As his eyelids began to droop, he thanked her again. Dropping the phone back in his pocket, a sign flashed by, telling him that they were only twenty-three miles from London. Heading in the right direction, he thought, and promptly fell asleep with a smile on his face.

After dropping Umar off at UCH and squaring things with Elizabeth Crane, it was almost 5 a.m. by the time Carlyle finally made it home.

'Bloody hell,' Helen mumbled as he crawled into bed, her voice deep with sleep, 'you are really late.'

'Sorry.'

'S'OK. Just try and get some rest. I've got to be up early.' Letting an arm drop across his chest, she immediately resumed her gentle snoring.

For a while, all that Carlyle could do was stare at the ceiling. After dozing fitfully in the car, he felt quite awake. Umar was being patched up before being sent home in a taxi. According to Dr Crane, the patient should rest – which apparently meant that he should take at least a fortnight off work. Knowing his sergeant, Carlyle expected that it would no doubt get stretched into three weeks, or even a month. He wondered what this latest turn of events would mean for Simpson's investigation into what he'd come to think of as 'the willy pictures', or 'Willygate'. Getting shot in the line of duty probably wouldn't do his sergeant much good when faced with several counts of inappropriate behaviour of a sexual nature.

*Bloody Umar.*

Eventually he let his breathing fall in step with Helen's and closed his eyes, confident that sleep would come in due course. All he needed was a couple of hours' rest and then he would be up and at 'em.

It was throwing-out time in Camden and a small crowd had spilled out of the Fristock Arms, gathering behind the tape to watch the firefighters clean up the mess. Some yummy mummy would find her Chelsea tractor missing in the morning. Standing at the end of the alley, Crew Commander Dave Wharton watched the smoking wreckage of the Porsche SUV and shook his head. What a waste of a great motor.

'Bloody kids,' someone grumbled. 'That's the second one this month.'

Third, actually, Wharton thought.

'I hope they're fully comp,' a woman shouted, prompting a round of drunken laughter.

Wharton took a couple of steps forward, putting a bit more space between himself and the rubberneckers. Where are the bloody police? he wondered. They should be moving these people on, not to mention checking where the vehicle had been stolen from.

Tuning out the voices behind him, the fireman watched his crew going about their jobs. Next week, they would be on strike. The dispute was over pensions being cut back. Wharton had voted to go on strike too. He didn't particularly see the point, but when the guys went out, you went out. If you didn't, working together afterwards would be impossible. When they came back to work, everyone would simply go on a go-slow and it would take for ever to get anything done. Already, he had started cutting back on his spending in anticipation of the loss of income. Next year's holiday was on hold and his daughter's riding lessons were under serious threat. The financial belt-tightening wasn't going down too well at home, but there was no way around it.

One of his men, Lewis Rotherby, a young lad from some-where out in the badlands of Essex, finished hosing down the car and popped open the boot. *Standard protocol.* Wharton nodded approvingly. Lewis was a good lad. Would make a decent fireman. Just wouldn't have any money when he retired.

At that moment, Rotherby dropped the hose and wheeled away, puking the contents of his stomach over the cobbles.

The drunken chatter went up a notch as Wharton reached for his phone.

# TWENTY-SEVEN

Opening his eyes, the inspector squinted at the green LED display of the clock on the bedside table: 3.15 p.m. 'Shit.' Sitting up in bed, he considered his options. Having slept for the best part of ten hours, he could head into the office and try to salvage something of the day, or simply say 'fuck it' and try again tomorrow. After thinking about it for several moments, he decided on the latter.

By the time Helen got home, just after 6.30, he had been to the gym, done some shopping at Tesco and even emptied the dishwasher.

Hovering in the hallway as she walked through the door, Carlyle brushed off her surprise at his presence. 'I thought we might go out for dinner,' he said, taking her coat. 'Alice said she'll come too.'

'To what do I owe this honour?' Helen's eyes narrowed. 'What have you been up to?'

'Nothing, nothing,' Carlyle said hastily, discomfited by his wife's ability to make him feel guilty at every turn. 'I just thought it would be a nice idea, that's all.'

'Yes, why not?' Clearly still suspicious, Helen slipped past him, heading for the bathroom. 'Just give me a minute and we can get going.'

After much debate, they decided on an Indian next to the Royal Opera House. It was part of a chain, but Alice liked it – the place had a nice, busy atmosphere, it was reasonably priced and the service was prompt and friendly. Hitting the post-work rush hour, they had to queue for ten minutes but were finally rewarded by a table next to the window. Waiting for the drinks to arrive, Carlyle watched as a group of work-men manoeuvred a series of massive sets out of the Opera House and into the back of a large lorry. After spending most of the day in bed, he felt unusually relaxed; successfully park-ing the cares of the night before, safe in the knowledge that they would be there waiting for him when he returned to his desk tomorrow.

Helen followed his gaze. 'There's a new production of *La Traviata* coming up. It's supposed to be good. I was thinking of taking Alice, if you'd like to come.'

'Not really my kind of thing,' he said immediately.

Alice looked up from the copy of *Maus*, the graphic novel about the Holocaust, which she had brought along for a little light reading at the dinner table. 'Peasant,' she teased him.

Carlyle smiled graciously. 'You are too kind, my dear.' Just then, the waitress arrived with their drinks, saving him from further abuse. He took a mouthful of his Kingfisher lager, and Alice took a gulp of her Coke and returned to her book.

'Christina called me this afternoon.' Helen looked at her wine but made no effort to reach for the glass.

*Uh, oh.* Carlyle wondered if he should have called Umar's wife on their way back to London. Too late to worry about that now.

'She said,' Helen lowered her voice so that, even sitting next to her, he had to strain to hear her over the hubbub, 'that Umar got *shot.*'

'Just a minor scratch.' Carlyle tried to calculate how much Umar would have told his wife and how much Christina, in turn, would have told Helen.

'Hmm.' Finally reaching for her glass, Helen took a sip of her wine. The poppadums arrived. Showing no interest in her parents' conversation, Alice began mechanically breaking them up and shovelling pieces into her mouth. 'According to Christina, it sounded like a gangland shooting.'

'Nothing so dramatic,' Carlyle said airily, grabbing a poppadum while he still had the chance. Breaking it in half he plastered some mango chutney on it. 'It was just an accident. You know what a drama queen he can be.'

'Christina says he wants to leave.'

*And he might get his wish, very soon.* Now, however, was not the time or the place to tell Helen about his sergeant's foray into photography. 'He's always said he fancied being a househusband but they can't afford it.' The waitress returned to take their order and Carlyle gave her a big smile, grateful that his grilling had been interrupted.

'And another thing,' Helen continued, 'why didn't you tell me about Chase Race?'

'Who?'

'The rapper,' Alice helpfully reminded him from behind her book. 'Likes to beat up his girlfriend. Mum wants to get her hands on his cash.'

'Alice.'

'Oh, *that* Chase Race,' Carlyle laughed, cheered by his wife's irritation. 'What's he done now?'

'He spent the night in your cells,' Alice told him. 'Didn't you know?'

'Ah. That would explain all the snappers hanging around the other day.'

'Honestly, John,' said Helen, exasperated, 'sometimes I think you walk around in a daze. You never pay any attention. What do you *do* all day?'

'Now you're sounding like my boss,' he said.

'There was a fight in a nightclub,' Alice giggled, 'and Mr Race was arrested. Now he's offering Avalon a hundred and fifty grand to try and rehabilitate his reputation.'

'Wow.' Carlyle looked at Helen. 'Is that right?'

'Yeah. Every time he does something stupid, he lumps in an extra £50,000.'

'You should sit tight,' Carlyle chuckled. 'It'll be a million soon enough.'

'I personally want to bite his hand off. The Board are still more than a bit sniffy about it though.'

'God. As if your job isn't hard enough.' As he gave her a consoling pat on the arm, an idea started to flicker in his brain. 'Have you met this guy?'

'Once. Why?'

'What was he like?'

'Like someone who was struggling to pretend he was house-trained,' Helen said drily. 'In a word, feral.'

'That's what kids are into these days,' Alice observed.

Carlyle thought about it for a moment. 'Do you think you could arrange for me to meet him?'

He had been at his desk long enough to switch on his computer and let a wave of ennui wash over him when Amelia Elmhirst sauntered over, grinning from ear to ear. Dressed in a pair of skinny jeans and a grey silk blouse, she looked totally out of place in the shabby surroundings of the third floor of Charing Cross police station. Deploying the willpower of a dozen men, Carlyle tried not to stare.

'I hear that you got Umar shot,' she said, perching on the edge of their absent colleague's desk.

'Not quite,' the inspector replied, keeping his eyes firmly on the screen of his computer. The cleaners had made a half-hearted attempt to remove Sonia Coverdale's lipstick but her faded message was still perfectly readable. Wondering how Sonia was getting on, he made a mental note to get some proper screen wipes the next time he passed a Superdrug store.

'It's the talk of the station,' the sergeant giggled. 'You walked him into an ambush and he nearly got his balls shot off.'

'That might have been a blessing,' Carlyle riposted, not

215

missing a beat. 'Put a stop to the boy's interest in photography.'
He was surprised to see Elmhirst blush slightly.

'Apparently he's gonna be off sick for months.'

At this, Carlyle sat back in his chair and folded his arms.
'I *followed* Umar into an ambush,' he informed her, 'and had
a nasty smack to my head, by the way. He took a minor flesh
wound to the thigh. Nothing serious and his famous wedding
tackle was never in any danger. The doctor says he should
take a week or two off. All this stuff you've been hearing is
just exaggerated nonsense.'

Elmhirst nodded solemnly. 'You know what it's like; the
truth is always the first casualty of war.'

'You shouldn't listen to the gossip,' Carlyle admonished her.

'Gossip or not,' she shot back, 'you'd better make a big con-
tribution to his collection.'

'Collection?'

'The guys on the front desk started it last night,' Elmhirst
explained. 'They've got more than £200 already.'

'It was just a bloody scratch,' Carlyle objected as he calculated how much he would have to drop into the pot; £30 at least.
'Anyway,' he sighed, 'was there something I could help you
with?'

'Well,' she said brightly, 'I'm Umar's replacement – in the
short-term at least.'

'Oh?' The inspector felt his mood lighten immediately.

'Commander Simpson asked me to step into the breach.'

'Excellent.'

'She said that my languages might be useful.' Noticing his baf-
fled look, she added, 'I speak French, Portuguese and German.'

As Elmhirst disappeared back downstairs, Carlyle idly specu-
lated on the possibility of having her as a full-time replacement
for the hapless Umar. After a while, the mobile on his desk
started vibrating and he picked it up. There was no Caller ID on
the screen but he took it anyway.

'Carlyle.'

'Inspector, you *are* sounding cheery this morning. Been busy locking up criminals?'

'Something like that,' Carlyle said coolly. 'How are things in the imploding world of the media?'

'Oh, you know. Same as ever – a constant struggle for survival in the face of the forces of progress.'

Carlyle glanced at the clock on the far wall. 'It's a bit early for you, Bernie, isn't it?'

'It's a 24-7 operation these days,' Bernie Gilmore replied sadly, 'constant rolling deadlines. We journalists never sleep.'

'My heart bleeds. What can I do for you then, at this early hour?'

'I have a little story that I'm lining up . . .'

Carlyle's heart sank. 'If this is about bloody Operation Oakwood—'

'No, no. That didn't really have any legs. This is something different.'

'Yes?' The inspector ran through a range of possibilities in his head, none of them good. Where did their little out-of-town adventure take place – Bedfordshire? Did Bernie have any contacts there?

'I was wondering if you might be able to give me some information about a hat.'

*A hat?*

'Inspector? Are you still there?'

'Yes, yes,' said Carlyle irritably. 'You want some information about what?'

'I'm running a story about the £1,000-headgear that your boss has bought for Trooping the Colour.'

'I thought it was only . . .' He stopped himself in mid-sentence.
'What?'

'N-nothing,' he stammered. 'What has Trooping the Colour got to do with anything?'

'I have a very good source.'

217

*Aren't they all?*

'This source tells me that Commander Simpson will be representing the Commissioner at the event this year. She has splashed out on a special Napoleonic-era hat to wear on her horse, Santa.'

'The horse is called Maverick.' *Oops.*

Bernie started scribbling away. 'Good to know. Anyway, the TAPW – Taxpayers Against Public Waste – are up in arms. Their chief executive, a Mr Clive Boyson, has given me a nice juicy quote complaining about the police wasting a couple of Monkeys on a hat at a time when there is no money to pay for good old bobbies to walk the streets, nicking vandals and deporting illegal immigrants, et cetera, et cetera. I'm going to ask Simpson for a quote but, seeing as you're her boy, I wondered if you could just confirm the number for me.'

'It wasn't a grand,' Carlyle sighed. 'It was only £800.'

'Maybe that was ex-VAT. A grand would be a better number.'

'Bernie, for fuck's sake.'

'Either way, it's a lot of money for a hat. Have you ever spent £800 on a titfer?'

'No,' Carlyle said, 'of course not. But what's with the rhyming slang, all of a sudden?'

'Fun stories like these,' Bernie explained. 'They just unleash my inner Cockney cheeky chappy. They make me smile and I know that they'll make the reader smile.'

'Glad to know we're keeping you amused.'

'With these kind of stories, as I'm writing them up, I hear them being narrated in my head by Sid James.'

'Maybe you should go and see a shrink for that,' Carlyle replied. 'Anyway, you know that Sid James was South African?'

'Get away.'

'Yeah. His real name was Solomon Cohen. I saw a documentary about him recently.'

'Well, well, you live and learn. Anyway, what were we talking about?'

'Simpson's £800 hat.' Carlyle lowered his voice as one of the other inspectors, a dour bloke called Beckett, walked past. 'Look, it's a special kind of hat she has to get specially fitted because it doesn't have a chin strap and she can't have it falling off on the day.'

'Yes, yes.' More scribbling.

'C'mon, Bernie,' Carlyle protested, 'it's not Simpson's fault. She only got the gig because some other woman fell off her horse.'

'Dangerous things, horses. Why anyone would want to get on one is beyond me.'

'Carole doesn't deserve to get a slagging in the press over this.'

'It's a story,' Bernie grunted. 'If I don't write it, someone else will.'

'You could sit on it for a while. Maybe it will just fade away.'

'Impossible.'

'What about if I give you something else?'

The sound of scribbling ceased instantly. 'What have you got?'

# TWENTY-EIGHT

'Well? Have you got something, or not?'

'Er,' Carlyle prevaricated, 'I might have something interesting on the Chelsea massacre.'

'That was *days* ago,' Bernie snorted. 'Tell me about something that's going to happen. Something sexy.'

*Sexy.*

'The hat,' Bernie reminded him, 'now that's a decent story. And, of course, I can always pad it out with a bit of backstory about her bent husband.'

'Her *late* bent husband,' Carlyle put in, 'as if that is relevant.'

'The fact that a senior police officer's husband was a convicted fraudster is always relevant,' Bernie said.

'She's not that senior.'

'She's senior enough to be doing Trooping the Colour.'

'C'mon Bernie, Simpson's all right. Give her a break.'

'I didn't say she wasn't. I don't decide what's a story. Gimme something else.'

'OK, OK. There are a couple of possibles.'

'Why don't you tell me them both,' Bernie coaxed, 'and I'll decide which one is the best.'

No fear, Carlyle thought. If I do that, you'll have both of them written up before I get off the bloody phone. The inspector would have preferred to give up the story of Werner Kortmann's disappearance – it was a miracle that it hadn't leaked already – but there were too many gaps still to be filled in. As things stood, he wouldn't put it past Bernie to run a *Keystone Cops lose German Bigwig* story. Worst of all, it would essentially be true. In the end, he recounted the story of Brian Yates and the alleged contravention of the Sale of Goods Act 1979.

'Is that it?' Bernie asked when he had finished. 'Who was the hooker?'

'No, no. Let's not go there. She's perfectly nice and doesn't deserve to be mocked.'

'Not a dog, then?'

'Not at all. I think she's quite pretty in a girl-next-door kind of a way.'

There was an awkward pause before Bernie asked: 'You haven't been . . .?'

'No, no,' Carlyle said hastily.

'Well then,' Bernie let out a long sigh, 'not much of a story, is it?'

'It's at least as good as the hat,' Carlyle countered. 'Sid James would find it funny.'

'At the very least, I need a picture: the hooker or the punter. Both would be best but either is fine. The hat story, we can always wait till Trooping the Colour and get a nice pic of the Commander all dolled up.'

Carlyle rummaged around in the top drawer of his desk until he found the business card that Yates had given him. After reading out the guy's mobile number, he recited the company's web address. 'I'm sure you'll get a picture on there.'

'Yeah, but will it be high-res?'

'I'm sure your picture desk can sort it out,' said Carlyle soothingly.

'We'll see.'

'So we have a deal?'

'Let's see what I can get out of this. I'll sit on the hat thing for now. I can tell the Taxpayers Against Public Waste that we are planning on running it to coincide with the ceremony.'

'Thanks, Bernie.'

'I can't promise that they won't try and take it to someone else though.'

'Understood.'

'I'd give Simpson a heads-up, if I were you. Just in case it does pop up somewhere else.'

'Good advice. Thanks.'

'I hope that she appreciates what you're doing for her.'

So do I, Carlyle thought.

'Now, what's that other story you mentioned?'

'It's early days yet. Too soon. I'll tell you when I've got a bit more, promise.'

'Fair enough. Oh, by the way, Seymour Erikssen . . .'

Carlyle frowned. Seymour Erikssen was a burglar who had been arrested so many times, the media had dubbed him '*London's crappest criminal*'. The time he had slipped through the inspector's fingers was a particular low point in Carlyle's career. 'Ye-e-s?'

'You haven't seen him lately, have you?'

'No, why?'

'It's just that I hear he's operating on your patch again, that's all.'

'Great,' Carlyle sighed. 'That's all we need.'


As always when he ended a conversation with Bernie Gilmore, Carlyle was conscious of feeling vaguely depressed, about life in general and his own circumstances in particular. On this occasion, he decided to remedy the situation with a trip to the canteen. Edna would doubtless tell him that it was closed, but he was sure he could talk her into selling him an iced doughnut and an Americano. Pushing up from his chair, he headed for the door only to be confronted by the wonderous Sergeant Elmhirst. Confusingly, she was accompanied by Alison Roche.

'She was looking for you downstairs,' Elmhirst explained, gesturing at Roche. 'I didn't know you had a female sergeant before.'

'These things happen.' Carlyle nodded at Roche. Dressed in a black T-shirt and an army surplus parka, SO15's finest looked tired and irritable. He hoped that she hadn't arrived to give him a bollocking for something.

'Boss.' Giving Elmhirst a sideways glance, Roche commented, 'I'd be careful. He gets through sergeants at quite a rate of knots, does the inspector.'

Elmhirst frowned but said nothing. For a moment, there was an awkward silence. Was there a bit of tension between the two women? Or was that just wishful thinking on his part?

'How's the beekeeping going?' he asked.

'It seems more like hard work than anything else,' Roche said truthfully, 'but I'll stick with it for a while.'

'Good for you.'

Nonplussed at the chit chat, Elmhirst stepped between them and thrust a sheet of paper into Carlyle's hand. 'I think you'd better take a look at this.'

Carlyle checked out the picture of an innocent-looking young man with thinning hair and a pair of John Lennon specs. He was smiling comfortably while looking directly into the camera. 'What's this?'

'That's Sebastian Gregori.'

'Eh?' Carlyle did a double take. The guy in the picture looked nothing like the man he knew.

'I printed it off his company's website,' Elmhirst said. 'Maybe we should have taken a look at that earlier.' *We* as in *you*.

Maybe I should, Carlyle thought glumly.

'I spoke to his boss in Berlin,' Elmhirst continued. 'Apparently he is with a client in South Africa right now. Has been for the last three weeks.'

'Ah.' Blushing, Carlyle refused to meet Roche's quizzical gaze.

'Once they check my bona fides, they will ask him to give me a call.'

Yes, yes, Carlyle thought, all right. Don't rub it in. But Elmhirst was already heading back down the stairs in triumph.

'I'll leave you two to *chat*,' was her parting shot.

'Quite a woman,' was Roche's only comment as Elmhirst disappeared from view.

'You're not here to beat me up as well, are you?' Carlyle asked.

'Me?' Roche widened her eyes in mock horror. 'Would I ever?'

He raised his eyebrows. 'So what can I do for you?'

Roche gestured towards his desk. 'Grab your coat. We're going out.'

Once they made it on to Chandos Place, Roche directed him towards a red Alfa Romeo.

'Nice car,' said Carlyle, as he slid into the passenger seat. 'Nothing but the best for SO15, eh?'

Roche mumbled something rude as she started the engine and pulled away from the kerb. Reaching the Strand, they made a right turn and were held up in a line of traffic at a red light.

'So where are we going?' he asked, finally tiring of waiting for an explanation.

'I thought we would go and see Gerald Howard,' she said, in a tone that suggested a casual social visit.

It took the inspector a moment or two to place the name. 'The drunk who saw the ninjas?'

'That's right.'

The lights changed and they began edging forward. At this rate, he reckoned they might make it under Admiralty Arch in about an hour. 'Any particular reason?'

'They found Michael Nicholson last night.'

Tallow Business Services. *Sonia Coverdale's client.*

'Yes, indeed.'

Roche kept her eyes firmly on the road ahead, even though they were travelling at barely five miles an hour. 'He was found in the back of a burned-out Porsche Cayenne up in Camden.'

'How did you identify him so quickly?'

'We didn't,' Roche said tartly. 'Some computer did. You find an incinerated corpse, you automatically cross-check it against the Missing Persons list. Nicholson was near the top, given he's so recent, and his dental records checked out.'

Carlyle nodded. 'Impressive.'

'Not as impressive as the way in which it's being buried.' She sent him a sideways glance. 'For some reason, not obviously apparent to the likes of me, SO15 has dropped this like a steaming dog turd. They just want it all to go away as quickly as possible.'

'So you came to me,' Carlyle groaned.

'Of course,' Roche said cheerily. 'I know that you'll want to get to the bottom of this. You don't look the other way.' Seeing the doubtful expression on his face, she added: 'Well, most of the time anyway.'

Carlyle thought about that for a moment. The pieces were slowly coming together. 'Ren Qi,' he said, as they finally made it past Nelson's Column.

'Who?'

The inspector ran through what the posh pimp Harry Cummins had told him about Ren Qi, aka Li Hang.

'OK, Mr Bond,' Roche said, changing gear, 'explain to me why some Chinese big shot wants to assassinate a small-time London businessman?'

'It might explain Mr Howard's ninjas,' he countered. 'This guy Ren does seem to have quite an interesting entourage. If we make a working assumption that his people are responsible for what happened in Chelsea, then we can move on to their motives. That, in turn, will lead us to why SO15 want to look the other way.'

'Simple, really.' Spotting a gap in the traffic, Roche stomped on the accelerator and they shot on to The Mall.

'Policework usually is,' Carlyle said.

'I'm not sure poor old Umar would agree,' Roche sniggered as they headed towards Buckingham Palace.

'Poor old Umar, my arse,' the inspector snorted. As they reached the next line of stationary traffic, he told Roche about his sergeant's photographic exploits.

Laughing, Roche shook her head. 'No way!'

'I'm afraid so.'

'Just as well the silly sod didn't send *me* anything like that.'

'Maybe he feels that your relationship hasn't quite reached the right level yet,' Carlyle chortled. Then: 'All joking aside, it's got serious consequences. It looks very much as if he's for the high jump. Even getting shot won't be enough to save him from the HR mullahs.'

'That's the problem with all this digital technology,' Roche observed, 'it allows boys to be even more badly behaved than they were before. In my day, they'd just sit in their bedrooms, playing with themselves. Now they want to share what they get up to with the world.'

'He's hardly a boy,' Carlyle corrected her.

'We live in an infantilized culture.'

'But why would you take pictures of your willy and send them to people you barely know?'

'Because you can.'

'I just don't get it.'

'Just as well,' were Roche's final words on the subject.

For a while, they sat in silence.

Heading along Constitution Hill, the inspector watched a steady stream of joggers making their way through Green Park. A statuesque blonde accelerated past a fat man who looked like he was about to have a heart attack, while an angry-looking bloke in a Radiohead T-shirt stopped by a tree to do a set of squats, moving up and down too quickly for the exercises to be of any use. Carlyle's mind drifted back to an evening, years earlier, when he himself had been jogging past that very tree. It was late in the day as the inspector stumbled across a young girl, alone and seemingly lost. The child spoke no English. Eventually, he discovered that her name was Alzbetha. She had been brought to London from the Ukraine by people traffickers. After he had placed her in the care of Social Services, the criminals had snatched her back.

Carlyle was not the kind of man who believed in things like 'fate' or 'destiny'. The fact that he had been in that park at the same time as the girl had temporarily eluded her captors was nothing more than a coincidence. Even so, from the first moment that he had come across her, something deep inside the inspector's being screamed that he had been meant to find this child. Having done so, it was his duty to look after her, keep her safe and do what he could to see that she had at least a chance of something approaching a decent life.

If he had been able to do only one thing of merit in his entire police career, that should have been it. He was a policeman. He should have been able to protect one single child.

*Alzbetha, I am truly sorry.*

Roche caught a glimpse of the look on his face. 'Are you all right?' she asked.

Remembering how she had always been good at reading what was going on in his head, the inspector turned his expression into a grimace. 'Just a bit of pain in my foot,' he told her. It was a convenient lie; the reality was that his foot had been much improved of late. 'Sprained ligaments.'

'You should get that looked at,' Roche said blandly. 'You're reaching that age where things start to go wrong.'

'I'm not *that* old.'

'I'm just talking about proper care and maintenance,' Roche scolded.

'You sound like Helen.'

'That's because we're both right.' Roche cackled. 'You don't know how lucky you are, having two smart women looking out for you.'

'How very true.' Placing his hands in his lap, Carlyle took a deep breath. Now felt like a good time to pop the question. 'If Umar does get the chop, would you be interested in coming back?' The words came out in a rush, causing Roche to do a double take.

'Seriously?'

'Yes, why not? I can't think of anyone better. There's certainly no one I'd rather have take the job.'

'I'm honoured,' Roche laughed, placing a hand on her chest. 'But what about that Amazon you've already got working for you back at Charing Cross?'

'Sergeant Elmhirst is great,' Carlyle explained, 'but she's only going to be temporary.'

'Things have a way of starting out as temporary,' Roche observed, 'and ending up as permanent. Anyway, I'm sure that you could get Simpson to extend her stay if you wanted to.'

The inspector shook his head. 'She's being fast tracked – that girl's going places. She'll be after Simpson's job before too long.'

'Ah. And you'd rather have someone who's going nowhere, like me?'

'No, no,' Carlyle protested. 'You know what I mean.'

Another red light loomed in front of them. Roche brought them to a gentle stop behind a sightseeing bus. 'Not really,' she said.

'If Umar *is* on the way out, I'm going to need a proper long-term replacement. And if you're not happy at SO15.'

'What makes you say that?' she shot back, shifting the car into gear as the lights changed in their favour.

'Why are we sitting here?' Carlyle countered 'If SO15 finds out you're going behind their back to breathe life into an investigation they want to bury, your days there are going to be numbered anyway. You'll need to have a contingency plan, if nothing else.'

'Get out the way, you bloody idiot!' Smacking the horn, Roche gestured angrily at a cyclist who suddenly cut across her.

Carlyle looked at her expectantly.

'One thing at a time,' Roche said crossly. 'Let's just go and see Gerald Howard and take it from there, shall we?'

# TWENTY-NINE

Gerald Howard was a small, trim man in a green cardigan and slippers. He had a couple of days' worth of stubble on his chin and his hair was in need of a comb. Clearly delighted to have some company, even if it was only a couple of coppers, he waved them inside his flat.

Standing in the living room, Howard announced that he had been enjoying a cigarette and a 'very nice bottle of Merlot' and immediately offered the pair of them something to drink. Not knowing a good Merlot from a smack in the face, the inspector found it easy to decline the offer of a glass of wine, accepting instead a black coffee. With Roche taking a cup of tea, Howard shuffled off into the kitchen after instructing the two police officers to make themselves at home.

Out of habit, Carlyle looked slowly round the room. It was barely large enough for a sofa and an armchair, with a coffee table in the middle, but it seemed cosy enough. In the corner, a small TV was surrounded by DVD box sets for TV shows that he didn't recognize. The far wall was lined with books from floor to ceiling; mainly world history and political biographies, with a sprinkling of management guides. On several shelves were framed photographs showing a younger Howard in various exotic locales. In each one he was smiling, with a protective arm around a small, mousey, uncomfortable-looking blonde woman, presumably, was Mrs Howard.

'What do you think?' Roche whispered, once their host started banging about in the kitchen.

The inspector's gaze returned to the coffee table, on which sat a wine glass and the half-empty bottle of red wine, along with an ashtray and a packet of cigarettes. 'He looks like a sozzled old maths teacher from a provincial fifties boarding school,' was the inspector's verdict. 'A nice enough sort of chap, but functioning on less than full power once you get into the afternoon.'

'Quite.'

Carlyle gestured at the photographs. 'I wonder what happened to the wife?'

'Dunno. But I certainly think he lives here on his own.'

'It would certainly help explain the boozing.' Carlyle wondered if he would go downhill if Helen wasn't around. Probably. He seemed to remember reading somewhere about how men needed marriage more than women and struggled to cope on their own. It wasn't a theory he felt any particular need to test himself.

'This is where he saw it happen.' Roche walked over to the window. When Carlyle joined her, she pointed to the street below. 'Marvin Taylor's car was down there, on the corner.'

Carlyle nodded. He could still see a scrap of police tape hanging limply from a nearby lamppost; the last remnants of an already forgotten crime scene.

'Marvin's guys were killed in an alley on this side,' Roche continued. 'You can't see it from here, but I'll walk you down there later. We didn't find much but you might as well have a look.'

'Quiet, isn't it?' was the inspector's only observation.

'You've got to be seriously loaded to live around here,' Roche reminded him. 'You don't get many people on the streets at any time of the day.'

'No, I suppose not. Why walk if you can take the Daimler?'

'Here we go.' Howard appeared with their drinks on a tray.

Much to the inspector's delight, there was also a large plate of chocolate biscuits. Placing the tray on the glass coffee table, Howard gestured towards the sofa. 'Please,' he said pleasantly, 'take a seat.'

For a few moments, they busied themselves with the drinks. Helping himself to a biscuit, the inspector took a nibble and beamed.

'Very nice.'

'You can't beat a chocolate digestive,' Howard agreed, offering the plate to Roche. When she declined, he placed it back on the table and grabbed one for himself. Breaking it in two, he popped half into his mouth and chewed happily. 'That's one of the nice things about being back in London. In my last posting, they were almost impossible to lay your hands on. In the end, my mother started sending us food parcels every month.'

'You were working abroad?' Roche asked.

'Oh, yes,' Howard smiled. 'I was in the Diplomatic Service.' He mentioned a country Carlyle had never heard of. 'In East Africa,' he added, helpfully. 'I was the Deputy Ambassador there until nine months ago.'

Carlyle had no particular interest in their host's career history, but he knew he was going to get it anyway, so he nodded politely.

'Then I had the misfortune to be sent on a team-building exercise in Wales by the Foreign Office. Run by a bunch of management consultants. Not surprisingly, they were total idiots. When I wouldn't join in with their silly games, they said I wasn't a team player. The next thing I knew, I was being sized up for a desk job back in London, to sit out the rest of my days.'

'So what did you do?' the sergeant enquired. Unlike her boss, Roche seemed genuinely interested in the man's story.

'I got the lawyers involved, threatened to sue for constructive dismissal and took them to the cleaners.' Howard raised a chuckle, but Carlyle could see that he considered it a pyrrhic victory. 'Got a lump sum and my full pension – five years early. A terrible waste of taxpayers' money really.'

'Not the first,' Carlyle mused, 'and it won't be the last.'

'Not to mention a thirty-year career down the drain.'

Roche gestured at one of the photographs with her mug. 'So where is Mrs Howard?'

Howard's bottom lip began to quiver and for a moment it looked as if he might burst into tears. However, much to the inspector's relief, he managed to pull himself together. 'Ellen is still out there. She works for the Service too. They won't let her come back to London and if she leaves now, well, she's a few years younger than me, so her pension wouldn't be up to much. For the moment, we have a bit of a long-distance relationship.'

*What you might call a trial separation*, Carlyle decided.

'Couldn't you have just stayed on, out there?' Roche asked.

Saying nothing, Howard simply shook his head. Popping the other half of the biscuit into his mouth, he chewed it with a grim determination.

You're not telling us the whole story, Carlyle thought, are you? Happily, it was none of his business. Tiring of the idle chit chat, he pointed at Roche. 'The reason we're here, sir, is that the sergeant thought that you might be able to explain to me what you saw on the night that Marvin Taylor and his colleagues were killed.'

Howard washed down the digestive with a mouthful of Merlot. 'I think I can do rather better than that, Inspector.'

Carlyle glanced at Roche who made a *no idea what he's taking about* gesture. 'Oh?'

'Yes.' Howard finished the wine left in his glass and reached for the bottle. 'I don't have to explain what I saw. I can show you.'

The spare bedroom was scarcely big enough for the three of them to stand in at the same time. In the corner, by the window, a large computer screen perched precariously on a tiny table. Switching on the machine, Howard tapped a couple of times on the keyboard, bringing up a video player. 'I shot this on my new phone,' he explained. 'My daughter-in-law got it for me as a retirement present. She showed me how to work it too. A lovely girl. Lives in Maidenhead with the grandkids.'

'The phone is registered to the daughter-in-law,' Roche explained, 'which is why it took us a while to track Mr Howard down.'

That, and the fact that he was too drunk to give his name, Carlyle thought.

'Ah yes,' said Howard sheepishly. 'I'm very sorry about that.'

'We got there in the end,' the inspector responded. 'It was lucky that you were filming in the first place.'

'It's not something I make a habit of,' Howard told them. 'I was playing with the phone, trying it out, when I saw what happened. I'd had one or two and, I have to say, I didn't know what to do, whether to record what was happening or call the police.'

Carlyle nodded.

'Anyway, this is what I got.' Enlarging the video so that it almost filled the whole screen, he hit the Play button and stood aside to allow them a better view. Carlyle and Roche stood in silence as they studied the shaky footage of the street outside. Parked on the corner, you could see the bonnet of Marvin Taylor's van but not the cab, or the man inside. The time code on the bottom of the screen showed fifteen seconds of nothing – just an empty street. Then the first figure appeared, dressed all in black, with a baseball cap pulled down over its eyes.

Then a second.

Then a third.

'The ninjas,' Howard said. 'It was the first word that came into my mind, I'm afraid.'

'As good a description as any.' Carlyle watched as two of the figures disappeared in the direction of the alley. The third – tall, sleek and athletic – disappeared around the side of the van. Instinctively, the inspector knew precisely who he was looking at.

Roche pointed at the screen. 'That was when Marvin got garrotted.'

'It's a woman.'

Roche and Howard both leaned forward, squinting at the screen. 'Maybe,' said the sergeant. 'Impossible to say. However, the statistics suggest otherwise.'

Carlyle grunted.

'The numbers don't lie,' Roche insisted. 'Even if you discount the upper-body strength that was required, you would not expect a woman to do something that savage. And so messy – urgh.'

'I've seen her,' Carlyle said, as much to himself as to Roche. 'I know who she is.' *Kind of.* Conscious of Howard's presence, he added: 'We can discuss it later.'

The picture wobbled and then the screen went blank.

'That was when I dropped the phone and called 999.' Howard scratched his nose. 'It's a truly amazing bit of kit though. Apparently you can film stories for the TV news on them, the quality's that good.'

Carlyle and Roche exchanged glances.

'You haven't put this on YouTube, have you, sir?'

Roche took Howard's bemused look as a 'no'.

'And you haven't given this footage to any journalists?'

Howard shook his head vigorously. 'Oh no. I wouldn't do anything that silly.'

'Good.' Carlyle let out a small sigh of relief.

'I know what a bunch of rapacious so-and-sos those fellows can be,' said Howard with some feeling.

'OK.' Carlyle tapped the screen. 'Let's take another look.'

'Why didn't you mention this when we talked last time?' Roche asked, once it had finished a second time.

'To be honest, I wasn't sure if I'd got it properly,' Howard explained. 'I thought I'd lost it. Once I finally managed to get it onto the computer, I sent it to your colleague, the young chap called . . .' for a moment he struggled to recall the name '. . . Oliver.'

Roche frowned. 'Oliver Steed?'

'That's right!' Howard said, pleased. 'I'm surprised he didn't show it to you.'

'Oliver's been put on another case.' Slipping easily into the lie, Carlyle gave the ex-Foreign Office man a conspiratorial wink. 'A bit of a crisis up North. Anyway, we've been left holding the baby on this one and are having to retrace some of his steps.' He glanced at Roche, who was staring at her shoes, trying not to blush. 'These things happen sometimes.'

'Don't worry, Inspector,' Howard chuckled. 'I know all about dysfunctional organizations.'

Carlyle nodded sagely.

'Anyway, once he'd got it, Oliver said I could delete my copy but, luckily for you, I hadn't quite got round to that yet.'

Pulling a business card from his pocket, Carlyle handed it to Howard. 'Maybe you could send it to me, as well? That way we've all got it.'


With Roche heading off to start her shift, the inspector made his way back into the centre of town. Walking through Leicester Square, he ducked up a side alley and approached a small black door marked STAFF ONLY. To the right of the door, at about head height, was an intercom with a keypad below it. Carlyle was just about to press the buzzer when a couple of tired-looking young women appeared at his side. Without a word, one of them punched in a code, pulled the door open, and disappeared inside with her friend. Grabbing the door handle before it shut, he counted to ten and then followed after them. Walking down a long, dark corridor, he came to a set of lifts. Picking the nearest one, he stepped inside and hit the button for the top floor.

Clanking and shuddering, the lift slowly ascended. When the door opened, Carlyle found himself on a spacious landing, with doors off to either side. On the far wall, under a massive print of Debbie Harry circa 1980, was an uncomfortable-looking sofa.

Reclining on it was a familiar giant, wheezing away, engrossed in a comic book.

'Kendrick!' Carlyle greeted him. 'How's it going?'

Kendrick Saunders looked up from his copy of *Justice League* and scowled. The bouncer had never forgotten – or forgiven – the inspector for trying to have him jailed for putting a customer in hospital after a dispute about a bill. In the event, Kendrick had escaped with fifty hours of community service and a £2,000 fine but he still resented the fact that the policeman had shown an undue zeal in trying to secure a custodial sentence. 'What do you want?'

'Where's Sammy?' Carlyle demanded, all trace of bonhomie extinguished.

Kendrick tipped his comic, gesturing towards the door on Carlyle's right.

'Thanks.'

'But he's busy,' Kendrick growled.

'Don't worry, I won't take up too much of his time.'

Watching the inspector stride towards the door, the bouncer thought about getting up before deciding that it would be too much effort. 'Suit yourself,' he muttered, returning to his reading.

If the inspector had been expecting to find Sammy Baldwin-Lee up to no good, he was sorely disappointed. Striding into the office, he found the club-owner sitting behind his desk engrossed in a copy of the *Financial Times*. Just about the last man in London still to be reading the actual printed newspaper, he scanned each word carefully, his mouth open just enough for his tongue to pop out. In a pair of jeans and a Fleetwood Mac T-shirt, he had the look of an off-duty accountant.

'Looking for tips?' Carlyle quipped.

'Looking for investors,' Sammy said glumly. 'Know any?'

'Yeah, sure,' Carlyle replied, casually looking around the

room. The place was a tip, with promotional materials and other club-related detritus scattered everywhere. Removing a box from the only other chair in the room, he sat down.

'Want a Racetrack T-shirt?' Sammy asked, pointing at the box with a stubby finger. 'On the house.'

The inspector held up a hand. 'Thank you, but no.'

'Hundred per cent cotton. Specially designed by, er, someone or other. They sell for £38.99 downstairs. Just make sure you wash it separately. Maybe the wife would like one?'

'I think she's sorted in the wardrobe department for now, ta.'

'OK, well, if you ever change your mind, the offer remains open.'

'Thanks. I'll let you know.'

'By the way,' tossing the newspaper on to his desk, Sammy gestured towards the door, 'isn't Kendrick out there? Keeping riffraff like you out is supposed to be part of his job description. At least it was last time I looked.'

'I said "hello" to him on the way in, but he's rather focused on reading his comic right now.'

'That damn boy spends half his life in *Forbidden Planet*,' Sammy griped, 'and the other half in Burger King. Maybe I should think about an upgrade.'

Carlyle gave a sympathetic cluck. 'I hear that he didn't do much to stop the fight the other night.'

Sammy's eyes narrowed. 'Is that why you're here? It was nothing at all, really. Just another average night on the town for our good friend Chase Race.'

'I suppose there's no such thing as bad publicity,' Carlyle reflected.

'I would never have thought I would say this, but he's becoming a bit of a pain in the arse. We don't want to be known as the kind of place where it's all just bling, bling, bling. It's all getting a bit too chavvy; very off-putting for the people who have serious money.'

'I suppose it must be,' the inspector sympathized. 'However, it's not Chase that I wanted to talk to you about.'

'No?' Sammy gave a disappointed shrug. 'I was hoping that you might be able to put the git away for a year or two; just long enough for everyone to forget who he is.'

'I'm here about the Chinese guy that Chase smacked.'

Sammy picked out a spot on the wall behind Carlyle and fixed his gaze upon it, bringing his hands together in silent contemplation.

'Some big shot called Ren Qi,' Carlyle continued. 'He was arrested along with a couple of Harry Cummins's hookers.'

'How is Harry?' Sammy asked genially. 'I haven't seen him for a while.'

'We can sit here and talk shit all day,' Carlyle said, 'or you can tell me where to find Ren and I'll let you get back to your reading.'

'The guy was just in the wrong place at the wrong time. When Chase loses it, you want to be at least twenty yards away and out of his line of vision.'

'He was in the VIP suite,' Carlyle pointed out, 'so don't give me that old cobblers.'

Leaning forward, Sammy scowled. 'Look,' he jabbed a stubby finger in the inspector's direction, 'this Chinese guy, from what I understand, well "big shot" is an understatement. He's a *major* player. I'm hoping that he might become an investor in the club.'

You can hope, Carlyle thought. 'Don't worry,' he said reassuringly. 'I just need to have a word with him about something completely different. He will never know that you and I have spoken.'

Sitting back in his chair, Sammy gave Stevie Nicks a scratch and folded his arms. 'So, if I do help you find him, what's in it for me?'

'The continuing support and regard of your local constabulary,' Carlyle said smoothly.

Sammy swatted the suggestion away with a wave of his hand. 'Too intangible.'

'That's just for starters.'

'Oh?'

'Yes,' Carlyle smiled. 'If you help me with this, I think there's possibly a way I can help you with your Chase Race problem.'

# THIRTY

Xue Xi wondered when they were going home. Their job in London was done but still there seemed no urgency on the part of her boss, Guo Miao to return to Beijing. When she asked about it, the major had simply smiled and said, 'Soon.'

Rather than protest, she had nodded and returned to her post. Her father had always told her that waiting was an important part of the job.

On the other side of the door, the screaming ticked up a notch. A gleeful Ren Qi had told his wife that Michael Nicholson was dead. The man simply could not control himself; he had to rub it in, reasserting his power. Wang Lei had worked herself up into a frenzy and was raging hysterically at her husband. Guo Miao had struggled to hold her back as she tried to scratch out Ren's eyes. It seemed inconceivable to Xue that the woman would now return to China voluntarily.

They were making life very difficult for themselves. Xue realized that things were different in England: harder to cover up. They had already caused a major furore with the killings of the security guards. When Nicholson's body was discovered, it wouldn't be long before someone made the connection between the crimes.

The tall, athletic woman shifted uneasily from foot to foot.

It was definitely time to go home.

After a few minutes, the shouting stopped. The door opened and Guo's head appeared. 'Get the boy,' he barked.

Xue nodded and made her way briskly along the corridor. Reaching Ren Jiong's room, she opened the door and stepped inside. The air was full of stale cigarette smoke. Xue had to do a little skip to avoid kicking over a full ashtray that had been left on the floor. Lying on the bed, Ren Junior was watching a porn movie on his iPad. Naked from the waist down, he bobbed his head in time to the grunts coming from the woman on the screen.

'Get dressed,' Xue commanded.

Ren rolled over and gave her a dopey grin. Tossing the iPad to one side, he slipped off the bed and stood to attention.

'Get dressed,' Xue repeated.

'What's the hurry?' he said thickly, stepping towards her. Dropping her right shoulder, Xue flicked out a jab. The punch caught him right on the chin and Ren toppled backwards, his skull cracking off the frame of the bed before he hit the floor with a thud.

'Your father is waiting.'

'Fuck you,' the boy wheezed, but she knew that he had no fight in him. He was soft and weak. Standing over him, Xue had to resist the temptation to give him a swift kick in the genitals to hurry him up. Ever since arriving in this country, she had endured problems with her impulse control and anger management.

Grabbing his hair, she pulled him up on to the bed. Disconcertingly, his erection remained intact. From the iPad, the groans of simulated ecstasy continued unabated. Switching off the tablet, Xue placed it on the bedside table.

'I'm not going back,' the boy warned, finally locating his underpants.

*Tell it to your father.*

Slowly, insolently, Ren recovered his jeans and pulled them on. Xue was reaching for the door handle when a buzzer sounded. She froze.

After a few moments, the buzzer sounded again.

Composing herself, Xue stepped out into the hallway; Guo

was already there. The buzzer sounded for a third time. The major glared at Xue, as if it was her fault. 'Make them go away.'

Ordering the boy to stay in his room, Xue walked nervously down the corridor. Opening the front door, she was confronted by the crumpled officer from the police station. Trying to keep him from seeing the look of recognition in her eyes, she immediately turned her attention to his associate, a tall blonde woman. Very beautiful, Xue thought.

'Yes?'

The man held up his ID. 'Police.' He let her stare at it blankly for a few seconds before stuffing it back into his pocket. 'I am here to see Ren Qi,' he barked.

*How did you know his real name? And how did you know he was here?* Gripping the door tightly, Xue tried to think of a response.

'I am here to see Ren Qi,' the man repeated, speaking more slowly this time, in the time-honoured tradition of Englishmen addressing foreigners. Edging forward, he had his foot in the door before she could consider slamming it in his face.

Carlyle recognized the woman immediately. Up close, she looked even stronger and more imposing than he had imagined. Happily, she didn't have any cheese wire in her hand. Still, the inspector had little doubt that he was looking at a good thrashing, should things come to fisticuffs. His mind went back to Gerald Howard's dancing ninjas and he wondered if it might have been wiser to organize some back-up. He wished that he had Roche with him, but she had cried off, citing a 'hot date'. Could Elmhirst look after herself in a ruck?

*A bit late to be worrying about that now.*

Pushing his way inside, he barrelled down the corridor. The woman tried to stop him, but Elmhirst cut her off. On his left was a door. As he reached for the handle, the door flew open. Carlyle jumped back in surprise.

'Inspector,' Ren Qi smiled. 'Please, come in.'

Ignoring Elmhirst's disapproving look, the inspector accepted a large glass of fifteen-year-old Dalwhinnie and settled into an armchair on one side of the fireplace, the better to enjoy the oppressive atmosphere. Cradling a glass of his own, Ren Qi took the chair opposite. The woman who had opened the door – the killer ninja as Carlyle had come to think of her – had disappeared, leaving an older woman and a short, intense middle-aged man to complete the numbers in the room. No one was making any introductions, so Carlyle sat back and savoured a mouthful of his whisky.

Ren did the same, giving a sigh of appreciation as he waited for the policeman to declare his intentions.

'Why did you give me a false name?' Looking up from his drink, Carlyle gave his host a *not that it's any skin off my nose* smile.

'I have to apologize for that,' Ren said smoothly, determined to outdo his guest with the depth of his insincerity. 'A man of my position, finding himself in such an unusual and unfortunate situation . . .' He shrugged. 'I'm afraid to say that I simply panicked.'

Carlyle nodded.

'An error of judgement for which I am deeply sorry. Of course, I will accept the appropriate punishment without demur.'

'Don't worry about that, sir.' Carlyle waved away his host's concerned look before taking another taste of the single malt. The Dalwhinnie burned on the back of his throat and his brain began to feel pleasingly warm. 'I completely understand how your state of mind could have been negatively impacted by the events of the evening in question.' *The evening in question.* Hurrah for the petty bureaucrat. 'I would like to assure you that the Metropolitan Police have no interest in making an issue of such a minor matter.'

Nodding graciously, Ren waited patiently for him to get to the point.

'Indeed,' Carlyle went on, continuing his meandering preamble, 'if I had been on duty at the time, I would have had you released immediately. I can only apologize that that did not happen.'

'Thank you.'

'Which brings me to the reason for my visit.' Finishing his drink, Carlyle held out his glass for a refill. After a moment's hesitation, the squat lackey fetched the whisky bottle and carefully placed half an inch in the bottom of the glass. 'Thank you.' The man exchanged glances with Ren and retreated to his position by the door. 'I was wondering,' said Carlyle, slowly looking up from his drink, 'if you could talk me through your relationship with Michael Nicholson?'

A strangled groan came from the woman in the corner. Ren shot her an angry look and the lackey put a restraining hand on her shoulder. Happy to watch events unfold, Carlyle took another mouthful of whisky. He was beginning to feel its effects now and told himself to slow down. Two drinks were more than enough.

'I'm sorry,' Ren said finally, 'but I don't think I recognize the name.'

*Lies, lies, lies.* Stifling a yawn, the inspector went on. 'He ran a company called Tallow Business Services. I asked you about it before.'

For a few moments, Ren mimed a man considering the name. 'No, as I said at the police station, I don't think we've come across it.'

'His body was found not far from here.' Carlyle was deliberately stringing out the conversation, letting the man hang himself. Finishing the Scotch, he watched Ren glare at the lackey. The drink was really getting to him now. 'I was wondering,' he continued rashly, unable to resist a smirk, 'why you had him, and three other men, killed?' As he turned to give Elmhirst a wink, the room began to spin. Clinging to his seat, he tried to return his attention to Ren. The smiling face of the politician was moving in and out of focus. Carlyle felt his stomach heave in a sudden lurch. What the hell's going on? he wondered, irritated. I only had a couple of small ones. Lifting the glass, he noticed a line of fine white residue that had collected, just below the rim.

*Oh, bollocks.*

The glass slipped from his fingers and he pitched forward into darkness.

'I thought we were on a date.' Pushing away the half-eaten pizza on his plate, Oliver Steed scratched at his Coldplay T-shirt and stared sullenly into his beer.

'Oli,' Alison Roche said, exasperated, 'I'm old enough to be your mother.' She took another mouthful of the rather acidic house white and grimaced. 'Well, almost.'

'But I like older women,' the boy whined. 'It's my thing. Cougars and all that.'

'I am *not* a bloody cougar,' Roche snapped, her voice a bit too loud. An older couple at the next table broke off their own conversation and started grinning at the two supposed lovebirds. The sergeant gripped her glass tightly. Dinner had been a mistake. She should have gone with the inspector to check out the Chinese bigwig instead. An hour in the presence of this snivelling brat had yielded no useful information whatsoever. Under the table, she felt a sweaty hand on her knee. 'For God's sake,' she hissed, grabbing one of his fingers and pulling it sharply backwards, 'behave.'

'Ow.' The boy sat upright, rubbing his finger. 'What did you do that for?'

'You can't put your hands on me.' Leaning across the table, her voice was barely a whisper now. 'If you don't get a grip, I'll go and speak to your mum. Now, for the last time, explain to me why you didn't properly log Gerald Howard's video.'

Oli's eyebrows knitted together as he struggled to assemble the building blocks of a vaguely credible story. 'Who says I didn't?'

'I do,' Roche insisted. 'And if you don't explain to me what's going on, I will make a formal complaint. Your career will be toast before it's even started.' She felt uncomfortable bullying the boy like this, but it was for his own good. If he didn't learn now, he would come a cropper sooner rather than later.

Oli took a sip of his beer and stifled a small burp.

God, Roche thought, some poor girl is really going to luck out, pulling you.

'Craven told me to ignore it,' Steed said finally, fingering Inspector John Craven, SO15's second-in-command, sidekick to the boss, Chief Inspector Will Dick.

*Finally, we're making some progress.* 'Why?'

'Dunno.' Oli stared at the table. 'He just said, this was going on the back burner. Not a priority.' Looking up, he smiled maliciously. 'And he said that I wasn't to talk to you about it because you were a loose cannon who had a problem with authority.'

Keeping her anger in check, Roche glided over the personal slight. 'Presumably this order came from Dick himself?'

'Dunno.'

'Don't know much, do you?'

Stung by the barb, the boy retorted, 'I heard some gossip that the spooks had asked for the matter to be shelved in the interests of national security.'

*In the interests of national security, my arse*, Roche reflected. *In the interests of doing business with China, no doubt.* 'Is that it?'

'That's all I heard.' Finishing his beer, the boy stood up. 'I've told you everything I know, so I'm going to push off.' He grabbed his jacket and began weaving his way past the other diners, heading for the door. The couple at the next table gave Roche a sympathetic smirk as she watched him disappear out into the street. With a sigh of relief, the sergeant took a final sip of her wine and signalled for the bill.

\* \* \*

Slowly coming to his senses, Carlyle blinked twice and wiggled first his toes and then his fingers. Everything seemed to be in working order, more or less. He had a thumping headache but at least the room wasn't spinning.

They had left him where he fell. Laboriously getting to his feet, the inspector headed out into the hallway. Moving at a glacial pace, he went from room to room in order to confirm what he already knew: the Chinese were gone.

He glanced at his watch.

'They're probably on a plane somewhere over Germany by now,' he grumbled to himself.

He slowly realised that the throbbing in his head was being accompanied by a banging that was external to his skull. He tracked the noise to a large, spotless and apparently unused kitchen, where his gaze fell on a small wooden door in the far corner.

*'Hey. Open this bloody door!'* came a muffled voice.

Despite his condition, Carlyle managed to muster the feeblest of smiles. 'Hold on a sec.' Fortunately, they had left the key in the lock. Opening it, he took a step back as Amelia Elmhirst staggered out of the pantry.

'The buggers locked me up,' she scowled.

'I can see that.'

Looking Carlyle up and down, her face darkened even further. 'What the hell did you take that bloody drink for?' she thundered.

Holding up his hand, Carlyle signalled that he was not in the mood for an argument; especially when the sergeant was one hundred per cent in the right. Turning, he headed for the door.

'What do we do now?' Elmhirst asked, following after him.

'Go home. Try and get some sleep.' Carlyle stopped and waggled a weary finger at his colleague. 'I'll see you in the office tomorrow.'

'But—'

'And,' Carlyle talked over her, 'most importantly, not a word about this to anyone.'

# THIRTY-ONE

Werner Kortmann munched listlessly on a slice of pizza. 'I have never really liked Italian food,' he said, tossing the crust back into the box and closing the garishly coloured lid. The pizza firm had an address in a town he had never heard of and a phone number he had no way of dialling.

'My most sincere apologies,' said Sebastian Gregori, cranking up the sarcasm, 'but the choice was rather limited.' Grabbing a slice of his own pepperoni pizza, he wolfed it down in three speedy bites.

Kortmann washed the taste away with a mouthful of cola. 'I have never really liked the Italians at all. Too theatrical, all of them. Everything has to be a drama . . . even lunch.'

'Well, don't worry,' Gregori reassured him, 'you won't be going there any time soon.'

'Why is that?' Kortmann looked around the dirty room, feebly illuminated by a couple of battery-powered lamps, and shivered. The concrete floor was cold and damp; within hours of being moved here, he found himself thinking wistfully of the straw-filled cage that had been his previous home. Their current accommodation was another countryside retreat, on the ground floor of a shell of a house. Gregori had explained that the development, a ghost estate in the middle of nowhere, had been abandoned when the developer went bust after the financial crash and had never been completed.

Through the gloom, Kortmann looked his captor in the eye. 'Are you going to kill me?'

Gregori patted the gun that bulged in his jacket pocket. 'That depends.'

Kortmann rubbed his ankle. His leg had been chained to a metal hook embedded in a block of concrete abandoned in the middle of the room when the builders had left. The dull ache in his lower back never left him and he would have paid a fortune for a few hours in a clean, crisp bed. Catching a whiff of his own body odour, he recoiled. 'Depends on what?'

The other man said nothing.

'People will be looking for me.' Kortmann tried to ignore his aching bladder. The chain only allowed him the freedom to move about a metre in any direction, and the place smelled enough like a toilet already.

Munching on another slice of pizza, Gregori nodded. 'Let them look,' he said with his mouth full. 'Do you really think that useless English policeman will find you in this – or any other – lifetime?'

'He almost found you once,' Kortmann countered, recalling when he had been bundled away from the farmhouse, Gregori screaming like a madman about *'those damn cops'*.

'Pure chance.' Gregori spat a mouthful of pizza towards his captive, the semi-masticated ball of cheese, dough and sausage landing at Kortmann's feet. 'He'll never manage it again.'

Kortmann sighed. Unfortunately, he shared his captor's view of the lugubrious police inspector. As a boy, he had grown up believing that the British police were the best in the world. It had taken just two days in London to fully disabuse him of that notion. He tried to change tack. 'So, what is it that you want?'

'You'll see.' Wiping his hands on his jeans, Gregori stood up. 'In the meantime, you should just sit back and enjoy the show.' He stepped up to the pizza box and kicked it into the corner. 'Don't think of this as being in captivity. Think of it more as an immersive interactive experience.' He gestured around the room. 'This is an opportunity to experience what Uli Eichinger went through all those years ago. It's your chance to get closer to him.'

When he finally made it home, Carlyle was surprised to find Helen still awake. The moment he walked into the bedroom, she dropped her iPad onto the bed and eyed him coolly over the top of her reading glasses.

'Have you been drinking?'

'Not really,' Carlyle said tiredly, his head still thick from the Mickey Finn. Stripping off his shirt, he was looking forward to having a shower before clambering into bed. 'Tough day.'

Helen grunted something that he chose to interpret as an expression of sympathy.

Carlyle gestured at the tablet. 'What are you reading?'

'Some stuff from Cancer Research.' She shot him another challenging look. 'You haven't forgotten about your dad's MRI scan tomorrow?'

*Oh, bollocks.* 'No, no,' he lied hastily, kicking off his trousers.

'Good. I spoke to him today. I think he's a little bit nervous about it.'

'I'm not surprised,' Carlyle quipped. '*I'm* quite nervous about it myself.'

'So nervous that you forgot all about it.'

'I didn't—'

Cutting him off, Helen reached over and switched off her bedside light, leaving the room in the weak orange gloom created by the light pollution from the city outside. 'Remember to look after his wallet and his keys. Otherwise the magnet in the machine will knacker them.'

'OK.'

'Apparently the machine is very noisy. You'll be able to see the scanning room through a window. And be prepared – the whole thing can take up to an hour and a half.'

'Great,' Carlyle sighed. He wished that Helen would just do it for him but he kept his mouth firmly shut. It was, after all, his responsibility. 'At least we'll know what's going on.'

'You won't know there and then,' Helen pointed out. 'It'll take a couple of weeks for the results to come through.'

'Bloody hell,' Carlyle groused, 'what a palaver.'

'Just be grateful that it's not you having the scan.' Plumping up her pillows, she disappeared under the duvet. 'Your dad needs you.' Suitably dismissed, he retreated to the shower.

Ignoring the alarm clock, Carlyle stayed in bed, only surfacing when both Alice and Helen had left the flat. After a shave, and a further shower, he threw on some clothes and headed out. On the back of the front door, Helen had stuck a Post-it note on which she had scribbled *Don't forget the scan x.*

'Don't worry,' Carlyle grumbled, 'I won't bloody forget.'

Feeling the need for a little personal time in order to improve his mood, he took a leisurely stroll across Covent Garden, heading for work via a detour to a new café that had opened up on Maiden Lane the week before. Ordering a flat white and a large pastry, he took his time going through a copy of that morning's *Metro*. The royal baby had finally popped out while Carlyle had been out for the count on Ren Qi's carpet and bookies were now taking millions of pounds in bets on what the sprog would be called. 'At least Bernie will be pleased,' Carlyle muttered as he turned to the sports pages, 'now that there'll be more space again for his muck-raking.'

Finally arriving at Charing Cross, he was dismayed to find Simpson waiting for him on the third floor. Perched on Umar's desk, the Commander was deep in conversation with Amelia Elmhirst. As he approached, it was apparent that the sergeant was showing no ill-effects from her unfortunate detention the previous evening. Indeed, clear-eyed and freshly scrubbed, dressed in a pair of black jeans and a red leather jacket over a grey blouse, she looked very much her usual elegant self. By comparison, the

Commander, dressed in what Carlyle imagined to be a trouser suit from M&S, looked positively dowdy.

Turning to face the latecomer, the Commander appraised him coolly. 'Inspector,' she said satirically, 'how nice to see you.'

'Boss.' Trying to gauge the lie of the land, Carlyle glanced at Elmhirst, but the sergeant was giving nothing away.

'Heavy night?' the Commander asked.

Carlyle flopped into his chair.

'I hear that you were off on another of your little adventures last night.'

*Ah.* He glared at Elmhirst.

'Don't blame Amelia, John.'

*Amelia?* The Sisterhood was ganging up on him. He made to protest but thought better of it. Better just to take his bollocking and move on.

'I had a call from a Chief Inspector Will Dick at four-thirty this morning.'

*Who?*

'He's the Head of SO15,' Simpson explained, recognizing his blank look.

*Hm.* Carlyle made a mental note to give Roche a call asap.

'The man whose investigation you and Roche blundered into.'

*Not much of an investigation.*

'Causing the targets to up and leave the country on a private jet less than three hours after you confronted them.'

Carlyle frowned. 'If the SO15 bods knew we were in there, why didn't they come and get us out?'

'They doubtless had better things to worry about.'

'Thanks a lot,' Carlyle huffed. 'Anything could have happened to us.'

But the Commander was in no mood for tea and sympathy. 'It was your own fault,' she snapped. 'I thought I told you to prioritize the Germans?'

'Well . . .'

Simpson shook her head. 'If I had told you *not* to focus on the Germans, you would probably be spending your every waking hour chasing the Teutonic buggers down, wouldn't you? Maybe I should be trying a bit more reverse psychology.'

*Maybe you should just get to the point.* Leaning forward, he switched on his computer, listening to it splutter into action like an asthmatic pensioner. 'Is there something I can help you with, boss?'

'Yes, there is.'

'Good.' Sitting up in his chair, Carlyle tried to look suitably keen.

'We've had a possible sighting of Sebastian Gregori.' Reaching into her bag, she pulled out a scrap of paper and handed it to him. The inspector scanned the address. 'It's about thirty-five miles from where you ran into him last time. I want you two to go and check it out. Gapper is downstairs ready to go.' Slipping off the desk, the Commander allowed herself the tiniest of grins. 'He can play the responsible adult role.'

'Ha, bloody, ha.'

'Just make sure you don't get another sergeant shot.' Simpson gestured at Elmhirst. 'This one we need to keep. She's got a great future ahead of her.'

'OK, OK.' Getting to his feet, Carlyle ignored the blushing Elmhirst, glancing instead at his computer screen, which was still wheezing into life. The clock on the wall told him that he should really think about heading off. 'That's fine. We'll leave when I get back.'

A black look descended on Simpson's face; she looked like she wanted to reach out and strangle him. 'John.'

'Sorry,' he said, jogging towards the lifts, 'but there's something important I just have to do first.'

*Maybe we should have gone private.* It was amazing how everyone could love the NHS in abstract but when it came to actually using the bloody thing it turned out to be a total pain in the arse. Sitting on a bench in an empty corridor, Carlyle looked at his watch. 'For God's sake.' He gritted his teeth in disbelief. They had been there for the best part of three hours and now he was having to wait for his father to get changed back into his regular clothes before they could finally leave the hospital. 'How long can it take?'

As if on cue, the door opened and Alexander Carlyle appeared.

'There you are.' The old man said nothing, concentrating on adjusting his tie. What do you need a tie for? Carlyle thought sullenly.

Alex tightened and straightened his knot. 'Sorry.'

'C'mon,' said Carlyle, already bouncing down the corridor. 'Let's get going.'

'Yes,' Alex replied, following his son, 'After all that, I could do with a bite to eat.'

*Nooo.* The inspector was about to protest, but caught himself in time. He imagined Helen giving him hell for not looking after his dad properly. 'Sure,' he said dully, 'good idea.'

Leaving the hospital at a brisk pace, they found a café a hundred yards down the road. Alexander took a seat at a window table while Carlyle went and ordered. Fifteen minutes later, he watched the old man shovel the last of his egg and chips into his mouth, washing it down with a swig from a large mug of builder's tea.

At least he hasn't lost his bloody appetite, Carlyle thought.

Alexander carefully placed his knife and fork together on the empty plate and sat back in his chair. 'I needed that. It's the first thing I've had to eat today.' He cast a covetous eye towards the selection of cakes lined up on the counter. 'They starve you before the scan, you know.'

'Yeah, Helen told me.' Carlyle sipped at a bottle of carbonated water, feeling virtuous.

Still looking at the counter, Alex took another slurp of

his tea. 'I think I might have one of those doughnuts. Want one?'

'Why not?' Getting to his feet, Carlyle asked the girl at the till for a couple of doughnuts and a black coffee for himself.

Returning to the table, he placed the food down and took a mouthful of his coffee. 'Urgh.' It was truly terrible, but he knew that it would complement the sugar rush well enough. Grabbing his doughnut, he took a large bite and watched his father do the same. For several minutes, they ate together in companionable silence.

All too soon, the doughnut was nothing but a guilty memory. Carlyle was wiping the crumbs from the corner of his mouth when his phone started ringing in his pocket. With some reluctance, he pulled it out and looked at the screen. *SIMPSON*. With a grimace, he dropped the handset back into his pocket.

'Don't you need to get that?' Alexander asked through a mouthful of saturated fat.

Finishing his coffee, Carlyle shook his head. 'It can wait.'

'I suppose you'll need to be getting back to work.' Gazing out of the window, Alex tracked the progress of a well-fed young baby as it made its way backwards down the street strapped to the chest of its exhausted-looking mother.

'Yes.' Carlyle made a determined attempt to study his father's face. The old bugger looked in decent shape, all things considering. 'How are you feeling?'

'Fine,' Alex said, 'that food's set me up nicely.'

'No, you know what I mean.' Even though no one else in the café was remotely interested in their conversation, he lowered his voice. 'How do you feel in general?'

'*Ach*.' Folding his arms, Alex did his best Grandpa Broon impersonation. 'I'm fine, son. More or less.'

Feeling Helen's presence at his shoulder, Carlyle continued to press. 'But are you worried about . . . you know?'

'Look,' leaning forward, Alexander smiled at his son, 'it's going to be bad news. There's no two ways around it.'

'You don't know that,' Carlyle said stiffly.

'Son,' Alex gestured back down the road, in the direction of the hospital, 'we wouldn't have been in there for all that time if they didn't think there was something wrong.' He clutched Carlyle's hand. The inspector was so surprised that he had to stop himself from pulling it away. 'Something *seriously* wrong.'

'And I thought *I* was the pessimist.' He tried to make it sound like a joke but the words crumbled as they came out of his mouth. The doughnut was settling in his stomach and he felt a little sick.

Alexander patted his hand. 'Don't worry, we'll deal with it.'

'Scottish grit.'

'Aye.' A flicker of amusement appeared in the old man's eyes. 'This is one of those times when some good old Presbyterian stoicism comes in useful.'

'I suppose so.'

'I'm just glad your mother isn't here to see this,' Alex chuckled. 'Could you imagine the fuss she'd make?'

Carlyle nodded. His late mother had always been very intolerant of anything that smacked of weakness. 'She'd be giving us both a kick up the backside right now.'

'That's one thing we don't have to worry about, at least.'

'Yes.'

'I have to say though, I'm very grateful for all your help and support, son.'

What support? Carlyle wondered guiltily. In his head, he could hear Helen laughing. 'Me? I've done nothing.'

'Just being there, son. Just being there. It means a lot.'

'Good,' was all he could think of to say by way of reply.

'A lot of people, they'd run a mile.'

'Hm.'

'I feel a lot better knowing that you are with me on this. Every step of the way.'

'Of course.'

'So now, we just have to get on with it, one thing at a time. No need to panic. Let's just wait and see what the results say.'

'OK.' Clearing the lump in his throat, Carlyle tried to smile. 'That sounds like a plan.'

'It's the only one we've got.'

'That's right,' he gave his father's hand a squeeze. 'I suppose it is.'

'You're a good lad,' Alexander smiled. 'But then you always were.'

# THIRTY-TWO

It was as if he was on a runaway train that would never stop until it crashed into the buffers at the end of the line, killing everyone on board. The fact that he had been sitting in a first-class compartment all the way would not save him. How could he get off the train? How could he jump to safety?

Ren Qi sipped his orange juice and stepped out on to the terrace. Under the shimmering blue sky, the Mediterranean stretched out in front of him. Reaching for the expensive sunglasses on the top of his head, he slipped them on. A private jet, just taken off from the airport at Mandelieu, was making a steady ascent, heading east, the vapour trail showing its serene progress. Lowering his gaze to sea level, he counted three, four, five superyachts lazily making their way towards St Tropez for lunch. On shore, off to his right, the ordinary people of Cannes went about their desultory business.

Ren wondered about the wisdom of operating his retirement fund out of grey, dreary London. No one in their right mind would set up their operations in France, especially not with the current President in situ, but Monaco was just down the road and, well, there were many quality of life issues to consider.

Trying to focus on the matter in hand, he ran through the events of the last thirty-six hours. Leaving the drugged policeman in the apartment, they had driven from London to Manston airport in Kent. From there, a private jet had taken them to Milan. After an extended argument, Wang Lei and Ren Junior had been placed on a commercial flight from Malpensa to China, accompanied by Guo Miao. The major would have several colleagues meet them on arrival at Beijing International airport. Wife and son would then be whisked off to effective house arrest at a discreet location until Ren Senior had decided how best to stop the pair of them damaging his political career any further.

Ren fretted over his decision to send them home. After all, what kind of man effectively kidnaps his wife and son? On the other hand, leaving them to their own devices in England was not a realistic option. How could a man unable to rule his own family ever hope to rule his country?

Getting them back to China, however, was the easy bit. What to do with them once they were repatriated would be far less straightforward. Ren knew that he needed time and space to come up with a sustainable plan for his unruly family, as well as a strategy for restoring his political fortunes. Fortunately, he had the perfect place where he could hunker down and clear his mind.

The Chemin des Collines villa had been a 'thank you' from a business associate following the completion of an extremely lucrative business deal. The property, done out in what the locals on the Côte d'Azur liked to call the 'English style', was worth something like €25 million. If things were to go badly for him back home, this place would doubtless feature prominently in any show trial cooked up by the Politburo.

For the hundredth time in the last week, Ren tried to calculate the chances of that doomsday scenario coming to pass. As always, the conclusion was simply that there was no way of knowing. The longer he spent out of the country, the less attuned his political antennae became. And yet something deep in his gut warned him not to go back. After the debacle of his London trip, Ren knew that he was more vulnerable than ever.

He was distracted from his thoughts by the vibration of

his mobile phone. Pulling it from the pocket of his shorts, he glanced at the screen and groaned. Baldwin-Lee. Another desperate plea for cash, no doubt. He should never have given his number to the wretched club-owner. Despite everything, Ren had to smile. According to his London accountant, the Racetrack was still losing cash at a steady rate. The expectation was that its investors would lose patience and pull the plug in less than a year – maybe even nine months. At that point, the place could probably be snapped up for something less than a third of the price of the debt. That would be the time to step in.

Always assuming that he wasn't languishing in jail by then.

The phone kept vibrating. Raising his arm, Ren threw it into the swimming pool.

'Hey,' said an amused voice. 'Watch what you're doing. That nearly hit me.'

Ren observed the girl pull herself out of the water. It took him a moment to recall her name: Cordelia. Drops of the heavily chlorinated water exploded across the concrete, evaporating almost immediately in the glare of the sun. Slowly, he let his gaze move up her naked body, taking in the smooth tan, no lines, no hint of a blemish of any sort. Perfection. Knowing what he liked, Madame Lee at the Golden Chrysanthemum, his preferred agency in these parts, had chosen well. Then again, she always did. Along with everything else, the prostitutes here were several notches above their London counterparts. *Quality of life issues.*

Hands on hips, she looked at him provocatively. 'Do you want to party now?'

*Yes*, said his head. *No*, his groin responded dolefully. Ren glanced at his shorts. The stress is getting to me, he thought. I can't even get it up any more. Wang Lei would laugh her head off if she knew how limp my dick was right now.

'I've got some Viagra,' Cordelia offered, sensing his despair. Walking past him, she plucked a towel from the sun-lounger and began drying her coal-black hair. 'That will solve any problems, guaranteed.'

A fifteen-second snatch of Beethoven's *Moonlight Sonata* echoed throughout the house. Ren sighed. Someone was at the door. The housekeeper would be at the market, choosing some fish for dinner. He watched as Cordelia began running the towel across her stomach, feeling the faintest stirrings of his own as she did so. *Maybe I won't need the Viagra, after all.*

The bell rang again. Still drying herself off, Cordelia looked at him expectantly. 'It looks like they want you to go and answer it,' she smiled.

'Yes.'

She gave him one of her trademark dirty grins. 'Do you want me to go? I could give them quite a surprise.'

'No, no,' Ren sighed. 'You stay here. I'll go.'

Striding into the hall, he stopped to check the rather obtrusive CCTV monitor that had been installed by the previous owner, a waif-like Russian singer who, in best rock star tradition, had been found one morning face down in the pool. Standing at the door was a familiar figure. Xue Xi stood tall and erect, eyes front, paying no heed to the watchful eye of the CCTV camera above the door. Ren frowned. He had assumed that Xue would have taken the flight back to Beijing with his family and Guo Miao. Presumably Guo had decided that she should stay behind, on the basis that his boss required some close protection capability while ensconced in his French haven. Ren's frown slowly morphed into a smile. Sometimes Guo's paranoia knew no bounds. That was one of his many positive attributes.

Even with the crappy resolution of the security camera image, the woman cut an impressive figure. His mind drifted off to thoughts of Xue, frolicking by the pool with Cordelia, and there was a definite twitch in his shorts. His smile grew wider.

His mood was spoiled by the appearance of a second woman, one whom he didn't recognize. She glared at the

261

camera with the stone-faced expression that had been patented by the MSS. It was as if she knew he was watching her at that very moment. After a few seconds, the woman ducked out of shot and, once again, he had to endure another short burst of Beethoven. Ren threw back his shoulders and took a couple of deep breaths. If the Ministry of State Security wanted to spy on him, that was fine; however, there were limits. He would be having strong words with Guo Miao about this. And, if these two overstepped the mark, he would have them immediately redeployed to Tibet, where they could eke out the remainder of their so-called careers dealing with self-immolating monks and other enemies of the state. 'Remember who you are,' he told himself. 'You are one of the most powerful men in the country. Act like it.'

Striding through the hallway, he pulled open the heavy door and stood in front of the two women, focusing his attention on the creature standing next to Xue Xi. Barely five feet tall, the unknown woman wore her hair short and had a deeply lined, tanned face. Ren tried to put an age on her but it was impossible; the woman could have been anything between fifty and seventy-five.

Meeting his gaze, she made no attempt to hide her contempt.

'Ren Qi, I am Commissar Zhou Xiaolan of the MSS.' She tapped the breast pocket of her tunic. 'I have papers here authorizing your arrest and immediate repatriation to the People's Republic.'

*So soon?* Stifling his surprise, Ren glanced at Xue but the young officer simply stared off into the middle distance. Sweat began beading on his brow and he pushed his sunglasses back up to the bridge of his nose.

Zhou gestured down the driveway, towards a black limousine waiting by the front gate. 'You must come with us.'

Ren's stomach did a somersault. *Remember who you are!* his brain screamed. Taking a step forward, he thrust out a hand. 'Show me the warrant.'

Moving slowly and mechanically, Zhou did as requested. 'It is all perfectly legal,' she intoned, 'having been drafted by the proper authorities, in line with the relevant legal statutes.'

*Spare me the window-dressing.* Slowly, Ren unfolded the sheet of thin paper. Under the stamp of the Judicial Affairs Department of the Supreme People's Court was a list of the charges against him: graft, bribery, abuse of power. If nothing else, his colleagues were predictable to the last.

Ren thought of Cordelia drying herself by the pool. Suddenly, he felt a vigorous erection in his shorts. He smiled.

'What's so funny?' Zhou demanded.

Ren glanced again at the inscrutable Xue. 'You would not understand.'

Zhou folded her arms. 'No?' This was the part of the job she liked the best – denial; when the guilty still thought that there could possibly be some way out, some means of escape from the firing squad or the prison cell.

'No.' Ren tore up the paper and the scraps fell at his feet. 'I will not go.'

*Quality of life.*

The Commissar was unmoved. 'I'm afraid, Ren Qi, that you have no choice in the matter. The court has issued the warrant. You must come with us.'

'There is always a choice.' Ren gestured over his shoulder. Whatever crimes he had had to commit, in order to get his mansion, whatever misdeeds had been required, in order to install his €1,500-an-hour German escort by the pool, they had all been worth it. 'Look around you,' he said, the pride clear in his voice. 'Look at what I have here. Why would I go back?'

'Because,' said Zhou slowly, 'as I said, you have no choice.' She watched impassively as Xue administered a swift kick to Ren's groin, sending the politician sinking to his knees.

'I . . . will . . . not . . . go.' Through tear-filled eyes, Ren watched as the young MSS killer stepped forward and placed a boot on his chest. A gentle push sent him sprawling backwards.

Fighting for breath, Ren could only look up at the blue sky and repeat his desperate mantra. 'I . . . will . . . not . . .'

A shadow passed across his face as Xue Xi hovered over him. In her hand was a hypodermic needle. Effortlessly, she found a vein and pushed down on the plunger. Almost immediately, the sky began to darken.

Quality of life, Ren thought dreamily. Quality of life.

# THIRTY-THREE

Walking along Maiden Lane, on the south side of the Piazza, Carlyle watched a rickshaw driver pull his vehicle up on to the pavement and take a small prayer mat from under the front seat. On the side of the dirty vehicle was an advert for a strip club called Everton's which had recently been closed down by the council. Umar's wife, Christina, had worked there; that was where the two of them had first met. With some embarrassment, the inspector realized that he had yet to enquire about his colleague's recovery from the unfortunate gunshot wound inflicted by Sebastian Gregori. Pausing to reach for his mobile, he pulled up Umar's number, then thought better of it.

Putting the phone back in his pocket, he watched as the rickshaw driver carefully placed his mat on the pavement. The guy, a spotty-looking white boy with a fine coating of bum fluff on his chin, dropped to his knees and began rocking gently backwards and forwards. Carlyle watched, bemused, as a steady stream of pedestrians stepped off the pavement and into the road, giving the boy sufficient space to continue with his prayers undisturbed. Aside from one woman who did a theatrical double take, no one seemed perturbed in the slightest.

Watching this performance, Carlyle calculated that the boy was praying towards Waterloo Bridge. Is that really the direction of Mecca? he wondered, as he continued on his way.

Approaching the police station, he was intercepted by Amelia

Elmhirst. 'Where have you been?' the sergeant demanded, grabbing his arm and marching them both off in the direction of Chandos Place. 'Commander Simpson has been calling me every ten minutes demanding to know why we haven't left on our hunt for Gregori yet. She says you've not been answering your phone.'

'I had stuff to attend to.' The inspector did not feel the need to share the details of his father's medical adventures with his colleague. Apart from anything else, the hospital visit seemed already to have been relegated to a distant memory. It was barely forty minutes since he had said goodbye to Alexander but, arriving back in Covent Garden, Carlyle had immediately been swallowed up by the relentless energy of the city and transported to a totally different world.

'That's what I told her. She didn't sound very impressed.'

*Tough.* Carlyle looked at his watch. He wanted to go home, pour himself a stiff drink and watch some football on the TV.

That's what he wanted to do.

'We're going to get caught in the rush hour,' Elmhirst said grimly.

'It's always the rush hour,' Carlyle pointed out. Why anyone tried to go anywhere by car in London was beyond him; it was the constant triumph of stupidity over bitter experience.

Slipping through a side door, Elmhirst led him into the cramped police garage. 'C'mon, Joel's waiting for us.' Once in the courtyard, the inspector was dismayed to find that Gapper was sitting behind the wheel of the same crappy green Astra that they'd been given last time. Through the open window came the sounds of some over-strenuous rap song that he didn't recognize.

'Turn that crap off,' Carlyle ordered, pulling open the door and climbing into the back seat. If nothing else, however, the music reminded him of his business with Mr Chase Race. Helen had yet to come good on her promise to set up a meeting. He sent a quick text, chivvying her along, before turning his attention back to the vehicle's various shortcomings: 'Is this the only bloody car we can get?'

' 'fraid so,' Gapper shrugged. He pointed to the sat nav that had been installed on the dashboard since their last adventure. 'At least they've given us that.'

'Great. Not exactly the bloody Sweeney, is it?'

Looking in the rear-view mirror, Gapper gave him a mystified look.

'Never mind.'

'Look on the bright side,' said Elmhirst cheerily in the front seat, as she pulled on her seatbelt. 'At least we'll blend in with the locals.'

'I don't want to blend in,' the inspector growled as Gapper slowly edged out of the garage, heading towards Charing Cross Road.

'It'll be fine,' Elmhirst chirped.

Her good humour was starting to grate. Carlyle wished he had Roche, or even Umar, joining him on the trip. He rested his head on the window and closed his eyes. If nothing else, at least he could catch up on his rest while they headed back to the provinces.

In the event, the inspector found it impossible to sleep in the back of the car. Inevitably, the traffic was appalling and it was almost an hour before they had made it past Archway. Feeling a little sick, he opened the window a couple of inches, in order to let in some fresh fumes. Seeing that he was awake, Elmhirst passed a thin A4 manila envelope over her shoulder.

'What's this?' he asked suspiciously.

'My homework,' she smirked. 'What I was busy finding out while you were AWOL.'

'I wasn't AWOL,' Carlyle groused. Tearing open the envelope, he pulled out an A5 black and white photograph and two sheets of A4 paper, photocopies of some kind of official forms, written in German. He held up the picture. The headshot was maybe ten or even more years old, the face had fewer lines and the hair was longer, but it was immediately identifiable.

'Sebastian Gregori.'

Elmhirst shook her head. 'No.'

'No?'

'That is the guy who *pretended* to be Gregori. His actual name is Marcus Popp. The real Gregori is still in Port Elizabeth. When his boss got hold of him last night, he was completely unaware that Popp had stolen his identity.'

'So who is Popp? Why is he playing this game? And how did you manage to identify him?'

'The German police made the ID.' The sergeant's grin grew wider. 'He was caught on CCTV getting on a flight to London with Kortmann. He was on some kind of a watchlist.'

'Obviously a very effective one, if no one actually stopped him.'

Elmhirst shrugged. 'These things happen. Not everyone gets stopped all the time, even if they do get flagged. Popp travelled to London on his own passport. Not that Werner Kortmann knew that. He would have thought Popp was Gregori.'

'One thing at a time.' Carlyle held up a hand. It was all getting very complicated. He wanted to line up all the bits of information and see if they added up to a vaguely coherent story. 'Why was Mr Popp on a watchlist?'

'Marcus has been a person of interest to the police for a long time. Abandoned by his mother as a baby, he was in and out of care homes until he was adopted by the Popp family when he was nine. Hats off to them, they stuck at it, although he was a difficult child. First arrest at eleven, for shoplifting, then a string of petty crimes; he crashed a stolen car when he was thirteen.'

'So far, so boring,' Carlyle yawned.

'He was bright though. Ended up going to university in Berlin. Became a student activist, racked up another four convictions, including one for arson and one for GBH. Then he dropped out of sight. I spoke to the Berlin police. They were surprised he had turned up in London.'

'So why did he hoodwink poor old Kortmann and pretend to be a private eye?'

'Because,' Elmhirst said triumphantly, finally playing her joker, 'he wants to find his mother – Sylvia Tosches.'

Carlyle slumped back in his seat. 'You are kidding me.'

'No.' The sergeant reached into her bag and pulled out a bright red apple. 'That's what the papers in the envelope say.'

The inspector lifted one of the closely typed forms to his face. It was still in German. He was still none the wiser.

'He's looking for his mum,' Elmhirst repeated.

'His mum the terrorist,' Carlyle said.

'She's still his mother.'

'OK, so he's looking for his dear old ma. The question is, why?'

'Because he's her son.' Taking a large bite out of the apple, the sergeant watched the Astra get overtaken by a minibus full of football fans. Clocking Elmhirst, they treated her to a series of obscene gestures as they edged past in the outside lane. As they pulled in front of the Astra, she flipped them the finger and was rewarded by an unflinching view of the chalky cheeks of one of the fat bastards in the back row. Elmhirst and Gapper giggled in unison, much to the inspector's irritation.

'For Pete's sake.' He felt like a schoolteacher on a fifth-form school trip.

Letting the minibus accelerate way from them, Gapper kept his eyes on the road. Elmhirst took another bite of her apple. 'People are funny when it comes to these type of things. Maybe he wants a tearful reunion or something?'

'He's not making much of a job of it, anyway.'

Devouring the apple core, Elmhirst dropped the stalk back into her bag. 'What's happened to the woman, by the way – the one that Kortmann thought was really Tosches?'

'Barbara Hutton?' Carlyle sniffed. 'There's still no sign of her or her husband.' Conscious that his 'to do' list was getting ever longer, he made a mental note to check in with the daughter when they got back to London. 'They'll turn up.'

'In Paraguay,' Elmhirst ventured. 'In twenty years' time, or something.'

'That was the Nazis, who fled to Latin America,' Carlyle corrected her. 'Tosches was a leftie.'

She rolled her eyes. 'You know what I mean.'

Not really, he thought coolly. Turning his attention to Gapper, he gestured at the road in front of them. 'How far away are we from this place, Joel?'

The driver looked at the sat nav. 'Should be about another forty minutes, I reckon.'

Elmhirst looked round at him expectantly. 'So what's the plan when we get there, boss?'

Good question, Carlyle thought, saying aloud: 'I'm working on it.'

# THIRTY-FOUR

Letting the car coast to a halt at the side of the road, Gapper switched off the headlights. For several moments, the three of them sat in silence.

'Is this it?' Carlyle stared out into the darkness. 'There's nothing here.'

The driver gestured down the single-lane road and into the night. 'According to the sat nav, it is 750 metres further on.'

'What is?' the inspector asked with a sense of foreboding. He'd had more than his fill of pastoral adventures the last time around.

'It's a housing development called Voisin Towers,' Elmhirst explained.

'But it's in the middle of nowhere,' Carlyle argued. 'You can even see the stars in the sky.'

'It was supposed to be elegant living for commuters,' the sergeant continued, 'a proposed total of 350 units – 230 flats and 120 houses – at prices of up to £1.8 million.'

'Nearly two million quid? Out here?' Carlyle made a disgusted sound. 'Bloody hell, those are almost London prices.'

'You know what it's like with the housing market,' Elmhirst said. 'Everyone talks it up and up – and then it crashes.'

'Yeah, I suppose so.' Carlyle gave silent thanks to his late father-in-law, who had conveniently keeled over, leaving Helen a small but cosy ex-council flat in Covent Garden. If it wasn't for that, they would have probably ended up living miles away from the centre of the city.

'The developer went bust in the crash. One day, everyone was working away as normal and the next they just never came back. The place is owned by a consortium of banks. It was number six on a list of the top fifty worst speculative developments in the UK. No one thinks it will ever be finished. The council is trying to get it demolished and returned to green fields, but the banks don't want to pay the twenty million that it is expected to cost. The whole thing is a bit of a mess, really.'

'You don't say. But how did they get planning permission in the first place? Aren't they supposed to protect the Green Belt from this sort of thing?'

'There's an investigation into that, apparently. The local paper ran a campaign.' Releasing her seatbelt, Elmhirst opened the door and got out of the car, while the inspector struggled out of the back of the Astra. Gapper, who seemed perfectly happy to stay behind the wheel, did not move.

Dressed in a pair of skinny jeans, black Converse All Stars and a black leather biker's jacket at least two sizes too big for her, the sergeant looked like one of the cool teenagers on the way to the village disco. Stuffing her hand in her pockets, she set off along the gentle incline. The inspector, definitely not one of the cool kids, lagged a respectful distance behind.

After a couple of minutes, Elmhirst came to a stop. Once Carlyle had caught up, she pointed at the vaguest of shapes in the distance. Squinting, the inspector could make out a feeble splash of light coming from one of them.

'That's Voisin Towers,' she told him. 'Kortmann's credit card was used yesterday at a petrol station three miles down the road. The CCTV shows that it was used by Gregori, aka Popp.'

'Not very clever,' Carlyle murmured, his mind already focusing on the shoeing that was going to be coming Marcus Popp's way once he caught up with him.

'He's obviously under a lot of stress.'

'We're all under a lot of stress.' He glanced back at the Astra. Gapper was happily ensconced inside, eating a Mars Bar and reading a newspaper; *he* didn't look like he was under any stress at all.

'With his mum and everything,' Elmhirst ventured, 'Marcus is under more stress than most.'

'We don't even know if she *is* his mum,' Carlyle reminded her. 'In fact, the more I understand about *both* of these two comedians, Popp and Kortmann, the less likely I am to believe anything that comes out of their respective mouths. I'm coming to the conclusion that poor old Barbara Hutton is nothing more than a posh Bloomsbury housewife with a rather unappealing husband.'

'But we have to confirm that.'

'Yes, we have to confirm that.' Fumbling in his jacket pocket, Carlyle pulled out his glasses, slipped them on and scanned the horizon. Quickly deciding that the glasses weren't helping him see any better, he put them back in his pocket. 'So, to recap, Popp used the credit card not far from here.'

'We got a copy of the receipt for his shopping: battery-operated lamps, blankets, a gas stove – like he was going camping or something.'

Once again, Carlyle peered into the distance. 'Which brought us to this place.'

'Which brought us to this place,' she echoed.

'Because it's not as if there are any other places they could go camping.'

'He doesn't have a tent,' Elmhirst said. 'At least, not as far as we know.'

'Jesus. It's all a bit thin.'

'Simpson was very keen that we check it out,' Elmhirst told him.

'Yes, she was, wasn't she? Very keen indeed.'

'Maybe she knows something that we don't.'

'Perhaps. But that's not really her style. The Commander is usually quite open. In my experience, she is very much a team player.'

Elmhirst grinned. 'You like her, don't you?'

'We work well together,' was all Carlyle would concede before he resumed his stroll down the road. 'For whatever reason, she wants the place checked out, so I suppose we'd better go down there and get on with it.'

The two of them approached the ghost estate at a gentle pace, each lost in their own thoughts. For no apparent reason, Carlyle's mind had turned to thoughts of 1980s music in general and Echo & the Bunnymen in particular. The chorus of 'Villiers Terrace' started playing on a loop in his head, growing in intensity with each repetition until he finally expelled it. Good band, he thought. They should have been more successful than they were. He wondered if, like everyone else, they had re-formed in recent years, to try and make some money on the nostalgia circuit. He vowed to find out; maybe he could persuade Alice to go to a gig with him.

By the time they passed a sign warning trespassers that they would be prosecuted, the inspector realized that he had long since lost sight of the flickering light that had been apparent when they had first left the car. From behind an overgrown hedge, the partially built properties stood in sullen silence, illuminated only by the light of a half-moon. Carlyle came to a halt at the main entrance, trying to gauge the size of the overall site. How long will it take me to search this place? he wondered. With the possibility of another debacle looming large, he glanced at the sergeant.

'A hundred and something acres,' Elmhirst said, reading his mind.

None the wiser, Carlyle nodded. 'You wait here and I'll go and see what I can find.'

'That's a lot of ground for one person to cover.'

Carlyle grinned. 'I don't want us *both* to get lost.'

'OK,' the sergeant nodded. 'Don't be too long though.'

'If I'm not back in an hour, go and get Gapper.'

'Will do.'

'And remember, if things get out of hand again and there's a problem you two can't deal with, your first call is to Simpson. Leave the local plod out of this. They don't even know we're here.' Registering her confused look, he added, 'We're not exactly playing this one by the book, are we?'

'I suppose not.'

'So let's try and get in and out without anyone noticing.'

'Yep.'

'Good . . .' he was just about to say *girl*, then thought better of it. No need to make his dinosaur tendencies any more apparent than was absolutely necessary. It was just that she was so terribly young; it brought out the worst in him in so many ways.

The sergeant looked at him solemnly, as if anticipating further pearls of wisdom.

'Remember,' the inspector joked, keen not to disappoint, 'this is the *how not to do it* module of your training.'

'I realize that,' Elmhirst smiled patronizingly. 'In fact, I think that's one of the main reasons why Commander Simpson sent me to work with you in the first place.'

'What?' said Carlyle, suddenly affronted. 'So that I could show you how to mess things up?'

'No, no,' she corrected him, 'more to show me that there is still some leeway for independent action by mid-ranking officers within the often confusing and sometimes conflicting parameters set down by the organization for choosing a particular course of action in different circumstances.'

Bamboozled by the gobbledygook, he frowned. 'Eh?'

'I think the Commander wants me to understand that you can't always hide behind the rule book and Health & Safety. Sometimes you have to simply trust your own judgement.'

'Amen to that,' said Carlyle, somewhat mollified by her simpler explanation.

'The Commander described you as "flexible, if occasionally reckless".'

*We-ell.* 'I'll take that as a compliment.'

'That's up to you.' Reaching forward, she placed a hand on his shoulder, making him jump. 'Just remember, however, that this is not the time to be reckless. Apart from everything else, we have to assume that Marcus Popp is armed.'

'But not very dangerous,' Carlyle quipped.

'That sounds like reckless talk to me. He's got a weapon, for heaven's sake.'

'I'm not worried about that,' Carlyle responded, stepping smartly away from her grasp. 'The gun is not going to be a factor here.'

'You don't know that,' she scolded.

'Look,' he gestured towards the rotting buildings behind him, 'if the two of them *are* holed up in this place, it really is game over. If he's sitting here, with no idea about what to do with Kortmann, Popp has basically run out of ideas – assuming he ever had any in the first place.'

'That's a bit of an assumption.'

'Always assume,' Carlyle retorted. 'You've always got to take an informed view, based on your experience. That's what we're paid to do, after all.'

'I suppose so.'

'Standing here, right now, we have to ask certain questions. What the hell's Popp doing way out here? What's that got to do with finding his mother? What does he want to do next?' Elmhirst started to say something, but he cut her off. 'The answer to each of the above is "nothing". If he didn't have a screw loose at the start of this whole escapade, he's certainly got one loose now. Sitting on the damp concrete, worrying about his piles, he's just waiting to be caught.'

'That's a *lot* of assumptions.'

'That's what being *flexible* is all about.'

'And if they're not here?'

'If they're not, we go home and I'll have a moan at Simpson in the morning.'

Hands on hips, Elmhirst changed tack. 'Maybe you should have brought a gun.'

The inspector was adamant. 'I don't like guns. Anyway, I'm not authorized to carry one. I've never shot a gun in my life.' If those first two statements were true, the last was an outright lie. Carlyle knew only too well what it felt like to pull the trigger with the blood pounding in his ears. But that was another time, another place; an operation that was so far *off piste* that none of his colleagues in the Met could ever know about it.

Elmhirst gave him a funny look.

'I know, I know. I'm a total dinosaur in so many ways. But look at it like this: Gregori, or Popp, whatever his name is, he could have killed Umar and me back at that farmhouse if he had wanted to. He has no intention of killing a cop.'

'Another assumption.'

'Another *reasonable* assumption.'

Clearly not convinced, Elmhirst pondered different scenarios. 'Even if that's right, he could always shoot Kortmann . . . or himself.'

'He won't shoot Kortmann,' Carlyle insisted. 'He needs him – or at least, he thinks he does. He's trying to find his mum, remember?'

'I just hope that you're right.'

'I'm always right,' Carlyle chuckled. 'That's how I made it to Inspector.'

The sergeant failed to look impressed. 'What if he shoots himself though?'

'That's not going to help him find his mum, is it?'

'No, but he could do something stupid.'

'Just for a change.'

'You know what I mean.'

'Well,' the inspector sniffed, 'if he does do something stupid, he won't get any complaints from me.'

Elmhirst gave a despairing sigh. 'Just be careful.'

'I'm always careful.'

As he stepped across the muddy entrance, Carlyle's foot brushed against something metallic. Looking down, he saw that it was a length of half-inch pipe. Picking it up, he weighed it in his hand. It felt good. What was the saying? *Speak softly and carry a big stick.* That seemed as good a plan as any. Waving at Elmhirst with the pipe, he continued on his way.

# THIRTY-FIVE

After five minutes of walking at a steady pace, Carlyle had completely lost his bearings. All of the plots on the abandoned development looked the same – square boxes squashed together, with barely enough space in between them to park a small family saloon. The only apparent difference was how far work had progressed on each unit. By the time the whole endeavour had come to a grinding halt, some were little more than a set of foundations, while others were almost a complete shell, with walls on both the ground and first floors. One or two even had the beginnings of a roof, a wooden skeleton waiting for tiles that would never be laid.

The main road through the estate went in a circle, with groups of eight or ten houses set on a series of cul-de-sacs, spokes leading off from the hub. In the centre of the development was a long, featureless building, three storeys high. Those must be the flats, Carlyle presumed. Stopping for a moment, to try and better get his bearings, he looked around. The place was completely dark, with no signs of activity. A gust of wind whistled down the road, making him shiver. Regardless of the time of year, it was cold at night. Moreover, the inspector was dressed for the city, rather than the countryside. His jacket was thin and offered little warmth.

Cursing to himself, Carlyle continued his slog round the site. After a couple of minutes largely spent trying not to fall into a series of large potholes, he caught a glimpse of a weak gleam coming from the ground floor of a property around 100 yards to his right.

An owl hooted in the darkness and he almost jumped out of his skin.

'Get a grip, you idiot.' After waiting for his heart rate to return to normal, he glanced at his watch. He had already been creeping round this place for more than half an hour. 'Get on with it,' he mumbled to himself, tightly gripping the salvaged length of pipe. 'You don't want Gapper to have to rescue you again.'

Cautiously approaching his target, the inspector saw that the light was coming from an empty window on the ground floor, gently illuminating the breezeblocks that formed the unfinished interior wall. As with its neighbours, the front of the property consisted of an area of deeply churned-up mud. Tiptoeing across this no man's land, the inspector crouched below the empty window, listening for any evidence of human activity inside.

The owl hooted again.

*Shut it.*

Holding his breath, he tried to block out extraneous distractions. A few moments later, proof of life from inside the house came in the unmistakable form of a loud, extended fart. This was followed by a second, much shorter expulsion of wind.

The inspector resumed breathing, counted to ten and then slowly edged to the side of the window, before taking a peek inside.

*Well, bugger me.* Although it pained him to admit it, it looked as if the Commander had been right. Lying under a dirty blanket on the concrete floor, surrounded by an array of empty pizza boxes and other fast-food packaging, Werner Kortmann had his back to the window. Despite the chain around his ankle, he semed to be sleeping soundly. There was no sign of Popp.

Moving away from the window, Carlyle cautiously slunk around to the doorway and stepped inside. 'Hey. It's the police.'

Lifting a foot an inch off the ground, he prodded Kortmann with his toe.

'*Geh zum Teufel*.' Kortmann brushed away the inspector's boot and sat bolt upright. '*Wer bist du?*'

'The po-lice,' Carlyle repeated, waiting for the guy to come to, recognize him and switch into his better-than-native English.

Kortmann obliged on all three fronts almost immediately. 'Well, get me out of here,' he snapped, yanking at his chain.

'Erm, yes.' Carlyle gave the chain a few desultory thwacks with the length of pipe he had discovered at the entrance to the site.

Kortmann grimaced at the sudden, discordant noise. 'That's not going to do it,' he shouted, 'is it?'

'No, I suppose not.' The inspector tossed the pipe into the corner of the room and looked around in the vain hope of finding a handy axe, or a pair of bolt cutters, nearby.

'Hurry up.'

Carlyle swiftly concluded that his search was not going to glean so much as a paper clip. Perhaps Gapper might have something handy in the boot of the Astra. Digging out his mobile, he was about to call the driver when he remembered he was in the middle of nowhere, with no signal. Scratching his head, he smiled weakly. 'I'm afraid this might take a little while.'

'*Schwachkopf.*'

From Kortmann's angry stare, Carlyle didn't feel the need to ask for a translation. 'Don't worry, we'll get it sorted.'

The German said nothing. Distracted by a noise from the darkness, he turned his attention to a point somewhere behind the inspector's head.

'Now, now,' said an amused voice from the doorway. Footsteps tapped across the concrete. 'That's no way to speak to the good inspector.'

The inspector looked longingly in the direction of his discarded weapon. 'Marcus Popp, I presume.'

'Good, good. Very good.'

Werner Kortmann's angry gaze flashed from the policeman to the kidnapper and back again. It was hard to determine which of the two wretched specimens standing in front of him the old man found the more annoying. 'Popp?' he thundered. 'Is that this criminal's real name?'

Carlyle made a face. 'It's kind of complicated.'

'Everything's complicated to you, isn't it, Mr Policeman?' Taking a step away from the inspector, Popp's eyes gleamed with a demented amusement. In the half-light, he looked like some kind of drugged-up Manga hoodlum. 'Maybe you should take a rest. Sit down.'

Reluctantly, Carlyle did as he was told, parking his backside a couple of feet from Kortmann.

Popp waved the gun at his two captives. 'Closer.' As Carlyle shuffled towards the grumpy businessman, Popp fumbled in his pocket, coming up with a short length of chain – like the kind of thing you might use to attach a bicycle to a lamppost – and a padlock. 'Here,' he tossed the chain towards the inspector. 'Tie yourself up, like Werner there.'

Catching the padlock in front of his face, the inspector did as he was told, tying the chain around his ankle and then running it carefully through the hook on the floor. 'What's the plan then, Marcus?'

'You'll see. It will be a surprise.'

Great, Carlyle thought gloomily, I love surprises. His analysis of Popp as a harmless nutter was now looking rather cavalier. Even the intervention of the local plod would have been welcome at this point. Some robust ribbing at the hands of a provincial flatfoot would be a price worth paying if they could get him out of this alive.

'Hurry up.'

'OK, OK.' Carlyle fiddled ineffectually with the chain. 'Locks were never really my strong point.' Simpson would have a fit when she heard about this, no matter that this whole fiasco had been her bloody idea in the first place. He knew that everything would get twisted, so that it ended up as his fault.

Feeling rather sorry for himself, he stared out into the darkness, wondering if Elmhirst had already set off on her mission to find Gapper. If nothing else, Carlyle was confident that he could rely on the up-and-coming young sergeant to follow his instructions. Whether those instructions would prove enough to save him, however, was another matter entirely.

'That's one of the things I was wondering about,' Popp chuckled. 'What exactly *is* your strong point, Inspector?'

*You'll find out when I'm giving you a good hiding, you little wanker.* Leaving the chain as loose as possible, he snapped the padlock shut and tossed the key back to his captor, deliberately sending it high and wide so that it flew past Popp's right shoulder. The gunman made a half-hearted attempt to catch it, but in the event seemed happy enough to let it bounce off the concrete, landing somewhere in the shadows.

Stepping forward, Popp inspected the chain from a safe distance. 'OK,' he said finally. 'You two sit tight, I won't be long.'

Watching Popp disappear through the doorway, Carlyle shifted on the concrete. His left buttock ached and the pain in his foot had returned. After a few moments of ineffectually rattling his chain, he lay down flat.

'It's no good,' Kortmann said bossily. 'You're not going to get comfortable.'

'Thanks for pointing that out.'

'I've been here for the last two days.' Kortmann scooped up his blanket and wrapped it tightly around his shoulders. 'I feel as if I've been run over by a truck'

Carlyle looked over at the dishevelled figure. 'You've been taken for a ride here, haven't you?'

Kortmann frowned. 'Taken for a ride?'

'Conned.' He gestured towards the darkness. 'This guy Popp has taken you for a right fool.'

'You don't say,' Kortmann responded drily, apparently

no longer particularly interested in his captor's true identity. 'Thank God you managed to see through him and rescue me from this rather unfortunate situation.'

'Is that an attempt at irony?' Sticking his hands behind his head, Carlyle stared up at the rusting metal rods sticking out of the ceiling. 'It's hardly my fault you ended up in this mess, is it?'

For several moments, they glared at each other.

Finally, the inspector asked: 'How did you end up on this wild-goose chase?'

Hawking up a gob of phlegm, Kortmann energetically spat it across the room into the gloom. Most of his anger seemed to go with it. When he spoke again, his tone was quieter, more reflective. 'We have been looking for Sylvia Tosches for decades. Well, I say "we" but I really mean "I". The rest of the family gave up long ago. After a few years, they wanted to forget all about what happened to Uli.'

'So why did you keep going?'

Kortmann allowed himself a grim chuckle. 'You know, that is the funny thing. I have been sitting here asking myself that very question.'

'And?'

'And I can't really remember.' Extending his leg, he listlessly pawed at the concrete with his boot. 'After all these years, it's just become a habit, I suppose.' He turned and looked at Carlyle. 'I don't expect you found her, did you?'

'Barbara Hutton? Er, no. She hasn't turned up yet. When she does though, how do you expect to prove if she is Tosches or not?' For a moment, he thought about his own question. 'Assuming that she won't confess, or voluntarily let us take a DNA sample.'

Kortmann simply grunted and stared off into space.

'God knows, if it was me, I wouldn't.'

Still the old man said nothing.

'Glad we sorted that out,' Carlyle mumbled. Closing his eyes,

284

he tried to imagine he was somewhere – anywhere – other than lying on a slab of cold concrete in the middle of a field. 'Now I can get back to my beauty sleep.'

Running, running, running. He was being chased down a dimly lit city street. Who was chasing him? All he knew was that he couldn't stop or something terrible would happen. Slowly, he became aware of shouting in the distance. A moment later, someone kicked his leg. Carlyle tried to shuffle away from his assailant – but all he got for his trouble was another kick, harder this time.

'Hey,' Kortmann grunted, 'policeman, wake up.'

'Fuck off,' Carlyle scowled. 'I was asleep.'

Waving away his protests, the German pointed towards the window. 'Listen . . .'

Shaking himself awake, the inspector realized that the voices were real, albeit indistinct as they ebbed and flowed on the wind. The rapid succession of gunshots that followed – one, two, three – were clear enough, however. In the subsequent silence, he glanced at Kortmann, who looked every inch a man who was resigned to his fate, before struggling to his feet. Still chained to the floor, he could make it almost to the doorway. Hands on hips, he stood and waited.

Behind him, Kortmann also pulled himself up on his feet. 'I hope that the little shit only has one bullet left,' he snorted, 'and that he shoots *you* with it.'

Just as long as he leaves you here to endure a slow, painful, lonely death, the inspector thought. A shadow appeared out of the darkness. He felt his heart get ready for take-off as the shadow moved towards them.

*This is it.*

'Inspector?'

Blinking, he slowly realized that the figure in front of him was not the psychotic Popp but, rather, the amused Elmhirst.

'What happened to you?' the sergeant grinned.

Carlyle simply stared at the semi-automatic hanging from her left hand.

'Just because *you* haven't been on the firearms course,' she explained, 'doesn't mean I haven't. I came third in my year in Hendon when it came to shooting.'

'Good for you,' the inspector responded tersely. Lifting his leg, he gave his chain a little jangle and pointed towards the corner of the room with his foot. 'Now, just get me the fucking key for this thing.'

# THIRTY-SIX

Carlyle gazed at the framed film poster on the kitchen wall as he tentatively sipped his oily coffee. Under the headline *Leisure Rules* a youthful Matthew Broderick grinned back at him. The inspector vaguely remembered seeing the movie, *Ferris Bueller's Day Off*, decades earlier; an eighties comedy about a slacker school kid bunking off.

Quite appropriate for our Mr Umar Sligo, he thought.

Moments later, the sergeant himself shuffled through the doorway, pulling a Green Day T-shirt over his head.

'Good morning,' said Carlyle cheerily.

'I hear that things went tits up again with that crazy German,' Umar yawned. 'Again.' Reaching for the kettle, he dumped some hot water into a mug. Adding a heaped teaspoon of Nescafé, he gave it a stir. 'Where's Christina?'

'She took Ella to the park.'

'Fair enough. This place is very small if we're all here all the time.'

'I can imagine.'

'One and a half bedrooms, £825 a month.' He shook his head. 'Shocking.'

The inspector mumbled something sympathetic.

'It's a long way from the station. Takes me more than an hour to get in, most days.'

'It took me something like that to get here.' Carlyle suddenly felt vaguely guilty about his own daily ten-minute walk to work.

'So, why *are* you here, boss?' Umar asked suddenly.

Carlyle shifted uneasily in his seat. It was a good question, to which he had no particular answer. 'Oh, you know. I just wanted to see how you were getting on.'

'I'm fine. It's you who's been pushing your luck. Again.'

'Hardly.'

'Don't you think he would have killed you?'

'Marcus Popp? Nah.'

'He might have done.'

'Not worth speculating about, really.'

'I suppose not.' There was a lull in the conversation before Umar said: 'This time it was Amelia Elmhirst who saved your bacon.'

'Not really,' said Carlyle tartly, irked that the latest gossip had made it all the way from WC2 to SE12 so speedily.

Umar started to pick his nose, then remembered his manners. 'At least she didn't get shot,' he observed, wiping a finger on his T-shirt.

'How is the leg?'

Resting his backside against the sink, Umar placed his mug on the draining board and folded his arms. 'I'll make a full recovery.'

'Good.'

'It's basically fine now, to be honest.' Recovering his mug, Umar took a slurp of his coffee. 'But there's no real need to hurry back, is there?'

Carlyle imagined Ferris Bueller giving them a cheeky wink. 'No, I suppose not.'

Umar gestured towards the letter lying on the kitchen table, the MPS logo at the top. 'Did you know about that?'

Having already seen the disciplinary hearing notice, Carlyle didn't bother trying to lie. 'Simpson mentioned it.'

Accepting this, Umar nodded. Then he asked: 'Want some toast?'

'Nah, I'm good, thanks.'

288

Reaching over to the bread bin, the sergeant removed a couple of slices of white bread, dropped them into the toaster and switched it on. 'It was only ever supposed to be a bit of fun.' Opening the fridge door, he took out the remains of a block of salted butter and a jar of marmalade. 'It's what people do these days; not a big deal.'

Licking his lips, Carlyle wondered if he had been a bit hasty declining the offer of something to eat. 'What does Christina make of it?'

'I told her that the hearing is to do with an investigation into a suspect who claims he was assaulted in police custody.'

A bus trundled past the window. The inspector looked at the miserable faces on the top deck as they headed slowly through the dusty badlands of South London.

'She's not happy.'

'She'd be a lot unhappier if she knew the truth,' Carlyle pointed out. Part of him wanted to understand why the sergeant had done it; an equal part of him didn't want to know. The pros and cons of photographing your genitals was not, to his mind, a suitable topic of conversation for two grown men.

'Who do you think complained?' Umar asked.

'I dunno.'

'Not Elmhirst.'

'No. She doesn't seem to be the sort of person who would be too stressed about that kind of thing.'

'Not at all,' Umar agreed. 'She's definitely one of the lads.'

'O-kay. How many other women did you, er – you know.'

'Not that many, five or six maybe.'

*Jesus.* 'Didn't you think it was asking for trouble? You send pictures of your willy to half the bloody station, sure enough someone is gonna take offence.'

'Come on,' Umar protested, 'half a dozen is hardly half the station.'

'But still.'

'It was just a bit of fun,' the sergeant repeated, sounding like an eight year old who had just been caught pushing a lit firework through his neighbour's letter box.

'What does the Federation say?' Carlyle asked.

The toast popped up. Dropping it onto a plate, Umar began smearing Lurpak across the first slice. 'I haven't spoken to them about it.'

'No?' Carlyle frowned. 'I would get on to the union asap, if I were you. The hearing's not that far away.'

Adding a dollop of marmalade, Umar took a bite of toast, chewing rapidly before washing it down with a mouthful of coffee. 'I'm not going to contest the hearing,' he said quietly.

'But—'

The rest of the toast disappeared in three swift bites. 'I emailed Simpson last night to inform her that I have decided to leave the Force.'

Not knowing what to say, Carlyle stared into his coffee.

'Better to jump before I'm pushed.'

'Well—'

'And anyway,' Umar said brightly, starting on his second slice of toast, 'I've got a new job.'

'Oh?' Carlyle looked up from his mug. 'House-husband?'

'Not at all. A proper job,' Umar grinned. 'I'm going to be working for Harry Cummins.'


'You are a very lucky boy. Amelia Elmhirst really saved your skin.'

'That is a fairly superficial reading of the actual situation, as it, er, evolved in real time on the ground,' said Carlyle, trying his best to smile through the grimace that had set, like concrete, on his visage. He was sitting outside a coffee shop on Garrick Street, the better to have a private conversation with the Commander about their little provincial adventure.

Carole Simpson allowed herself a chuckle. 'The sergeant handled herself extremely well. Under different circumstances, she would be in line for a commendation.'

'Under different circumstances,' Carlyle grumbled, 'we wouldn't have bloody been there in the first place.'

'Now, now, John,' she chided, 'things worked out well enough. Herr Kortmann has given up his search for the terrorist Sylvia Tosches and gone home.'

'I'm not surprised.'

'Yes,' Simpson continued. 'He couldn't get out of here quick enough, heading back to Germany as soon as a doctor had given him the all clear.'

'And what about Popp?'

'All been dealt with,' Simpson said cheerily, meaning: *don't ask*. 'We have earned some brownie points with our German colleagues, now that one of their leading criminals has been caught.'

'Marcus Popp was hardly big-time,' Carlyle said.

'You can be so negative,' Simpson scolded. 'I'll have you know that he was number 2,356 on the Europol Most Wanted list.'

Decidedly unimpressed, Carlyle replied. '*You're* probably higher on the Europol list than that. I *certainly* am.'

'The point is,' Simpson said primly, 'that things could have turned out a lot worse.'

'Yeah, I could have been shot in the head. Game over.'

'There's no need to be so melodramatic.'

'Why not? I was the one chained to the ground.'

The Commander raised an amused eyebrow. 'A moment ago you were claiming it was no big deal.'

'You could have been burying me round about now. Coffin wrapped in the Union Jack, twenty-one-gun salute, the whole works.'

'I'm not sure that you would merit a twenty-one-gun salute, Inspector.'

'Bloody typical.' He toyed with his empty coffee cup.

'All's well that ends well,' the Commander persisted. 'There's really no need for you to be so ungracious.'

'Me? Ungracious?'

'Yes, you are. There are plenty of times when it seems like I spend half my working day trying to keep you out of trouble of one sort or another. I do that – willingly, for the most part – because I know that you have certain qualities that many modern law-enforcement officers lack.'

Carlyle felt himself begin to blush. 'Don't try and butter me up,' he stammered.

'Qualities,' Simpson continued, ignoring his discomfort, 'that young, up-and-coming officers like Elmhirst should be exposed to, if only for a short while, under controlled circumstances.'

'Ha.'

'Qualities,' Simpson persisted, 'that mean that when we are confronted with very tricky situations like Voisin Towers you are my go-to guy.'

*Go-to guy. How very American.* Blushing harder now, he kept his jaw clamped tightly shut.

'Anyway, I knew that Amelia would back you up. That girl really is something special. She will go far.'

'She can certainly shoot,' Carlyle reluctantly conceded.

'You should be grateful that Elmhirst had your back. Not everyone can be so confident about their colleagues.'

'I suppose not.' He gestured down the road, in the direction of the police station. 'Where is she, by the way? I haven't seen her around since the incident with Popp.'

Simpson eyed him over her cup of tea. 'As of this morning, Sergeant Elmhirst is seconded to SO15.'

'Oh? For how long?'

'That remains to be seen. For six months, at least – probably nine. It will be an important part of her career development.'

'So where does that leave me?' Carlyle whined.

'Well,' Simpson took a sip of her tea, 'given that Umar Sligo is headed out the door, you're going to be on your own for a while.'

'Great.' The inspector watched as a familiar face came down

the road. With a couple of oversized tourists sitting in the back of his rickshaw, the pimply driver with the prayer mat was sweating heavily as he pedalled towards Trafalgar Square. You poor sod, Carlyle thought. There's got to be an easier way to make a living.

'But not for too long.'

'No?' Carlyle turned back to look at his boss.

'In return the Chief Inspector over there has agreed to let us have Alison Roche back.'

'Oh yes?' Carlyle tried not to seem too chuffed at this extremely positive development.

Simpson's eyes narrowed. 'I thought you'd like that.'

'It's fine by me,' was the most expansive response he could muster.

'As it goes, the powers that be in Counter Terrorism seem quite happy to see the back of her,' Simpson revealed. 'From what I can gather, Sergeant Roche can be a bit of a trouble-maker.' She arched an eyebrow. 'Asking difficult questions. Tilting at windmills. That sort of thing.'

'Better to keep us troublemakers together, I suppose,' Carlyle quipped. 'Easier for the top brass to manage.'

'That's exactly what I thought,' the Commander grinned. Reaching under the table, she took a hold of the handle of the outsized hat box at her feet and stood up.

Carlyle remembered that Trooping the Colour was less than a week away. 'Ready for the big day?'

'I'll be glad when it's all over,' Simpson admitted.

The inspector thought about mentioning Bernie Gilmore and his interest in her £800 hat but thought better of it. The poor woman was under enough stress already. 'Good luck. Break a leg.'

'I'll try not to,' Simpson laughed. 'You just see if you can behave yourself for the rest of the week.'

'No problem, boss,' he promised, beaming. 'No problem at all.'

# THIRTY-SEVEN

As he entered the station, Carlyle immediately clocked the headline on a newspaper lying on the front desk: PUNTER CALLS *999 OVER UGLY HOOKER.*

'Looks like Bernie caught up with Brian Yates, then.'

Underneath the headline was a picture of the hapless Yates trying to hide from a snapper dogging him by holding up a hand to the lens. It made for a good picture – Yates looked as guilty as sin.

The inspector felt a momentary pang of shame at having so casually thrown Yates to the wolves, even if it was to save Simpson from getting a public kicking over her expensive hat. Scanning the story, he saw that Sonia Coverdale had not been mentioned.

His sense of embarrassment evaporated as the desk sergeant appeared in front of him. 'There's a friend of yours downstairs. We've Seymour Erikssen in again.'

*London's crappest burglar.* Carlyle shook his head. 'I don't know why they bother letting him out. What happened this time?' As if he needed to ask.

'Mr Erikssen was caught carrying a bag of gear out of a house on Rugby Street at one-fifteen this morning. iPads, laptops – the usual.'

'Rugby Street.' Carlyle frowned. 'Where's that?'

'Up near Great Ormond Street,' the sergeant explained. 'The constable who came across him had to give chase all the way to the Piazza before he caught him.'

'Blimey.'

'The daft sod almost got run over by a night bus in the process. For such a scrawny old git, it seems that Seymour's still got quite a turn of speed.'

'Yeah. The silly bugger keeps on getting caught though, doesn't he?' the inspector said.

'He must be entitled to his pension by now.' The sergeant started to laugh.

'If only he would call it a day and retire.'

'Do me a favour.' The sergeant took a sheet of paper from a printer behind the desk and handed it to Carlyle, 'Take this downstairs, will you? Seymour just needs to sign it and then we'll pack him off back home to the Scrubs.'

The inspector looked at the confession, which was little more than a list of addresses. 'He's copping to all this lot?'

The sergeant shrugged.

Carlyle waved the sheet of paper in dismay. 'This must be just about every unsolved burglary this side of King's Cross.'

'Only about three-quarters of them,' the sergeant said defensively.

'Bloody Seymour.' Carlyle shook his head. 'Once we get him in here, he'll sign anything.'

'It helps with the clean-up rate,' the sergeant countered. 'Ticks a few boxes. Gets a few break-ins off the books and allows us to deal with other things. Plus, it allows Seymour to maintain his reputation as a hard-working criminal.'

'Some reputation.' Carlyle ran his eye down the list for a second time, looking for one address in particular. And there it was, third from the bottom: *46 Doughty Street.* 'Good old Seymour, taking one for the team.' He placed the old lag's confession back on the desk, ignoring the disgruntled look on the sergeant's face. 'Sorry,' he smiled, 'but you'll have to take this down there yourself. I'm late for a meeting.'

\* \* \*

Kendrick, the giant American Samoan bodyguard, lifted his head out of his bag of Monster Munch long enough to nod at the inspector as he breezed into Sammy Baldwin-Lee's office. Inside, the Racetrack's owner was in familiar pose, feet up on his desk, leafing through a copy of that morning's *Financial Times*. 'Listen to this,' he said as the inspector dusted off a chair and sat down. 'Apparently scientists have created an artificial brain.'

Carlyle gestured towards the man sitting on the ratty sofa in the corner playing on his iPhone. 'Maybe they can give him one, then.'

Chase Race, engrossed in a game of Fruit Ninja, didn't look up or acknowledge his presence in any way.

Chuckling, Sammy quoted from the newspaper article. 'According to this, *"human stem-cells have been turned into pea-sized mini-brains with a neural structure similar to the brain of a developing embryo"*.'

'You can't believe what you read in the papers, Sammy.'

'But it's the *FT*,' the nightclub-owner protested. 'They at least try to get it right.'

Being more of a *Daily Mirror* man, Carlyle had no real view on the pink paper, one way or the other.

'Anyway, it's a more interesting story than this one.' Holding up the paper, Sammy pointed at the headline on the next page: REN QI SHOW TRIAL DESCENDS INTO FARCE.

'It's all about power, corruption and lies,' Carlyle observed tritely.

'They reckon he's going to get twenty years, at least. He might even get the death penalty.' Letting the newspaper fall on to the desk, Sammy remarked sadly, 'You lost me a serious investor there.'

'Me?' Carlyle spluttered. 'How is that possibly my fault?'

'He could have put millions into this place, *millions*. We could have signed Oscar 451 on a twelve-month residency.'

The inspector had no idea what the club-owner was talking

about. 'Never mind,' he said cheerfully, 'there are plenty more fish in the sea.'

'Easy for you to say. You've never had to raise a bean in your life.' Sammy shot Carlyle a look of utter exasperation. 'Have you ever tried to get a rich man to part with his money? It's damn near impossible.'

Still focused on his game, Chase let out a cackle. 'You tell him, man.'

'Speaking of which,' said Carlyle, keen to move the conversation along, 'I have found a way of properly utilizing your excess funds, Mr Race.'

Dropping his iPhone on the sofa, the rapper finally looked up. 'What?'

'The money that you wanted to donate to the Avalon charity, in order to boost your reputation,' Carlyle explained. 'I've found a suitable home for it.'

# THIRTY-EIGHT

Sitting in a busy Soho restaurant, Carlyle allowed himself to be distracted by the TV screen, which dominated the back wall. Less than a mile down the road, Trooping the Colour, the Queen's Birthday Parade, was progressing smoothly. It suddenly struck him that Her Maj had to be at least ten years older than his father. Despite her advanced years the old girl seemed happy enough as she waved from the back of her phaeton. It was the best part of thirty years now since she had done the ceremony on horseback but, other than decamping to her carriage, she showed no real sign of her advancing years.

The benefits of a pampered lifestyle, the inspector mused.

Peering at the various horses trotting past the camera, he tried to pick out Simpson amidst the sea of uniforms. However, of the Commander he could find no sign. Let's hope her damn hat's stayed on, he thought.

Sitting next to him, Helen sent a sharp elbow into his ribs. 'This is hardly the time to be watching telly,' she nagged, 'is it?'

'No, sorry.' Sitting up straight, Carlyle returned his attention to the table.

'There was a guy I read about,' Alice took a slurp of her Coke, 'a musician. He was diagnosed with cancer too – of the pancreas, I think. And *he* decided not to get treatment – went on a farewell tour instead.'

'Alice,' Helen tutted, 'for God's sake.'

'She's got a point.' Alexander Carlyle patted his

granddaughter on the shoulder. 'Why bother? I feel fine at the moment. They say I could have another eight or nine months like this. Every day now is a gift. Why go through the hassle of treatment?' He looked at Carlyle and Helen. 'It will make me feel terrible. And for what? Another month or two? Maybe not even that.'

Helen gave him a consoling squeeze of the hand. Carlyle simply stared at the large plate of garlic bread in the middle of the table.

Folding up the letter from the hospital, Alexander slipped it back inside his jacket pocket. 'At least we know now. To be honest, I feel quite cheerful about it.'

Looking up, Carlyle frowned. 'Cheerful?'

'I don't know why, really, but ever since I spoke to the GP and got the letter, I've felt – I dunno – *calm*.' Alexander took a sip of his lager. 'It's like the game's almost over. We're in injury time. You don't have to worry about the result any more.'

Carlyle reached for a slice of garlic bread. Good for you, he thought grumpily. I just hope I don't have to be terminally ill before I can feel relaxed.

'I'm just going to enjoy my farewell tour. When it ends, it ends.'

*I suppose when you're staring death in the face you can mix your metaphors too.* Carlyle made a mental note to get a couple of season tickets for Fulham. If nothing else, it would be a decent gesture. As the conversation lapsed, a procession of waiters appeared with their pizzas and began distributing them around the table. Keen to be distracted by the food, everyone assaulted their plates and began happily munching.

'One bit of good news,' said Helen, between slices of Padana, 'is that Wilf has finally turned up.'

'Wilf's a cat who lived in our block,' Alice explained to her granddad, who was busy wiping a globule of tomato sauce from his chin with a napkin. 'He ran away from home and the owners put up *Missing* posters everywhere.'

'Cats do that sometimes,' Alexander observed. 'They like to roam.'

'He turned up somewhere in Camden,' Alice continued.

'Lucky he made it across the Euston Road then,' Carlyle said through a mouthful of Fiorentina, 'without being run over.'

'Da-ad.'

'His owner is an alternative comedian.' Helen mentioned the name of a guy Carlyle assumed had died years ago. 'I didn't even know that he lived in our building.'

'Obviously not making much money,' Carlyle observed.

'What's an *alternative* comedian?' Alice asked.

'One who isn't funny,' both parents chirped in unison.

Once they had demolished the pizzas and a selection of desserts, Alice dragged Alexander off to Foyles bookstore on Charing Cross Road so that her grandfather could have the honour of buying her the latest L.J. Smith novel. On the TV, Trooping the Colour was still in full swing.

Helen turned to her husband as he stirred his double macchiato. 'It was a nice thing that you did for Naomi Taylor.'

'It won't bring her husband back,' he said, taking a sip of his coffee. Feeling more than a little full, he signalled to a waitress for the bill.

'No, but still, it was a good idea, to get Chase Race to give her that cash. It will help tide them over for a bit.'

'It's money out of your pocket though,' Carlyle said.

'It doesn't matter.' But the frustration in his wife's face told another story.

'I'm sure Avalon could have put it to good use.'

'Oh, hell, yes.' Lifting her cup to her lips, Helen blew on her tea and took a cautious sip. 'But the Board were never going to accept his money. They thought it was tainted.'

'All money is tainted.'

Helen grinned. 'Maybe I should have got *you* to come and talk to them. Make them see sense.'

'Ha.' Reaching over, he gave her a peck on the cheek. 'As if that would have done any good.'

'Anyway,' Helen sighed, 'the papers will lap it up. Chase probably gets better PR this way than if he had given the cash to Avalon.'

'It's a nice picture story,' Carlyle agreed, 'rapper with the grieving widow. Charity begins at home and all that. Once Bernie Gilmore starts weaving his magic, we'll probably discover that Marvin was a big Chase Race fan on the quiet and that Chase is big on law and order.'

'Don't believe the hype.'

'You gotta fight the power.'

'Seriously though, well done. The money has been put to a good use – even if it wasn't *my* good use.'

'Thank you.' Finishing his coffee, he took the bill from the approaching waitress and glanced at the total, trying not to wince.

Helen reached into her bag and pulled out her purse. 'Let me.'

'OK,' Carlyle shrugged. 'It's all from the same pot, anyway.'

'What I don't understand,' Helen said, checking the total before dropping her Visa card onto the plate, 'is what Sammy Baldwin-Lee gets out of all this. I mean, Naomi gets the cash, Chase gets some good PR, but his club still needs some investors.'

'He's getting a good deal. Chase is going to improve his standards of behaviour and stop lowering the tone at the Racetrack.'

The waitress appeared with the card reader and Helen typed in her PIN. 'That simply means his champagne sales will take a hit. It doesn't seem like such a good deal to me.'

'I also said that I'd introduce him to Dom.' Dominic Silver was a former copper turned drug dealer. He was also a mate, a family friend for more than thirty years. 'He always has cash burning a hole in his pocket that he can use for suitable investments.'

Retrieving her card, Helen waited for the waitress to retreat to the till before commenting. 'Yeah,' she said finally, 'I can see how that would be the case. Cash generation is pretty good in the drugs business. And you don't have to pay any taxes.'

'Pur-lease,' Carlyle protested. 'Dom's straight these days.'

Helen shot him a doubtful look.

'I spoke to him not so long ago. His art gallery is doing really well. He's thinking about opening another one, in Shoreditch.'

'Shoreditch?' Helen raised an eyebrow. 'Handy for the hipster trade, I suppose.'

'Art is his thing now,' Carlyle insisted, 'but he's looking for other opportunities as well.'

Still looking less than convinced, Helen put the card back in her purse and stuffed the purse back in her bag.

'It's just an introduction,' he pointed out. 'All I'm doing is bringing the two of them together. It will be up to them whether they want to take it any further.'

'John Carlyle,' his wife grinned, 'mover and shaker.'

# THIRTY-NINE

His foot had started hurting again. Carlyle grimaced as he hobbled down the road. Turning off Northington Street, his phone
began vibrating in his jacket pocket. Checking the number on
the screen, he let out a heavy sigh.

'How's it going, Bernie?'

'Not bad, Inspector – how about you?'

'Fine, fine,' Carlyle muttered. Ignoring the pain in his foot,
he quickened his pace.

'Did your boss enjoy Trooping the Colour?' Bernie Gilmore
asked.

'Dunno. Haven't spoken to her about it.'

'At least she managed to keep her hat on.'

*That's £800 of taxpayers' money well spent, then.* 'You're not
thinking about running the story, are you?'

'No, no, no,' the journalist reassured him. 'That's been and
gone. The public only have the attention span of a dying gnat.
We must move on.'

'Good.' *Feel free to get to the point.*

'I hear,' said Bernie, 'that your friend and mine, Seymour
Erikssen, has returned to his natural habitat.'

'Eh?'

'The silly old bugger is back behind bars.'

'Oh, right. Yes, he is.'

'What has he done this time?'

'The usual.' Carlyle explained the background to the master

criminal's latest arrest. 'He confessed to a dozen or so burglaries in Bloomsbury.'

'The legend continues,' Bernie opined. 'Virginia Woolf will be turning in her grave.'

'Ach. Who's afraid of her?' Carlyle replied, pleased with his speedy quip.

'Yes, yes. Very good. But getting back to the matter in hand, I just need a nice quote for my story, from sources close to the investigation. You know the kind of thing.'

The inspector thought about it for a moment. 'What did you have in mind?' Dodging an old man walking his dog, he listened to the journalist outline a few frothy soundbites.

'What do you reckon?'

'Sure,' Carlyle smiled. 'That sounds fine. No problem at all. You go for it.'

Ending the call, the inspector realized that he hadn't asked Bernie whether he would be interested in doing a feature on Chase Race and Naomi Taylor. Ah well, it could wait.

With Seymour taking the fall for his little spot of breaking and entering, Carlyle felt comfortable in the familiar surroundings of the back parlour of 46 Doughty Street.

Looking up at the peaceful visage of Ulrike Meinhof, Carlyle wondered if his father might not be right, after all. The inspector could see how, when the game's finally over, all life's hassles just melt away. Knowing that no minor irritant can really stress you out any more must be very liberating.

His morbid musings were interrupted by his host taking a seat on the sofa opposite.

'It was quite a shock to come home and find that our home had been,' Barbara Hutton paused, searching for the right word, 'violated.'

Automatically, the inspector slipped into pseudo-social worker mode. 'I can imagine,' he purred, sitting forward and clasping his hands together. 'This type of event can be very upsetting. It can take a while for people to get over it, for them to again feel confident and secure in their own home.'

'Yes, I can see that.' Placing her hands on her knees, Hutton did not appear either insecure or lacking in confidence. Poised and relaxed, she was dressed in a pale blue dress underneath a grey cardigan. 'Derek was furious when we got back. I thought he was going to have a fit.' For a moment, Carlyle thought she was about to giggle but she quickly got her amusement under control. 'It was as if all the benefit of the yoga workshop had been undone within five minutes of us getting home. He stomped off back to work wound up as tightly as ever.' She shook her head sadly. 'And a Blue Spirit Retreat doesn't come cheap, I can tell you.'

'No, I suppose it doesn't,' the inspector said blandly.

'Now I think I'm going to have to take the poor soul back to Costa Rica again quite soon. Otherwise, he will struggle to make it through the winter.'

The inspector's mind turned to his upcoming summer holiday – five days at his mother-in-law's place in Brighton – and tried not to feel too sorry for himself.

'But I suppose these things happen,' Hutton said, injecting a little brightness into her voice. 'And the good news is that I hear that you caught the man responsible?'

'Yes, indeed.' Carlyle offered up a summary of Seymour Erikssen's confession.

'Quite a fellow,' Hutton observed. She glanced around the room, as if doing a quick inventory. 'The thing is, apart from making a bit of a mess, he didn't seem to take anything.'

*Ah*. Carlyle made a face.

'He went rooting around in Derek's study. I don't know what he thought he would find in there.'

'Seymour's not the sharpest tool in the box,' Carlyle ventured.

Hutton looked at him, uncomprehending.

'He's not very smart,' the inspector explained. 'That's why he gets caught so often.'

She nodded. 'Still, you would have thought he would have taken *something*, wouldn't you? After all, that was the whole point of the exercise, wasn't it?'

'Maybe he was disturbed when the police turned up.'

'Ah, yes. That might be it.' Getting up, Hutton signalled that the conversation had run its course and it was now time for him to leave. 'Of course, you did warn us of the dangers, Inspector.'

'Just part of the job,' Carlyle replied, struggling to his feet.

'Thank you for keeping such a close eye on things while we were away.'

She began ushering him towards the door. 'And thank you for coming back to check on everything.'

'No problem. Maybe you should look at upgrading your alarm system.'

'That is a very good idea. Derek said the same thing. He was particularly annoyed that the security cameras didn't work.'

'Technology can be tricky,' the inspector observed. Reaching the entrance to the hallway, he paused. 'There was just one other matter.'

A brittle smile crept across the woman's face. 'Yes?'

He gestured towards the painting. 'I was just wondering, given your interest in recent German history, whether you knew a woman called Sylvia Tosches?'

Staring at the front door, Hutton appeared lost in thought. 'I know *of* her,' she said quietly. 'She was an associate of Baader, Meinhof and the rest. Not a major player, but part of the wider ensemble.'

The inspector eyed her carefully, waiting to see if she would say more.

'She escaped from police custody, as I recall.' Hutton restarted along the hall, walking like a deep-sea diver edging along the sea bed. 'Vanished.'

'That's a hard trick to pull off.'

'Yes, I suppose it is.' With an excess of concentration showing on her face, Hutton reached for the door handle. 'Why do you ask?'

'I had a run-in with her son recently.'

'Oh?' Opening the door, she took a moment to compose herself. 'I didn't know that she had children.'

'No reason that you would.' Carlyle stepped past her, out onto the street.

'And what was the son doing in London, Inspector?'

'He was looking for his mother.'

'And did he find her?' Standing on the doorstep, Barbara Hutton wrapped the cardigan tightly around her chest, scanning the heavens as if searching for Divine salvation.

'I'm afraid not.' Carlyle gave a rueful smile. 'Some things just don't get resolved, do they?'